WHERE THE WEAVER BIRDS FLY

JOHN ELLWOOD NICHOLSON

ACORN INDEPENDENT PRESS

ISBN 978-1-908318-31-2

www.acornindependentpress.com

About the Author

John Ellwood Nicholson is a native of Cheshire but now lives with his wife in Dorset. His love of Africa and the African people, which he hopes is obvious to the reader, goes back over forty years. He attended Kings School, Macclesfield, and the University of British Columbia, and his career has taken him to North America, South East Asia, Europe and more than fifteen years in various sub-Saharan African countries.

Acknowledgements

I would like to thank my daughter Lynne and son Mark, for their great ideas, as well as other friends; specifically Dina Pavey, who inspired me to write in the first place, and Mike Wright for his artistic ideas. I would also like to thank members of the Ringwood Writers' Circle for their help in completing this novel, and, last but not least, my editor at Acorn, Leila Dewji

For my wife Isobel

*Without whose continued support, I would
never have finished this book*

CHAPTER ONE

BUZAMBA, CENTRAL AFRICA

'What does my daddy look like?'

They were only a couple of hours from landing when suddenly Gilly started to cry. Not a great howling, just terrible, tragic tears. 'I won't know him, will I?'

'Of course you will, darling, and he'll know you.' Jane reached across the armrest and put her arm around her daughter's shoulder, cuddling up to her. 'Anyhow, we'll be arriving soon and Robert will be there to meet us.'

Gilly's eyelashes were heavy with tears and her little body shook as if she had an attack of hiccups. Since Jane had first told Gilly the news that she was going to marry Robert and they would live with him in Africa, the little girl seemed to have taken everything in her stride. She'd had to say goodbye to everyone at home including her school friends, the lady in the sweetshop and the postman who always made her laugh as she walked to school. Nothing seemed to have fazed her. It was only now, with this sudden outburst, that Jane knew she should have given more thought to the impact of this venture on her six-year-old daughter, instead of worrying about her own misgivings.

But how good was her own recollection of her new husband? If he stood in a line-up of similar-sized men she might struggle to recognise him – except for his chin, she thought to herself, a slight smile playing on her lips. How crazy is that? Her own husband! With that niggling thought, Jane did her best to settle back in her seat for the final part of their flight, thinking back to her rushed wedding day just seven weeks earlier.

Everything had been hurried as Robert was leaving the next day for Buzamba. Summer weddings were popular in Ringwood and the only date the Registry Office had available was three o'clock on Thursday afternoon 20th July; surely, the most important date of her adult life. Or would it be? Jane fervently hoped so. At least it had been warm and sunny and the few who'd witnessed the occasion said she looked very happy…which was a bit of a surprise considering she'd been on the verge of pulling out of the ceremony a dozen times, and on the actual day, Poppy almost had to drag her there. Unaware of her mother's doubts, Gilly had thought it was all wonderful, thoroughly enjoying the dressing up and all the fuss she received being her mum's bridesmaid. The honeymoon was one night at the plush Rhinefield Hotel where the marriage was consummated, although the actual act could hardly have been described as earth-moving. Ah well, Jane thought, the dastardly deed was done, the ring was firmly on her finger and a new name in her passport. There's no going back now, she thought apprehensively, settling back in her seat for the final part of the journey.

British Airways flight BA2011 carrying the newly-wed Mrs Jane Kimber and her daughter, together with two hundred and ten other passengers and crew, touched down at Ouverru International Airport at 7.35 p.m. local time, two hours ahead of GMT. As the plane came to a halt and the engines switched off, Jane and Gilly peered through the tiny window of the Boeing 747 into the African darkness. They could see the airport terminal lights in varying shades of white and yellow through to deep amber; some very bright like floodlights and others so dim it was difficult to tell if they were lights or just reflections.

After getting up at five o'clock that morning, they were both very tired because Poppy and Tony Partington had insisted on getting them to Heathrow well over three hours before departure which gave them plenty of time for breakfast before the emotional farewells. At least, the three girls were close to tears and even Tony was a little misty-eyed. He liked Jane and was afraid that the rugged Mr Robert Kimber might not be quite the knight in shining armour that Poppy insisted he was.

Reaching the departure gate, Tony gave Jane a small parcel as a farewell gift. 'Put all that training I've given you to good use.' It was a diary to keep a record of her new life in Africa but he also hoped there could be a story in it for him. Poppy was annoyed with her mercenary husband and complained that he could never think of anything other than business – they were there to say goodbye to Jane and Gilly heading off into the great unknown and all he could think about was a story for his lousy newspapers. Jane had assured an irritable Poppy that she would enjoy writing about her experiences and, with Tony's proven skills at twisting the facts as only a journalist could, they should make a fortune.

And now, eight hours later, she and Gilly had arrived. On reaching the open aircraft door, the heat of the night air hit them like a blast from a damp furnace. Joining the other disembarking passengers they walked towards a brightly lit door in the terminal building.

The queue at immigration and customs was extremely slow and annoying but Jane, being well versed by Robert on how to handle these officials, placed a ten pound note in her passport and another attached to her customs declaration form. These backhanders smoothed their way through. At first, she hadn't believed Robert when he'd told her that the officials would almost certainly be unpleasant when she arrived in Buzamba for the first time. Unlike countries such as Kenya and Tanzania, Buzamba was not a popular tourist destination and consequently, airport officials hadn't been forced to be more welcoming to visitors.

As they proceeded through the terminal building, Jane was intrigued by her first sight of Africa, not at all as she'd imagined. The building looked fairly new but there was an unpleasant smell about the place as if it needed a good airing. She wondered if it had been designed to be air-conditioned but if so, she couldn't feel any cooling effect and she was uncomfortably hot and sticky.

With immigration and customs out of the way, Jane and Gilly excitedly went through the swing doors into the arrivals hall. Jane was sure Robert would be at the front of the crowd with a huge smile over his big chin, but she couldn't see him. She stood on tiptoes as she pushed the trolley through the chaotic, noisy throng, ignoring calls from numerous taxi drivers and hanging onto Gilly, trying to stop them grabbing their luggage and dragging them to their taxis.

'I'm being met,' she shouted, 'no taxi, no taxi, someone is here to collect us,' she kept repeating until they reluctantly left her alone and went after other prey. Their arrival with nobody to meet them had not been part of the plan, so what now? Where was he? She looked around the arrivals hall which was just a long, dingy corridor and saw several white people waiting to meet friends or family. Around thirty or so local people were hanging around, but no Robert.

'Isn't Daddy here?' Gilly asked in a tired, little voice.

Jane knew that she was close to tears. She'd had a long, tiring day and it was now past her bedtime. Also, this was a strange country which was sweltering, smelly and noisy, and they were surrounded by strangers.

'No, not yet darling, he'll be here soon. Maybe the traffic's bad.'

'I'm tired Mummy and I want to go home,' Gilly sobbed.

'It won't be long now. You've been such a good girl and I'm very proud of you, and Robert will be proud of you too.' Jane comforted Gilly trying to keep her going a little longer. Surely Robert would be here soon.

Jane found two seats on one side of the corridor and wearily sat down with the trolley at their side. She wiped the sweat from her own brow and Gilly's and tried to relax as much as she could while keeping a close watch on their possessions. Looking around, she noticed most of the white people were leaving the terminal and only the locals were left, probably hoping for a final taxi fare before the night was out. She wondered whether it was time to start worrying. Surely he couldn't have changed his mind. But, even if he had, he wouldn't just leave them at the airport. No, not Robert; not the Robert she knew. But there again, she acknowledged, she hardly knew him.

As they sat waiting, Jane noticed a strange-looking woman leaning against the opposite wall who seemed to have been staring at them ever since they sat down. Without staring back, Jane couldn't quite make out what was so strange about her; something seemed to be wrong with her face. Robert had warned Jane that there were a few unfortunate people in Buzamba who had mental problems of one kind or another and, with only limited facilities, they were forced to roam the streets. It was best to steer clear of them as their behaviour could be erratic and occasionally hostile.

After what seemed like hours, Jane checked her watch for the umpteenth time and found it was only fifteen minutes since they'd entered the arrivals hall. The strange woman started to walk in their direction and Jane stared at her hoping the intensity of her stare would stop her, but she only hesitated slightly before continuing in their direction. Jane could now see clearly that her face was badly disfigured; the skin on one side of her face was badly scarred and lumpy. Jane grabbed hold of Gilly's hand and held it as firmly as she could without hurting her.

'What's wrong, Mummy. Who's that lady? I don't like her.'

'It's all right darling, everything's fine.' She looked round to see if there was any help at hand but now all the white people had left, and still no sign of Robert.

Suddenly, the main lights went off as if the arrival of this strange woman had triggered the abrupt darkness; more like semi-darkness as dim security lights were still on. Now, she was frightened, very frightened.

'Madam,' the disfigured woman said in heavily accented English, 'I take you right now.'

Chapter Two

Ringwood, England
Three Months Earlier

'Now listen very carefully and tell me if this sends your heart racing.' Poppy Partington paused momentarily to give her next piece of information more impact. 'He's twenty-nine, six feet tall, brown hair and blue eyes.' Ever the dramatist, Poppy gave her listener a little time to take it all in. 'And...' putting a heavy emphasis on the *and*... 'he wants to get married within six weeks and take his blushing young bride back with him to live in... wait for it... Africa.'

'You're on those happy pills again, aren't you?' was Jane Hart's curt response.

'Not at all, Madam. You know I don't need artificial stimulants to give me my constant *joie de vivre*.' Poppy was smiling to herself as she hurried through the bustling Wednesday market and along High Street to her office above Lords Barbers, her mobile phone pressed firmly to her ear.

Jane and Poppy were the best of friends and had been since they started school together when they were five years old; twenty years ago. They even started dating boys at the same time but here their experiences differed. Jane had gone out with Peter Collins while Poppy had dated Tony Partington. Jane had ended up with a baby girl but no husband. Peter Collins, a surveyor on temporary assignment with the New Forest District Council, had only been in Ringwood for a year, and had done a runner as soon as she told him she was pregnant. Poppy, on the other hand, had struck gold. She and Tony had been married for three years but so far had no children. Tony was a freelance journalist who, along with two colleagues, owned the Bournemouth and Boscombe News Cooperative – BBNC.

Poppy's office, one room, a small kitchenette and cloakroom, was where she made dreams for the unattached come true, or at least that was what she was meant to do. The introduction agency was partly a hobby to give her an interest, but also to help find the perfect man for her best friend.

Sitting behind her desk, Poppy had an inscrutable smile on her face as a flustered Jane hurried in. 'Is that it?' she growled nodding towards the e-mail. 'Don't just sit there smirking like a juvenile adolescent, tell me more.'

'Well,' Poppy did her best to smirk, 'he wants to meet six young ladies and the winner – the chosen one – goes back with him to Buzamba.'

'You're out of your tree! Six dates in six weeks as well as getting married! He must be some kind of psycho! Count me out.'

Poppy passed the e-mail over. 'Okay then, his name is Robert Kimber and he arrives in Ringwood in ten days. Mmm, I wonder, do you think he's English living in Buzamba, or an African coming over for a white bride, a piece of white mischief?' Jane had seen the film of that name on TV just a few days earlier.

'It's hard to say,' mused Poppy, 'but as he says he has brown hair and blue eyes, I think Miss Marple might deduce he's a white man. But how did he get my address? Why Ringwood? Why does he want a wife in six weeks?'

'He's probably a white slaver. Count me out, let Amanda have him.'

They both disliked Amanda Clegg, a glamorous twenty-six-year-old who was usually the first choice of any new man registering with Poppy's agency. But Amanda was very fussy; not about their looks but the size of their bank balance, and she hadn't found a rich enough catch yet.

'I'll reply to my African friend Robert Kimber, as I smell a little money for me. And when you think about it,' she said thoughtfully, 'expatriates are paid a lot of money, and six weeks… well, maybe that's his annual leave so, if he doesn't organise a wife this time around, he'll have to wait another year. At least he didn't ask for six virgins because that would have been impossible.'

As always, Jane ignored Poppy's predictable vulgarity. 'Well, good luck with that one. I think you'll need it.'

Although Jane desperately wanted to meet her Mr Right, she'd more or less accepted that, for a couple of reasons, this would never happen. Being an impoverished single mother, she worked hard just to keep a roof over her head and food on the table for herself and her daughter. She now worked as a part-time accounts clerk but, a few years earlier, when she'd been in serious financial difficulties, she'd earned money in what could have been called a less than savoury occupation. This had ended tragically when a deranged client had gone berserk and slashed her face, leaving a permanent scar from just below her left eye down to the middle of her cheek. Only knowing part of the truth about how it happened, a very concerned Poppy had twisted Tony's arm to employ Jane as his Ringwood news correspondent. When he'd refused, she'd threatened to cut off his conjugal rights and burn her Ann Summers maid's outfit, and it was this subtle persuasion that convinced him to take on Jane for fifteen hours a week.

'This is strictly on probation,' he warned Poppy, 'and if she doesn't perform and earn her pay, then she's out.'

Poppy knew this was Tony's best offer, and accepted on Jane's behalf, on the condition that he and/or a colleague would help by introducing her to the usual sources of news such as the police, hospitals, council offices, courts and the Greyfriars Community Centre. She struggled for several months, but never gave up and gradually became more confident and adept in all aspects of the work. Her reports (with some judicious editing by Tony) began to fill many column inches in the region's press. Tony also wanted Jane to keep an ear close to the ground and tip him off if she got wind of any big story that he might be able to sell to the national press – this was where the big money was; a juicy sex scandal involving a celebrity or politician would be perfect. So far, however, nothing of that nature had come Jane's way.

As soon as Poppy received Robert Kimber's reply, she excitedly phoned Jane. 'Guess what, oh ye of little faith, I've got a reply from the African dream-boat himself, and he accepts my terms of business.'

'Well, I'm pleased for you, but I still think he's a psycho.'

'No, I disagree. I have a good feeling about this gent, and your file will be the first one I'll give him. Just imagine,' she said dreamily, 'hot tropical nights sipping cocktails as the sun passes over the yard arm, with a Brad Pitt lookalike tending your every need. What more could a girl ask for?'

'Ha! Just you wait and see when he comes and instead of Brad Pitt he looks more like Worzel Gummidge after a night on the tiles. Make sure you grab the money before he realises he's been shafted.'

'We shall see,' Poppy smugly replied, 'we shall see.'

Four days later, just as Jane left her accounts job, her phone rang. 'The love-god has landed!' Poppy announced like a theatrical newsreader. 'Mr Brad Pitt, oh, sorry, Mr Robert Kimber has arrived. In fact, the jungle stud only just left the office. Come on in, baby, I've got all the fascinating details.'

This piqued her curiosity and Jane dutifully did as she was told. 'Now then Miss Matchmaker,' Jane gave her friend the sternest look she could muster, 'give me all the lurid details, and be serious… if that's possible.'

'You know very well Miss Hart that I'm a professional to my fingertips. Of course I'll be serious.'

'That'll be a first then!'

Ignoring Jane's sarcasm, Poppy began her summary. 'Well, he's originally from London and has worked in Buzamba for three years. Why Ringwood? Well, it's like this; an English chap he knows owned a flat here which he'd bought when he was single and working for New Forest District Council. Because he's now married with twin baby girls and has no desire to return, he decided to sell it. Robert snapped it up, sight-unseen, to use when he's on leave – six weeks annual leave, as I'd assumed. Robert's friend happened to have an old copy of our local paper and found the name of my agency. So, there we are; all mysteries solved.'

'Aren't you the clever one? Now, tell me, what's he really like?'

Poppy thought carefully before answering. 'I think he's nice. He's no Brad Pitt but he's not bad looking. But, oh boy, he's very, very shy.' She paused for a moment. 'Definitely not experienced with women. Before he went to Buzamba he lived with his parents in Maidenhead.'

'So he's a geek.'

'No, he isn't, he's just shy. He told me that in Buzamba there are virtually no single females that he can date.'

'So seriously, is he determined to get married in six weeks?'

'Oh, he's serious all right. Unless he's wed he can't get married housing – the bachelor flat he has is very basic. But what makes matrimony essential is that the Buzamban government won't issue a residents' visa to a partner; you have to be married to get a visa – end of story.'

Jane shook her head. 'Well, I don't care what he says, it's still crazy. Six weeks is much too short… unless you're desperate… and I'm not.'

'Anyhow, you have a date with him tomorrow, 7 p.m. at The Old Cottage restaurant. You'll recognise him because he wears a grass skirt and has a bone through his nose.' Poppy thought it so funny that she struggled to stop laughing.

'You couldn't resist it, could you?' Jane admonished as Poppy eventually dried her eyes on a tissue.

'Ah, well,' Poppy sighed. 'And I've also lined up five more of our Ringwood beauties, including dear, sweet Amanda.'

'What have you told him about me? Does he know about Gilly?'

'I asked him if it was important if the lady was divorced or had children and he didn't seem to mind one way or the other. He just wants to make sure 'the chosen one' is willing to live in Africa.'

Waiting apprehensively for the taxi to take her on her big date, Jane took stock of all five feet three inches of herself in the floor length mirror. She thought her short auburn hair looked OK, having been brushed vigorously until it had a bit of a shine. She'd always been reasonably pleased with her face, with an attractive high forehead, dark eyebrows that rarely needed any attention, hazel eyes edged with thick, long lashes, a short nose which was a little too plump around the bridge to be perfect, and a small full-lipped mouth above a slightly receding chin. But then... there was her scar.

The scar looked like a deep groove, as if a jagged line had been drawn with force using a flesh-coloured pencil, but unlike a pencil mark, the indentation didn't fade, it remained forever. Poppy and other friends had assured her that it was only a minor problem and jokily said it gave her face more character; a sense of mystery and mystique, like a James Bond heroine. When anyone asked, her explanation was that she had been in a car accident and to stop further questions, added that she didn't want to talk about it.

So, would Mr Robert Kimber be the man of her dreams? Jane had reached the stage when she wanted a man in her life. She wanted the physical intimacy that only a man could provide; in other words she wanted regular sex, but with love. In reality she wanted what Poppy had – a wonderful shagging husband. Was she getting desperate? Yes. But she came with baggage. The scar on her face didn't help, she also had Gilly, who was six, and her previous choice of occupation would put most men off. Her thoughts ended abruptly as the taxi arrived sooner than expected.

In the restaurant, the waitress led Jane and Gilly to a table where a man was sitting with his back towards them. He was unaware of their arrival.

'Hello Mr Kimber, my name's Jane Hart,' she said cautiously as they drew level with the table. 'Oh, and this is my daughter, Gilly,' Jane put her hand on her daughter's shoulder. 'I hope you don't mind but I was let down by my babysitter at the very last minute.'

A self-conscious-looking Robert Kimber stood and looked at them, blinking as if the overhead light was too bright. He was tall and towered over them standing straight and stationary as if he was waiting for something else to happen. Why he paused for so long before speaking, Jane had no idea. The awkwardness of the moment soon passed and, surprisingly, he held out his hand to Gilly who, much to Jane's surprise, shook it. Realising he'd missed Jane out, he then held his hand out to her.

'Hello, I'm Robert Kimber.' His voice was soft but pleasant. It appeared to Jane as though he wanted to smile at the same time as his introduction, but the ill-at-ease contortion of his mouth suggested that this feat was too much for him.

Poppy had been right... he was terribly shy.

After taking their seats, he passed the menu to Jane with a trembling hand. Even though she was starving, Jane ordered one of the cheapest items on the menu. Choosing the cheapest of anything and everything was a habit of a lifetime brought about by her perpetual state of poverty, even when a meal was free.

Nervously, he smiled at them both and then turned to Gilly. 'And how old are you, Gilly?'

She answered him, and he then asked about school. Again, she replied without looking at her mother for help. Although Jane was pleased he had accepted Gilly's presence, she was starting to feel left out of things, but it was a chance to size up her blind date. First of all, he didn't look like a geek; apart from his very obvious shyness, he looked quite normal. He had short brown hair which had started to recede at the temples, the palest of blue eyes, a longish nose and protruding chin. In fact, his chin was the most noticeable feature. In a way, it was very masculine, not just sticking out but also broad and square with a dimple in the middle, like Kirk Douglas', but bigger. He was smartly dressed in a navy sports jacket, tan chinos, a light blue shirt and a dark striped tie. She thought his appearance quite acceptable – in fact, he looked pretty good even with his big chin. But why would a successful man with a reasonable appearance be so shy? She didn't think that he had anything to be shy about.

One big plus factor, however, was that on the few occasions he managed to look directly at her face, he hadn't done a double-take on seeing her scar. Whenever she was out, she couldn't help but be aware that some people stared at her facial imperfection, even pointing when they thought she wasn't looking.

Finishing his conversation with Gilly, he turned to Jane and tried to smile, but had difficulty holding eye contact; he seemed to be trying to start a conversation.

'I believe you live in Africa,' Jane tried to get things moving.

'Yes, that's right, in Buzamba. Have you heard of it?'

'Oh, yes,' she answered. 'Isn't it somewhere in central Africa around Uganda, Congo and Rwanda and that general area?'

'Yes, that's right. Your geography's good.'

'I used to collect foreign stamps, so I know where most countries are.'

They continued a stilted conversation about Africa and Buzamba, with Jane asking the questions and Robert managing brief answers without elaborating on anything. They ate their meal in silence, and Jane began to feel irritated. What was it with this man?

Waiting for dessert, Jane hoped he would ask her some questions. If he was desperate to find a wife within six weeks then surely he would want to know as much as possible about her. Maybe he'd already decided that he wasn't interested, so to go through the charade was a waste of time. She wondered if it was Gilly, or her scar which put him off.

'When do you expect to return to Buzamba?' She tried once again to get an exchange going.

'I only get six weeks holiday each year,' was all he managed as a reply.

Jane gave up. It was like holding a conversation with a brick wall.

After the meal, Robert drove them home and Jane politely asked if he would like to come in for a coffee, certain he would say no. Shock horror, he accepted! Jane started to panic, the house was in such a mess after their rush to get ready but then she thought – so what, he wasn't interested in her anyway.

She put the coffee on and helped Gilly into her pyjamas, making no effort to clear up in the living room. When Gilly was in bed, she asked if Robert could say good night to her and

Robert, who had obviously overheard, said he was coming and appeared at the bedroom door. Gilly held out her arms and when he went to her bed she wrapped them around his neck and gave him a kiss. Jane was amazed; it certainly wasn't Gilly's normal behaviour. Robert also was surprised and banged his head on the cupboard door as he straightened up. He rubbed it and gave a silly grin while Gilly laughed, thinking it was very funny.

Back in the living room, complete silence reigned while they drank their coffee. Why doesn't he say something instead of studying the stains on the carpet? She wondered if he'd misconstrued the offer of coffee as an invitation to seduce her, which had sometimes been the case with other men she'd dated. Surely, he wouldn't try anything on. A one-night-stand was the last thing she wanted. But sitting looking at him, it was hard to imagine that he would have the nerve to try anything like that, not unless he suddenly flung himself on her without warning. She started to smile at the very thought but stopped herself laughing by asking about his plans for the weekend.

'I'm going to see my parents in London for a few days. I haven't seen them for a year.'

Well, that was that as far as Jane was concerned. Goodbye Mr Kimber and the best of British luck with your quest, but the 'chosen one' will die of boredom within six months. She now knew why he was still single.

As soon as he'd finished coffee, he stood and remained motionless for a few moments as he'd done in the restaurant; it reminded Jane of little children playing musical statues at Gilly's last birthday party. It was obvious that he wanted to say something but no words were uttered, so she ushered him out of the door and thanked him for the meal. They shook hands formally and he drove off in the direction of Ringwood town centre.

A cautiously optimistic Poppy phoned Jane the following morning to find out how the date had gone. Listening to Jane's grumpy account, she felt a mixture of annoyance and disappointment. Biting her tongue, she tried to calm herself, although all she really wanted to do was shout at Jane to stop being so silly. 'Look

Jane, it's probably a confidence thing. He's successful in business but falls apart socially. He's insecure and needs someone to bring out the exciting side of his personality.'

'Huh! He's about as exciting as thermal knickers.' Feeling depressed, Jane didn't want to talk about Robert any more. Poppy said she'd keep in touch but Jane was adamant that she didn't want to see him again.

CHAPTER THREE

BUZAMBA, CENTRAL AFRICA

In the dim light of the airport arrivals hall, the sinister-looking woman waited for an answer. Jane was momentarily struck dumb, her mind in turmoil as she went into panic mode. What should she do? Yell and scream at the top of her voice? But what good would that do? There was nobody she could yell and scream to, only a few Africans who, she thought, were probably all in league with each other. Was this the first step for the two of them into the white slave trade? Had Robert tricked her into this situation?

The dimming of the lights had made matters worse and a shiver went down Jane's spine even though the dank heat was almost overpowering. Her silence seemed to intimidate the strange woman as it was a few seconds before she spoke again.

'Madam, I take you and the girl now.'

'No thank you,' Jane replied as firmly and loudly as she could, desperately looking round for some kind of help. There was none.

'You come now.'

'No, leave us alone.' Jane repeated her refusal in an even louder voice.

The woman stood her ground. 'Mr Kumba say I take you to the house.'

Jane gave a sharp intake of breath. Mr Kumba – did she mean Mr Kimber? She repeated this to the woman. 'Did you say Mr Kimber?'

'Yeah, Madam, you come now, please.'

'But where is Mr Kimber?' Jane was now baffled as well as frightened.

'He can't come. I think he at police station.'

'But who are you and why is Mr Kimber at the police station?'

'I not know, Madam, but he say...' she paused trying to find the right words, 'he say he can't get you, I must get you.'

'But who are you?' Jane almost shouted at her. All this was unreal and utterly confusing. Was Robert really at the police station and if so, why? If for some reason he hadn't been able to collect them, then surely he would have sent a note with one of his friends; a white person whom she would have believed. Not a malformed, frightening woman straight out of a Frankenstein movie. What was she to do?

'I Sellie. I work in Mr Kimber's house.'

Jane continued her questioning but didn't know what to do. There was still no sign of Robert and, in the semi-darkness, she could just make out a few local people chatting to each other.

Jane tried another tack. 'Do you have a car?'

'Yea, Madam.' The woman looked relieved and called to one of the local men in a strange language. The stockiest of the men came over.

'*Karibu*,' he said, giving Jane a faint smile. But from the look in his eyes, she couldn't tell if he was being friendly or not.

'Where's the car?'

'Outside,' the man replied pointing in the direction of the exit, 'it parked right there.'

What choice do I have, she thought and the answer quickly came back – none. 'OK then, let's go.'

The man took the trolley and, still clasping Gilly's hand, Jane followed closely making sure that nothing was snatched. Her heart was pounding and she realised that if anyone did take anything there was nothing she could do about it. She was in their hands and said a silent prayer to keep her and Gilly safe, and prayed even harder that this was not the first step towards the white slave trade.

Her fixation with the white slave trade went back to when she was fifteen and a friend had given her a book because the heroine's name was similar to hers – Jane Hartmoor. The heroine had been kidnapped by slavers whilst on holiday in France and sent to a harem in North Africa. She managed to escape on horseback into the desert, only to be captured by an evil Sheik, but was finally saved by the handsome and brave Captain Brennan from HMS Fury. After further adventures, they settled in England and lived happily ever after. But that was schoolgirl fiction – this was reality.

'Where are we going?' Gilly tearfully whispered.

Jane explained that Robert had sent these nice people to take them to their new home and they would be there soon. She made her voice sound as calm as she possibly could, which was the complete opposite of how she felt.

The man pushed the trolley into the night and Jane took a deep breath of the fresher air which was several degrees cooler and less humid than inside the terminal. The noise of the cicadas rose as they passed a tree and the sickly-sweet smell of frangipani flowers filled Jane's nostrils. They walked over to a Range Rover which looked brand new parked under a tree. The man and Sellie loaded the bags under Jane's close supervision and then they all climbed in; the man behind the wheel, Sellie next to him, and Jane and Gilly in the back.

Jane tapped Sellie on her shoulder. 'Who is this?' she asked nodding in the man's direction.

The man answered for himself. 'I Basil.'

Basil! Fawlty Towers Basil? Even in her troubled state, she almost smiled at the thought that this huge black man had such a name.

Her heart pumping ten to the dozen, they set off in the air-conditioned car and within a few minutes Gilly was fast asleep resting her head on Jane's shoulder. For her part, Jane tried to follow the direction they were taking just in case they had to find their way back, but after a short distance involving many corners and the constant shock of the vehicle hitting potholes, she gave up. With one hand gripping the armrest and her other holding onto Gilly, she just did her best to hang on. Gilly was so tired that not even the bumpiest car ride could awaken her.

After a journey of about forty minutes, partly on bad roads, Basil brought the vehicle to a halt at some sort of check point.

He wound down his window and the warm, scented air rushed in and enveloped them like a warm, damp blanket. Basil called to a uniformed man sitting at a desk under a three-sided shelter who looked up and came towards the car. Jane thought, oh my God, what now?

The man came right up to her window, his large, black face pressed against the glass. '*Karibu*,' the man stared at Jane. She just sat staring apprehensively at this apparition.

Without waiting for Jane to react Sellie said, 'this Alfred; he security.'

Jane recovered quickly. 'Oh, hello Alfred. . . err. . . nice to meet you,' she said lamely not sure whether she should be more, or less, frightened.

With the introduction over, Basil drove the car through the gates and stopped at the fourth house along a brightly lit street. Basil and Sellie got out.

'This Mr Kimber's house,' Sellie announced.

Jane opened the car door and gently shook Gilly's arm to see if she would wake up. 'We're home now darling, can you wake up?'

With a few grunts and little whimpers of sheer exhaustion, Gilly struggled to sit upright and looked outside. 'This isn't home, mummy,' she sobbed.

'This is our new home, my darling, and look how beautiful it is.' This seemed to trigger something in Gilly's mind, because she immediately got out of the car. 'Doesn't it look nice?'

They stood and looked up at the bungalow. It was certainly a lot bigger than their rented place in Ringwood. There were many bright lights all around the outside which reflected on trees and shrubs in front and at the side of the building. Even in the dark, Jane could see it was a gleaming white detached bungalow with a long frontage and very imposing pillars either side of what Jane assumed was the front door. They both stood rooted to the spot, far too hot and exhausted to say or do anything. An earthy, damp smell assailed her nostrils. She heard the sounds of the night. The cicadas seemed to surround them and other tropical noises, including the screech of some nocturnal animal, came intermittently from a number of directions. This sound, combined with the smell, heat and humidity, did seem like the Africa she had expected.

Holding a large bunch of keys, Sellie skittered up the steps and opened the front door while Basil started unloading the bags. Sellie soon had the internal lights on and beckoned for them to go in.

'But where's Daddy?' Tears were not far from Gilly's tired eyes.

'He'll be here very soon now,' Jane tried to sound convincing even though she wasn't sure she'd ever see him again. The fact was that Jane had no idea where they were and she only had the word of two total strangers that this was Robert's house. Her mind was racing with dark thoughts. Why had she allowed herself and Gilly to get into this situation? Why had she married this stranger and left the security of their life in Ringwood? She wished, oh! how she wished she'd never, ever listened to Poppy. This house could belong to anyone or even be some form of prison. She took a deep breath and tried to tell herself she was overreacting – she was tired and being silly. There would be a simple explanation, there had to be.

She looked round one last time to try and see some sign of Robert, but there was none. Left with no other option, she tightly clutched her daughter's hand and, with her heart pounding, they slowly climbed the steps not knowing what awaited them beyond the open front door.

Not daring to move away from the entrance of the bungalow, Jane and Gilly slowly surveyed the scene in front of them. Although the room was basically furnished, it had an empty, unlived-in feel about it. The only sound came from the creatures that filled the tropical night outside and, inside, from the whirring of two large ceiling fans. The bleak room was quite large with doors leading off to both the left and right. There were a few chairs and tables, but no carpets or rugs although there were patterned curtains at the windows. The windows...

oh, my God... Jane suddenly noticed that there were heavy-looking bars on all the windows. And with the front door now firmly closed behind them, there was no way out.

CHAPTER FOUR

RINGWOOD, ENGLAND
THREE MONTHS EARLIER

Just when Jane thought she'd heard the last of Robert Kimber, Poppy contacted her again. 'One thing about Robert, he completes the Comment Form like a real businessman. And… you should see what he's written about you!'

'Are you sure I would want to?'

'Well, of course. Come and see for yourself.'

As a curious Jane entered the office, Poppy smiled cheerfully. 'Have a look at this.'

After glancing at the form for few seconds, she gave Poppy a puzzled look. 'There's hardly anything here!' He'd only written that '*she is a very pleasant and intelligent lady with a nice daughter*'. And that was it. At the bottom of the form, where clients were asked if they would like another meeting, he'd written 'yes'.

'What! He actually wants to see me again! I can't believe it! He's not just shy… he's… he's the most tedious man I've ever met. There is no way I could live with this man. My answer to Mr Kimber is no, no way, definitely NO.'

'So, I'll put that down as a 'maybe',' Poppy smiled. 'Oh, by the way, our mutual friend Amanda is looking forward to meeting him and says she would love the colonial life. She's taking the day off work just to get herself dolled-up. So poor Robert had better watch out, he won't know what's hit him once the Venus Flytrap gets her claws into him. I'm feeling sorry for him already.'

There were peaks and troughs working as Tony's 'newshound' in Ringwood, but this week was particularly hard as, in addition to her routine work, she'd then been told to write about a bunch of travellers who'd suddenly set-up camp in Carver's Field, but getting an interview with Ringwood Council had proved a nightmare. Anyhow, she'd managed to meet the pesky deadline and was looking forward to a restful evening watching a film on TV; *Out of Africa* starring Meryl Streep and Robert Redford. It seemed strange that two films about Africa had been on TV recently; was this some sort of creepy omen? The insistent sound of the phone ringing interrupted her thoughts.

'Guess what Miss Hart.' Poppy's voice was bright and chirpy, 'it's nearly time to pack your bags.'

'Oh, no,' sighed Jane. 'What is it this time?'

'Mr Robert with the chin, remember?' Poppy paused for effect which, at times like this, Jane found extremely irritating… 'you are the chosen one.'

'Look, Poppy, don't mess me around. I just can't be bothered. I've already made it as clear as possible. I… am… not… interested. *Comprenez*?'

'OK, I'm sorry, but let me tell you what's happened. He's not interested in any of the other five, including Amanda, and doesn't want me to fix any new dates. He only wants to see you again.'

'But why?' Jane almost screamed down the phone. 'Did he tell you that virtually ignored me in favour of Gilly, that he knows nothing about me?'

'Err. . . well, I've filled him in on a lot of that – you know – your struggle to bring up Gilly and trying to find as much work as you could.'

'Did you now?'

'Look, please give him another chance. He told me that he really liked you.'

Jane was quiet for a few moments. She knew she would have to see him again even if it was only for Poppy's sake. 'Yes, okay then, I'll see him once more but this time it'll be without Gilly so he'll have to talk to me, and only me.'

'Good girl,' Poppy said with relief. 'Oh! you'll like this – he didn't like Amanda one bit. He thought she was shallow and vain.'

'Well, he's right there.' At least, this bit of news cheered Jane up a bit.

'And to cap it all, I had Amanda on the phone saying how much she liked him and hoping for a second date. She said he was her ideal man. I bet she must have checked his bank account before saying that.'

The following afternoon, Jane hesitantly answered Robert's call. He sounded nervous. 'I was wondering if you would be available for dinner tonight.'

What could she say? She'd promised Poppy she would see him. 'Err... well, it would be nice but my sitter's been looking after Gilly all day and it wouldn't be fair on either of them if I went out again. Maybe another night.' She hoped he would take the hint. She could tell from his faltering hesitation on the other end of the phone that he was disappointed and wondered if he was going to stick out his very British chest and announce *let me take you away from all this.*'

Instead, he managed, 'Oh dear, I was hoping . . .err . . .to see you and take you out for dinner.'

'Look,' Jane said, questioning her own sanity, 'come round to my house about eight o'clock and I'll rustle up something for us both. And by that time, I'll have sorted myself out and Gilly will be in bed.'

Robert's voice brightened immediately. 'I'll tell you what, why don't I bring a take-away meal to save you the trouble? Is Chinese OK?'

'Yes, that's fine. Okay then, I'll see you at eight.'

Although she was tired after a hard day, putting in four hours at her main job in the accounts office and then following up on the travellers' story, she played with Gilly before bath time and putting her to bed. She then showered and changed into comfortable, as opposed to dressy clothes. Tidying the living room, she left the dusting and vacuuming for another day, cleared her small dining table and set two places, deliberately not using candles or any other touches that could possibly be considered as romantic. She had told Gilly that Robert was coming for dinner and they didn't want to be disturbed.

Carrying a bottle of wine and two bags from a nearby Chinese restaurant, a nervous-looking Robert arrived punctually. Taking dishes from the cupboard, Jane told him to empty the contents into them quickly so the food wouldn't get cold. She passed him a corkscrew to open the wine but in doing so, he managed to cut his thumb, which took several minutes to clean and to put on a couple of plasters. This stopped the bleeding but by then, the food had cooled and had to be reheated in the microwave.

'I think you're a little accident prone.' Sipping her wine, she remembered the mishap during his last visit.

'Yes, I guess I am a little.' As he said it, he lifted his hand to his head where she noticed another plaster near the top of his forehead.

'What happened there?' she tried to keep a straight face.

'Err. . . I was helping a lady called Amanda into the car and caught my head on the top edge of the car door.' He said it in such a guilty manner that Jane couldn't help laughing. This brought a smile to Robert's face. 'Hopeless, aren't I?'

Apart from a few pleasantries about the weather, no leading questions were raised, but Jane was determined that once the meal was over, she would take the initiative and tell Robert how she felt. She was about to start but Robert beat her to it.

Preparing for this second date, he'd thought long and hard about his approach. The five other women he'd met through Poppy had made him realise, beyond any shadow of doubt, that Jane was the one. He'd questioned himself over and over about why he had chosen Jane... after just one date... how could he feel this way? Was he mad or just desperate? No, it was neither of those although any normal person might think so. There was something wonderful about her, but it had taken several days for it to dawn on him. Now, when he thought about her, he got that strange tingling feeling that made his heart skip a few beats. He knew it wasn't just infatuation... it was much more than that...

he was well on the way to falling in love. But he'd made such a mess of their first date, desperately wanting to act differently and say more, that he'd fluffed it. So this was it, he had to snap out of his pathetic shell and show her that he was the man for her. His careful planning paid dividends as he was almost word-perfect while telling Jane about himself and his background.

She listened carefully. Although there was nothing to change her mind, it had obviously been difficult for him, and she held a grudging respect that he'd fought his shyness to make his pitch. 'Why didn't you show more interest when we first met? You gave me the clear impression that you weren't keen.'

'Oh dear, I'm sorry about that. I think you've probably guessed by now that I have difficulty in showing my feelings.'

While Jane felt sorry for him, this feeling was certainly not the basis for a relationship. 'As you have only three weeks of your holiday left, there's no point in beating about the bush. I'm afraid I haven't felt anything between us. What is it that makes you think a relationship is possible?'

He was disappointed but not yet ready to throw in the towel. 'I know there's a lot of nonsense spoken about love at first sight but the moment we met in the restaurant, I felt there was something special about you.'

'Special? I don't understand.' But as he had turned down all the others, including Amanda, it did give her a boost. 'But tell me, another puzzle about your... err... shall we say 'mission', is why you want to marry a virtual stranger, in just six weeks. Why not ask someone to join you out there for a month or so before committing to marriage. That would make more sense.' Poppy had already told her this couldn't be done without a visa, but she wanted to hear it from him.

'Yes, it is rushed, I know.' He went on to explain that the owner of the company, Dr Otto Schulz, was an authoritarian German Presbyterian and it was his strict rule that overseas staff must be married, not just living together. Also, unlike other countries like Kenya and Uganda, Buzamba wouldn't grant residents' visas to the unmarried.

'But six weeks! How can anyone fall in love and get married in six weeks? I'm used to tight deadlines at work, but this seems crazy.'

Robert wondered if Jane was beginning to show an interest, even in a negative way. 'I know half a dozen expats in Buzamba who've done just that. They went on leave as bachelors and returned married.'

This interested Jane enough to ask, 'did those half dozen marriages work? Are they still living in married bliss?'

'Err… well… err… two of them seem fairly happy.'

'Two out of six! Fairly happy! That's no good, is it?'

'But the other four were… how should I put it, bad choices.'

'How do you mean, bad choices? No, don't bother answering. It's too bizarre.'

Not to be beaten, he added 'The bad choices were because they weren't compatible. But I think we are.'

That's one road she definitely wasn't going down and she wanted to end it there and then. She stood hoping he would take the hint. She'd already let him know she wasn't interested and there was no point in prolonging the agony.

Robert knew that this was his last chance. Like a knight of old, he girded his loins and made one last stab; the one he'd planned if, as he'd expected Jane to turn him down. 'I'd like to make a proposition.'

Whether or not it was because she was tired that her concentration lapsed for a second or because she felt a little sorry for him, she wasn't sure, but what she said would change her life for ever. 'OK then, what's your proposition?'

Chapter Five

Buzamba, Central Africa

Neither Jane nor Gilly said a word as they stared into the room. Gilly was too tired to have an opinion and just sat down on one of the chairs and closed her eyes.

Inwardly, Jane was panicking. She felt trapped. And why were Sellie and Basil staring at her like that? Did they know what was going to happen to them?

Basil asked if there was anything else he could do.

'Only one thing, Basil, please find my husband . . . err . . . Mr Kimber.'

'I not know where he is, but I go to police stations to find him.'

'I don't think so,' Sellie interrupted. 'Mr Kimber say Basil wait with car after bring you from airport; he call when he come home.'

This made Jane feel even more worried. Sellie seemed to be the one in charge and she wasn't letting Basil leave the house.

'You need food or drink?' Sellie asked.

'Do you have tea?'

'Yes, Madam, we have tea and cola for the girl.'

'Good. We may be here a long time.' Why she said that she wasn't sure but Sellie appeared to do as she asked. This, she thought, clutching at straws, was a positive sign.

Jane felt a little better after her tea and, while Gilly slept in the chair, she asked Sellie to show her around the house, thinking that this might give her some more clues as to whether she was in the right place or a prison. Sellie happily agreed. The door on the left led to three bedrooms; the main one had a double bed already made up with cream sheets and pillows, and an en suite bathroom with several fresh towels. The second bedroom had obviously been prepared for a child as there was a large teddy bear tucked up in bed and there was a single bed and wardrobe in the third. Jane noted with alarm that these rooms also had barred windows. Jane followed Sellie back into the living room and through the opposite door into the kitchen and utility room. Sellie pointed to the back door explaining that her own quarters were through there.

Thinking that she'd never see Robert again, she suddenly heard a car pull up outside and a man's voice speaking to someone as the car doors closed, followed by hurried footsteps and a loud knock on the door. Sellie unlocked it. An African man stood there. He was tall, stockily built and looked older than Basil and the other men she'd seen so far. But... he was black. Although she'd seen many black people on TV and in films, they were seldom in Ringwood and she couldn't remember ever talking to a black man before. But now here she was, surrounded by black people. Apart from them looking and speaking differently, they even smelt different; not a bad smell but strange to her. She knew she was way out of her depth and hated it.

'Hello,' the man said looking directly at Jane. 'My name's Ken Kasansa and I work with Robert.' He hesitated before taking a couple of steps inside the house, nervously scratching his head.

Jane didn't rise to meet him. If a white man had come in with the same line, she would have relaxed and been reassured that Robert was okay and would soon be home, but now she had no sense of security. She was in such a state that she was suspicious of all three of them and their motives. 'Where is he then? Why isn't he here?'

The man awkwardly moved from side to side and nervously cleared his throat before answering. 'I'm afraid he's at the police station. He was taken there earlier today. I'm trying to get him released but these things take time.'

'But why is he there? Has he been arrested?' Jane felt her dander rising but tried to keep her voice under control so as not to wake Gilly.

'There was a misunderstanding with the contractor. It's not Robert's fault and they shouldn't have arrested him.'

'But they did. Can't the British Embassy get him out?'

'Err… well, I did try the High Commission but they were closed and no one answered the emergency number.'

'But surely there must be something you can do. You say you work with him so go and tell them… the police to let him go.'

'I spoke with the German Embassy three hours ago and they said they would send someone round.'

'And have they?'

'As far as I know.'

'Do you know which police station he's at?'

'Yes, it's Kinchea Police Station.'

As soon as he said that both Sellie and Basil gave a sharp intake of breath.

'Do you know the place?' Jane spoke sharply to Sellie.

She nodded but gave no further reaction.

Jane turned her attention back to Ken Kasansa. 'Why don't you go there and see if he's all right and if the German Embassy has been? Do something. You can't do anything here, can you?'

'I wanted you to know what was happening first. I'll go now.' Sellie opened the door for him and as he left the house, he turned. 'I'm really sorry about this Mrs Kimber, really I am. I'll do my best to bring him here as quickly as I can.'

Sellie closed the door and they heard him drive off.

'Do you know that man?' Jane asked Sellie.

She shook her head. 'No, I not know him but he looks fine. I think he a good man.'

'I know Mr Kasansa,' Basil chipped in. 'He works with Mr Kimber.'

'Well, I gathered that, Basil, thank you very much,' her temper was getting the better of her. 'Do you know him well?'

'Oh, yes. He the manager down at Ogola. He a good man.'

Feeling slightly relieved that something was apparently being done, she looked at her watch and saw it was already after eleven o'clock and way past Gilly's bedtime. She looked comfortable enough sleeping in the chair, and Jane decided to leave her there and not put her to bed in a strange room.

'Can you get me something to eat, Sellie? I'm hungry now. A couple of sandwiches would do and another cup of tea.'

Sellie went through to the kitchen while Basil sat in an armchair.

Almost half an hour later they heard another car pull up outside their house followed by the sound of people arguing; a woman's voice mixed with the deeper tones of a man, the finale culminating with the woman shouting what sounded like abuse, followed by a car door being slammed and a vehicle driving away at speed.

The doorbell rang and Sellie opened it. The strangest-looking African woman pushed her way in.

'I hear this is new house belong Robert Kimber. Is that right?' She spoke to Sellie ignoring Jane and the sleeping Gilly.

'This Mr Kimber's house. Who are you? What you want?' Jane was surprised that Sellie's voice was hostile.

'I Precious. I know him,' the woman announced.

Precious! She looks anything but precious, Jane thought. She was taken aback by the woman's appearance. She was small, little more than five feet, even in high heels. Like many local women, she'd had her hair straightened and set in a series of stiffly lacquered waves but an attempt had been made to colour her naturally black hair a reddish hue; this had only been partially successful, resulting in an irregular patchwork of varying shades of reds, browns and black. Her cheeks were heavily rouged, almost the same colour as her brightly smeared lips, and the tight, pink satin dress with a revealing top only just covered her ample backside. Jane thought she looked like a cheap prostitute and couldn't believe that Robert would know anyone like her.

'So, this his new woman,' Precious leered contemptuously at Jane. Her accent was thick and coarse and hard to understand. She gave Jane a mutinous look and then turned back to Sellie. 'Jimmy tell me he bring *mzungu* woman to Buzamba.'

'But who are you?' Jane asked, matching Sellie's hostile tone.

The woman gave a big smile. 'I already tell you. I'm Precious and I Robert's wife. I'm Mrs Kimber.'

CHAPTER SIX

RINGWOOD, ENGLAND
THREE MONTHS EARLIER

'Why don't I take you and Gilly away for the weekend?' This was Robert's *last-gasp* proposition – his final chance and, when he saw the look of hesitation on Jane's face, his bravado managed to marshal some inner confidence. 'I know it's peak season but I'll find somewhere.'

'But wouldn't you be better off taking someone else?'

'Now, you already know there isn't anybody else,' his voice had taken on a note of resolve. 'Give me this last chance . . . please.' What he said next was a mixture between a plea and an order. 'I'll collect you and Gilly at five thirty on Friday and bring you back on Sunday afternoon. If, after that, you don't want to see me again, then I'll go forever. How does that sound?'

For reasons which were unfathomable, she found herself accepting his proposition. How on earth had she let herself be talked into this by a man who didn't seem to have an ounce of excitement in him? Later, getting ready for bed, she wondered fleetingly if there was more to Robert than met the eye.

When Jane phoned Poppy the next morning, she was surprised but also concerned. At the time when Poppy had told Amanda that Robert had no plans to see her again, she became very upset saying that Robert had tried to assault her, but she'd managed to fight him off by hitting him on his head with an ornament.

'Well, well, how interesting.' Jane was also starting to worry. 'He has a plaster on his head and said he'd caught it on his car door. He didn't say that she'd hit him on the head! So ... who's telling the truth?'

'And that's not the worst thing,' Poppy continued, 'She also said Robert has an unhealthy attitude towards children, especially little girls.'

'Oh, no!' Jane cried out. 'Hey, hang on a moment, Poppy. When you told Amanda that Robert only wanted to see me again, was that before she accused him of the assault?'

Poppy thought for a moment. 'Yes, it was. But surely, not even Amanda would stoop so low... or would she?'

'It could be, couldn't it? She can be a spiteful cow if it suits her.'

'Yes, come to think of it, I think she probably is lying. She's trying to ruin everything for you.'

Weighing up the difference between the two stories and knowing from past experience that Amanda could be vindictive, they decided that Jane should still go away as planned, but to keep in touch just in case a rescue mission had to be mounted.

As Jane had predicted, Robert arrived promptly at half past five and soon had the cases and bags in the car boot. Before getting in, Jane asked where he was taking them but Robert wanted it to be a surprise. 'Gilly and I are not going until you tell us where you are taking us.' She held tightly on to Gilly's hand looking directly into his eyes.

Robert was taken aback. This wasn't how he'd planned things but, on reflection, he thought he could understand Jane's concern. 'We're staying in two separate rooms at a hotel in Studland. Separate rooms,' he emphasised, 'is that OK?'

Jane was pleasantly surprised. Although Studland was only about fifteen miles from Ringwood, she'd never been as it was more difficult to reach than the nearby beaches of Bournemouth and Boscombe. 'Yes, that sounds fine, thank you,' she said in a much calmer voice. 'Let's go.'

Robert drove south out of Ringwood on the A31, and at the Ashley Heath roundabout, turned onto the dual-carriage Wessex Way to Bournemouth and Poole. The sun was still high in the sky and they kept the two front windows open to enjoy the breeze. It had been a very hot day. Starting to relax, Jane felt that with all her experience of men, she could be almost certain that Robert was not a molester but, just in case, she would make sure that she and Gilly were not in position where he could take any kind of advantage.

Luckily, by the time they'd reached the ferry which linked Sandbanks with the Isle of Purbeck, the queue of cars was short and they didn't have long to wait before driving on behind an open-top bus. Robert explained that technically, the ferry was a 'chain bridge' and it crossed the entrance to Poole Harbour.

Seeing some bus passengers going up to the upper deck, Gilly pointed, 'Can I go up there?'

'Yes, I'll take you,' Robert happily agreed. 'In fact let's all go.' He helped Jane and Gilly climb some stairs to get a better look at where they were going.

'It's really like being on holiday now,' Jane said as they looked over the narrow band of water to the long expanse of beach stretching into the distance. 'Is that the beach we're going to?'

'No, I think we'll be going a bit further on, but I'm told it's very nice.'

Jane smiled to herself just as Robert turned to look at her. 'What are you smiling at?' he asked as they went back to the car.

'I'm just looking forward to a nice break from work, housework, shopping, and preparing meals. Gilly and I haven't had a break for such a long time.'

'I'm glad you're looking forward to it. If I hadn't twisted your arm, you'd still be in Ringwood.'

Jane knew this was true, but didn't say anything.

They checked into their rooms which were at the front with partial sea views. 'This is lovely, Gilly,' Jane said as they entered their twin-bedded room.

'Can I sleep in that bed?' Gilly pointed to the one nearest the window and, before either of them could answer, she ran and put her little bag on it showing that it was reserved for her. Looking out of the window, she said excitedly, 'Look, the beach is just there across the sand dunes.'

The adjoining room was Robert's which was connected by a door linking the two. She raised her eyebrows a little and said in a slightly concerned voice. 'That's very convenient for you, isn't it?'

'Don't worry, the bolt is on your side so you'll be quite safe.'

Seeming moderately relaxed at dinner, Robert was visibly more confident in himself. He chatted to them both and made funny remarks about some of the other guests, which Gilly found so hilarious to the point where Jane was concerned that she might repeat some of these comments within earshot of those being sent-up.

After dinner Jane suggested that a leisurely stroll into Studland village would help to digest their meal before bed. Before they'd gone far, Gilly was tired and without hesitation, Robert picked her up, swinging her round onto his shoulders, with one leg on either side of his head, holding her hands while she whooped with delight. Bearing in mind Amanda's accusation, Jane was uneasy and kept checking to make sure there was nothing untoward happening.

'Are you sure you can manage her?'

'She's as light as a feather, how far shall we go?'

There wasn't much to see in the village so on the way back they took a detour along the beach and agreed that they would go there the following day. The forecast was for wall-to-wall sunshine with temperatures around 80 degrees. Even Jane was catching some of Gilly's excitement. A full day on the beach with nothing to worry about, what bliss!

Returning to the hotel, they went to their separate rooms. Jane bathed Gilly and put her to bed before knocking on the connecting door. Robert, who was under orders to kiss Gilly good night, put his arms gently around her and kissed her. He then left the door ajar so that Gilly could hear them in the next room.

Jane sat on the one chair while Robert perched on the end of a bed.

'How about a night-cap?' he asked with ever-growing confidence. They both fancied cognac. There was no room service, so Robert went down to the bar. While Jane was waiting, she wondered if the new relaxed Robert was winning her round; today he'd certainly not been boring, although she wasn't quite ready to surrender herself to his macho charms – if he had any. It was still most peculiar that he hadn't asked anything about her. How could he want to date and marry her when he knew nothing about her life, her family, Gilly's father, other love affairs, or even her bra size? She smiled at her own funny just as Robert came in carrying two huge glasses of cognac.

Seeing the size of them she exclaimed, 'Wow, they're enormous – are you trying to get me drunk, Mr Kimber?'

'But of course, Miss Hart, how else can I convince you that I'm a wonderful catch?'

Slowing sipping and enjoying their drinks, they talked generally about the hotel and made plans for the next two days.

'I want to mention one thing that has bothered me from the first time we met.'

Robert looked a little wary but said, 'OK then.'

'You have gone to a lot of trouble and expense to show you are interested in me as a possible partner whereas I haven't given you any encouragement. And yet you haven't asked me any questions – you know virtually nothing about me.'

Robert paused before answering. 'I do know something about you, and it was Poppy who told me.'

'Oh, did she?' Poppy was really doing her best to match them up... what did she see in him that she herself didn't? 'What I find difficult to get my head round is that you're only here for six weeks, and during that time, you're first of all looking for a woman to spend the rest of your life with, and...'

'I've already found her,' he interrupted with something approaching a smile on his face.

Jane flushed but continued, 'and the second thing is you want to take her away from her family and friends back to Africa with you... all in six weeks.'

'Correct. All I've got to do is convince you.'

She laughed. 'At least I don't have a family to worry about, but I do have friends. And I've got a little girl to worry about. You should choose someone with no ties and no children... like Amanda.'

The mention of Amanda made him pull a face which cheered Jane up no end. 'Believe me, Buzamba is a great place for families and children. There are hundreds of expat families there and the schools are very good. I'm sure you and Gilly would have a great time.'

'But Africa is full of terrible diseases and malaria and stuff.'

'Yes, of course it is, but with vaccinations and modern medicine, most people keep very well. The only ones who get ill are people who don't take care of themselves. And Schultec has an excellent company doctor.'

Jane hadn't wanted to get into so much detail and now her head was spinning with confused and conflicting thoughts. After finishing their nightcaps, she stood to go to her room. She found it hard to believe that he hadn't tried to make a move on her, considering he was paying a lot for the weekend and they'd consumed a good amount of alcohol. Even more pertinently, they were in his bedroom. Every other man she'd known would have started a seduction routine right from the off; maybe he wasn't a sexual person. Though his lack of fervour suited Jane for now, she was still surprised and – could it be? – a little disappointed that he hadn't shown any sign of wanting to take things further. Perhaps he wanted more of a personal secretary than a sexual partner.

As Robert held the door, Jane stood on her tiptoes to give him a brief kiss on the lips. She was very grateful for this holiday with Gilly, and was pretty well convinced that he was a decent man.

That night, Jane dreamt she was in a strange building – like a hotel but with bars and steel shutters – more like a prison than a hotel. Amanda, dressed in long flowing robes, was standing high on a pedestal and grinning down at her in a malicious way, wagging her finger and repeating over and over 'I told you so, I told you so'. And then, out of a window, she saw Robert carrying Gilly away on his shoulders, and she was paralysed, unable to move to stop him. She tried to shout but nothing came and then everything clouded over and she was back in her bed. She woke in a panic, her heart pounding, and looked in the direction of Gilly's bed. The light in the room was sufficient to see that Gilly was sleeping soundly. . . and safely. The adjoining door was still shut and bolted and there was no sign of Robert. Bloody Amanda, she thought to herself, she wanted Amanda-free dreams from now on.

After a hearty breakfast, they strolled the short way down to the beach on a path meandering through the marram grass covered sand dunes, Gilly suddenly took off yelling, 'I'll be first on the beach.' Robert glanced at Jane, shrugged his shoulders in resignation and, weighed down by the day's essentials in his backpack, scrambled manfully after her. Soon lost to sight, Jane, still enjoying the freedom of being on holiday, heard Gilly's faint shout of triumph in the distance. 'I won!' By the time she arrived, Robert had unpacked the backpack, a bit like Mary Poppins, from which he produced a bucket and spade and lots of colourful flags for Gilly, and was now in the process of hiring two deck chairs. Jane held her breath as she watched him perform all sorts of contortions trying to put the deck chairs into the right position and, sure enough, managing to trap of his finger between two of the wooden uprights. Licking his sore digit, he smiled at Jane as she gave a little laugh. At least he didn't poke his eye out. She wondered if he was always accident prone.

After that little incident, they settled themselves down with plenty of sunscreen conscious that the temperature was rapidly rising. Jane started reading her novel while Robert played with Gilly. Jane had debated with herself which of her two swimming costumes to wear, the modest one piece or the slightly skimpy bikini – the latter winning the day. She was pleased with her slim but firm figure which she put down to a very active working life and running a home. Not having a car, she walked a lot, partly for the exercise and partly because she was always short of money – even for a bus fare.

While Robert was busy scooping out a tunnel through Gilly's sand castle, she was able to check out his physique which, to say the least, was eye-catching. He obviously kept in good shape. After playing with Gilly for about half an hour, Robert sat himself down in his deck chair and after checking that his two ladies were happy, started to read a newspaper. Mid-morning he brought them an ice cream and at lunchtime they ambled slowly along to the beach cafe. Gilly had a cola with her lunch and Robert talked Jane into sharing a bottle of wine.

'I could get used to this life, Kimber. Are you always this perfect?' Jane asked as she sipped her second glass of wine.

'Always Miss Hart, always.'

Jane couldn't remember having had such a good time in her adult life, and the three of them seemed to make a wonderful family unit. Could this be real? No, it couldn't possibly be; she wasn't that lucky. Where was the catch? When would the dream come crashing down? It may well be that her earlier life would be too much for Robert to come to terms with, but Jane was determined to tell all; if it had to fail sometime, the sooner the better. It was obvious that Gilly loved having a man in her family, and must be wondering if Robert would become her daddy. Near them on the beach, there were several other family groups and excited children kept calling their daddies to help with building sand castles and fetching buckets of water from the sea. All the mothers seemed to be very thankful to be left out of this activity.

After lunch, Jane and Robert sank back into their deck chairs and Gilly to her ever-growing number of sand castles. She was used to playing on her own, but hoped Robert would play with her again later.

It was interesting watching people walking to and fro along the beach, and a couple of very attractive young ladies went past wearing only their bikini bottoms, pretending to be oblivious to the stares they were receiving. Jane could tell they were enjoying the attention. Going topless was acceptable for sunbathing at Studland but not many women paraded that way. Jane watched Robert studying the two women and then suddenly, realising Jane was watching him, he turned round guiltily. He smiled self-consciously. 'There's nothing wrong with that,' he blurted out.

'No, nothing at all,' Jane smiled at him knowing she had caught him out like a naughty schoolboy.

Gaining confidence and boosted by the wine he'd recently consumed, Robert looked from Jane's face down to her bikini top, studied it for a moment, and then up at her face again and gave her an enquiring look.

Jane gave him a very school-mistressy look and exaggeratedly mouthed, 'No way.'

'Ah well,' Robert said shrugging his shoulders, 'it was worth a try.'

Jane thought that he might not be so boring after all as he clearly hoped she would take her top off. She craftily glanced down at the crotch area of his trunks and instantly knew he wasn't impotent. That was a relief!

She didn't think it would be long before the subject of sex was raised, knowing from the way he had looked at the two topless women that sex wasn't far from his mind – typical man she thought.

By four o'clock all of them felt that they had had enough of the beach and walked leisurely back in the warm afternoon sun. Going to their separate rooms, they had relaxing baths and changed for dinner. The evening and dinner were an enjoyable repeat of the previous day. A thoroughly tired but happy Gilly snuggled into bed, shortly after which, Jane knocked on the connecting door so that Robert could give Gilly a good night kiss again.

'Thank you very much for such a wonderful day,' Jane said giving him a peck on his lips.

Immediately, he retreated into his shy mode, and didn't kiss her back or even put his arms around her. She didn't want sex with him – she just thought he would have reacted more positively. Better to leave well alone she thought to herself.

'I'm glad you had a good time, I enjoyed it as well. Weren't we lucky with the weather?'

'Yes, it was great day and more of the same is forecast for tomorrow. Do you have the same weather in Buzamba?'

Pleased that Jane was showing an interest in Buzamba, he hoped it was a breakthrough and proceeded to tell her about the two rainy seasons (called locally *the big wet* and *the little wet*). The farmers managed their planting and harvesting around these periods, in a temperature that hardly varying from one month to the next, ranging between 22 and 32 degrees.

'Most expat wives settle well into the life there, but not all.'

'Why's that?'

Robert gave a little smile. 'It's a bit like those Brits who go to live in Spain. They're only happy as long as they can have their fish and chips and Coronation Street on TV. Without those, they'd prefer to stay at home.'

'Oh, I see. But there's a big difference between Spain and Africa.' She asked more about the country and the way of life amongst the expatriate community.

'In the capital, Ouverru, there are several social clubs with tennis courts and swimming pools and there's a choice of Western-type supermarkets; in fact, everything you need to live a comfortable life.'

'It sounds a bit too good to be true,' Jane said, 'and do you belong to these clubs?'

He frowned slightly. 'It's not so easy for bachelors as some of us have a reputation for excessive drinking. The clubs are more geared to families.'

'So you're a boozer then.'

'Not really, although I have occasionally been led astray.' He gave an awkward smile.

'What else do you do out there... socially I mean?'

'Oh, there's a group of us who meet most weekends. I play tennis and swim quite a bit. I read a lot, play music, listen to the BBC on the radio, watch TV occasionally. I keep quite busy.'

'And what about girlfriends?'

Silence. Why should such a simple question make him look awkward, she wondered. Had she touched a raw nerve?

'No girlfriends,' he stuttered, trying to regain his composure. 'There are hardly any single women there... well, European that is.'

'There must be lots of African girls though.'

More silence. She had touched a raw nerve after all.

'I've been out with one or two local ladies...' why did he say ladies instead of girls or even women? He'd hoped this subject would never be raised.

'Well, that's all right, isn't it?'

More awkward pauses. 'Yes, but not romantically.'

Jane let his last remark hang in the air. What did he mean? The eager conversationalist had reverted to being an introvert. She decided not to explore that subject as he was clearly embarrassed. Apart from that, it all sounded very interesting, but it wouldn't be the country that would convince her to go... it would be the man. She realised that Robert was not such a bore and put down his lack of confidence at their earlier meetings to shyness. So, should she think the unthinkable? The first two days of this break had been great and all three of them got on very well. This was beginning to look like the family unit she had dreamed about.

She knew that if she wanted to take things a stage further, she would soon have to tell Robert about her life, family, and how she'd got her scar, and when he'd heard it all, his mind may well change.

After a sunny and pleasant drive through the Dorset and Hampshire countryside, Robert dropped them back at their house, whereupon Jane immediately phoned Poppy with the news of the weekend. And big news it was! Something had changed Robert into being a normal human being.

'There was no assault then?'

'It's not in his nature. I'm sure he's one of life's true gentlemen. Obviously, I watched him like a hawk when he was with Gilly and he was quite normal. He played with her like any daddy would play with his daughter. That bloody Amanda needs locking up.'

'And how was it otherwise?'

'Pretty good actually. Conversation-wise... well... he struggled at first but after a while he was ... I'm trying to think of the right word... well, he was normal. We talked well into the early hours sipping nightcaps in his bedroom.'

'So, you were in his bedroom were you, you saucy girl? How long before he'd got your knickers off?' Poppy laughed.

'You are so crude, Mrs Partington. Don't you ever have anything else on your mind besides sex?'

'No, not often. But anyway, how was the sex?'

'As I've already told you, Robert was the perfect gentleman and nothing happened to satisfy your filthy mind.'

'Oh, poor you!'

Jane was quiet for a few moments before continuing. 'It was quite strange really. On both evenings, just before I left his room, I gave him a kiss to thank him for making everything so nice, and not, using one of your course expressions, tonsil-tennis, just a gentle kiss one on the lips.'

'And?'

'Well, he didn't return the kiss, he didn't even put his arms round me.'

'Oh dear. That doesn't sound good. Maybe he's impotent.'

'I was thinking that myself but when we were on the beach this morning, two topless girls walked past and... let's say he had to adjust his shorts, if you know what I mean.'

'Oh, that's interesting. So as long as you walk around topless all

43

day, you'll be able to get your leg over regularly. But going topless could be a bit awkward when shopping in Sainsbury's!'

As usual, Jane ignored Poppy's childish comments. 'Anyhow, I'm beginning to think there might be a chance we can get along and the outcome is that we're meeting at the Fisherman's Arms tomorrow evening for a cards on the table talk.'

'Ooh! Does this mean wedding bells are due to ring out over Ringwood?'

'It's far too early for that,' laughed Jane. 'I'll have to give it a lot of thought. But seriously Poppy, if you were in my shoes, what would you do? And no stupid jokes.'

Poppy was thoughtful, taking a few moments to come up with an answer. 'If I thought there was a chance, a good chance, we could live happily together, then I would bite the bullet and say "yes". Take my advice as a professional, it's not all about passion and lust, it's about being comfortable together, and being best friends.'

'You sound so old and wise. I was afraid you'd say something like that.'

'Well, look at it this way. What have you got to lose? He said he'd give you open return tickets, so if things don't work out, you and Gilly can always come home.'

'Yes, but I'd be married. If wedlock wasn't involved then it would be easier, but marriage… wow… it's a big commitment.'

'*Au contraire,* my little innocent. From my experience, being married is a bonus. A divorcee with a child is much more fascinating to my clients than an unmarried mother.'

Jane didn't think she could treat it so lightly.

'Now here's an offer you can't refuse,' Poppy was determined not to leave the matter unresolved.

'What do you mean?'

'I was talking to Tony last night about you and Robert… you know, about having to make such a big commitment and all that, and we agreed that we'd come out and visit you in Buzamba after say, three months. Then, if you're not happy, you and Gilly can come back with us. How does that sound?'

'Wow! You'd do that? You're more certain than I am about Robert, aren't you?'

'I am. I like him. Of all the guys I've checked out through my agency over the past few years, Robert is the best… by far.'

'Well, thanks for the offer. I'll keep it in mind.' For the rest of the day, she thought of little else. At times she felt very positive that they could be a family and living in Africa sounded really exciting. What an amazing change in lifestyle and a wonderful experience for Gilly. But at other times, she thought she was crazy to even think about it. One of her problems was to work out which was the real Robert Kimber. Was it the tongue-tied, shy geek with no personality who would drive her crazy in no time, or was it the Mr Wonderful she'd spent the last two days with?

The Fisherman's Arms was almost empty and they easily found a quiet corner where they wouldn't be overheard. Jane found the whole thing weird; two strangers summarising their lives, trying to decide whether or not to make a lifelong commitment. During the weekend, he'd been interesting and, occasionally, even verged on being exciting. But now he sat opposite her, nervously fiddling with his glass and fidgeting around in his chair. Was he reverting back to boring? It was difficult to know.

Trying to ease the tension, Jane said, 'So, my friend from darkest Africa, where do we begin?'

This brought a slightly relieved smile to his face. 'How about I tell you a bit about myself?'

'Okay.'

He was born in London when both his parents were well into their 40s. He had one sister, Barbara, who was fourteen years older, so he tended towards the idea that his arrival was a mistake during a night of passion. He had a scholarship to a boys' public school where he stayed until he was eighteen. That explained his shyness with women, Jane thought. Going to Sheffield University, he obtained a degree in civil engineering, and his first job was with Ealing Council. He stayed there until he joined Schultec Consult in Buzamba as the resident manager.

'That's about it I'm afraid – not very exciting is it?'

No, she thought to herself, it's as boring as he is. 'So you're a public schoolboy,' she teased. 'I've read many naughty things about them.'

'What do you mean?' He was obviously offended by her last remark.

'You know… dirty deeds in the dorm.'

'That's rubbish,' he retorted. 'Anyway, I was a day pupil.'

'Okay, but I still don't know much about you. Were you happy at home… at school? Did you do lots of exciting things? And why did you go to Africa when you already had a good job in Ealing?'

He knew exactly what she was getting at, but this was an area he found very awkward. There were so many things about his weaknesses and lack of confidence, mainly to do with the opposite sex, that even he found difficult to admit to himself. Being shy was a terrible affliction but strangely, this wasn't a problem in relationships with men and the public at large… only with women… and white women at that. He found he wasn't at all shy with African women. Explain that one, Dr Freud. But obviously, if he was going to make a go of things with Jane, he'd have to change. He'd come this far and would do everything he could to show her he was good catch. So, taking a deep breath as though he was about to dive under water, he opened up his heart and told her things he'd never told anybody before, only leaving out the bit about African women.

At first she was dumbstruck, and there was an awkward pause as he held his breath. 'Wow, that must have been difficult for you.' She reached across the table and took his hands in hers. 'Thank you very much. I feel I know you a lot better now. It's a bit difficult for me to understand your shyness – it has never affected anyone in my family… in fact quite the opposite,' she gave him a warm smile.

'So there you are. That's me, warts and more warts, in a nutshell… err… more like in a nutcase.'

She drained her first drink and started on her second, feeling that she knew him better and liked what she saw. She also knew he could be outgoing as he'd been over the weekend, so his occasional lapses into his shy mode should not be a problem. Anyhow, if he lived with her, she'd soon bring him out of his shell – she would see to that. 'I guess it's my turn now,' she smiled. 'Are you ready?' A few more people had come into the pub but it was still quiet and nobody was within earshot.

Robert nodded and took another nervous drink from his glass.

She hadn't planned what she was going to say so her summary was a bit jumpy. She was an only child, very close to her mother who died from cancer when Jane was only seventeen. Within four weeks of the funeral, her father had gone off with one of his fancy women, and the last she'd heard he was living in Norfolk. She'd never been close to her father – in fact she'd never liked him as he treated her mother badly even when she was ill. They never had much money – her mother had been the main breadwinner. She never received a call or letter when she wrote and told him about Gilly, so she considered he was out of her life for ever. She'd been a straight A-level student at school with a very enquiring mind (her teachers had told her mother) and her ambition had been to go to university, but the death of her mother and then her pregnancy had put paid to that.

It was now his turn to reach over and take her hand. 'I'm sorry. Things must have been hard.'

She squeezed his hand to show she appreciated his gesture. Now that she was thinking there was a chance they could make a go of it, she had to tell him something important. This was her 'skeleton in the closet' moment which she hadn't mentioned before, thinking that there wasn't any chance of a relationship. But now... well... he'd made it obvious that he loved her and wanted to marry her. She took a nervous sip from her glass before saying, 'I'm not sure which stage we're at but there is something I have to tell you before we go any further.'

'This sounds a bit ominous,' he studied her inquisitively.

'A few years ago I worked as an escort.'

'An escort for what?'

'It was actually four years ago. I'd been silly and got into serious debt, which is easy when you're a single mum. I was several months behind in my rent and the landlord was about to send in the bailiffs and throw us out. I owed money . . . lots...on credit cards and, stupidly, I'd even borrowed a few hundred pounds from a loan shark. I deliberately avoided the benefit system because I was afraid Social Services would take Gilly into care; it's happened to other women I know – that's what they do. Overall, my situation was so desperate that I would have done anything to keep us together.'

Robert nervously gulped down his drink, uncertain where this was leading.

Holding direct eye contact with him, she continued with her story. 'I was in deep, deep trouble. I thought of taking Gilly and running away, somewhere nobody would find us, but common sense told me that it wouldn't solve anything. It was then that I saw an ad in the paper for escorts in Bournemouth: start immediately; good pay etcetera, etcetera. At that stage I didn't know what was expected.'

'And what was it?'

'It varied. Sometimes men wanted a female companion to go with them to formal events, like a business dinner, because if they were alone, they felt uncomfortable amongst other couples. So they would contact the agency and ask for an escort for the evening.'

'Ha. I know the feeling about not having a date,' he said grimly, having been there himself.

'But sometimes it was different.' Jane hesitated and the next sentence was blurted out. 'On occasions, I went to men's hotel rooms and had sex with them.'

The enormity of her last statement left him open-mouthed and stunned. His throat felt closed and he struggled to get words out. 'You mean... y-you're a prostitute. Oh my God, you're a prostitute!' He repeated it again, hoping he'd somehow misunderstood, and Jane would deny it... but she didn't. He felt numb. All his dreams had suddenly come crashing down. Brusquely, he stood to leave, his chair crashing to the floor. He looked at her one last time, his face drained of colour. 'Well... that's that then.' He turned and rushed unseeingly out of the pub.

A few moments later, Jane wearily trudged home where she consoled herself with the little that was left in a bottle of brandy. Her emotions were all over the place but she didn't feel like crying. Neither did she think that Robert had behaved unreasonably; it was clearly something he couldn't handle. Draining the dregs, she fell into bed, the events of the evening playing over and over in her mind. Perhaps she'd been silly to be so honest. Had she ruined her chances of a secure life with a man who, she now acknowledged, was as good a catch as she could possibly hope for?

Chapter Seven

Buzamba, Central Africa

Losing her temper, the horror of the situation finally got to Jane. 'Get her out of here,' she yelled looking from Sellie to Basil and back to Sellie, trying to avoid direct eye contact with this appalling apparition who described herself as Mrs Kimber. 'Get that woman out of here.' As she shouted the command, it suddenly dawned on her that maybe she wasn't in the position to give any orders, and that this woman, Mrs bloody Precious Kimber, had more right to be there than she had. Holding her breath, she waited to see what would happen. Much to her relief, and without delay, Sellie and Basil escorted Precious to the door, pushed her out, ensuring it was relocked.

'I call security,' Sellie said authoritatively. 'They get rid of her.' Picking up the phone, she made a quick call in a language Jane didn't understand, but presumably it was the order to accompany Precious out of the compound.

Jane was close to tears. What the hell was happening to her? And Gilly, who Jane was relieved to see, was still sound asleep, not having stirred in her chair during all the commotion. This was an utter nightmare and she felt she was about to lose her mind.

'I want to go home' Jane said to herself; wanting to click her heels and keep saying, 'There's no place like home, there's no place like home,' just like Dorothy in *The Wizard of Oz*. The thought of going home was now foremost in her mind, but she wasn't actually sure if she was free to go. Was she a prisoner in this barred and locked house, with two people guarding her? Emotionally drained, she desperately wanted to cry but that would do no good. She didn't want to show any sign of weakness and she steeled herself to hold back her tears and give an outward appearance of calm.

'Was that woman's name really Precious?' Jane asked Sellie. It seemed a strange word to use as a first name but, there again, neither 'Sellie' nor 'Basil' would have easily rolled off the tongue in Ringwood.

' Yeah, her name Precious.'

Jane wasn't sure whether to continue the conversation, especially if Sellie was a guard. She had regained some of her composure and the fact that Sellie had spoken harshly to Precious made her feel a bit better. 'In England,' Jane continued, 'precious means something very valuable.'

'It same here. Very valuable. She a Peelee woman.'

'What do you mean?' What Sellie said didn't seem to make any sense, and her accent was so different from anything she'd heard before.

'She from the Peelee tribe. They the big tribe in Buzamba.'

'I Peelee also,' Basil spoke up for the first time. 'I see that Precious woman once in Mr Kimber's office.'

So Robert did know her. Surely she wasn't the African girlfriend he'd told her about. This woman looked horrible… at least to her. But maybe she was the girlfriend, and maybe that's why she called herself Mrs Kimber. Jane couldn't understand why Robert would choose a woman who looked like a cheap whore.

She asked Sellie if she thought it was true that Precious was married to Mr Kimber.

'I think not.' Sellie explained that tribal marriages were often arranged when a suitor paid the bride price but it only happened when the two families arranged everything beforehand. She didn't think that Precious was Mr Kimber's wife but she wanted to cause trouble and get money from him.

Suddenly, the shrill sound of the phone ringing broke the tension. If Jane had been a bit quicker, she would have grabbed it herself, but Sellie got there first. The conversation was in her native tongue and she kept looking in Jane's direction as she talked. After a couple of minutes, she replaced the phone.

'It Mr Kasansa.'

'Who?'

'Mr Kasansa.' Sellie repeated. 'The man here earlier who say he work with Mr Kimber.'

'Ah, yes. What did he say? Has he seen Mr Kimber?'

'Mr Kasansa say he at police station but he not able to see him.'

'But why not? Why won't they let him see him?'

'I can't say, Madam. But he say a man from German Embassy been there.'

'Is he still there? Surely can get Mr Kimber out.'

'The German man only stay short time. He gone now.'

'So what's Mr Kasansa doing then?'

'He say he stay there and talk to police officers. He gave them money to let Mr Kimber out but they say no. If he not out by morning Mr Kasansa get a lawyer to help.'

This was too much for Jane; it was more than she could take. Her handbag was on the coffee table next to her and she double-checked to make sure their open return tickets were there. They were.

'Basil,' she said, trying to keep her voice calm, 'I've had enough. I want you to take us back to the airport.'

A look of opened-mouthed astonishment crossed his face.

'I think you stay here, Madam,' Sellie looked worried and nervously crossed and uncrossed her arms.

'I think it best if I go back to England now,' Jane repeated. 'I have tickets.'

'But it night,' Sellie persisted. 'The airport closed.'

Damn. Yes of course, it was closing when they left several hours ago. She wondered when the next flight to London would be. 'Can I phone the airline then? British Airways.'

'They closed, Madam. They not open till morning.'

Jane had naively thought British Airways office would be open all night but accepted that what Sellie had said was probably correct. After all, Buzamba was in a remote part of Africa. It now looked clear they would at least have to stay the night in this house. She decided she and Gilly would sleep in the main bedroom although she was reluctant to get undressed in case something happened in the night; something that might need an urgent departure. Sellie looked relieved when Jane told her what she was going to do.

She had hoped there would be a lock on the inside of the bedroom door but no such luck. After settling a still sleeping Gilly on half of the double bed, she tried to lodge a chair under the door handle, but either the chair back was the wrong height or she was too exhausted to do it properly.

Although she hadn't done it since she was a young girl, she knelt by the side of the bed and prayed. She prayed that she and Gilly would be safe, and that they'd somehow get back to England unscathed and as quickly as possible.

Before lying down, Jane put the bedside lamp on so if she dozed, she would instantly know where they were; she didn't expect to sleep, but sheer exhaustion combined with a very long day took over, and she soon fell into a deep slumber.

As Jane and Gilly slept soundly, still wearing the same clothes they'd had on since leaving Ringwood, there was a light knock on the bedroom door. Neither of them heard it.

The handle was slowly turned and, although the chair Jane had placed there hindered entry, the door was quietly forced open, and the silhouette of a large man stood looking at them in the faint light of the bedside lamp. Standing stock still for almost five minutes, he carefully retraced his steps, closing the door quietly behind him.

CHAPTER EIGHT

RINGWOOD, ENGLAND
THREE MONTHS EARLIER

'My escort confession was too much for poor old Robert,' Jane told an angry Poppy the following morning.

'Why did you tell him all that?' Poppy snapped. 'It's something he didn't need to know!'

Previously, Jane hadn't told Poppy everything about her time as an escort, only a sanitised version to explain the scar on her face. Now she told all, and Poppy found it almost unbelievable.

'Being an escort doesn't mean I'm a bad person.'

'No, of course not. You know I'm on your side.' This explained why Robert hadn't been in touch. Still persevering, Poppy decided to try and arrange another meeting even though Jane insisted that it would be a waste of time.

Later that afternoon, Jane had just finished her follow-up story on the travellers' eviction from Carvers Field when her mobile rang. It was Poppy with a quick message. Jane MUST be at her office at four o'clock and she MUST get her babysitter to stay with Gilly and, if necessary, tell her it was a matter of life or death, or even worse.

A defiant Jane strode into Poppy's office at four fifteen, taken aback to see Robert also there, deliberately avoiding any eye contact with her. His prominent chin had somehow shrunk and disappeared into his shirt collar.

Immediately, Poppy took charge and talked about their earlier dates and pointed out that they were getting on swimmingly until Jane confessed that she had once been an escort. She then urged Jane to explain what led her to do that sort of work.

Jane's demeanour changed. She gritted her teeth and tightly clenched her fists. She was now angry, not only with herself, but also with Poppy and Robert who were sitting on their high pedestals as judge and jury to give their verdict on her sordid past.

'How dare you both sit there to pass judgement?' she yelled.

They were startled by Jane's sudden outburst and, as she turned to look directly at Robert, she was close to screaming. 'Tell me, have you ever been poor?'

Robert was dumbstruck; this was a side of Jane he hadn't seen before. 'Err . . . no, I g-guess I've never been poor,' he stuttered.

'And another thing – I told you I'd been an escort but you immediately labelled me a prostitute. How dare you! I wasn't out touting for business on street corners or in a massage parlour. I was out on dates and it was my own choice whether I was prepared to have sex or not.'

A duly reprimanded Robert mumbled an apology.

'You've no idea, either of you. I've already told you what a mess I was in. If I hadn't had Gilly, I would probably have jumped in front of a bus, but that wasn't an option.' All the time she was shouting, her anger rose in her chest. 'I couldn't think of anything else. I needed big bucks and I needed it quickly and working as an escort was the only way.'

Cowed by Jane's verbal onslaught, Poppy and Robert sat motionless while she took another deep breath and slowly unclenched her fists. When she next spoke, her voice dropped to a whisper. 'I thought I'd be okay... you know, cope with it all.' She gave a little sob. 'The first time I had sex with a client I cried the whole time.' She gave them a pained smile, 'but I made a lot of money.' She asked for a glass of water, taking her time before continuing. 'After six months I'd cleared all my debts and was up-to-date with the rent.' She glared at them both then sat back and waited for one of them to say something, somehow knowing it wouldn't be Robert.

Poppy rose, put her arm around Jane's shoulders and gave her a hug. 'I had no idea things were so bad, why didn't you tell me, I could have helped?'

Too emotionally drained to say anything, Jane glared at Robert who was sitting upright in his chair, his expression difficult to read.

'Why did you stop?'

Slowly, Jane drew her finger down from the top of her scar to the bottom. 'This stopped me. I thought I could look after myself but one night it all went wrong. I went to this guy's house in Boscombe and as soon as I entered, he locked the door. I knew then I was in trouble. He screamed obscenities while he beat and kicked me, ripped my clothes and went berserk.' She felt herself trembling and took a deep breath. 'He broke a bottle then slashed my face.' She was crying now, tears streaming down her cheeks, her voice barely audible.

Looking directly at Jane, Robert slowly rubbed his chin, shook his head from side to side but didn't say anything. She had no idea what he was thinking.

Poppy looked at Robert. 'I think it's time to call it a day.' She motioned him to leave. 'I'll call you tomorrow.'

Uncharacteristically, Jane didn't go to work the following morning. The events of the past few weeks, culminating with the showdown in Poppy's office, had left her exhausted. It had been an emotional roller coaster and now everything had fallen apart. Poppy wanted to give it one last try although it was obvious to Jane that she was flogging a dead horse. Robert was history and she didn't blame him, but she certainly wasn't going to apologise.

When her phone rang, it wasn't surprising that it was Poppy. 'I've arranged for you to meet Robert this afternoon.' Before Jane could object she continued, 'now don't say "no", because Robert has asked to see you.'

'Liar. If he asked to see me again, it's because you made him.'

'No, it's not like that. He would just like to see you one last time, to say goodbye.'

'I'm not sure.'

'He would like to talk to you privately and suggested his flat at, say, three o'clock.'

'I can't go to his flat, remember, that's what prostitutes do.'

'Don't be so silly. Just go round and say goodbye. Is that too much to ask?'

'I hate you.'

Poppy laughed. 'Go and see him or I'll tell Amanda you're a slapper.'

Jane ignored this last comment. 'OK then, I guess I owe him that much. It's not his fault I'm a whore.'

There was a shared feeling of uneasiness when she arrived, Robert nervously showing her into the living room before going into the kitchen to make coffee. While waiting, she looked around the room which somehow seemed familiar, almost as if she'd been there before. She was still trying to unravel this puzzle when he returned with a tray of coffee and biscuits.

'I guess you feel your holiday's been a failure,' Jane said, trying to get a conversation going.

'Well, in a way, yes, although I did know it was a tall order to return with the love of my life, but it was worth a try.'

She eyed him cautiously. 'So what will you do now?'

He thought for a moment. 'I'm not sure. In the two weeks I have left I'll see my parents and maybe spend a few days in London doing some last minute shopping and also take in a couple of shows; try and get a quick culture fix before I return to darkest Africa.' Now that his hapless quest was over, he seemed less stressed and more relaxed in Jane's company. Looking up to see her smiling, a feeling of desolation came over him knowing that she wouldn't be joining him in Buzamba.

She interrupted his thoughts. 'Can I ask you a personal question? You don't have to answer if you don't want to.'

'Sure, go ahead.'

'Well,' she paused, knowing that she was being cheeky but to her it was important. 'I'd like to know if you've ever been with a prostitute – have you ever paid for sex?'

Robert was slow to answer, unsure of where it was leading. 'Why do you ask?'

'I'm curious. I'd like to know.'

He struggled to know what to say. Since he'd stormed out after Jane had confessed to being an escort, he'd gone over and over in his mind whether he'd overreacted. Did he owe her a reply, an honest one? 'OK, I find it very embarrassing but I will tell you. I went with girls in Buzamba, and every so often, I gave them money.'

'So they were prostitutes.'

This was getting harder. He hadn't revealed to anyone that he'd never had sex with a girlfriend in England. On the few occasions he'd taken a girl out, he hadn't had the nerve to take it that one step further. He'd managed the occasional kiss, but his technique was so inept that the girls didn't respond, and time and again, he'd returned home furiously kicking himself for being so timid. He decided he would answer Jane's question because he knew that he himself had to change and overcome his reserve and shyness, in the hope that next time, he would have a better chance of making a go of it.

For a few moments neither of them spoke.

'You're not alone you know,' Jane said sympathetically. 'I met several men with similar problems. They were often successful in business but, sadly for them, they had the same difficulty as you.'

Robert looked down at the floor as if he'd confessed to some heinous crime. 'So there you are – bloody pathetic isn't it?'

'One more question.'

'No. I think that's enough.'

But Jane wasn't prepared to leave it there. 'I want to know if you felt contempt for the prostitutes.'

'No, of course not.' For a moment he sat motionless. 'You mean you, don't you? I don't have contempt for what you did. I guess I was worried you wouldn't be… you know, faithful. I wouldn't want a wife who slept around.'

This made Jane stop for a second. 'Is that what you think?'

'I didn't know what to think. It was such a shock… you know.'

'Let me tell you something, I hated every minute of it.'

Before answering, he paused to collect his thoughts, giving a pensive smile. 'I've already told you that I fell in love with you the very first time we met.'

'And do you still love me… now you know about the escort business?'

Sitting on the edge of the settee and gazing down at the carpet, he nodded his head and mumbled what she thought was a 'yes'.

She sat down opposite him. 'Although I regret what I did, I'm not going to apologise, but I can tell you this. Now that I've cleared all my debts and I'm working – partly thanks to Tony, I'm okay financially and I've got my independence back.'

Standing and pacing round the room, he stroked his chin, put his hands in and out of his pockets, scratched his head and fidgeted like a nervous teenager. Why idiotic thoughts flash into one's mind at times like this he couldn't fathom, but for some crazy reason, he remembered one of Tony Blair's crass statements that the 'hand of history' was on his shoulder. Well, while Tony Blair could look for a new scriptwriter, this was a momentous time for him; maybe the hand of destiny was on his shoulder. He steeled himself. 'Do you think we could go back to where we were before?'

'Before what?'

'You know. Before I left you in the Fisherman's Arms.'

'And…'

'I was on the point of asking you marry me.'

There was a moment's silence as they cautiously looked at each other.

'Am I getting the picture clearly? Are you now asking me to marry you?'

'Yes, I am. With every fibre of my body, I love you. I love you so much it actually hurts; and I'm old enough to know it's not just infatuation.'

Jane was in turmoil not knowing what to think. 'Hang on a moment. I think we need a small recap here. And I'm totally confused,' she looked at her watch, 'and I have to get home to relieve my babysitter.'

Robert took Jane's hands in his. 'Well, you haven't yet said "no", so am I in with a chance?'

'Look, take me home and I'll make some dinner. If I can clear my head of all this muddle, I'll give you an answer before the evening's out. How's that?'

Walking in the front door of her home, Jane watched Gilly run up to Robert who picked her up and whirled her around. Her happy laughter plucked at Jane's heartstrings. She thought again how marvellous it would be for her little girl to have a man in her life; more to the point, a daddy in her life.

Later that evening, she tried to unravel her thoughts, repeating to Robert that although she didn't love him, she had a great affection for him, but was that a good enough basis for a marriage?

Robert took the bull by the horns. 'I honestly believe we'll make a go of it. In some societies, it's quite common for couples to marry without being in love, believing that love will follow. And it usually does. But on my side… I'm certain I'm in love.'

'I'm not sure we're suitably matched,' Jane smiled. 'Are you?'

'I'm certain we are. Please say yes.'

Jane felt the pressure. If only her mother was still alive – she would know. She looked heavenward, I need help, Mum, she thought, what should I do? If his proposal hadn't included marriage, she would definitely have gone, just to see if it worked. But as it did, could she make that massive leap of faith? Ever since her teenage years, she'd wanted to be married with children and, bearing in mind the total mess she'd made of her life so far, that dream had virtually disappeared. Was this her big chance? Yes, dammit, this is it. 'Before I agree, you must think again because I don't want you to have any regrets about your hasty decision. I can't think of anything else to put you off,' she added cautiously. 'You now know me… warts and all.'

'Please believe me, it's not a hasty decision.' He knew Jane needed a little longer to make the final commitment, so he broke the tension. 'God, I'd love a drink. Have you got anything?'

'The cupboard's bare I'm afraid, but I need a drink myself.'

'Why don't I go to the Fisherman's and get a couple of bottles so we can get back to where we were?'

What a turnaround. Jane felt she was being tossed around in a whirlwind. Oddly though, everything seemed to have clicked into place. With a little frisson of excitement, she was preparing to make the biggest commitment of her life. It hadn't been easy and had taken some time to realise that this was a golden opportunity not only for her, but also for Gilly. She was taking a big risk but, then again, so was he. She'd known this man for little over a month and, if she accepted, he would be taking them away from all their friends to a remote part of Africa. But what had they to lose? If things didn't work out, Poppy would mount her rescue mission and they could return to Ringwood and take up life almost as they'd left it. Her final decision would have to be made when he returned with the wine. For the first time in years, fortune had come calling and she wouldn't turn it away this time. She felt really alive, and was looking forward to an exciting future. A married future in Africa.

Chapter Nine

Buzamba, Central Africa

On awakening, Jane found the bedroom bathed in the early morning light. She looked around to get her bearings and, immediately, her heart sank. What new catastrophe would this day bring? As if on cue, Gilly rolled over and opened her eyes.

'Where are we Mummy?' Her sleepy little voice sounded so pathetic that Jane hated herself for exposing her to this terrible situation.

If the circumstances had been different, Jane would have told her they were in their wonderful new home and how lovely it was, but her present plans were to get the first plane back to England... if that was possible. She took her in her arms and gave her a kiss. 'Remember our long journey yesterday, sweetheart?'

Gilly slowly nodded her head as she looked round the room.

'Well,' Jane continued, 'we are going to get something to eat and then decide what to do next. Is that okay, darling?' Jane gave her another cuddle and kiss before rolling out of bed. 'You stay here, and I'll see if we can get some breakfast.' Still dressed the same as when they'd left England and hot and sweaty, Jane desperately wanted a shower and some lighter clothes. But for the moment, they'd have to manage as they were, in case they had to leave quickly.

Walking towards the bedroom door, she noticed that the chair she'd placed behind it had moved; someone must have been in during the night. With her heart beating wildly, she carefully opened the door and looked down the short corridor towards the living room. Her heart almost stopped. There, at the end of the corridor stood Robert, grinning the same way as he had whenever he banged himself when they first met in Ringwood.

'Hi,' he said quietly, 'welcome to Buzamba.'

Jane fought back the urge to burst into tears, and suddenly felt incredibly angry. Was he for real? Welcome to Buzamba was all he could say. She tried to think of a suitably abusive reply but her head was in too much of a turmoil.

'Hey, hey,' he said noting her hesitation. 'What's the matter?'

Her initial reaction when he asked this disingenuous question was to reach for something heavy to throw at him. What's the matter? She and Gilly had been subjected to the most frightening and upsetting experience of their lives and all he could say was, "what's the matter?"'

'What-the-hell-do-you-think? No, it's bloody awful here and all we want is to get back to England as quickly as possible. Right now won't be soon enough.'

Neither of them moved. Robert was bewildered by Jane's outburst, unsure of what to do. He slowly walked towards her.

'Stay away from me,' she barked.

The look of bewilderment turned to shock. He opened his mouth to say something but no words came.

Gilly must have heard Robert's voice because just then, she came out of the bedroom and, on seeing Robert, rushed up to him. 'Daddy, Daddy,' she cried and let Robert pick her up. 'Do you remember me?' she asked piteously.

'Of course I remember you, Gilly. Of course I do.' He ignored the motionless figure of Jane and carried Gilly into the living room. 'You're home now. Your new home.'

Jane was completely at a loss. Was yesterday just a bad dream or was there still a sinister reason for them being here? Had she misinterpreted everything and was it just unlucky that Robert had been detained, and would everything now be fine? Robert had taken Gilly into the living room and she had no option but to follow. There was no sign of Sellie or Basil... only the three of them.

'Look Jane, I'm really sorry about yesterday. You know, being at the police station when you arrived. It's never happened to me before.' He nodded in the direction of Gilly. 'I'll explain everything later. In the meantime, would you like breakfast?'

'Not yet. I'd like a cup of tea though.' She replied curtly. She thought she knew how a schizophrenic person must feel; half of her wanted to attack Robert and beat him senseless, and the other half would calmly want answers to a hundred and one questions she had for him.

'By the way, you're not serious about leaving, are you?'

'We might be.'

He looked imploringly at her. 'Please don't leave, Jane. Everything will be all right now. I promise. Anyhow, I'll get you some tea right away. You sit out there,' he pointed to the veranda, 'and admire the African sunrise.'

Jane decided to say nothing else for the moment as she didn't want to alarm Gilly. Apprehensively, she went outside and sat on a brightly upholstered bamboo chair and looked around, her tenseness gradually subsiding. Spreading out before her was a large lawn, as wide as the house, with flowers and shrubs in front of a striking hibiscus hedge covered in bright, red flowers. The cloudless sky was in the process of changing from a pale and a misty mix of pastel blue and yellow to pure bright blue, heralding a hot, sunny day. She had no idea of the time but thought it would probably get much hotter later in the day.

Robert brought their drinks and joined them. Busy sparrow-sized weaver birds with bright yellow bodies and black and yellow wings were chattering away in a couple of palm trees in the corner of the garden. They flitted from branch to branch with long, thin strands of palm fronds in their beaks, which they somehow plaited into elaborate tubular nests shaped like chunky question marks, dangling from the branches. There were some other less frenetic, but equally noisy, birds flying in and out of bushes near the edge of the lawn. It was beautiful.

Gilly settled herself comfortably on Jane's lap.

'Why are we in a prison?' Jane asked, hoping Gilly's attention was taken up by the activity in the garden.

Robert laughed. 'This isn't a prison. It's our home.'

'Then why the barred windows and locked doors?'

'Oh, you mean the rogue bars. They're just a precaution against burglars. All houses have them.'

'What do you mean, rogue bars?'

'Burglars, thieves and the like are called rogues in Buzamba. But here inside Basu compound, they're not really needed. We have very good security.'

'So we're free to go out at any time?'

'Yes, of course you are. In fact, we'll all have a walk this afternoon and you'll see for yourself.'

'And Sellie and Basil. Do they really work for you?'

'Yes. Sellie is the house-girl and Basil my driver. I hope they looked after you well yesterday.'

'What's wrong with Sellie's face? She's a bit frightening.'

'I don't know. I haven't asked her. But she's very good in the house and kitchen and she came with excellent references.'

'But more importantly, I had the pleasure of meeting your wife last night.'

'Oh God.' Robert's expression changed. 'Yes, Sellie told me she'd been here. Jimmy must have told her. Anyway, she is not my wife. Please believe me, I never married her. She was the girlfriend I told you about, but that's all she was... a friend. Why she said that I've no idea.'

'She seemed pretty certain last night. And, by the way, she looked horrible. What on earth did you see in her? She's just a cheap prostitute.' Jane added the word cheap, having worked in the same profession herself not too long ago. She hoped the comparison ended there.

'I don't know what's happened to her. She looked okay when I took her out.'

'Who's this Jimmy you mentioned?'

'Oh, Jimmy's a friend of mine. You'll meet him later. He's a nice chap when he's sober so I can only assume he was drunk when he told Precious my new address. I'll read him the riot act when I see him.'

'So you're definitely not married to that woman.'

'Definitely not. In fact I haven't seen her since we broke up six months ago.'

Jane wasn't sure what to think or whether to believe him. She had many more worries and questions which needed answers and reassurances before she committed to staying. 'Before we go any further, Gilly and I want baths and a change of clothes. Is there any hot water?'

'Yes, the heater's been on all night. You go and have showers or baths and I'll get breakfast ready. Is that okay?' He took orders for breakfast, giving them firm instructions to return to the veranda when they were ready.

While the bath was running, Jane did some unpacking to find their summer clothes and half an hour later, they both reappeared looking refreshed, with Jane looking a bit happier than before. The veranda table had been set with fresh orange juice, bacon and eggs with toast and marmalade.

Both Jane and Gilly were hungry and enjoyed the meal. After breakfast, Jane was beginning to think that last night was just one of those dreadful coincidences that could happen to anyone. Being unaware of the extent of her mother's ordeal the night before, Gilly felt happy with her new surroundings and new daddy. She loved her bedroom, especially as it was already occupied by a large teddy bear.

After coffee, Gilly went to play in her bedroom while Jane and Robert sat and talked. As the subject of Precious had been covered, next on Jane's agenda was why had he been at the police station instead of meeting them at the airport, and how petrified she'd been, not knowing what to do.

He apologised once again saying how sorry he was. He explained that his company were the supervising engineers for a slum project financed by the German government. The day before, the contractor, Zanga Construction, had tried to cheat on the contract. There followed an argument which resulted in Robert telling them that they wouldn't be paid until it was completed to his satisfaction. What he didn't know was that one of the President's brothers owned Zanga Construction and, on hearing about the dispute, he had Robert arrested on a charge of sabotaging the project.

'So what happened then?'

'Two policemen came to the office and took me to the police station. I had my mobile with me so I called the British High Commission and the German Embassy asking for their help, but I figured it would take a long time to sort out, and you were due to arrive just a few hours later.' He rubbed his chin and added ruefully. 'That's when I phoned Sellie. I would have contacted Jimmy or one of my other friends but it's a new phone and I hadn't got round to putting their numbers into the memory.'

After hearing Robert's explanation, Jane thought it could be plausible. 'So what you're telling me, correct me if I'm wrong, is that Zanga tried to cheat and you found them out.'

Robert gave his chin another rub. 'In a way, yes.'

'In every way, yes,' countered Jane, 'it's a form of corruption. And all because it's owned by the President's brother.'

'There's not much we can do about it.' He shrugged his shoulders. 'If it means paying a bit extra... then so be it.' Once again, he smiled at Jane. 'Welcome to Africa!'

'What's that supposed to mean?'

He thought for a moment. 'Things aren't the same here as in England. You know about corruption because it's in the media all the time and it's associated with the top people in government. But in fact corruption is at every level.'

'Is that why you told me how to pay bribes to the customs at the airport? Isn't that corruption?'

'Yes, it is, I'm afraid. Even we expats add to the corruption industry.'

'I've obviously got a lot to learn,' she was feeling more relaxed now. Jane then told Robert about their arrival at the airport; the frustrating tussle with immigration and customs, and then waiting half an hour until Sellie came over to them.

'I don't know why she waited all that time, maybe she was nervous,' Robert said. 'I've only had her for a week so it was a lot to ask of her. In fact, I've only been in this house a week. She was recommended by a Swiss couple who have just left the country, so she is on probation for the first month.'

'Well, apart from the wait, both Sellie and Basil... Oh, by the way, what a name, Basil! Wait till Poppy hears this, she'll be in hysterics – but both of them were very helpful.'

'That's good to hear. May I assume then, that you are staying?'

'For the moment,' Jane managed to smile. 'Yesterday, I hated you, I hated this country and I hated the Africans. I was so frightened.'

He took her hand and held it close to his chest. 'I don't blame you. But I think you can see that it was all a terrible misunderstanding.'

'Well, I hope so. But I've still got our return tickets if we need them.'

'I'm sure you'll love it here. I won't pretend it's as easy as living in England, but it's interesting and... well, different.'

'It's different all right. So, what does Sellie do for you?'

'She does the housework and laundry but she told me she is also a cook, so I tried her out a couple of times and she did well. She made spaghetti Bolognese once, and two days ago she made cottage pie.'

'Cottage pie in Africa, wow, that's terrific!'

'But now she will take her orders from you.'

'Me? I can't give orders.' Jane, rapidly forgetting about the previous day's nightmare, was a little overawed with the prospect of being in charge of someone. 'Well, I'll do my best. But let's get back to the police problem, we seemed to get side-tracked. What happened after you phoned for help?'

'Well, I'm not too sure but it appears the British High Commission phoned the police station although I don't know what was said. The German Embassy, however, sent someone round, a chap called Hans Schulz. When I told him what had happened he spoke harshly to the officer in charge saying I must be released within the next four hours. It seems he had to give them this time to save face. Saving face is important here. Ken Kasansa came, and although they wouldn't let him see me, he stayed outside until Hans Schulz came back. Hans told the officers that he was taking me away. They didn't try to stop us and Ken brought me home. I agreed I would go back there sometime on Monday, and that's how it was left.'

'What will happen then?'

'According to Hans, they'll do nothing. I won't be charged and everyone will want to forget it ever happened. I hope he's right. Certainly when I involved the German Embassy it made the police a little nervous.'

'Well, I hope nothing else happens as I don't want a criminal for a husband, do I?' Jane smiled. 'You told me the job was interesting and challenging and you weren't kidding. Why was it the Germans and not the British who got you out?'

'Partly because I work for a German company and partly because the British High Commission prefers someone else to sort out problems.'

'So, when a country was once a colony of Britain, the embassy isn't called an embassy but a High Commission. Is that right?'

'Yes, as long as it's still in the Commonwealth. Buzamba gained its independence in 1964 and our beloved President, Amos Mutua, who took control following a rebel uprising in 1996, enjoys going on his *jollies* to Commonwealth conferences. And, like most African rulers, he flies there in his private jet.'

'Do they have elections here, like a democracy?'

Robert gave a short laugh. 'Elections don't bring democracy, only chaos. There haven't been elections since Amos took power but he's under pressure from the UN to hold them soon.'

'If there are no elections, then what?'

'I honestly don't know. Some form of benevolent dictator, I guess. Anyhow,' Robert said, changing the subject, 'I suggest that, on the basis that you're not planning on running away, I show you the ins and outs of the house. After that I'll make lunch and then we can have a walk round the compound; there are thirty-five houses.'

'Okay,' agreed Jane. 'I'm beginning to think we'll be all right now.'

'One thing that works well, surprising in a way, is the mobile phone network. A South African company installed the system two years ago but, just like England, the handsets are targets for criminals.' Robert went to his desk and took out a mobile phone and gave it to Jane. 'This is for you. I've already entered all the important numbers, including the German Embassy,' he smiled, 'and it would be good if you take it with you whenever you go out of the compound. Most women carry them in an inside pocket which is safer than a handbag.'

'Yes. It makes sense.'

After exploring part of the garden, a happy-looking Gilly joined them on the veranda.

'And, while I remember, the locals call us white people *mzungus*, and you'll hear that quite often when you're in town, but it's not threatening so don't worry.'

'Am I a zungoos?' asked Gilly, struggling with the pronunciation.

'Yes, we're all *mzungus*,' laughed Robert.

Curious to see the rest of the compound, after a light lunch and wearing shorts and T-shirts, they set off to explore. A generous covering of sunscreen protected them from the burning sun, although both Jane and Gilly were already tanned from the English summer.

'Look, you can now see that all the houses have rogue bars,' Robert pointed them out as they strolled along the road.

'Yes, I see. Who lives there?' Jane pointed to a large imposing house.

'Almost certainly the owner will be a rich local. I don't know anyone in the compound except a chap called Gregg Bond from InterBank but I'm told the residents are a mixture of expats and locals.'

'Mr Bond is it? Sounds exciting,' Jane laughed.

'Please. He's heard every possible joke about his name a hundred times over, so I'd avoid it if I were you.'

Lying in the middle of the road they saw a weaver bird's nest. Gilly looked up to Robert and hesitantly asked if she could pick it up.

'Yes, of course.' Looking up at the overhanging tree, they saw it was alive with noisy little yellow and black birds busy with the dozen or so nests hanging perilously from the branches. 'It must have just fallen; the nests are not only for breeding but are a year-long lodging house, so some poor little blighter will need to get busy.'

Gilly gingerly handed it to Robert who looked inside and shook it. 'It looks all right but we'll spray it with insecticide when we get home.'

'It's beautiful,' Jane examined the woven tubular nest with a tiny entrance hole at the bottom.

'Yes. It's the most elaborate nest of any bird in the world. They use four different knots to build a roof, walls and entrance. It's the male that builds the nest on spec, and then tries to tempt a female inside. If she likes it, they mate.'

'What a lovely story. Aha,' Jane suddenly smiled, making a connection that Robert hadn't even considered. 'Just a moment, I get it. You tempt me with your big house here... your nest, and now you expect to... you naughty man.'

He gave an embarrassed smile. 'Well, you've already said you like my house so it's too late now.'

Jane gave him a little poke in the ribs as the path turned a corner, revealing a recreation area with a swimming pool and a tennis court. Several people, some wearing swimming costumes, were standing about in random groups near a large barbecue billowing smoke.

'Ah, I forgot to tell you, we also have this communal pool and tennis court,' Robert said awkwardly.

'You forgot! How could you forget that?'

'I guess it must have slipped my mind, what with everything... and those noisy weaver birds.'

'Are we allowed to use it?' Gilly asked.

'Oh sure. It's for all the residents of the compound.'

One of the men waved at them. 'Hi Robert, come and join us.'

'No, that's OK,' Robert shouted back and gave him an uneasy wave.

'Well that's not very polite is it?' Jane hissed through clenched teeth. 'Let's go and meet them.'

She could see that Robert was reverting to his timid mode but she wasn't going to let him get away with it. She wasn't shy. 'Tell that man over there – who is it by the way? – that we'll go and meet them.'

'That's the Gregg Bond I mentioned, but I don't know any of the others. Are you sure you want to?'

'Yes, I do. They're probably our neighbours.'

Robert reluctantly agreed, and gave Gregg another wave to indicate they were on their way. There were a series of 'hellos' and greetings from about twenty men, women and children of varying ages and sizes. Around half were white and the others various shades of brown and black.

'Welcome,' Gregg said shaking Robert's hand. Being confronted by so many new people, he was looking ill at ease.

Jane quickly took over. 'Hello,' she said, proffering her hand, 'I'm Jane and this is our daughter Gilly.'

Gregg gave them both a big smile. 'Welcome to the Bazu Compound, come and meet some of your neighbours.' He also gave a kindly smile to Gilly who was tightly holding her mum's hand.

'Thank you.' Jane saw that some of the people had turned in their direction.

'They're all a grotty lot,' Gregg joked, 'but you'll just have to make the best of them.'

Jane took an instant liking to Gregg. He was about Robert's age and height and had an easy charm that was very attractive.

'Meet Josie and Lester,' Gregg announced. A slightly older couple held out their hands. 'They're from the colonies and speak funny.'

'Ignore him,' smiled the man. 'He's only a disreputable banker. I'm Lester and my wife here is Josie. Welcome to Basu compound. And if you haven't already guessed, we're from God's own country – Canada.'

'Ah, so that's where God lives,' Jane said, 'I've always wondered.' She was pleased with her quick-witted reply, and the responsive reaction from the others. Her adrenalin levels must still be high.

'We normally keep it a secret,' chimed in a laughing Josie, he lives just up the road from Santa Claus.'

'And all these years I thought they were both English.' Robert managed to come out of his shell and gave a nervy grin when they laughed.

Lester and Josie, after asking a few questions about her first impressions, said they looked forward to seeing them later.

What nice people, Jane thought. First Gregg and then Lester and Josie seemed to have a certain aura of confidence about them which Jane thought might be because they were well-educated and well-travelled, and although she wasn't necessarily intimidated by them, she wondered if she would be able to hold her own if and when she got to know them better.

'And this old man,' Gregg continued in his droll derogatory manner, 'is Old Man Quentin McKeever, another bloody colonial, this time from South Africa.'

'You're a cheeky bugger, Gregg,' the man barked, 'I'm no age at all. Hello you two, I'm Quentin.' As he shook hands with Jane, he openly stared at her scar and gave a puzzled look at Robert, as though he was responsible for it; Jane was annoyed at his impertinence. Then he noticed Gilly and gave her a big smile. It was clear that Quentin had an overpowering personality and wouldn't ever be overshadowed by anyone, even Gregg.

Quentin turned and called loudly to his wife. 'Kath, come and meet our two newcomers, Jane and Robert.' It was more of an order than a request.

Kath, who had been talking with another group, obediently came straight over. She was quite small and seemed more timid than the others. 'Hello and welcome,' she smiled. 'If you need any help in settling in, please let me know.'

Jane and a nervous Robert thanked them all for their welcome and remarked how beautiful it was there.

After introducing them to some others, Gregg took them to meet a stunning looking lady, the blackest there, who was wearing a brief bikini which, in Jane's eyes, was only just decent. 'This is my wife, Cindy,' he said proudly, 'and over there,' he pointed in the direction of two light brown girls who had just got out of the pool, 'are our daughters.'

Cindy gave them all a huge smile. 'Welcome to paradise,' she laughed. She had an attractive English accent and made it obvious that she was very pleased to meet them. Even though she was skimpily dressed, she gave all three of them a hug and a kiss on their cheeks. This embarrassed Robert and made Gilly giggle.

'Thank you for the welcome,' Jane laughed. 'It certainly looks like paradise.'

Holding Jane and Gilly's hands, Cindy took them over to meet her daughters, while Robert and Gregg stood and watched. Trish, aged nine, was the tallest and Susie, six, was about the same size as Gilly.

Very quickly, they were all provided with drinks and food from the barbecue and Jane was relieved to see that Robert looked more relaxed and seemed to be getting on well with Gregg. Jane chatted with many of the other residents and found them friendly but the one she was most relaxed with was the shameless Cindy in her brief bikini. It was good to see Gilly happily playing with Trish and Susie. Next time they came they would be prepared for swimming.

During a brief lull, Jane took stock and couldn't quite believe what had happened to her in the last twenty-four hours. After travelling halfway round the world and to be frightened half to death, here she was with a brand new husband (who now seemed to be genuine), mixing with complete strangers of various races and nationalities in the most beautiful tropical setting. A way of life she had only seen in films or read about in books – a way of life she had never, ever dreamt could be hers. She thought about pinching herself just to see if it was all a dream and felt that it just couldn't last. Something would happen to bring it all tumbling down, and would that something be Robert?

CHAPTER TEN

Tentatively, Robert put the question which he'd mulled over for the last couple of days. 'So, what do you think?' They were sitting on the sofa, Robert, his arm around Jane's shoulders, was enjoying the intimacy and the feel of her leaning against him.

'What do I think of what?'

'You know, living with me and everything you've seen here so far.'

She turned and gave him a smile. 'Give me time. I've only been here three days but apart from you being "missing without trace" when I arrived, it's been good.'

'And Gilly, she's adapted amazingly well.'

'Yes, hasn't she? It's fantastic that she's started school already and loved her first day. Going with the Bond girls and sitting next to Susie must have done the trick, and having only fifteen children in the class must be good.'

'Having not had kids before, it was hard for me to judge what the schools were like, but other parents I know were very pleased with this one.'

'Yes, it reminds me of an old-fashioned village school... you know, small and friendly. And having mainly black teachers didn't faze Gilly at all; I was worried about her education before coming out here, I don't think I needed to.'

He put his arms around her and planted a tender kiss on her lips. 'I love you, Mrs Kimber.'

She wasn't yet ready to declare her love for him – it was much too early. However, she liked him and his company and had a good feeling that at the very least, they'd be good friends.... well, that was a bit silly, they'd have to be more than friends considering they shared a bed together... and the sex was pleasant enough... no, that's unfair, it was more than just pleasant, he was gentle and caring and tender when they made love and, she had to admit, she enjoyed it. 'I think you're pretty good yourself, Mr Kimber.'

He would have liked a bit more enthusiasm, but time was on his side to prove that he was more than 'pretty good'.

'I love the house and everyone I've met has been very friendly, although Quentin is a bit hard-going.' She repositioned herself to get the benefit of the cooling air from the ceiling fan. 'It's so much nicer than I'd imagined.'

This was exactly what Robert was hoping to hear.

'But, there is something.' She turned and eyed him thoughtfully.

'Ah! I thought there may be a 'but' with you.' There was a note of caution in his voice.

'The 'but' is that I can see myself getting bored even though there's a pool. I'll definitely need something to do especially as Sellie does all the housework and laundry. Perhaps I could get a job.'

'That's not easy as there aren't many jobs for foreign women. The embassies employ a few but those jobs get snapped up and there's always a waiting list. There's a chance of voluntary work if that's of interest.'

'I'll do anything. As you know, I'm a super-sleuth investigative journalist, ha ha, and I'm okay with computers and accounting systems. Can I work for you?'

'No, the company definitely wouldn't allow that and, Akuko, my secretary would be a bit miffed. I'll tell you what, I'll speak to Ken Kasansa. Remember, you met him the other night. He's our project manager at the Ogola slum project. He might know of something.'

'That's settled then.'

'In fact, I'll take you there. How about after you're settled in better, say sometime next week? He's a brilliant chap and I'm sure you'll like him.'

'Well, I only saw him briefly the other night and I wasn't in the right mood to be nice to him.'

'Oh, he'll understand. Next week it is then.'

The smell of freshly ground coffee assailed Cindy's nostrils as it bubbled and popped in the percolator. She had called round to see how Jane was getting used to her new environment. They chatted about various things including their children, the social life, and the dos and don'ts of living in Africa.

'Always be careful how you speak to Africans; they can be very tetchy.'

'How do you mean?'

She listed some of the things which could be misconstrued with the advice to be very careful as offence is often taken when none is intended.

'Oh dear, well, thanks for the warning.'

Finishing coffee and in need of a breath of fresh air, Jane sauntered back with Cindy to her house, along the mango tree and palm shaded road; the sun was so bright it seemed to bleach all the colour out of the sky. On their way, they met Kath, carrying a parasol, who told them she and Quentin were planning a dinner party later in the month and hoped that the two of them and their spouses would come. So, thought Jane, was this the 'social dining' Robert had put in his first letter to Poppy?

It was fresh and cool inside Cindy's house and she suggested that after lunch, she should take Jane to see what food was available in the local supermarkets. Jane already had Sellie's shopping list and willingly accepted. It was a novelty for Jane to be driven in style by the Bond's chauffeur, Solomon.

'Why are the traffic lights only red and green... there's no amber?' Jane looked puzzled.

Cindy laughed. 'The story is that the extra money for amber lights was pocketed by the President.'

'Ah, I see, more corruption,' Jane sighed.

When they reached the store, Jane couldn't believe her eyes when she saw beggars and cripples crowding round the entrance. There were the old and infirm, children holding the hands of the blind, and many with wasted lower limbs who used small blocks of wood to propel themselves amongst the other poor and disabled. They called out to them, holding up their often withered hands for money.

Feeling sick and helpless, Jane looked for guidance from Cindy who was already giving coins to half a dozen beggars. Noting Jane looking lost, she passed her some coins to give to those who had been missed, and then they scurried inside the supermarket.

'Wow, is it always like this?' Jane was visibly shaken.

'Unfortunately, yes. But you get used to it.'

Jane was sceptical about that – how could anyone get used to it?

Surprisingly, the inside was similar to small supermarkets in England, with a row of fruit and vegetables, some local and some imported, a good variety of tinned food, a freezer section for meats, and a selection of ice cream. There were also shelves of beer, wine and spirits. What was even more surprising was one long shelf filled with good quality children's books and toys.

'Whatever you do, don't try and convert these prices into UK money,' Cindy told Jane. 'You buy whatever you need and that's that. Oh, and don't look at 'sell-by' dates either!' she laughed. 'But the things to be careful about are imported wine and spirits which are incredibly expensive. The local beer and gin and even the brandy are OK, but the local wine is ghastly.'

Armed with Sellie's list and guided by Cindy, Jane managed to buy almost everything she needed and was pleasantly surprised to find many of the British and European tinned, bottled and packaged foods that she bought at home.

Solomon was waiting at the exit to carry their bags to the car. No beggars were in sight; for some reason they restricted their begging to the entrance.

With each day dawning hot and dry with clear blue skies, the compound pool was a boon and a popular place for many of the wives to meet. After only a few days, Jane had made several new acquaintances. Apart from Cindy, Kath and Josie who she'd already met, there was Mona and Jewel who were Buzambans, and married to Aaron and Frank respectively. Jane found that meeting so many new people in such a short time was confusing, but Cindy assured her she would soon be placing names and faces together, while remembering who was married to whom. And most importantly, who was playing around with whom. But that would come later. Jane got the distinct impression that Cindy had her ear to the ground as far as any gossip was concerned which, once again, reminded her of Poppy.

One thing Jane found unnerving was having a house-girl in her house. Every day except Sunday, it was Sellie's job to clean the house and make the beds. At first, Jane wanted to do their bedrooms and bathrooms herself but Robert explained that this would upset Sellie who would think she wasn't trusted. And besides, it was too hot for physical work. It wasn't long before Jane was only too pleased to let Sellie do it all, her only input being to check it was done properly.

Gradually, Jane became relaxed enough with Sellie to ask her about her family and why she did this kind of work. She explained that she came from a village near Lake Arthur in the north east of the country where her family made a living from farming and fishing.

The one thing Jane did want to ask Sellie about was her badly disfigured face, but she didn't feel she knew her well enough to broach the subject, so it caught her by surprise when Sellie asked about the scar on her face. Jane told her about the *car crash,* and then she felt free to ask Sellie the same question. The blotching on the left side of her face happened when she was twelve. Following a girl's first period, it was traditional in her tribe to make two small cuts on either side of the face just below the level of the eyes; this was an outward sign of being ready for marriage. She pointed to the two small scars on the right side of her face that had healed over. Unfortunately, one of the cuts on the left side had turned septic and the family called the local traditional doctor, or witch doctor as they are known to *mzungus.* He used some medicine which badly burnt her face, leaving her permanently scarred. His excuse was that she had evil spirits in her body which the medicine had driven out, leavingher disfigured as a punishment. Her parents, being primitive people in awe of the spirit person, accepted the situation. But she didn't.

'What did you do, or what could you do?' Jane asked.

'We people believe there are always big reasons why good things happen and why bad things happen. We believe sickness and accidents are not caused by virus or bad luck like you people believe, it always bad juju magic that makes sickness and bad things happen.'

'I think I understand.' Jane was still confused but didn't want to say so.

'There many kind of traditional doctor in Africa; they do different, different things, like make sick people better, mend broken bones, but other spirit people make bad juju and people get sick or die.'

'They make people die! Why would they do that?'

'For revenge. I wanted revenge for my face… so I did it.'

'Hang on… you had the man killed?' Jane was now getting worried.

'No,' Sellie replied thoughtfully, as if she was only now justifying what she had done. 'I not want him killed, the man what scar me, I want him punished. A spirit man near my village strike people with sky-fire… so… I meet this man and he learn me things. I pay him to do this thing for me.'

Jane's alarm was growing by the minute. Who was this woman sharing their house? Sellie seemed so nice but now Jane wasn't sure. She thought of leaving it there but curiosity got the better of her. 'So what happened?'

'One month after I make contract, there this big storm, and fire from sky, you call lightning, hit that bad man on his head, he scarred now… just like me.' Sellie said in a very satisfied manner. 'Like the Bible say, *"an eye for an eye and a tooth for a tooth"*. I get revenge.'

'Now you've really frightened me, Sellie. I hope I don't meet any bad juju witch doctor.'

'Ha! Witch doctors can't hurt you, Madam.' Sellie laughed. 'They can't hurt *mzungus* people.'

'But why not?'

'Because you people not believe in African magic. It only our people who believe this thing. But I think you have same thing in England.'

'No, Sellie, I don't think we have anything like that.'

'I think so. I read… err… book about a so-so treasure place, and bad person gave some man the *black spot*… to make him die. It's the same thing.'

'Oh, yes, you're right,' Jane laughed, 'but that was a long time ago. It doesn't happen now, and *Treasure Island* was a book of fiction, it was pretend.'

Sellie wasn't convinced. In fact she looked very pleased as she had shown the *mzungu* madam that it wasn't only in Africa that people made bad magic.

Jane dropped the subject of witch doctors and spirit people and returned to their shared facial disfigurements.

Sellie said that her appearance made it impossible for her to get married. 'No man want a wife who look like me.' She said it without any sign of emotion. Her main regret was that she would never have children. She'd had six years' education at a Catholic mission school in her village and, unlike her parents, was able to read and write. The main reason for coming to Ouverru was to find work in an office and send money home. This didn't happen because there were very few jobs for semi-educated girls and her appearance put off potential employers. Eventually, through a woman from her village who was housekeeper to a Swiss family, she found a job as a laundry girl. For two years she did all the laundry as well as some housework, but all the time she watched the cook preparing meals and she helped her with the recipes. When the cook was fired for stealing some of the madam's jewellery, Sellie was given her job and the madam was very pleased with her work. Entertaining was a big part of the family life, and Sellie gradually learnt to do all the catering without any help. Unfortunately, the family had had to leave Buzamba two months ago and it was then that she got the job with Mr Kimber.

Cindy Bond rapidly became Jane's best friend and confidante. She was also one of the sexiest women she had ever met, with beautiful features and a great figure, albeit on the plumpish side. It was not only the way she held herself when standing or sitting but it was the way she walked that really caught the eye. She was so confident, swaying her hips slightly from side to side rather like Marilyn Monroe's famous walk in the film *Some Like It Hot* – 'like jello on springs' was Jack Lemon's famous line. And not only was Cindy at the top of the 'sex appeal charts' but her husband, Gregg, was one of the most attractive men she'd met for a long time. What a couple! Did she hear alarm bells ringing?

It wasn't long before Jane and Cindy swapped stories about their earlier lives and how they had met their husbands.

Born twenty-nine years ago in Jamaica, Cindy was the younger of two daughters. Her father worked for the Jamaican High Commission in London and the two girls were sent to a private school where they picked up their cultured accents. 'I'm as black as the ace of spades but I speak like the Queen,' she said, laughing at the irony.

At her first job as a trainee bank clerk, Gregg was her immediate boss. The moment she set eyes on him she fell head over heels in love, although her feelings were not reciprocated at the time. In fact, he already had a girlfriend but, luckily for Cindy, they gradually drifted apart. That's when Cindy struck. She and some friends planned a drinks party one Saturday and invited Gregg. After a few relaxing drinks she worked her spell on him like a sorceress with a magic potion, ending up making love under a pile of clothes in her bedroom. A few weeks later, she moved in with him. Gregg did well at the bank and, three years ago, the company had offered him the position as deputy to InterBank's general manager in Buzamba. They were excited at the thought of living in Africa but Gregg told her that to satisfy Buzamban visa regulations, they had to get married. Although his parents weren't pleased he was going to marry a black girl, Gregg was determined to go ahead, and by the time the big day arrived, they had reluctantly accepted it.

While Gregg was at work and the girls at school, Cindy kept herself occupied by playing bridge twice a week and mah-jongg every Friday afternoon. The family spent most Saturday mornings at the golf club and, while Gregg and Cindy played, the girls used the club's pool and other facilities. They usually spent Sundays in the compound having a barbecue and swimming. Both of them were members of the Ouverru Amateur Dramatic Society which put on a drama or musical twice a year, and a pantomime at Christmas. 'And that, my dear,' Cindy said, 'is the life of an expat's wife. I love it and here's hoping you do too.'

Then it was Jane's turn. She gave a sanitised version of her parents and how her first heartthrob, Peter Collins had left her pregnant – left being the operative word as she'd not seen him again. She went into detail about her best friends, Poppy and Tony, and finished by telling her how she'd met Robert. Cindy was amazed to hear her story and the way in which Robert had gradually worn her down.

'I hope you tried him out in the bedroom a few times before you said yes,' Cindy eyed her cheekily.

'No. Not until after the wedding. In fact it was the night before he left to come out here.'

'That was one hell of a risk, wasn't it?' Cindy said in mock horror. 'It's golden rule number one, darling… have sex with him a dozen times before you commit, to make sure he can fulfil his marital responsibilities.'

'You sound just like my friend Poppy,' Jane laughed. 'That's exactly the crude sort of thing she would say. Anyway, I've no complaints in that department, thank you very much for your concern.'

'Well that's all right then. So instead of knowing his sexual prowess, what was it that won you over? Was he fantastically exciting?'

This brought a smile to Jane's lips. 'No, not really. I must admit, at first, I found him boring.'

'I wouldn't call Robert boring,' retorted Cindy. 'Maybe he's quiet and a little shy but, in fact, I think he's very attractive.'

Jane thought about that for a moment. Should she be anxious that *sexy Cindy* showed an interest in him? 'He was shy when we first met and that put me off. He later told me his parents and sister were just the same.'

'Wow, what a fun family they must have been,' Cindy said flippantly.

'I think coming to Africa helped him to gain confidence. He had a girlfriend here before he met me.'

'Ooh,' smirked Cindy. 'He likes black girls then. If I play my cards right…'

Although she knew Cindy was joking, Jane thought she'd better bring a halt to any thoughts she might have in that direction. 'Hey, hands off Robert – he's mine.'

'Just my sense of humour, my dear,' laughed Cindy with an impish sparkle in her eye. 'Did he do the same as Gregg and tell you that you had to be married to get a visa?'

'Yes.'

'Devious bloody buggers – both of them.'

'Why do you say that?'

'Well, it is the law in Buzamba but it hasn't been enforced for at least ten years. You could have come out here without being married.'

It took Jane a few seconds for this to sink in. 'You think he tricked me then?'

'I think so, honey. I know several single women who've come out here and cohabited.'

This made Jane angry. 'The sneaky bastard, I think I'll have a word with bloody Kimber this evening.'

'Be easy with him, honey. Don't go and spoil a perfect marriage. Anyway,' she thought it opportune to change the subject, 'your little girl, Gilly seems to be settling in well. Trish and Rosie are thrilled to have her here – they get on so well and Rosie says she's doing well at school.'

'Yes. It's amazing how quickly she's adapted to her new life. I think having Robert as her daddy has been a big factor.'

'There you are then. Maybe tricking you worked out just fine. And as well as Trish and Rosie having a new best friend, Gregg and I have also got new best friends in you and Robert. I just know we're going to get on well together,' Cindy gave Jane a mischievous smirk and then reached over and kissed her on both cheeks.

Jane did her best to show how much she appreciated Cindy's gesture, but they hardly knew each other and, deep down, she preferred best friend declarations to take a little longer to develop.

She decided she wouldn't raise the visa question with Robert for the time being, but she'd hold it back for another day… there may come a day when she'd need it.

That night, she sent her first article to Tony giving him her initial reaction to life as an expat wife living in Africa

CHAPTER ELEVEN

The following week, Jane reminded Robert that he'd promised to help her find some kind of job to keep her occupied, instead of just living in the bubble of Basu compound. As he'd already mentioned it to Ken Kasansa in Ogola, he arranged that they'd go the following morning, calling at his main office on the way so she could see where he worked most of the time.

Schultec's office was situated in a drab block near the centre of Ouverru and, as they entered, Jane saw a short chubby African lady sitting in the reception area, industriously tapping away at her computer keyboard. Robert introduced Patience Akuku, his secretary, who looked up and smiled. Comfortably sprawled on a battered looking basket chair near the entrance, Basil was the only other person in the office.

'So this is where I park myself,' Robert said stepping into a relatively small room containing a cluttered desk, two visitors' chairs and a couple of filing cabinets, one of which acted as a table for a photocopier. He had a few e-mails and papers which needed his immediate attention and when he started taking phone calls, Jane quietly closed his door and went to talk to Patience Akuku. Meeting strangers had always been easy for Jane; being a confident person, she found it no more difficult talking to the Africans in Buzamba than the English in Ringwood. Once the ice was broken, she and Patience were soon chatting and exchanging details of their respective families and when politeness allowed, Patience asked how she and Mr Kimber had met and married in just six weeks.

Before answering, Jane turned and looked behind her. 'This is woman's talk Basil; you're not to listen, OK?'

'Ma ear close, Madam,' he replied as all three of them laughed.

Jane told an astonished Patience about Poppy and her introduction agency; how they were introduced and the whirlwind courtship, leading to marriage on the day before Robert returned to Buzamba.

Patience's open mouth turned into a big grin. 'It must have been love at first sight,' she laughed. Like many Africans, she loved to laugh, her face lighting up and her laugh showing her perfect white teeth.

When Jane and Patience turned round, Basil was also laughing but, seeing he'd been caught, he put his hands over his ears. 'I not hear nothing, Madam,' making them laugh even louder.

'Keep quiet out there,' Robert's voice came through from his office, 'this is a work place, not a playground.'

Putting on guilty expressions, they all grinned widely. Patience then continued in a much lower voice. 'And I'm so glad he found such a nice lady like you.'

'Well, thank you,' Jane smiled back.

'I didn't like the girlfriend he had before.' Patience's expression suddenly changed to one of alarm as she realised she'd said too much. 'Oh dear, I'm sorry.' She put her hand over her mouth and Jane thought she was probably blushing bright red under her dark skin.

Seeing her embarrassment, Jane reached across and took hold of her hand in a token of friendship. 'It's OK, Patience, he told me he'd had a girlfriend before he met me. Did she come to the office?'

'A few times, but Mr Kimber got annoyed and kept telling her to stay away. She wasn't very nice,' Patience concluded, immediately changing the subject. 'Tell me about your little girl.'

They talked for a few more minutes, feeling that a bond had been forged between them.

'Here's the keys, Basil,' Robert came out of his office and threw them over before turning to Patience. 'I'm taking Jane to have a look at Ogola but I'll be back later this afternoon.'

'Yes, Mr Kimber,' she replied. 'It's not very nice there,' she said to Jane showing concern as they shook hands. 'I hope you've been warned.'

'Yes, thank you, Patience. Anyhow, it's been nice to meet you and I'll look forward to seeing you again shortly.'

Cutty Road, leading to Ogola Slum, was full of potholes, like a rough farm track, with mounds of fly-covered garbage and clouds of dust and litter blowing in gusts, seemingly from all directions. Single storey shacks of differing shapes and states of disrepair, made from corrugated iron, and ragged pieces of canvas, lined both sides of the road. From the air-conditioned comfort of their vehicle, Jane's overall impression was of a dirty, run-down crowded shambles. Large numbers of brightly dressed men, women and children, threaded their way between the obstacles, among numerous market stalls selling items ranging from fruit and vegetables to cooking pots and second-hand clothing. Despite their surroundings, many of the people looked cheerful enough, and some of the women looked very smart wearing long colourful dresses, in bright reds, yellows and blues, with matching turban-style hats. A group of giggling school children, wearing colour co-ordinated red shirts and khaki shorts or skirts, jostled their way through the crowds under the control of a male teacher.

As they wove around the deepest craters, drivers of mini-buses called *matatus*, cars, trucks, motor bikes and bicycles honked their horns at everything and everybody who was conceivably in their way.

After travelling for about a mile, Basil turned onto a dirt track which was even more litter-strewn than the main road. Two large concrete posts with rusted iron hinges stood like sentries at either side of the track but there was no sign of the gates which had once hung there. A few yards beyond the posts was a large corrugated-iron shed which had seen better days, the roof slanting at an unnatural angle and years of rust and corrosion evident on the dust-covered walls. Two windows with iron bars were open and a straggly group of people queued outside. On the nearest side of the building was an unpainted wooden door marked 'OFFICE'.

'Welcome to Ogola.' Robert held the vehicle door open for her. The air buzzed with insects and it was stifling hot like a steam bath, supplemented with a mixture of dust and strange smells.

'Is this the office?' She was shocked that this rundown, rusty old shed appeared to be the office. 'Do you work here?'

'I come for a few hours two or three times a week, yes. This is the Africa tourists never see,' he said with a touch of irony.

Since her arrival in Ouverru, Jane hadn't been anywhere remotely like this and the few tourists to Buzamba wouldn't even know such places existed.

Inside was almost as dusty as outside. There were some dark-stained plywood partitions between three individual offices. By the light from four bare light bulbs hanging from the ceiling, she could see the concrete floor was also dusty. As well as the two barred windows she'd seen when they arrived, there were similar ones in the other two offices, none of which were glazed, but had steel-reinforced shutters resting beneath, to be fixed over the openings when the office was closed.

Robert could see that Jane was shaken and tried to lift her spirits. 'Don't worry, this is only temporary. We start constructing the new head office in a couple of weeks.'

It was all a bit overwhelming for Jane to say anything positive.

'Ah, here's Ken Kasansa.' Robert introduced him properly to Jane this time, and she took the opportunity to apologise for being curt when he came round to the house on that fateful first night. He smiled graciously saying he fully understood.

'If you two don't mind, Ken, I need to have a meeting with the contractor over an unpaid bill. I won't be more than an hour.'

'That's okay with me as long as Jane doesn't mind.'

Robert smiled encouragingly at his hesitant wife. 'Ken's the expert here. He runs the show.'

Jane was reassured by Ken's friendly nature and she was pleased that he was easier to understand than most locals. She later learned that when he was a boy, Buzamba was still a British colony and his father, being a top official in the colonial administration had, with his family, socialised with the British. When Buzamba gained its independence, the British had proposed Ken for a senior position but this was rejected because he was from the *wrong tribe*.

The first and all succeeding presidents were from the majority Peelee tribe so it naturally followed that most of the top jobs were held by them; the Vice-President was always from the second largest Solu tribe. Ken was from the smaller elite Busti tribe which, prior to colonisation, had ruled a large area of the country. Although many Bustis had the knowledge and experience to help the young country through the initial tribulations of independence, they were only allowed minor roles under the control of the Peelees or Solus.

Through a family connection, Ken got a job with the EU based in Brussels, and was assigned to work with several European development agencies. He spent five years in Europe before returning to Buzamba to get married and settle down.

After Robert left, Ken took Jane round the office and introduced her to the accountant, Hani, the two cashiers, Momo and Amos, the accounts clerk Lola, and Ruth, the cleaner who also made tea and coffee for them all. They then returned to Ken's office.

'Poor girl, she must have a hard job trying to keep this place clean with all the dust blowing in through the windows.'

'Yes, she is a poor girl,' Ken nodded. 'She was diagnosed HIV positive last month,' he paused. 'She has four young children and... her husband died last year.'

This was Jane's first direct contact with anything to do with AIDS. She gave a sharp intake of breath, unable to speak for a moment, and glanced at Ruth who was taking cups of tea to the other staff. She tried to see if her face showed any sign of her illness, but she looked normal.

'Is Hani good at his job?'

Ken shrugged his shoulders. 'To be perfectly honest, I don't really know. He has a certificate showing he passed an accounting exam, but that doesn't necessarily mean much here. But he's never used a computer.'

'Oh wow. That doesn't sound good.'

'But he comes from a top family – the Oburus. His uncle, Samuel Oburu, happens to be the Vice-President but, his father fell out with him years ago and that's why Hani works here instead of having a big job in government.'

'Poor chap... well, maybe not! Is it good to be connected to the Vice-President?'

'It can be a mixed blessing. Because most power here is tribal-related, he could have as many enemies as friends.'

Ken led her into another office to show her a plan of the project area. 'The total Ogola slum is about two square miles with a mind-boggling population of some nine-hundred thousand; the section of the German-sponsored project houses around 150,000 people; bounded on one side by Cutty Road ,on another by the Sambula River... oh, by the way, Sambula means blue in the Peelee language but this river hasn't been blue in living memory. On the third side is an old basalt quarry, and the rear borders onto the grounds of the Catholic High School.'

'You say almost one million people live in two square miles! Surely not.'

'Amazing, isn't it?' Ken saw the look of disbelief on Jane's face. 'It's not the most congested slum though. For example, Kibera in Nairobi has one million people in only one and a half square miles.'

All Jane could do was shake her head in disbelief.

'Oh, and incidentally,' he added, 'one of the people owning a lot of buildings in Ogola is the local MP, a man called K.K. Machuri, who is also the main troublemaker.'

'You're joking,' Jane said in disbelief.

'I wish I was. He and a few other well-connected people are constantly giving us a hard time.'

'But why? Don't they want the people to have better lives?'

Ken sighed and gave a despondent shrug. 'Where there's foreign money coming in, they want to grab as much of it as they can. I shouldn't be saying this as I could get into trouble but the answer to your question is "no" – they don't care about the poor, only themselves.'

Jane found herself sighing and shaking her head again. If she was to cope with life in Buzamba, she knew she would have to stop doing this.

When Robert had mentioned that Jane was looking for a job, Ken had immediately thought of his own needs. He was an engineer knowing little about accounting and desperately needed help with it. If Jane was willing and able, it could be the answer to his prayers.

'If you don't mind, Jane, while I make a couple of phone calls, would you look in on Hani and the accounts office. I'd like to know what you think.'

On entering the cramped office, baking hot under the corrugated roof, they all smiled politely. Wow! How could anyone work in these conditions? With sweat dribbling down his face, Hani was using a calculator to tot-up figures on a raft of papers, while the two cashiers rapidly scribbled receipts for a queue of people waiting outside to make payments. Jane waited for a lull, hoping they wouldn't think she was interfering if she asked some questions.

'Has anyone considered using computers?' she eventually asked.

'We got computers.' Hani pointed to some dusty cartons piled up against the rear wall but didn't offer any explanation as to why they weren't in use.

Not wanting to probe too much, Jane said nothing.

Hani turned to Ken who had just walked in. 'Mrs Kimber ask if we have computers.'

Ken pulled a face. 'Yes, DGA agreed to provide computers but...' his expression changed to frustration. 'The expert sent by Schultec placed the order in Germany and these boxes,' he pointed to the cartons, 'arrived three months ago but two are still missing. We looked inside these boxes but the manuals are in German – none of us can read German!'

Jane was staggered that Schultec would make this kind of mistake. 'So what happens now?'

'We don't know,' Ken replied.

After Jane thanked Hani for showing her around, she accompanied Ken back to his office.

'Robert tells me you're looking for a job.'

'Yes, not a full-time job but maybe two or three days a week. Why, do you know of anything?'

A sheepish smile creased Ken's face. 'The only job I know of for an expat wife would be here in Ogola. Helping Hani and the accounts staff. If we're to computerise our accounts as DGA demand, then you could be a godsend.'

'Oh!' she was taken by surprise by Ken's immediate offer. When she'd thought of a job, she was thinking of something in an office and not in a filthy baking hot slum.

Seeing the disappointed expression on Jane's face, Ken suggested she think about it. 'Next time you come here, I'll give you the grand tour of the slum.' He laughed and said that would probably put her off for ever.

'Yes, okay then,' Jane said knowing she had plenty of time to decide.

'Ah, there you are,' Robert joined them and turned to Jane. 'So what do you think?'

Jane laughed. 'Well, it's a bit early to say yet but it seems a very ambitious scheme. Next time I'm here, Ken has promised to take me on a tour of the slum.'

'Oh well, you've been warned.'

'And I've seen the accounts office and those unused computers. I'm told the manuals are in German and two boxes are missing.'

'Yes,' Robert sighed.

'So, what happened to the other two?'

'Gone! We searched the warehouse high and low and filled out a "missing item" form; even the German Embassy became involved, but to no avail. Schultec didn't even want to claim on its insurance.'

'Why not?'

'Beats me. I'm still following it up with them but they're in no hurry to answer.'

'Ah, I forgot to tell you,' Robert announced when they arrived home, 'a good friend of mine is coming round for a drink this evening.'

'But the house is a mess, and I'm feeling tired.'

'It's OK, he'll only stay for a short while but I promised he could come. He's very keen to meet you.'

'Who is this friend?'

'He's Jimmy, who was my neighbour in my old bachelor pad and is my best friend here. I think you'll like him. He's a little strange but he's harmless.'

'Ah! He must be the 'Jimmy' who told lovely Precious your new address.'

'Yes, that's him. But please don't say anything as I've already given him an earful. He'll be more careful in future.'

Gilly had just gone to bed when the doorbell rang.

'That'll be him.' Robert opened the door, ushering in a somewhat hesitant visitor. Robert looked in Jane's direction, stood to attention and gave a slight cough as if he was starting to address a huge audience. 'Jane, may I introduce you to Mr f-Fearless f-Faversham, spinster of this parish,' Robert gave a mock bow as his friend entered the room.

'I thought you said his name was Jimmy?' Jane stood and held out her hand to whoever he was.

'Your new husband is sadly p-predictable and trying to be h-hilariously humorous or, at least, he thinks he is,' the man rolled his eyes in Robert's direction. 'My name is Jimmy or, more formally, James Faversham and... err... welcome to Buzamba,' he shook Jane's hand in a slightly nervous manner.

'Thank you, but why the f-Fearless?'

'Well, some people, present c-company included, think I have a slight st-stutter, and the f-fearless bit stuck as it was erroneously reported that I ran away from a threatening situation.'

Robert mocked his last remark. 'He wouldn't pay his bar bill or...'

'All lies,' f-Fearless interrupted.

'I believe you, Jimmy.' It was easy to see that Robert and Jimmy were close friends, probably because they shared the same silly sense of humour.

Jane was a little surprised because Jimmy looked older than Robert and was nothing like the macho Gregg or any of the other men she'd met earlier. He was fairly short, only an inch or two taller than her, very thin and drawn looking, with sallow skin which appeared to have been stretched tight to cover his skull. She wondered if he'd been ill. Over a large forehead, he had thinning brown hair that was turning grey at the sides, and wore thick horn-rimmed, bifocals, which gave him the look of someone who found everything a bit of a puzzle. His eyes, behind the thick lenses, matched his grey pallor and he seemed to blink a lot as if there was dust in the air. Jane could tell that he was uneasy and thought that he was probably another shy type – just like Robert. She wondered if it was living in Africa that made men that way.

It was obvious that Robert had told Jimmy all about her and Gilly, and probably how they'd met so, to keep the conversation going, she found out as much as she could about her husband's friend. Jimmy was English, had been in the country two years longer than Robert and worked as an engineer in the Water Department of the Ouverru City Council. His wife had divorced him eight years earlier and she and their eleven-year-old son lived in Leeds. Jimmy explained, with sardonic gravitas that, as a Buzamban government employee, he did not get the high salary or fringe benefits enjoyed by Robert, but he soldiered on to improve the lot of the citizens of Buzamba. Immediately Robert ridiculed this, countering that Jimmy had the best of everything: a very easy job with no pressure, good pay, never worked overtime, and any *soldiering on* he did was for the sole benefit of f-Fearless f-Faversham. ·

'You can be cruel at times, Kimber,' Jimmy said, 'but I'm sure Jane believes me and not you, you bounder.'

'Of course I do Jimmy, I'm sure you're a credit to your profession.'

They talked a bit longer but Jimmy could see that Jane was tired, so he excused himself just after eight o'clock, saying he hoped to see them again very soon.

'So, what did you think of him?' Robert asked after he'd gone.

'He seemed nice and quite funny but isn't he a lot older than you?'

'He's only about 34 or maybe 35 but he doesn't look well. He had a bad dose of malaria two months ago and lost a lot of weight, but he's on the mend now.'

'I thought he looked a bit haggard but I wasn't sure if it was due to overindulgence of one kind or another.'

'Ha, you mean booze. Yes, he does drink a lot but that's very common here, especially amongst the bachelors. I drank too much myself; but not any longer.'

New experiences were coming thick and fast for Jane, the next being dinner at the home of Kath and Quentin McKeever. Several days earlier, Jane had commandeered the help of Cindy on what was *de rigueur* for such events. Looking round Ouverru at the few dress shops which supplied western clothes, Jane was horrified at the prices of even the simplest outfits.

'What? How much? That's crazy, I can't pay over £200 for a skimpy little top and skirt when I'd pay well under twenty in Sainsbury's.'

'You won't find any Western clothes cheap here.' Cindy laughed at the shocked look on Jane's face. 'Go ahead and buy it. Robert can afford it.'

'Absolutely no way,' Jane was adamant. 'I don't care how much money Robert's got, I couldn't spend such a ridiculous amount on that top. I'd prefer to wear an old T-shirt and go as a scruff.'

'No way! You can't go as Cinderella to the McKeevers' ball. I'll tell you what, I'll lend you one of my outfits and we'll mix-and-match so nobody will know.'

'That'd be fantastic, thanks very much. And I'll make sure that any alterations I make can be taken out afterwards.' Jane had almost put her foot in it by saying she'd have to 'slim everything down', but she'd managed to stop herself just in time.

She'd also quizzed Cindy on what she should expect at dinner parties in Buzamba knowing that Robert wouldn't have a clue. Apparently, they were usually enjoyable but Cindy did warn her that Quentin could be difficult. 'Although he's South African, he's the senior partner of a British accounting firm and considers himself to be one of the leading businessmen in the country. He usually drinks too much, is very opinionated and dominates the conversation.'

'Oh dear. That doesn't sound enjoyable to me.'

'Not only that, but he's a bloody racist. He frequently makes racist comments, but at the same time always going out of his way to exclude me, a Jamaican. His one saving grace is that he can also be extremely funny.

'I'm not sure I'm looking forward to the dinner after all,' said Jane looking worried.

'You'll be fine. From what I know of you, I think you'll be able to hold your own with anybody.'

As they dressed to go out, Jane confided in Robert that she would need help from him that evening because she wasn't sure what to do or say.

'You'll be all right,' he put his arm around her. 'If anyone needs help in these situations it's me. I'm the shy one, remember, not you.' As an afterthought, he added, 'there's a chap called Rex who's also coming to the dinner; he's the fellow I told you about who sold me the flat in Ringwood. So if you sit next to him, you'll have something to talk about.'

Although they were a little late after settling Gilly in bed, with Sellie happily doing the babysitting, they took their time to stroll the short distance to the McKeever's house enjoying the warm evening. There was a light breeze and the tangy smell of orange blossom was almost overpowering. Being slightly behind schedule, they found Cindy and Gregg, as well as Josie and Lester already there.

The gregarious Quentin had a voice that seemed to enter the room before he did. He ushered them in with a flourish, a handshake for Robert and an old fashioned kiss on Jane's hand, before introducing them to the earlier arrivals. They were moving into the living room as Rex and his wife Stella arrived. Jane froze. No, it couldn't be – just couldn't be! But horror of horrors, he was an ex-client from her escort days! Now it was obvious why Robert's flat in Ringwood had looked familiar; she'd been there with Rex and he'd paid £300 to have sex with her. She felt she must have stared at him, mouth agape, for minutes whereas she knew it couldn't have been for more than a second. Would he recognise her? Hoping that nobody had seen her reaction, she put on a smile as she was introduced. After greeting Stella she stood, trying to stop shaking, for what she thought would be a peck on the cheek from Rex but he planted a firm kiss directly on her lips. He reeked of alcohol and as he pulled away, gave her the sort of inept smile that only a drunk can manage. She swore anxiously under her breath certain now that Rex had recognised her.

During their pre-dinner drinks, Jane kept a wary eye on Rex who was downing his drinks as if there was no tomorrow. A few moments later Quentin announced that they should all go into the dining room. He sat at the head of the table in his role as host and Kath sat at the other end nearest to the kitchen. Quentin, looking rather arrogant, surveyed the guests from his top position, whereas Kath looked nervous and kept glancing in his direction like a schoolchild seeking approval from a teacher. To Jane's horror, she was placed between Lester and Rex. She made light conversation with Lester, who worked at the Canadian Trade Commission, and was thankful that Rex concentrated more on getting his glass refilled than trying to talk about their meeting in Ringwood. She was very relieved when the first course was served.

It wasn't long before Quentin interrupted the meal, reprimanding the stewards for their slightest error. His booming voice took no prisoners. 'God, these people!' he glanced heavenward. 'If only they could be more like us,' he quipped. 'But they can't be, can they? It was Cecil Rhodes who once said that to be born and Englishman was to win the lottery of life.'

'Well, you lost out there then, Quentin,' smirked Cindy. 'You're a ruddy South African.'

'Ah, but of good English stock.' He definitely would not concede anything to a black Jamaican. He then shifted his attention to Jane. 'Jane, m'dear, you've been here for a few weeks now. How do you find these bloody people?'

There was silence as all eyes focused on Jane. She knew that Quentin was unfairly targeting her – the newcomer – and she hated the way he had said "m'dear" in such a condescending manner. She was probably the youngest there, but Quentin was about to learn that she could more than hold her own in any company. Her dander was well and truly up. 'Actually Quentin, all these bloody people…'

she repeated *these bloody people* in the same tone he'd used, 'I've met are extremely friendly. I like them.' Jane knew she had already said enough but couldn't help adding. 'And I also think your stewards are doing an excellent job.'

The tension around the table was palpable as all eyes switched to Quentin. Kath held her breath. Robert wasn't sure if he should say something to support her but the words wouldn't come.

'Oh! I've been told off in my own house!' Quentin's expression was more humorous than angry and when he looked back at Jane he realised she was a significant adversary. 'Well, I've obviously been naughty. I promise I'll be a good boy now, Miss,' he smiled warily at her.

The tension that had built up was suddenly released and everyone laughed, including a much happier-looking Kath. Cindy even clapped her hands.

Quentin gave her a shocked look. 'God, you're clapping – am I that much of a bastard?'

'Yes, you are, Quentin. You're really rotten to your staff at times and I agree with Jane that most of the locals are fine.'

Although Quentin had been taken aback by Jane and Cindy, he seemed to enjoy the confrontation. Jane wondered whether he knew he got his own way too much and it was a pleasant experience to be challenged now and again.

'I can see I'll have to turn over a new leaf now I've been shown the error of my ways,' Quentin was clearly amused. He then turned to his two stewards who both looked nervous, being unsure about what was happening. 'You're doing a wonderful job, chaps,' he said. 'Now clear away these bloody plates and bring in the next course.'

Wine glasses were regularly topped up and the repartee was lively with occasional bursts of laughter around the table. They were nearing the end of the main course when, to Jane's horror, she felt Rex's sweaty hand caressing her leg under the table. What the hell was he doing? Each time she pushed it away it stealthily slithered back for another grope. Jane knew she had to do something.

'Excuse me, Quentin, but do you have a dog in the house?'

Quentin looked puzzled. 'No, but we have two in the yard.'

'Well, it's just because something damp keeps rubbing itself on my leg under the table and I can't think what else it could be.'

Rex was seriously inebriated by now and everyone saw his

hand suddenly appear above the tablecloth. His expression of embarrassment was partly masked by his drooling grin.

'For God's sake, Rex,' Quentin boomed as he glared at Rex. 'Stop groping my guests, there's a good fellow.'

Realising he'd acted badly, Rex anxiously looked first at his wife and then at Robert.

'What are you doing?' Stella asked her guilty-looking husband.

'Well… it's… err… her fault; she led me on,' was Rex's slurred response. 'Last time I met her in Ringwood she didn't… err… object then.'

'What the hell do you mean by that?' Quentin shouted angrily.

At last Robert found his tongue. 'Yes, Rex, how dare you? I think you should apologise now or…' Robert's mind was racing and he realised that Rex must have known Jane when she was an escort. He had to stick up for her… but how?

'Hang on a moment,' Quentin stepped in again. 'Is there a simple explanation to all this?' His question wasn't directed at anyone in particular.

Rex started to say something but, in his semi-comatose state, he was struggling to find a way out that would let him save face. 'Well… err… yes, there is…err…'

Trying to keep her composure, Jane knew she had to take the initiative away from the floundering Rex. Her heart was pounding. She would lie through her teeth if necessary. 'Yes, Quentin,' she said, 'there is an explanation. When I lived in Ringwood before I met Robert, I was a single mother and took on various jobs to make extra money.'

Robert was extremely nervous about where this was leading. 'Are you sure you want to continue with this, darling? We can leave now if you like.'

Jane knew she couldn't leave matters there. If Rex was able to label her as a prostitute, then how could she remain in Buzamba? She couldn't. She decided to start with a straightforward explanation, hoping that something – an inspired brainwave – would come to her before she finished. 'A good friend of mine,' she started, 'occasionally did escort work for a legit company in Bournemouth, it was all above board, nothing seedy. The clients were mainly closet homosexuals who'd been invited to a function where they were asked to take their partner. For whatever reason, these men had not 'outed' themselves, so they would hire a lady for the evening. Due to the men's sexual orientation, the ladies never had a problem, and usually received a good tip.'

Rex kept trying to interrupt but Quentin glared at him to keep quiet. As she continued her story, her voice involuntarily started to tremble. 'If my friend had to cancel, she would ask me to fill in for her and I always jumped at the chance. It was money for old rope.'

'I hope you're not suggesting I'm bloody faggot,' Rex tried to stand but the effort seemed beyond him. 'Anyway, it's all lies, don't believe a word she's shaying,' he slurred. 'She was on the game.'

There was a chorus of protest from around the table.

Jane turned and stared directly at Rex. She knew that at the moment, the others were on her side. 'When we first met I thought you were gay, it was only when we went back to your apartment that I discovered you weren't… you were just weird.' Turning to face the others, she couldn't believe her luck; tears were coming to her eyes and, for extra effect, she sobbed quietly as she continued. 'When I went inside his apartment the table was covered in…' she gave another little sob before pretending to struggle to continue… 'dirty magazines… and there was one of those blow-up dolls.' The tears were flowing now.

Robert rushed to her side, put his arm round her shoulders and gave her a handkerchief to wipe her eyes. 'You bastard,' he seethed. He thrust out his chin and grabbed Rex by his shirt collar. Quentin rushed round to stop any violence and the three of them stood locked together for a couple of seconds.

'Take me home, Rex,' Stella commanded, rising from her chair and walking towards the door.

'But it's all lies, I tell you,' Rex was almost screaming by this time.

'Go home, Rex,' Quentin ordered in his commanding voice. 'Take Stella home and I'll call you tomorrow.'

Rex had noticeably sobered up and realised there was nothing he could do. Jane had crucified him and it was clear the others believed her. As Quentin helped him out of the room, he hoped he would be able to convince Stella of his innocence – or at least his side of the story. But that wouldn't be easy because when they first started going out together, she'd found a pile of porno magazines in his desk.

Quentin and Kath were determined to continue with their dinner party. They wouldn't let Rex's bad behaviour spoil their evening. Quentin apologised for Rex's conduct and said that although he'd known him for a couple of years, this was the first time he'd invited the couple for dinner. Jane basked in the sympathy she was receiving, but deep down she felt a tiny bit guilty. Rex didn't have dirty magazines or a blow-up doll, nor had he behaved any worse than her other clients. But, he had groped her leg and who knows what he would have tried if she hadn't put a stop to it? So, she'd got the son of a bitch: revenge against him and all those other sad losers she'd had to put up with.

After the final course, and a significant consumption of wine, the fully satiated diners had a feeling of splendid, alcohol-induced contentment. The seductive sounds of dance music inspired Cindy to totter to her feet and shimmy suggestively in tune to the beat. She obviously loved centre stage. Making erotic gestures with her hands and arms, she slowly traced the contours of her body, simultaneously swaying her hips like some exotic dancer. Her performance got everybody's undivided attention.

'Come and dance with me, Quentin,' she purred towards her host.

Ignoring the hostile glare of his wife, Quentin obeyed, but made sure he didn't make a fool of himself. He was more of a heave-twist-and-throw man when it came to dancing – twisting and twirling Cindy round and round until she had to sit down. Jane thought that would teach her a lesson.

After that brief but frenetic performance, the others gradually took partners for a more sedate dance. A very drunk-looking Gregg invited Jane who, thanks to more wine than she was used to, was more than pleased to dance with him. He was by far the most attractive man present, and his comforting hand on her waist was just what she needed to get Rex completely out of her mind.

'Do you normally dance at a dinner party?' Jane's speech was slightly slurred as she arched her neck to look up into his eyes.

'Not always, but we do at our house. Cindy insists.' Gregg was also having speech difficulties, and Cindy came out as 'Shindy inshists'.

As they danced, Gregg gradually held Jane tighter and took every opportunity to rub his thigh against her. What's all this about, her muddled mind tried to figure out? Does he think that Rex was right and I'm a whore? Like everyone else there, with the exception of Kath, they'd all had too much to drink and she thought it was just the excess of alcohol making Gregg so amorous... but, she had to admit, she liked it.

It was well after midnight when the exhausted Kimbers eventually staggered home, trying unsuccessfully to clear their heads in the sticky night air. Thinking back to Gregg's attempt at *dirty dancing*, she decided she wouldn't say anything to Robert – it was definitely something best forgotten. But she did confess to Robert that she'd lied to humiliate Rex and felt confident that everyone, including Stella, believed her.

'But what a lousy, stinking coincidence!' she said. 'All the time I'd worked as an escort, I'd made it clear that I wouldn't go with anybody from Ringwood. But one night when they were short-handed, I'd agreed to escort Rex as a favour. Sod's law wasn't it?' she said with a rueful smile.

If Robert hadn't been sure before, he was now certain that he had married a formidable woman. She obviously had the guts to stand up for herself against Quentin and Rex, whilst all he could do was panic and flounder.

'Care for a nightcap?' he asked, opening the drinks cabinet.

'Oh, yes, please, I need it. I'm sorry I caused you all that embarrassment, but thanks for coming to my rescue. I think you'd have punched Rex if Quentin hadn't stepped in.'

'I almost did – the slime ball.'

'My hero!' She smiled as she cuddled up to him, enjoying the security of his embrace. 'Let's go to bed. I want to show you just how proud I am!'

About ten o'clock the following morning, after Jane had sent another article to Tony focusing on the computer fiasco, Cindy, still nursing a sore head, and Kath called to see that Jane was all right after Rex's accusations. They thought he must have some serious sexual problems and felt very sorry for his wife. What must it be like to be married to someone like him, they wondered? Jane was very relieved that everybody had believed her. What a great liar I must be, was her uneasy thought.

Sitting in the relative cool of the terrace they finished analysing the previous evening's events. Cindy soon left, but Kath stayed behind as she wanted a private word with Jane. Cindy assumed it would be to do with Quentin's rudeness… but it wasn't.

'You're new to Africa and the expat lifestyle.' Kath nervously fiddled with her empty cup. 'I hope you don't mind if I give you some friendly advice.'

'No, not at all.'

'I think it's partly to do with the heat, cheap alcohol and the fact that we all have servants.'

'What is?' Jane couldn't understand what she was getting at.

Again Kath hesitated before placing her cup on the table. 'I couldn't help noticing the way Gregg danced with you last night.'

'Oh!'

'I understand that Gregg and Cindy are – how should I say? – a little lax in their attitude to sexual partners.'

Jane didn't say anything.

'The amateur dramatic society they belong to is known for occasional wife swapping and I've heard rumours that the golf club is… err… well, things happen there as well.'

'But they seem very nice people,' Jane countered.

'And they are, very nice, and we socialise with them regularly but, as you and Robert are new here, I… I hope you don't mind me telling you this. The moral rules of the outside world don't appear to apply here.'

Jane was reluctant to accept Kath's word at face value. But maybe the way Cindy dressed showed she was open to offers and Gregg's behaviour last night was mischievous to say the least. In fact, the more she thought about it, there had been one or two occasions when Cindy had dropped some non-too-subtle hints about Robert. When she'd said she liked him, what did she really mean?

She thanked Kath for her well-intentioned advice and said they would be careful. The last thing she wanted was to get mixed up in anything like that.

Chapter Twelve

It was amazing, Jane thought, that although she and Gilly had only been in Buzamba a short time, they'd both adjusted to their new lives. 'It doesn't seem possible,' she told Robert when they'd settled down in the living room after another of Sellie's impressive dinners, that Gilly has settled down at school without any of the usual grumbles.'

'I've heard the same from other new arrivals,' Robert gently put his arm around her, hoping it would become their evening ritual, especially when Jane responded positively. 'It's a bit like when I was young and went on a week's holiday to France with my parents. After the first couple of days, I began to feel settled and by the end of the week, our cottage seemed like home.'

'Well, I wouldn't know about that, never going on a family holiday. The only time I was away from home was either with the school, or a few days with my mum at her friend's in Weymouth.'

'Oh, poor you,' he teased, 'I'm so sad, it's making me cry.'

'Okay, rich public school boy,' she poked him in the ribs, 'but seriously, I think having Sellie in the house has helped, and Cindy seems determined we'll like it here.'

'And married life?' questioned Robert with slight apprehension in his voice.

Jane turned and looked him straight in the face. 'You keep asking me that. Don't worry, if I start to have a problem I'll let you know quickly enough.'

'Okay, okay. Sorry I asked. It's just that...'

'Yes, I know,' she interrupted, 'it was a huge step for both of us, but I think it's worked out surprising well... so far, that is. You're not a molester or a wife-beater. In fact, I think you're a kind and decent man.'

'And you're madly in love with me.'

'Don't push it Kimber, just count your blessings. You're getting your sex and my scintillating company... okay?'

Smiling at each other, Jane gave him a tender kiss; she didn't want to kiss him passionately yet. Without a doubt, he was all those things she'd said, and Gilly loved him to bits. But one thing he wasn't... he wasn't sexually exciting.

Leaving Basu Compound, Basil tried to control the swaying and bouncing car as he manoeuvred his way along Cutty Road to Ogola. It seemed to Jane that the potholes and piles of rubbish were even worse than on her first visit. On reaching the dilapidated building, she pushed open the creaking door into the 'so-called' management office where Ken was waiting for her.

'*Karibu*, Jane. Welcome once again.'

'Thanks, Ken.'

Ken was pleased. 'Stay for as long as you like and I'll give you the grand tour.' His motive was not only to be friendly, but also that she might take him up on the offer of helping with the accounts. 'I've nothing urgent on this morning, so I could give you more on the background of our little venture.'

Sitting in the dusty shack of an office in the middle of an African slum, Ken filled Jane in. 'Originally, it was a political initiative from Berlin because the Green Party felt that most of the money given to African governments ended up in Swiss bank accounts, and even though all international donors knew this, they did nothing about it.'

'But why?' Jane found this hard to believe. 'Why don't these donors insist on their money being spent properly? Otherwise, stop the aid.'

'Yes, it's interesting isn't it?' Ken saw the doubt on Jane's face. 'From what I learnt when I was with the EU, all developed nations have budgets for overseas development. Electorates pressure them into doing so. I think it's the same in the UK.'

'Yes,' Jane replied. 'Our politicians and pop stars are always going on TV asking people to give more to Africa.'

'Every donor country has created its own aid agency staffed, or more usually overstaffed, by workers whose performances are often below the standards tolerated in the private sector. In your country it's DfID.'

'You're not filling me with much confidence,' Jane needled him lightly. 'Tell me, if all the donors scrutinized every payment, would this stop the corruption?'

'In theory you are right of course, but in practice it's different,' Ken sighed. 'As I've already mentioned, all EU countries have cash to spend in Africa and, this may sound very cynical, their priorities are to look after their own nation's interests and protect their well-paid jobs. Helping the African poor seems to be of a lesser concern.'

'But that's terrible.' Jane was finding it difficult to believe. 'As an African, you must find this hard to take.'

Ken gave a philosophical smile. 'Yes, I do, but Western bureaucrats and most expatriates rely on Africa to secure their high standards of living.'

'You mean like Robert?' There was a hint of accusation in Jane's question.

This made Ken look a little uncomfortable. 'Well, yes, in a way. I'm sure Robert earns more here than he would in a similar job in England and also, he gets a free house, a car, airfares and medical, etcetera. His total pay package will be more than treble the amount he would cost a UK employer.'

'Well, that must apply to all expats then.' She wasn't sure how to take Ken's inference that Robert was on a sort of cash bandwagon.

'Yes, of course it does. But let me tell you this in Robert's defence. He is one of the few who deserves to be well paid. Without him, this project would struggle. But, from my knowledge of many expats, they are just here for the money and nothing else.'

Jane decided not to say any more until she had talked it over with Robert.

As they left the office, Ken explained that *mzungu* women were a bit of a curiosity and some residents would be suspicious of her motive for being there. 'However,' he added, 'the children will be pleased to see you.'

The first part of Ogola had recently been completely rebuilt. There were two rows of five buildings, each consisting of ten rooms, five on each side set back-to-back. All were of a uniform size and measured around twelve feet by twelve, with a variety of brightly-coloured wooden doors and shuttered windows. The outer walls were made of rammed earth mixed with cement moulded into blocks, and painted with a white protective coat. Inside partitions were wattle and mud with roofs of clay tiles and compressed earth floors. Considering it was a slum, Jane thought the area had quite a cheery appearance.

While Ken was showing Jane these first buildings, her attention was suddenly drawn to two little girls, aged about two or three, squatting in a small gully next to the block, playing with a greenish-brown lizard which was frantically trying to escape. A piece of string had been tied around the creature's body and the girls took it in turns to yank the poor thing, this way and that, just as infants back home would do with a toy. Jane looked away; there was nothing she could do.

She caught up with Ken who was pointing out concrete walkways with drainage ditches between buildings, and 'the big extra' at one end of each block, was a wetcore consisting of a small room with a shower and a second with a flush toilet. On the outside of the end wall were three large sinks, each with a cold water tap.

'So each block has running water and flush toilets,' Jane looked to Ken for confirmation. 'I guess that makes all the difference.'

'Believe me, having clean running water on tap is amazing.'

Walking on to the next block where most of the doors were open, women stood around talking to neighbours, often laughing loudly, while children played with bits of rubbish, some breaking into little song and dance routines. Just then, the two infant girls she had seen earlier tottered round the corner, one of them sobbing and pulling what was now the lifeless form of the lizard. They went to a lady who had a pot on a charcoal fire emitting a dreadful smell. Speaking sharply to the girls, she pulled the string off the dead lizard and popped it into her pot. This made the girls cry even louder.

'What's in the pot... apart from the lizard, that is?' Jane asked.

Ken took a look. 'It's pig's intestine. She will share it with the other women and they will mix it with whatever vegetables they've got in their pots.'

Ken approached one of the women and asked if Jane could see her room. Looking inside, she saw a couple of narrow beds covered in shabby blankets, a small chair, and a shelf stacked high with a variety of pots and personal items. Everything was cramped with virtually no vacant floor space.

Jane put out her hand which the woman took shyly. 'Thank you for letting me see where you live... it's nice.'

They started to move away. 'How many people live in a room like this?'

'Well, it's for a family so it could be anywhere from one up to seven or eight.'

Jane was incredulous. 'You mean eight people live in one room which is only twelve foot square? That doesn't seem possible.'

'Oh, it's possible all right. There are some rooms in the old part of Ogola which are smaller, and some households haven't any adults – only children.'

'How's that?'

'The parents are dead or missing, so the children have to cope alone. I could show you some rooms where the head of a household of, say, four or five children is only eleven or twelve themselves.'

'Oh my God,' was all Jane could say.

'But rooms aren't used during the day, only for sleeping; it's a hot climate and more comfortable outside.'

While Ken talked to some of the other people nearby, Jane looked around trying to get a feel for the place; what she had seen so far looked tolerable. As the fresher morning air gave way to the heat and humidity, she was starting to feel sweaty.

She became aware that a couple of little girls were staring at her. Both had short hair and one sported a faded red hair band and had a runny nose, but was seemingly unaware of the greyish, green slime stuck to her upper lip. Jane gave them a brief smile which was obviously taken as an invitation, as they both ran in her direction.

'Ow are you?' they shouted in high-pitched, patchy English. With broad smiles they each took one of Jane's hands and held on tight. 'Ow are you, ow are you?' they kept repeating in their squeaky voices.

'I'm fine thank you, how are you?' Jane smiled and looked at Ken for guidance.

He spoke sharply to the girls. They stopped smiling but held onto Jane's hands even tighter. 'Do you mind them?' Ken asked.

'No. I don't mind at all.' Both girls looked at Jane to see what her reaction would be and, as Ken didn't chase them off, they jigged around with delight.

'Well if you really don't mind they can come with us. They're used to wandering around on their own – it's normal here.'

Jane spoke to the two girls. 'My name is Jane, what are your names?' They didn't answer so Ken translated and found out that the one with the hairband and runny nose was Grace and the other one Kaba. 'By the way,' Jane asked, 'what language do they speak?'

'There are many different tribal languages and dialects but the lingua franca is Kiswahili, even if it's not their first tongue.'

'Do they speak English?'

'No, not really. They can all ask "how are you?" and you hear that every time a *mzungu* comes here, and they may know "yes" and "no" and one or two other words but that's all. Most of the adults have a reasonable grasp of English as it is spoken on the radio and TV, and some of them will have mixed with English speaking people, either at work or as domestic staff.' He pointed in the general direction of the slum area. 'OK then, let's go and see the rest of the place.' Slipping down a slight slope, they rounded a corner and, in a matter of thirty yards, the change was dramatic. Huge mounds of foul-looking stinking garbage spilled over every spare bit of land, some having been set alight sent even worse smelling smoke swirling around in the air. Scrawny-looking chickens scratched and pecked in the piles of rubbish, with a couple of goats competing for anything edible.

'We start building the new head office and five new blocks here next week,' Ken was pointing to a recently cleared area.

Apart from the increase in garbage, it took Jane a few moments to see what was different in this area they were now entering – it was something to do with the total lack of colour. Everything in front of her was the dusty, rusty brown of corrugated iron with no white walls or brightly coloured doors. Even the people's clothes seemed to lack colour. She turned to Ken. 'Nobody grows flowers here, do they?'

He laughed. 'If they did they wouldn't last long and anyway, there's no space for them to grow. Outside the slum areas, you see flowers and shrubs everywhere... but not here. Ah,' he suddenly remembered, 'I forgot, there are some flowers. I'll show you in a few minutes.'

'I'll look forward to that.'

'Ow are you, ow are you?' came a cry from several more little children scampering up to the group; they also wanted to hold Jane's hands, trying to force theirs between hers and Grace's and Kaba's. Grace held on tightly but Kaba had to share with a little boy. It was then that Jane noticed that Kaba had something wrong with her other hand – a bone between her wrist and fingers was sticking out at an unnatural angle and some of her fingers were bent inwards.

'I'll send them packing if you like,' Ken said firmly. 'I'm afraid there will be even more children all wanting to hold your hand.'

'It's no problem, Ken, honestly, I'm fine.'

They were now in the old part of Ogola, full of the noise, smoke, smell and squalor of overcrowded living. There was no uniformity to these buildings, either in size or layout, but what Jane found interesting was that every room was more or less the same twelve foot square as in the new blocks. These walls were made from corrugated iron with upright poles held together with intertwined twigs and small branches, not unlike the wattle and daub houses built in the UK in olden times. The main difference was that the walls were very thin – no more than four or five inches – and most were in very poor condition. Holes were patched with anything that could be found, such as plywood and plastic, and the roofs were all made from rusty corrugated iron.

Ken saw Jane's expression. 'All of Ogola has buildings like this. There's no water, sanitation or electricity. The buildings are packed together so closely that it's sometimes hard to walk through the area. In parts, we have to scrape round corners and duck to avoid getting our heads cut open by rusting zinc. You still want to carry on?'

'Oh yes, I want to see as much as I can. Aren't there any roads or paths?'

'No, but under our project, there'll be a paved road with interlinking pathways.'

They continued their tour, scrambling up and down garbage-filled, stinking ditches, ducking under overhanging pieces of corrugated iron, made all the more difficult for Jane with the children still holding her hands. When one had had enough another child would take over, repeating the 'ow are you?' greeting. When Jane reached an obstacle where she needed both hands free to climb over a small fence, Ken spoke sharply to the children who immediately let go.

'What's that tree over there?' Jane pointed slightly to the left of where they were heading. 'It looks out of place amongst all this...' her sentence was left unfinished, as she couldn't decide the politically correct word to describe the wretchedness that surrounded them.

Ken smiled. 'That's our one and only tree. The others were cut down long ago.'

'So why was this one left?'

'It's supposed to have some spiritual meaning to the locals. You'll see it for yourself later.'

As they continued, Jane noticed women and children carrying large, heavy-looking, jerry cans on their heads. 'What's in the cans?'

'Water. Some of the more industrious residents have a standpipe and sell a jerry can of water for 10 shillings – that's about twenty pence in your money. The standpipes aren't legal though.'

Jane slowly shook her head despairingly. 'Wow, are there any toilets?'

A hesitant smile crept around Ken's lips. 'Are you sure you want to know?'

'Oh dear, it's as bad as that, is it? Well, in for a penny – oh, pardon the pun,' she said dryly. 'Tell me the worst.'

'Apart from the Sambula River and the quarry, there are "flying toilets".'

She looked baffled. 'And they are...?'

'Well, people... err... perform onto a piece of old plastic, carefully fold it up, and then throw it as far as they can.'

Jane involuntarily ducked at the very thought of it. 'Should we be wearing hats?'

Ken laughed. 'If you're unlucky then, yes. Fortunately, the missiles usually end up on roofs, hence the smell and the flies. You can see a mass of flies over there look,' he said pointing to the next block.

She only gave a brief look before turning away.

Ken led her down a few roughly-hewn steps to the Sambula River. The smell hit her before she could even see it but she deliberately tried not to react too sharply to the stench. It was hardly more than a stream; the distance between the two banks was around fifteen feet, and the actual water flow about two feet wide, as it slowly wound its way through the deepest part, desperately trying to push through all the litter. The water was very dark, liquid sludge, with swarms of flies and other insects busily hovering around the more obnoxious areas.

'I guess it could be worse,' she managed to stop herself gagging.

'It would have been worse yesterday, but last night's rain flushed a lot of it away,' he met her gaze briefly. 'But look up there... you see... right on the horizon.'

Jane looked to see where he was pointing. The land rose in a series of low hills and, screwing up her eyes against the glare of the sun, she could just make out some large gleaming buildings, shafts of light reflected in the numerous glass windows, all surrounded by brightly coloured hedges and trees. 'What is it?'

'That's where the President and all his cronies live,' he sighed loudly. 'They're all ultra-modern mansions, with swimming pools, tennis courts . . . and the rest'

'Wow,' Jane shook her head in incredulity. The contrast between the filth and squalor, and those luxurious houses, probably no more than a mile away, was mind-boggling. She turned to look at Ken. 'Well, that says it all.'

'How do you mean?'

'Well, look around here, and now look back to the horizon. It puts into a nutshell everything that's wrong with Buzamba.

Standing here, we are in absolute poverty with people struggling to survive, but the money meant to relieve this poverty is being stolen by those...' she lowered her voice so that only Ken could hear, '... those bastards up on the hill.'

He gave a sad smile and nodded to show he agreed. 'And that's not all.'

'Oh no,' she gave a quiet groan, 'please don't say there's more.'

'The source of the water in the Sambula,' he pointed to the oily-sludge they called a river, 'is from a spring up on the hill. About six years ago, the President had a dam built to keep the bulk of the water for their own use, and it's only opened in the heavy rainy season.'

Jane closed her eyes and rested her head on one of her hands, shaking it ever so slightly from side to side.

'And when they do release the water, the volume is often too much and a large part of the slum floods.'

Jane stood, hands on her hips, taking in the vista and absorbing everything Ken had just told her.

'Shall we go?' he asked.

'I think we'd better,' she turned her back on what reminded her of Dorothy's vision of the Wizard's town in the film of *The Wizard of Oz*. Fiction is so much better than reality, she thought.

'So,' continued Ken, 'apart from the river, there are other areas of sewage and whenever there's heavy rain, much of it flows round, and sometimes through people's rooms.' He then added to the horror of the day by telling Jane that human embryos were occasionally found amongst the sewage.

'Oh! Surely not,' was all she could say, knowing it was the shocking truth. She desperately wanted to leave now and run away. Away from this hell-hole of a place, but she knew she couldn't; not yet at any rate. She told herself she would see it through.

Ken hadn't noticed the inner trauma that Jane was going through. 'Our design will have a piped sewer system from every wetcore, taking all the sewage to a treatment plant two miles from here,' he smiled, 'so it's conceivable that in a few years' time, the river may become blue again! Now, I'd like you to meet the lady who lives in the room over there,' he pointed back up the slope, 'and you'll see one of the major problems we have.'

The building was probably in a worse condition than any Jane had seen. The door was open and Ken looked in and spoke to someone inside. He then beckoned Jane over. 'This is Blessing Okonyo and she is dying from AIDS.' He spoke loudly enough so that anybody close by would hear. There was no hiding the truth about terminal illness here.

As Jane went to the doorway, Ken placed his hand on her arm to stop her going any further. There was an overpowering damp, fetid smell in the airless room where an emaciated woman of indeterminate age lay on a low bed. A young child was sitting silently on the floor next to her, its eyes clouded with flies. A clutter of old boxes and pieces of clothing filled the rest. Her eyes appeared large, protruding from her gaunt skull, and her skin had a pale grey sheen to it. Even though it was uncomfortably hot in the room, she was covered with several layers of tattered blankets. While they were looking inside, a group of children, including Kaba, gathered behind them. Two of them pushed past and stood between the seated child and the woman's bed.

'Is this your mum?' Jane asked Kaba.

Ken translated. 'Yes, Blessing is Kaba's mother.'

Jane took Kaba's good hand. 'She looks very ill,' was all Jane could say. A lump formed in her throat and she felt a wave of despair spread over her.

Ken spoke to the two children inside the room and then the others pushed their way in, all squashed together to form a line by their mother's bed. There were five in all, two boys, two girls and the infant. The tallest, a boy, stood at one end of the informal line and the infant at the other. Kaba was in the middle. It was as if they were infant soldiers guarding some important dignitary. 'These are all Blessing's children,' Ken told Jane, 'and I believe that the two youngest are HIV positive.'

'Oh my God!' Jane said under her breath. She felt tears coming to her eyes. 'What will happen to them when... she...?'

'I don't know. The next time you come to Ogola, I'll get our Social Department to give you the details.'

Jane felt sick. She had been warned that she would see people with AIDS in Buzamba and especially in Ogola, but nothing had prepared her for this. This poor woman, who was probably only a little older than her, dying in squalor in a room that would be condemned for cattle back in the UK, with five little children to be cared for and no husband. She wanted to help but what could she do? She felt as though she wanted to sit down with this dying lady, hold her hand, give her some comfort and take her somewhere clean and bright, so she could live her last days with some dignity. But, of course, she couldn't. The dreadful truth was that there were millions more like Blessing, in Ogola and every African country.

As they were leaving, all Jane could think of to say to Blessing was 'good luck and God bless'. She gave a big smile and wave to the children who were still lined up, like soldiers waiting to be given an order to dismiss. None of them was crying – they just seemed resigned to their situation. In response to her wave one of the little girls put on a smile and said 'ow are you?' Jane turned her head and walked briskly away, not wanting any of them to see the tears streaming down her face.

They pushed on further, coming across more or less the same as they had just left. Large numbers of shabbily dressed children greeted them with amazingly cheeriness, many, like Grace, with runny noses. 'Ow are you,' they chorused, but when Ken spoke to them sternly, they walked along with them listening but not understanding.

'Over here is one of the bars. Beer is sold as well as homemade liquor. Strictly speaking, it is against the law to make this moonshine known locally as *chang'aa* or black man's whisky. Unfortunately, it's sometimes toxic with variable effects, but the main outcome is mental illness, blindness, or very occasionally, death.'

'Is alcohol a big problem in Ogola?'

'Oh yes, huge,' he said sadly. 'Not only alcohol but also drugs and glue.

'Glue?' questioned Jane.

'People sniff glue and it eventually melts their brains. I've even seen mothers giving babies the glue bottle to sniff to make them forget their hunger.'

Jane shook her head in despair.

Ken pointed to a larger building in better condition than the others and, although there seemed to be two doorways, there were no windows. 'And another problem is over there.' Some unsavoury-looking men drinking from plastic bottles and wearing dark sunglasses were milling around, smoking in an aimless fashion; two of them were using mobile phones. A couple of vendors were selling cigarettes – not in packs but singly.

'What is it?'

'It's a brothel,' he replied bitterly. 'This is yet another way of fleecing the men. On payday after work, some start off in the bar, then onto the brothel and by the time they get home most of their pay has gone. That's why on Friday evenings, many wives wait at Ogola's entrance, trying to catch their husbands before they get to the bars. Some people find it amusing when there are blazing rows and fights but, in reality, I think it's one of the most depressing sights. I wouldn't recommend it.'

Round the corner of the brothel, the ground rose slightly and, from a vantage point, Ken pointed out where they had started the tour – the office, then traced the route of the Sambula River to where Ogola backed onto the recreational field of the Catholic High School in the distance, and then finally, the line of the quarry back to Cutty Road.

'And just down there is "The Tree". Come, I'll show you.'

The tree grew from a slight hollow in the ground and as they got close, Jane was amazed by its beauty. It was much bigger than she'd thought – tall and slender like a Corinthian column. The branches spread out symmetrically and large yellow and red striped flowers, shaped like giant tulips, could be glimpsed on the tips of the highest branches. Jane thought it would have looked more at home in Kew Gardens rather than in this dreadful place.

'This is the African Tulip Tree,' explained Ken, 'and… there are the flowers I promised you.' He pointed to the upper branches. 'Some locals believe it has magic powers. I'm told that these trees only flower for four months of the year, whereas this one has never been without flowers.'

'Is that true, or have they made it up?'

'As far as I know it's true.'

'And someone keeps it clean,' Jane added. 'There's no rubbish. Amazing.'

'As I said, it is revered by many who live here. And once a year, when it's covered in flowers, it cries.'

Jane laughed. 'Trees don't cry, Ken. Not even magic trees.'

'This one does,' he smiled. 'Well, let's put it this way. Once a year the flowers drip a liquid – probably nectar – and hundreds of people gather underneath and let it fall on them. It's sweet and gooey and they lick it off themselves and other people. I've only witnessed it once but it's quite a spectacle.'

'It sounds fantastic.'

'And they say that when their special African Tulip Tree cries, it's crying for them. Crying for their suffering and crying for Africa.'

'What a fantastic story. I'd love to see it crying,' Jane said.

'I don't think that would go down well. Remember, most people blame Westerners for their suffering.'

Jane sighed. She didn't normally pray but from now on she would pray that maybe, just maybe, this project would succeed. She looked up and caught Ken's attention. 'Can you give me any cheerful news, or is it all bad?'

Ending the tour on a brighter note, he said the project would help everybody, and the German Embassy had promised to build a primary school and to pay the wages of a headmaster and two teachers.

'That sounds good,' Jane said with little enthusiasm. She was attempting to ignore the worst of what she had seen and think only of how much better it could be in the future. She felt an empathy with the African Tulip Tree and wanted to cry to relieve the suffering she had just seen. Thinking about how top government officials were putting obstacles in the way of the work Ken and others were trying to do, she was angry and wanted to blame someone – but who?

'But don't make the mistake of thinking their lives are a constant misery and nothing else,' Ken finished with this final homily. 'As you saw for yourself, most people have an amazing spirit to make the best of the life that has been dealt them and when you walk around, you'll see more laughter than weeping.'

Leaning against the rusting, corrugated-iron wall of the office, Jane wiped the grimy perspiration from her brow while waiting for Ken to complete some urgent paperwork, a light breeze kicking up dust patterns around her feet. Only a short while ago she'd been leading what she now realised was a safe, sheltered life in Dorset with only her daughter to worry about. But worry about what? Whether to buy the luxury or bargain ice cream, or what channel to let Gilly watch on TV? And yet, just eight hours away, she found herself in… she struggled to form words that could possibly describe this super-slum… hell on earth.

While reflecting on the futility of it all, she was rudely jolted out of her dreamlike state by the unmistakable sound of gunfire… and it was coming her way.

Nearby, people screamed and began running chaotically in all directions, but Jane stood paralysed with fear, her brain unable to take in what was happening. Within a few seconds, Ken rushed to her side, dragging her unceremoniously to the office door, at the same time as three men, carrying AK47s, ran into the space left by the scattered inhabitants. One of the men was running wildly, being chased by the other two, until the nearest pursuer aimed and shot him in full flight. The deafening bang, so close at hand, shocked Jane to the core, and she instinctively clamped her hands over her ears. In the split second before closing her eyes, she saw the injured man scream and fall to the ground, bright red blood spurting from his abdomen.

Amongst the shouts and utter mayhem, Jane's scream was by far the loudest, attracting the attention of everyone within earshot. Was she going to be the next target? It didn't register that, in fact, the opposite was true as the two gunmen disappeared just as quickly as they'd arrived. Puffing hard, Ken at last managed to manhandle Jane into the office, shutting the door with a crash.

She was trembling, and without hesitation, he put his arms around her until she gradually began to calm down. 'What… what the hell was all that?'

'I'm sorry you had to see it,' He was relieved that Jane was calming down.

'But what happened? It looked like they were trying to kill that man.'

Ken sat her down and phoned Robert to come as quickly as he could, trying to decide how he should handle this tricky situation. He thought carefully before answering Jane's question. 'Just what happened, Jane, I don't know. Some people in Ogola have guns which are usually used in tribal conflicts or by drug gangs.'

'But what about the injured man? Should we call an ambulance?'

'Somebody will have already done it.' He sat down next to her. 'If we were to look outside now, you can be certain he will have disappeared; whether to the clinic or somewhere else, I've no idea, but... he will have gone.'

'Can you do something? Can you find out if he's still alive?'

Ken sighed and using a handkerchief to wipe the perspiration from his face, admitted, 'I can't do anything.'

'But why?'

'In Ouverru, I'm considered to be from the wrong tribe. If I ask questions or get involved in any way, I'd probably be accused of the shooting.'

It took a while for Jane to understand. 'Oh, I think I know what you mean. Being from the minority Busti tribe, you have to keep a low profile.'

'Yes. Relationships between the tribes are very complex.' He smiled now that he could see she was recovering from her ordeal. 'And you saw how everyone reacted when they saw you.'

'Yes, that was amazing. Was it me or something else?'

'Oh no, it was you all right.'

'But why?'

Quickly, Ken came up with the best story he could think of. 'Every Buzamban, even gangsters, know that if a white person is injured or, worse still, killed then the there is no escape from the law. Not only the Buzamban authorities but the police from the victim's home country would be here in no time, and everyone would suffer.'

'Wow. That's madness.' She shook her head in disbelief. 'Anyhow, thanks for looking after me Ken. You were great.'

Ken wondered if this would be the end of any thoughts she might have on accepting his job offer? Probably. Of all the lousy coincidences. He was just about to say more when Robert burst into the room.

'What's all this about a gun fight? Are you both all right?' He went up to Jane and put his arms around her. 'Are you all right, darling?' he repeated.

Jane and Ken between them recounted the whole story. Still holding onto Jane, Robert gave her a kiss before thanking Ken for everything he'd done. They decided to leave for home before there was any more drama.

Ken was left in a dilemma. Had he done the right thing by Jane, being economical with the truth? He was a little ashamed with himself for letting her believe it was the sight of a white woman that had sent the gunmen running. He went through to the office where Hani's brother, Ben, a uniformed police officer, was waiting for him. 'It was our good luck, Ben, that you'd just arrived. The sight of you must have scared them off.'

Ben saw the funny side of it. He'd earlier warned Ken about the ever-increasing number of guns held by criminals in Ogola, and that the police knew things were getting out of hand. Ben left the office a happy man, pocketing a thousand shillings given to him by Ken. He'd make a point of calling more often.

Ken, on the other hand, was far from happy. He desperately needed Jane's help with the accounts, but on the other hand, he didn't want to put her in danger. For the time being, he would keep to his story that it was the sight of her that sent the gunmen running, but if things got worse, he'd have to tell Robert.

On their way home, Jane asked Robert if shoot-outs were common in Ogola. Now that she was safely in the car, her feeling of danger had abated. Robert admitted that there were occasional minor skirmishes, but these rarely took place during daylight. She was just unlucky. 'The trouble is far too many people have guns.'

'But aren't guns too expensive for people who live in a slum?'

'I'm told guns kill more people in Africa than AIDS. They're smuggled in from Sudan and Ethiopia or even the Congo. A lot of the aid money sent to Africa for food is used to buy guns. That's why they're so cheap and drug bosses give them out free to their supporters. Although Bob Geldof fumes whenever anybody says it, out of the hundred million dollars raised by Live-Aid, ninety five per cent bought guns.'

'Oh, surely not!'

'I don't really know myself, but that's what many people say.'

The events of the day had taken their toll on Jane. She tried to put the shooting out of her mind for now; she still had a home to run. Wearily, she asked Sellie to prepare dinner, after which she bathed Gilly and got her ready for bed. It was earlier than usual so she stayed with her longer, holding her very close while she read stories. Lying in the lovely bedroom with clean walls, fresh sheets and Gilly's school uniform laid out for the following morning, upsetting images floated around her head of all those other little girls, no more than two or three miles away, living in abject squalor. It seemed obscene, especially when it dawned on her that Gilly's bedroom was considerably larger than the rooms occupied by a whole family. She wondered how such a family would feel if they suddenly found themselves in a bedroom with an adjoining bathroom. Would they think they were in heaven?

Whilst being a single mother in England, struggling to bring up a child on very little money, Jane had thought she was hard done by, but today's experience had changed that notion forever. After kissing Gilly good night, she flopped into her favourite chair in the living room. Before the shooting incident, she'd planned to talk to Robert about her tour of the slum but she knew all of that would have to wait. She was shell-shocked and, without warning, started to cry.

'Hey,' Robert gently kissed the top of her head. 'It's all right, I'm here. Was it seeing the man shot that's upset you?'

Between her sobs, Jane explained that it had all been too much for her. Yes, of course the shooting was upsetting but also seeing Blessing Okonyo dying of AIDS in her squalid hovel of a room and her young children standing by her bed, almost as if she was just suffering from a heavy cold and would soon be better. Instead, they would shortly be orphans with only some distant relatives to look after them, who would, in turn, have their own problems of sickness and poverty. Suddenly, the thought came to her that Kaba was probably around the same age as Gilly and this made everything even harder to take.

'Was it worse than you expected?' Robert asked.

'Bloody hell, yes!' she sobbed. She'd earlier steeled herself for what she'd see in the slum but in her mind the worst was something like the Soweto slums near Johannesburg which she'd seen on television. But Soweto was well laid out with roads and pathways and electricity. 'Yes, it was worse,' she said. 'Much worse.'

She wished she'd misunderstood the situation and that it had all been a bad dream. But this wasn't the case. This was everyday life in the real slums of Africa. She wanted to help but what could she do? What could anybody do? At least some Western countries and NGOs were trying to improve the housing and provide medication for the sick, but obstacles were being placed in their paths by corrupt leaders whose only interest was to feather their own nests and to hell with the people they were to serve.

Jane tried to get her thoughts together. For a moment she thought she wanted to go back to Ringwood and take Gilly with her but what would that solve? Her running away would not help Blessing Okonyo's children. Could she help them, she wondered? She knew it was possibly stupid to even think about getting involved but even so, fleeting thoughts were going round in her head that perhaps she could do something to help, especially Kaba. Yes, she gritted her teeth, regardless of what Robert or Ken or anyone else said she would definitely do something to help Kaba and her siblings. She might accept Ken's offer to help with the accounts... at least she'd be on the scene.

After tossing and turning for most of the night, Jane, shivering slightly in the early chill of the morning, crept out of bed to make herself a cup of tea. Sunrise wouldn't be for another hour. As she sipped from her mug, she tried to make sense of yesterday's shooting – was she just unlucky being in the wrong place at the wrong time? To overreact was probably unnecessary because, after all, gun crime was all too common in the UK, and the world over for that matter. But surprisingly, it wasn't the shooting that had upset her the most but the terrible conditions in the slum and, in particular, that poor lady Blessing Okonyo, dying of AIDS.

Later in the morning, after Robert had gone to work and Gilly to school, there was a knock on the door and a cheery Cindy burst in, happily accepting an offer of coffee. After saying how pleased she was that Gilly had settled in at school so well, Jane told her about her visit to Ogola, and how terrible the slum conditions were.

'Look, Jane,' Cindy said. 'There's lots of poverty here, mainly brought on by themselves. Expats like Gregg and Robert do their best, but...' she shrugged her shoulders showing that she wasn't particularly interested.

Jane then casually mentioned the shooting but saying it had been some distance away and there'd been no danger. She thought that if she'd told the truth, Cindy and all the other expats would tell her not to go there again... but for the moment, she didn't want to hear that.

'Gregg says the town is full of guns,' Cindy continued, 'but you rarely hear of expats being shot. I've never felt in danger myself but , then again, I always keep to the safe areas, though from what you say, Ogola isn't one of them.'

'Don't worry, I'll take care if I ever go back again,' Jane assured her.

It took Jane a couple of hours to work out just what she should put in her article to Tony about her dramatic day in Ogola. What would anyone in England want to know about African slums? Maybe this was a hot topic after the success of the film *Slumdog Millionaire* but... was there much difference between Indian and African slums? Probably not. They all had poverty and squalor at their heart, with man's inhumanity to man as a centrepiece. But how to put in writing the filth, smells and dust? Reporting on court cases, car accidents and news stories in Ringwood and the New Forest had not prepared her for this. She did her best to describe what she had seen; meeting a lady dying from AIDS with her soon-to-be orphaned children cramped into a room the size of a single garage. But she emphasized the remarkable spirit of those who lived there and the efforts being made by the German Government to improve the living conditions. She decided not to mention the shooting incident for the time being, as she had a niggling feeling that the explanations from Ken and Robert were not the full story... maybe they were both a little too casual, but she wanted to find out more about it before putting it in a report.

CHAPTER THIRTEEN

Although Jane had a head full of questions after her two visits to Ogola, she didn't want to bombard Robert with them all at once.

'By the way,' Robert smiled, as they sat down to breakfast, 'you were quite a hit with Ken.'

'Really? You know he asked me if I wanted to help with the accounts. I forgot to tell you with all the other excitement going on.'

'Yes, he told me. Do you want to do it?'

'I'm not sure. What do you think?'

'I think you can forget about the shooting and all that business. I'm sure it was a one-off.'

'In a way, I would like to help, but I'm not sure I'd be up to it.'

'With your knowledge of accounting systems and computers, you'd be ideal. He thinks you're very mature for your age. Hani and the accounts staff also seem to like you – I wonder why that is...? Ow... don't poke me like that. I might have to retaliate!'

'Don't you dare, Kimber,' Jane said, looking very pleased with herself. 'Anyhow, I think Ken's very nice and doing a great job in terrible conditions.'

'He even said you were intelligent, but I had to correct him on that score... Ow... You've done it again!'

It was nice to know that Ken and the others liked her and thought her mature! It gave her a bit of a fillip. 'It may seem odd,' she said, 'but when I was an escort, I often mixed with older business men, mature men. Something must have rubbed off on me!'

Leaving that thought hanging in the air, she asked if he'd heard anything else about the missing computers.

'Yes, I heard this morning from DGA that we've been authorised to buy new computers locally.'

'But what about the first ones and who'll pay for the new ones? Ken told me the first shipment has already been charged to the project at an extortionate price.'

'That's as may be.' Robert didn't appear to be concerned and said DGA would pay for the new equipment, including staff training.

'That's crazy. What a waste of money. Hani told me he has a contact at the airport. Did you ask him to find out what happened to the two missing boxes?'

'No, I didn't know. Anyhow, we're getting new ones and this time we'll be sure to get everything in English.'

'You shouldn't just give up. You know all six boxes arrived so someone must have them.'

Robert just shook his head, obviously not interested. She decided that on her next visit to Ogola, she'd talk to Hani to see if he could do anything to find the missing boxes. After all, she'd had a two-hat job in Ringwood; an investigative journalist as well as an accounts clerk.

Not long after Robert left for work, Basil brought the day's mail. There were a couple of letters for Robert and one for her. Recognising Poppy's handwriting, she poured herself a glass of Sellie's homemade lemonade and settled herself comfortably on the terrace. Poppy's news was mainly about Tony and herself: still not pregnant, thinking of talking to their doctor; Tony's business doing well; two large articles in the national press; general news on Jane's friends in Ringwood ; and looking forward to their holiday in Buzamba. Then she dropped her bombshell. Amanda, their dear friend, was married and living in Africa. What? Jane could hardly believe it. Amanda had written to Poppy telling her that, after meeting the lovely Robert (I think she still fancies him, Poppy wrote), she'd realised that there must be lots of men working overseas who, during their annual leave, would be on the lookout for a wife. With this in mind, she'd checked the web and found that one of the biggest employers of British men working abroad was Coast Global Ltd based in Manchester, so she'd upped-sticks, moved there and somehow managed to land a job with them as a receptionist. This was perfect for her as every man returning on leave had to report to head office, where Amanda would direct them to the appropriate section. After two non-starters she'd found her man, a Mr Paul York who worked in the company's Nairobi office. Poppy wrote that the arms of the Venus flytrap would have snapped round poor old Yorkie before he could come up for air.

How about that? Whatever else was said about Amanda, you had to admire her single-track ambition to ensnare the bank account of her dreams.

Having an early night, they sat in bed reading when Jane remembered she hadn't told Robert of Kath's warning about Cindy and Gregg.

He pursed his lips. 'Oh dear, that could be a problem.'

'How do you mean?'

'We'll have to be careful when we're in their company.'

'Cindy and Gregg are our friends and… well, we won't be forced to join in any hanky-panky.'

He thought for a moment. 'I guess you're right.'

'Well, we've been warned,' Jane said. 'And now for my second scoop.' She filled Robert in about Amanda's marriage.

'You say she got the idea after meeting me?'

'That's what Poppy says. Do you know of Coast Global?'

'Oh yes, they're a big conglomerate with offices all over Africa. They have quite a big place here in Buzamba.' He then added mischievously, 'if Yorkie could get a transfer to Ouverru then we'd all be friends together.'

'God forbid,' Jane responded tersely, 'she's the last person I want to see again.' She decided that now would be the ideal moment to tell Robert that Amanda had accused him of trying to assault her on their date in Ringwood. Jane thought that even the timorous Robert would explode with indignation and waited for his vigorous denial. She waited… and waited… 'Oh no, say it's not true… it can't be!' She jumped up and confronted him. 'Look at me and tell me it's not true – please.'

Struggling to find the right words of explanation, she interpreted his silence as an admission of guilt.

'It's true then, you did molest Amanda,' Jane screeched.

'No, it wasn't like that… it was just a misunderstanding. I didn't assault her.'

'But something happened didn't it?' Jane was still horror-struck at Robert's failure to deny Amanda's story. 'You'd better tell me what happened, and tell me the truth because if you don't, I'll ask Amanda herself. And don't forget, Poppy and Tony may arrive soon so I can ask her as well.'

'I'll tell you all that happened but keep your voice down, you'll wake Gilly.' Robert sat on the edge of the bed. 'You'll remember we were in the middle of a heat wave at the time. My date with Amanda was at the Indian restaurant on the High Street. It was very hot inside. To make matters worse, we ordered a spicy meal, which would have been okay on any other day, but Amanda was complaining that she was wearing the wrong kind of dress… it was made from some type of synthetic material which was sticking to her. We finished the meal quickly, I drove her home and she invited me in for a nightcap.'

Jane sat motionless, arms folded across her chest.

'The second we got inside, she unbuttoned the front of her dress and, as she went into the bedroom, she… err… slipped it down to her waist. I assumed she would come back wearing something else but… she didn't. She'd poured two brandies and brought them into the lounge still without…'

'She was wearing a bra I assume,' Jane questioned sharply.

'Oh yes.'

'Go on then.'

'I didn't know what message she was trying to send. I wondered if, by unbuttoning her dress, she was just trying to cool down or whether she was inviting me to do something… you know, make a…a pass or something.'

'Make a pass?' Jane was deliberately making it more difficult for him. She could picture the scene where the would-be Romeo was dithering like an inexperienced schoolboy trying to pluck up courage to make an advance on a half-naked female. But so far, she couldn't see the funny side of it.

'You know what I mean,' he said crossly. 'Although I was uncertain what to do, I thought she probably *did* want me to do something… make a… a move… I didn't want her to think that I didn't find her attractive… if you see what I mean?'

'So, you found her attractive, *and* she'd unbuttoned her dress, *and* you didn't want to hurt her feelings, so you thought you'd have sex with her. She was obviously far more attractive than me because I don't remember you making a pass at me on our first date.'

'Look, I felt I had to do something.' He was beginning to resent Jane's aggressive questioning.

'So what did you do?'

'Well, Amanda turned her back to put some music on, so I went behind her and tried to undo her bra.'

'You what?'

'Oh shut up a minute. I'm trying to tell you what happened.' Robert's voice was getting louder and he was becoming irritated.

'OK then, I'm listening.'

'So when I tried – unsuccessfully, by the way – she turned round and said something… I forget what exactly… about me being naughty, or something like that, and she gave my shoulder a little push. She wasn't angry, in fact I think she was smiling. But I lost my balance and had to take a step backwards not realising that the coffee table was directly behind my leg. As the back of my leg caught the edge of the table I completely lost my balance and fell over, knocking the brandy over the floor and banging my head on an ornament… that's when I cut my head.' Robert paused for a moment and looked at Jane who was sitting impassively listening to his tale of woe.

'I panicked and Amanda screamed. The drinks spilt over the carpet and I was bleeding from the cut on my head. She rushed to get some cloths and I didn't know what to do. My head really hurt and I felt so embarrassed. My attempt to be romantic had created all this chaos. I stayed a short while to help mop up the spilt drinks and then left.'

'And that's it?' Jane demanded.

'Yes, that's it.'

'Didn't she say anything else?'

'As I left, she said I shouldn't worry about the mess I'd made and… something like… to keep in touch. That was all.'

'And did you keep in touch?'

'No. I told Poppy that I wasn't interested in her, I was only interested in you.'

'So what was wrong with Amanda? You obviously found her more attractive than me and tried to seduce her like a dirty old man, so why didn't you want to see her again?'

Robert began to lose his temper. 'You're being silly now. I've already told you she wasn't my type. All she wanted to know was whether she could get her hair and nails done in Buzamba and could she get designer clothes and shoes, and were there lots of parties to attend. She didn't even know where Buzamba was, for

God's sake. Anyway,' Robert started to smirk, 'you didn't strip down to your bra for me on our first date.'

Jane ignored the last cheeky remark. 'Well, now for the next subject. Amanda told Poppy that you had an unhealthy obsession with little girls.'

'That's bloody ridiculous and you know it,' Robert was beginning to shout, not caring whether he woke Gilly or even Sellie. 'That's a terrible thing to say. You know yourself that it's total rubbish.'

'So why did she say it?'

'The only time I mentioned anything about any young girl was when I told her I had been out with you and how much I liked your daughter.'

Jane pondered this last piece of information. It made sense. She could imagine Amanda twisting events around and doing her best to spoil Jane's chances. 'OK then, I believe you, but you lied to me about how you cut your head and you didn't tell me the full story of your encounter with Amanda. You should have.'

'It wasn't important and that's why I didn't tell you. If I had you'd have gone on and on like you're doing now. Give me a break will you?'

It was Jane's turn to pause for a moment. She softened her tone because she knew he was telling the truth and for the very first time, he was getting angry with her.

'Is that why you didn't like me picking Gilly up when we were in Studland?'

Jane nodded. 'I was watching you like a hawk. But you behaved impeccably; in fact that was the first time I thought you may be… well… OK.'

By now, Robert had calmed down. 'In the circumstances, I guess *OK* was pretty good,' Robert was slightly reassured.

'I think she's still got the hots for you.'

'Well, she's only human… ouch. What was that for?'

'You know very well.'

'And you think Amanda was jealous of you… over me! I think that's the first time I've ever been fought over!'

'Nobody fought over you, you moron. Don't go and get any big ideas or your head will grow as big as your chin.'

'That's fighting talk, Mrs Kimber; you're in for it now,' he said, launching himself at Jane. He'd recently found that she was very sensitive and hated being tickled, so he honed in on all her most responsive areas, sending her into girlish squeals, wriggling and twisting to get away. But he wasn't having any of it, pinning her down he whispered, 'prepare yourself for a night of passion, Mrs Kimber.'

'Oh *Bwana*, you're so masterful,' Jane said in anticipation.

As she tried to sleep next to her lightly-snoring but fully satiated husband, she couldn't help a slight feeling of disappointment as the *night of passion* wasn't quite the earth-moving experience she'd hoped for. Would it always be like this? Since their first few nights together and, after one or two awkward moments, their lovemaking had gradually developed into a routine which Jane found pleasant enough but something – she wasn't sure what, but that indefinable something – was missing.

Receiving another of Ken's invites to see more of Ogola, Jane was pleased to go to the office the following day.

'Before we start,' Jane said, 'I wonder if you know the editors of any of the local newspapers. I did a bit of reporting before leaving England, and my boss there asked me to make some contacts here, just in case there's something worth reporting.'

Ken pursed his lips. 'There are about five newspapers in Ouverru, but all bar one are just government propaganda outlets. I'd be very careful, though, if I were you as anything to do with politics can be a bit of a minefield.'

'Thanks for that Ken, I promise I won't rock the boat. Which is the good paper, by the way?'

'The *Buzamban Times*, and the editor is a man called Elphic Chuchu.'

'Do you know him?'

'I've met him once or twice and he seems a good man. I'll see if I can arrange something for you.'

'That would be great. Thanks Ken.'

As usual, a smiling Ruth brought them coffee and biscuits.

'I was wondering for today,' Ken said, 'if you'd like to see the feeding station.'

'I'd like to but... what is it exactly?'

'It's where the destitute can get two free meals a day. And, believe me, the list is getting longer by the day.'

'I'd love to see it, thank you.'

The feeding station was about fifty yards past the new blocks on the quarry side of the project. The structure had recently been built in the same material as the new blocks but with electricity and plumbing. Two ladies were busy behind a long counter, cutting up various types of vegetables and putting them into two huge pots which were being heated on charcoal stoves. Ken introduced Jane to Isata and Mona. They explained that they were volunteers from the Catholic Church and took it in turns, with a group of fifteen other ladies, to provide two meals a day to those residents who were destitute. In most cases the food was eaten at the feeding station because if it was taken away, it would either be sold or stolen. The midday meal had already been served and preparation of the evening meal was underway. The contents were almost always the same, consisting of maize meal, sweet potato, cassava greens, some root crops, and either fish or meat. The fish was tinned mackerel and the meat was scrag ends of chicken, cattle or goat from the nearby abattoir. The German Embassy provided some of the money whilst the Catholic Church and other charities gave the rest.

'But remember,' Ken added, 'if it wasn't for the project, this feeding station wouldn't be here. Unless you have money, you go hungry. There are people here whose only thought when they awake is to find food and water to survive the day, usually by scavenging in rubbish tips.'

'Is this where Blessing Okonyo's children are fed?' Jane asked.

Ken spoke to Isata who referred to a stained piece of paper attached to a clipboard. 'It's a bit confusing,' he checked the list for himself. 'It says here that a man called Toma Obayo collects Blessing Okonyo's meal and some of her children eat here.'

He questioned Isata again. 'She thinks Toma Obayo is a relation, and he's told them not to give any food to the girl with the broken hand.'

'That must be Kaba,' Jane was shocked. 'Why would he say that?'

'It seems,' he checked once again with Isata, 'he told them that the broken hand was a sign that she had evil spirits in her, and she must die.'

'But that's ridiculous,' Jane turned from Isata to Ken. 'Isn't it?' she demanded.

'Yes, of course it is. I'll check with the Social Department. They'll be able to sort it out.'

Jane reached into her inside pocket and took out some money. 'If, for some reason, they won't feed her, I'll pay for her food myself.' She handed the money over to Ken.

He gave her a wary look. The last thing he wanted was Jane getting personally caught up with any of the slum dwellers or the internal politics in Ogola. He had more than enough headaches already. In different circumstances he would have told her not to get involved, but he was still hoping she would help with the accounts. Reluctantly, he said he would give the money to someone in the Social Department to ensure Kaba got fed.

Leaving the feeding station, they walked over a small piece of rough, litter-strewn waste ground to return to the office.

Lola met them just inside the door. 'Mrs Kimber, what you think of Ogola?'

'Oh, please call me Jane and, to be honest, I've never seen anything like it before.' She was trying to choose her words carefully. 'Before coming to Buzamba, I'd never been outside England so everything here is new. Parts of Ogola are not very nice and life must be very hard, but the new blocks with the wetcores are good and it'll be wonderful when it's all like that.'

Ken spoke to the staff. 'Tell Jane what you think of the wetcores.'

They all said they were good but Ken turned on them and said that was not what they'd told him and they should tell the truth. They tried not to make eye contact with either Ken or Jane.

'This is another of our problems,' Ken said despondently to Jane. 'We don't say what we really mean; it's partly because it would be impolite to criticize anyone who gives us money but the main reason is the ex-colonial problem.' This made the staff look uncomfortable. 'You will find this everywhere you go, Buzambans don't like hearing the truth because, in a way, it's humiliating for us.'

Jane felt a change in the atmosphere.

'All Africans have a complex about white people,' Ken said. 'Why? Well, when the white man first came, we were told we were primitive and backward. They took our land and our chiefdoms, and between them, the British, French, Germans and others drew lines across the continent and told us that we now had a new nationality and language. They even imposed their religion on us – we were *saved*... or so we were told. So, from being a member of the Busti or Peelee or Solu or one of the many other tribes with our own lands, cultures and languages, we were told we were now Buzambans and belonged to the British Crown; the main language would be English and we must all learn to be good Christians. The first colonists were ruthless, very clever and stamped down hard on any resistance.'

Nobody in the office said anything but every so often one of them would nod, acknowledging that what Ken was saying was true.

'Although the Africans did all the labour,' Ken continued, 'it was the white man who built wonderful new buildings, roads, and railways and made big farms from our small ones. They introduced British law which we had to obey; they educated us and we even fought their wars for them; we were totally subjugated. Anyone stepping out of line would be harshly treated. So, with all that history, it's not surprising we have this problem, it's become part of our DNA. Somehow, we have to show that we are intelligent people capable of deciding what's best for ourselves. African leaders like Idi Amin and Mugabe stood up to the white man, and that is why they are heroes in the eyes of many Africans. The fact that both men inflicted huge suffering on their own people is overshadowed by the fact that they did not take orders from the white man... Wow, I got on my high horse again,' Ken gave a laugh as he saw the reaction from the staff. 'Sorry about that. And all we were talking about was the wetcores.'

Jane didn't know what to say. What could she say?

'So let's get back to wetcores,' Ken said. 'You've heard me rant on, so now it's your turn. Come on Hani, tell Jane what you think of the wetcores.'

Poor Hani looked embarrassed. 'We agree, wetcores are very good. We get clean water, we get flush toilets. But, we say, the design is not good. The German people didn't ask we slum people what we wanted.'

Lola wasn't embarrassed about speaking up and she took over from Hani. 'The people don't use the showers, they not like them, they put water in a bowl on the ground, and wash that way.'

'This the traditional way,' Hani continued. 'The Germans could save a lot of money with no shower and one standpipe.'

'Does Mr Kimber know this?' Jane asked.

'The trouble is,' Ken said, 'that Robert and I were employed after the design had been completed.'

'Have you heard that we can buy our own computers?' Ken asked.

'Yes, Robert told me - that's good news. Have you done anything about it yet?'

Hani told her that he had asked three suppliers to send representatives to their office later that day. Hesitating, he asked if she would sit in on these meetings.

'I'd be pleased to,' Jane assured him. 'I'll be here all day.'

Ken was pleased. Maybe Jane would take the job after all. The computer suppliers from Ouverru had probably never been to Ogola and would be shocked at the state of the office. Seeing that a white person was involved could be reassuring and although Jane understood why, it still made her sad; you could be the stupidest person in town but having a white skin impressed more than intellect.

'But what about those two missing boxes? Hani tells me he has a contact at the airport. Shouldn't we try one last time to find them?'

'I'm not sure. I couldn't stir up trouble myself because I'm from the wrong tribe, but Hani may be able get some sense out of someone.'

'Why don't I go with him? Between us, we might just get to the bottom of things.'

Ken pursed his lips. 'I don't know, it could be a bit awkward.' After rubbing his chin for a second – Jane thought he must have picked up the habit from Robert – he said that white people could often open doors where locals couldn't. 'Okay then, give it a try, but at the first sign of trouble, come back quickly. Okay?'

Later that afternoon after the three computer representatives had been, the consensus was that the second company, BuzanComp, was the most impressive.

'So what's next on the agenda?' Jane smiled enquiringly at Ken, as a very satisfied Hani returned to the accounts section.

'As you know, Jane, I'm an engineer and my experience of accounting is nil. Have you thought any more about helping us out?'

'I'm not an expert, you know, but I'll give it a go. See how it works out.'

'That's great news,' a look of relief crossed Ken's face. 'Thanks very much. We'll need a lot of training but nobody here will know whether the training is any good... except you.'

'I'll certainly do what I can. But there's one important thing which everybody must know. I'd be an unpaid volunteer. I will simply be here to assist.'

Ken had no hesitation in agreeing. 'What would be useful is if you would give us your CV,' he gave a little laugh, 'and make it... how can I put it? Exaggerate your qualifications and work experience because if any government busybody wants to know what you are doing here, even though you're a volunteer, we'll have to prove your professional skills are important to the project.'

She looked amused, never having been a *professional*. 'I'll do what I can and I'm sure Robert will help with some creative writing.'

Jane found that putting the day's events in writing helped to crystallize in her own mind how international aid to Africa was actually being implemented. When she lived in England it all seemed fairly straightforward that benevolent western governments taxed their rich citizens to help those in the developing world out of poverty. The reality, she was learning by the day, was that there was nothing straightforward about it at all. It was very complicated. Dealing with the minutia in Buzamba and especially Ogola left her struggling to get a grip on the bigger picture. Putting to one side her own experiences, she was intrigued... even excited about learning more about how everything worked. She could report some snippets of this to Tony that might be of journalistic interest but this would be her secondary objective; her priority was caring for Gilly and keeping her new family together.

CHAPTER FOURTEEN

Another of Robert's responsibilities was, for one week every month or so, to go to the provincial town of Kabara to supervise another Schultec project. As it was only a four hour drive south-east of Ouverru, leaving Jane and Gilly for five days shouldn't be a problem, living as they did in a secure compound with good neighbours to keep an eye on them.

'Don't go and get arrested up there.' Jane said flippantly. 'The forces of the German Embassy may not be so keen to come to your rescue you next time.'

Robert grimaced at the very thought, and promised not to upset anybody, especially if they were related to the President.

Two days after Robert left, Cindy mentioned to Jane that Gregg had flown to Kabara that morning on urgent business, and she wondered which hotel Robert used; Jane had no idea, but hoped they would meet, even if it was only for dinner.

While Robert was away, Jane decided she must talk to Sellie about taking in Kaba, but how to broach this was difficult. An opportunity presented itself when Sellie was doing the housework, singing quietly in her usual manner. Jane asked her about their earlier conversation when Sellie had said she was sad that she couldn't have children of her own.

Sellie, looking puzzled, nodded to show she remembered.

'Have you ever been asked to look after someone else's children, orphans for instance, as part of an extended family?'

'No, not in Ouverru,' Sellie replied. 'If I live in my village, then I would care for many, many children from my tribe.'

'Oh, what is your tribe?'

'I Lindu tribe, Madam, from Lake Arthur.'

'Is that one of the larger tribes, like the Peelee or Solu?'

Sellie paused for a moment. 'No, not too big, but Lindu best tribe.' She laughed and Jane, joining in, made a mental note to ask Ken which tribe Blessing Okonyo belonged to.

Also, while Robert was away, Jane thought it would be a good time for her and Hani to investigate the whereabouts of the two missing boxes of computers. She felt certain that if Robert knew what she was planning, he would tell her not to interfere. Using his computer, she'd made some new business cards for herself printing in bold letters "BBnC", and then smaller, and fainter, Bournemouth and Boscombe News Cooperative, International Division. She hoped that anyone taking a casual glance would think it was the BBC. Even in Africa, the BBC had a large number of listeners so it could help to open a few doors.

Basil had driven Robert to Kabara, so Jane took a taxi from Basu compound and picked up Hani from Ogola who was carrying the file on the shipment. He was a tall, well-built man and, Jane thought, that if he had worn a dark suit instead of an open-necked shirt, he would have looked very striking. She made a mental note to point it out to him next time. Tony had always impressed upon her that appearance and presence were all important if you wanted to get beyond any manager's defences and get down to the details.

The taxi took them straight to the airport warehouse, which was situated some distance from the main terminal. Hani asked to see his friend, Mr Wasubu, the manager of the cargo delivery section. There were about fifty people working in a chaotic-looking office, and all heads turned towards this tall local man leading a small *mzungu* woman with a ritual scar on her face, to Mr Wasubu's private office. She looked very much like his assistant. Very strange.

Mr Wasubu made them welcome and ordered one of the office girls to bring tea and biscuits immediately. He was delighted to have such an important lady in his office, especially as Hani had given her a big build-up. The tea was horribly sweet but, like a true investigative newshound, she dutifully swallowed it and thanked Mr Wasubu for his kind hospitality.

At his request, a young man brought in the cargo delivery slips which showed that Ogola had signed for four boxes and two were unsigned.

'What we'd like to know,' Jane smiled warmly at Mr Wasubu, 'is what happened to the two missing boxes.'

'We can't find them. They're definitely not here.'

'We want to know who took them… maybe by mistake… so that we can recover them.'

Wasubu looked blank and shook his head. Much to Jane's relief, Hani then took the initiative and he and Wasubu had a long, occasionally heated discussion in their own language and she could only guess what was being said. The only part she understood was when Hani nodded in her direction and said in English "BBC investigating reporter" – there mustn't have been a translation in their own language describing her title. This seemed to have the required affect as Wasubu called the same young man back to join them. There was another lengthy debate before another man, looking terrified, was called. Jane almost laughed as she'd never seen anyone look so scared in all her life. All the men took turns to launch verbal assaults on this petrified-looking fellow who timidly said a few words before leaving the office.

'I think we may be able to get to the bottom of your problem,' Wasubu said to Jane. 'I'll look into things further and let Hani know when we have a result.'

'Thank you very much, Mr Wasubu,' she gave him a positive smile. 'We have every confidence in you,' and, for reasons which she didn't understand, added, 'London will be pleased.'

Jane and Hani went back to Ogola to report to Ken.

'I'm relying on you, Hani, not to get Jane into any trouble,' Ken looked a little uneasy.

'It's okay, Ken,' Hani replied with a tone of confidence in his voice, 'I'll be very careful. But Jane can probably get things done that I can't on my own.'

'Yes, I realise that. Just take care.'

'I will,' Hani smiled in Jane's direction.

'Oh, by the way Jane, I've arranged for you to meet the editor of the *Buzamban Times* next week, but whatever you do, don't tell him what you're up to with Wasubu, it could get even him into trouble.'

Thanking Ken for his help, and Hani for fixing the meeting with Wasubu, Jane went back home for a well-earned rest.

At the end of the week, Robert arrived home late in the evening and was pleased they hadn't had any problems. Sitting on the terrace with their usual gin and tonics, they took great pleasure in the unmistakable sounds and smells of Africa. She loved the continuous noise of various nocturnal creatures, it was so tropical, so Africa. Tree frogs were particularly noisy that evening, their croaks seemingly in synchronicity with the twinkling fireflies that danced and sparkled over the lawn and bushes. The night was beautiful, velvety, and millions of stars shone brightly in the midnight-blue sky competing with the laser show put on by the fireflies. The only downside was that they had to cover themselves in mosquito repellent and, when the breeze shifted, inhale the occasional whiff from the half-dozen mosquito coils simmering around the terrace.

She suddenly remembered that Gregg had also been in Kabara and asked Robert if he'd seen him. She noticed an uneasy flicker cross his face before he quickly answered that they hadn't met. Was it unease, and if so, why? No matter, it was too nice to worry about it at the moment.

'Why don't you fly to Kabara like Gregg?'

'I have flown once or twice, but the road has now been completely rebuilt by the Chinese, and I need the vehicle to visit Kabara's two satellite towns which the project also covers.'

'Oh, I see.'

'I'll tell you something I've done, though. Unbeknownst to DGA or Schultec, I've arranged to extend the water system to a mission hospital which presently has no running water.'

'Wow, you're being brave,' she smiled. 'Won't you get into trouble over that?'

'I hope not. I've managed to hide the extra costs so, hopefully, nobody will be any the wiser.'

They sat with their own thoughts for a few minutes, Jane eventually breaking the silence by asking how the project was progressing. She was sorry to hear that the situation wasn't good; of the three German Schultec employees, one was regularly off work with a tropical fever, another had cut his hand and could only do office work for the next few weeks, and the third, the project leader, had had a row with the mayor over a bar girl and was desperately trying to avoid being arrested.

'That's terrible,' she looked sympathetically at her husband, 'what'll happen now?'

'Oh, it'll probably be all right. I did what I could to ensure that things keep going and I'll go there again in a month's time. And, of course, I'll send my report to Schultec to keep them in the picture.'

'Did anything else happen?' Jane asked.

'No, not really, although an English chap I know there told me a story and I wasn't sure whether to laugh or cry.'

'Let's hear it then.'

'Well, he was driving past the hospital when he noticed smoke coming from one end of the building. A man in a white coat came running out shouting at him to go and get the fire brigade; the hospital's phones had been disconnected for non-payment of their bills.'

'What! They actually disconnect a hospital?'

'Oh yes. Ted raced to the fire station, only to find the fire engine was out of fuel and water; they couldn't get any because they hadn't paid the bills for months. So Ted bought fuel with his own money and the men said they could get the water at the nearby lake.'

'But weren't they wasting time? The hospital was still burning.'

'That's right. Ted was frantic. So eventually, they shot off to the lake and reversed down a ramp to pump lake water into the tanks but the driver misjudged the distance and the bloody fire engine ended up in the lake.'

Jane now knew why Robert hadn't known whether to laugh or cry. 'No, no. It's too far-fetched to be true, surely he must have exaggerated.'

'Ted's a straightforward chap and I'm sure he didn't make it up. Anyhow, what is certain is that part of the hospital did burn down with several casualties, and the fire engine did end up in the lake. That much was reported in the local paper.'

'You wonder at times what's wrong with people here,' Jane said.

'Yes. I wish I knew. I think the explanation is complicated. It's not as though the people, like the firemen for example, aren't clever or well-trained because most of them are, and they're quite capable of doing the job, just as well as blokes back in England.'

'Is that only when they're supervised?'

'Yes. Maybe it is.'

'And what about the… shall I say, the professionals? Are they any good?'

'Some are very good. Unfortunately, most of them now live in Europe.'

'So it's not a lack of knowledge and it's not a lack of training,' Jane said, 'so what is the problem?'

'I think it could be to do with their environment, or even evolution.'

'How do you mean?'

'In England, well, let's say the developed world, the majority of children are brought up to read and write from an early age. They learn discipline at home and school, and help is there for any who slip through the net. And keeping time is important whether it's for school or even to watch a TV programme.'

'Yes, I see what you mean.'

'Getting to school or work on time for Africans can be stressful.'

'Does that mean it will take generations to… well, catch up?'

'Maybe. I think today's youngsters whose parents are educated will be far more capable.'

'Well,' Jane sighed. 'I hope you're right.'

Jane wanted to go to Ogola again to find out if Kaba was all right, but before that, Ken had made arrangements for her to meet

Elphic Chuchu, the editor of the *Buzamban Times*. Although she was keen to see him, particularly as Tony had told her to make this contact, she hoped she wouldn't be delayed for long.

'Please come in and make yourself comfortable,' Elphic greeted Jane with a big smile and immediately sent for tea. He looked very dapper in a pinstripe suit, white shirt and tie, a folded white handkerchief in his top jacket pocket and, distinctively, a red carnation in his buttonhole.

'I appreciate you taking the time to see me,' Jane immediately relaxed after his friendly welcome.

'Mr Kasansa tells me you're a journalist.'

'Only in a very minor way,' Jane modestly replied. She told Elphic about her part-time job in the small market town of Ringwood, and how she reported local events to a nearby news agency. 'It wasn't very exciting but I really enjoyed it.'

'Well, good for you. I've been in newspapers all my life, and I wouldn't change it for anything... well, that's not quite true... what I would change in Buzamba is being able to write the truth. I learnt my craft many years ago with an agency in London where freedom of the press is sacrosanct.'

'I wondered about that,' Jane said. 'How bad is it here?'

'I have to be careful not to offend those in power. I criticise where I can but there's a line I dare not cross. I've been arrested three times so far but because I'm a Kenyan citizen and have a very good lawyer, I've managed to stay out of prison. My wife is Buzamban and that's the main reason I'm here.'

'Is she well connected?' Jane wasn't sure whether this was a bit cheeky.

Elphic thought her question very funny. 'She's not a Peelee or Solu if that's what you mean,' he laughed. 'She's a Lindu and comes from a family of tribal chiefs, but since independence most of them now live in England.'

'Oh, from near Lake Arthur,'

He gave her a respectful glance. 'Yes indeed, you have learnt a lot in your short time here.'

'I try,' she replied. 'The main reason for coming today... apart from meeting you, of course, is that my boss from England will be coming here for a holiday soon, and he's expressed a wish to meet you. Would that be all right?'

'Of course. It would be my pleasure. You never know, we might be able to do some business together.'

After thanking him once again for his kind reception, Jane said her farewell and headed for Ogola.

During the night, there had been several rain showers and the skies were leaden with the threat of more to come. The blanket of cloud seemed to compress the humidity in the air, making everything damp and musty. Cutty Road was awash with muddy, garbage-filled puddles and vehicles had to crawl along, navigating their way around the largest craters. The market sellers were huddled under umbrellas and Jane felt sorry for them and the pedestrians who were struggling to keep the mud off their clothes by trying to avoid being anywhere near a puddle when a vehicle passed.

'*Karibu*, Jane,' Ken greeted her when Basil dropped her off at the office. Ruth, as usual, rushed to get her a cup of tea; their acceptance of her made Jane feel almost humble and she really wanted to help if she could.

'Did you see Elphic Chuchu?' Ken asked.

'Yes, thanks very much for arranging it; he gave me a very useful slant on the newspaper business here. I'll go and see him again when Tony comes out.'

'Oh, that's good,' Ken was pleased.

Deciding to leave this subject for the time being, Jane wanted to bring up the tricky topic of Kaba, bearing in mind Ken's warning about getting involved. However, she was determined not to let it drop and asked if he could get someone to find out the actual situation and make sure that the little girl was being fed.

'I handed the money you gave me last time to a lady in the Social Department. You'd have to ask them if she's still around. Would you like to talk to the manager, Nelson Lamu?'

'If it's no trouble, Ken, I'd appreciate it.'

Ken was once again caught between two dilemmas. First, he wanted to keep Jane happy so that she'd help with the computers and accounts, but on the other hand, it could be awkward if she started to act as a charity by getting too involved with this girl.

On the way to Nelson Lamu's office, Ken told Jane that he and Nelson were second cousins and that Nelson's grandfather had held a senior post in the old colonial government. Following independence he'd fallen out with the Peelees and had then been imprisoned for over five years on a trumped-up charge of trying to overthrow the government. Nelson and his family had been forced to keep a low profile and had changed their family name.

'That's too bad,' Jane said sadly.

Nelson gave Jane a friendly welcome. He was slightly shorter and slimmer than Ken but it was obvious from his facial features that they were from the same ethnic background. Without delay, she was introduced to three of his staff; the fourth member, a lady called Constance Wanjiku, was away in Italy attending a seminar on low-cost housing which was financed by UNDP.

'That sounds interesting,' Jane said. 'Anyhow, I'll look forward to meeting Constance when she returns.'

Whispering softly, Nelson told Jane that Constance was very well connected to the top Peelees and the UNDP.

'Oh, I see,' Jane gave him a knowing wink, and told him about her interest in Kaba Okonyo who was recently orphaned.

He called one of his clerks to bring in their records. 'Ah, yes,' he said looking puzzled. 'You gave money for this girl to be fed. Is that right?'

Jane nodded.

Nelson continued. 'Yes, she has a bad hand and some man called Toma told the feeding station ladies not to feed her as she had evil spirits.' He paused again to clarify some of the information he'd been given. 'The mother died last week... I think... and the children were sent back to her village. It looks as if Kaba is still here but is not living in their old room – someone else has moved in.'

143

This piece of information worried Jane. 'Would it be possible to find out where she is living?'

'We can make enquiries but… why are you getting involved?'

'You see, Nelson, when Ken took me to see Blessing Okonyo, I met all her children and felt sorry for them, especially Kaba.' Jane held her breath, not being sure what Nelson's reaction would be.

He told Jane that it was up to the extended family to look after any dependents. However, to keep Jane happy, he reluctantly asked one of his ladies to make enquiries. Jane thanked him for his help and went back to the main office.

Jane didn't consider herself a religious person but, for the first time in her life, she felt there was something… something she couldn't quite get her head around… that had brought her to this place and at this time. There was no clap of thunder nor a beam of light but a sense that fate had brought her here for a purpose – and that purpose, she reasoned, was that as well as caring for her own daughter, she should also take care of a less fortunate little girl, Kaba. She wasn't sure how it could be done and it would be difficult as everyone, including Robert, would certainly be against her, but there was a compelling inner voice telling her that she must to do it.

CHAPTER FIFTEEN

Exhausted after a hot, clammy day in Ogola, Jane stood under the cooling water in her spotlessly clean shower, wondering how the people of Ogola managed to keep clean. At least, those living in the new blocks had water and could wash, but life for the other poor souls must be appalling. But what about Kaba? Did she have somewhere to live and was she still being fed?

The wonderful aroma of roasting pork greeted her as she wandered into the kitchen for a much needed cup of tea. Sellie called all roast meat '*nyama choma*'. Not only was the meat cooking in the oven but Sellie had also prepared the potatoes and vegetables and only wanted to know what time they would be eating. This was the only decision Jane had to make, as Sellie would also set the table and do all the washing-up. Perching herself on a kitchen stool sipping her tea, Jane thought what a cushy life she had.

After making the challenging decision on what time their dinner should be ready, she told Sellie about her day in Ogola.

Sellie's expression was one of contempt. 'Ogola people lazy. That why the slum be too bad.'

'But most of them are too poor to make their rooms nicer... aren't they?' Jane asked guardedly, not knowing quite what point Sellie was making.

'They wait for *mzungu* people to do it. They too lazy to do it they self.'

This was a bit of a puzzle for Jane. 'Have you actually been there?'

'I been plenty times. People from my tribe there. Some men have money, they spend it on beer and girls.' She paused for a few moments. 'Do people say "thank you" for work you do? No. Do people help with work? No. Do they pay rent? No. They see rich white people so they sit and wait for work to be done... for free.'

She'd almost finished her condemnation before adding, 'that's the way it is.'

This was the strongest condemnation she'd heard of Buzambans and it had come from one of them, not from Quentin as she might have expected.

Jane could tell that Sellie wanted to say more but something was holding her back. 'I'd like to hear what you think. I won't tell anyone, I promise.'

Sellie hesitated before continuing. 'Many people think they wait long time, then white man fix things. They say white man stole everything in old days; you get rich from suffering of African slaves.'

'Is that what you think?' she asked warily.

Sellie gave a little laugh and her face relaxed before she answered. 'No, Madam. I think white people help us… most of time. What happen in old days was very bad. They take our land, send people as slaves, they now sorry for their sins and wickedness and try to make things better.'

Not being sure how to continue, Jane was relieved to be saved by the bell – the telephone was ringing in the living room. It was Robert confirming that f-Fearless would be coming round for a drink after dinner, although he'd already sounded drunk when he'd called from a local bar.

'I'd prefer if he didn't come tonight. I'm tired and want an early night and, if he's been drinking all afternoon, then…'

'I'll cancel it, he can come another night.'

Jane didn't go back into the kitchen, her discussion with Sellie could wait for another day.

Settling down on the sofa with their usual after-dinner nightcap, Robert wanted to hear all about Jane's day in Ogola. She was pleased to be able to talk about it without the emotion she'd felt after her last visit.

For the next five minutes, Robert felt wonderful. He couldn't believe how well everything was working out with his new family; life couldn't get any better than this. But, his blissful state was about to be well and truly shattered.

First, they heard a car pull up outside the house followed by the sound of people arguing; a woman's voice mixed with the deeper tones of one or two men. The finale culminated with a woman's scream and loud aggressive shouting, followed by a car door being slammed and a vehicle driving away at speed.

Then their doorbell rang. Exchanging puzzled looks Robert crossed the room and opened the door. Quickly, he stepped back, almost pushed over by a very drunk and dishevelled f-Fearless staggering into the room, desperately trying to keep his balance; his legs seemed to have minds of their own insisting on going in different directions. He stank of alcohol. His glasses were hanging precariously from one ear. Clutching the arm of a chair, he made a supreme effort to steady himself, straightened his glasses, and tried to say something, but his stuttering words came out as gibberish. He looked a mess. His face was blotchy, his thinning hair splayed in all directions, only one button on his shirt fastened, and there was a nasty stain down the front of his trousers. 'I w-wish… wish to… err… intro..,' was as far as he got before Precious barged her way through the open door.

She rushed straight at Robert. 'Hello Bigman,' she said trying to give what she thought was a sexy smile, but the effect was somewhat spoilt by a lipstick stain on her teeth. Ignoring f-Fearless and Jane, she flung herself at Robert, unsuccessfully trying to plant a kiss on his mouth.

The blood drained from Robert's face as he looked from Precious to Jane. 'What are you doing here?' he stammered.

Jane could hardly believe her eyes or her ears. Precious looked just as horrible as the first time she saw her and the patchy discolouration on her face she now knew was the effect of skin-lightening cream.

Robert quickly changed tack. 'Jimmy,' he shouted, 'get her out of here.' But f-Fearless was sprawled in a chair with his eyes closed.

'Please go away. You're not wanted here, and you've no right to come here.' Robert's raised voice was trying to be masterful.

'So, this your new wife.' Her drawn-on eyebrows rose as she looked at Jane. Her accent was thick and coarse and hard to follow. She gave Jane a mutinous look and then turned back to Robert.

'I see her before. Jimmy tell me you bring *mzungu* woman to Buzamba. She wife number two – I wife number one!' She gave a big smile. 'You tell she wife number two.'

'Don't be silly, you know damned well you're not my wife.'

'I am so. Everyone know it. You bought me from my pa. Tell him Jimmy.'

Jimmy f-Fearless f-Faversham was gradually coming round and endeavoured to sit upright in the chair. He tried to focus using the top and bottom halves of his bifocal glasses which were now attached to both ears, but he was obviously having trouble focusing on anything and any form of sensible speech was still too difficult.

Robert took a deep breath and stuck out his chin. He was really angry now. 'Jimmy, get this woman out of here… now,' he shouted.

Jimmy gave a weak, drooling smile and tried to shake his head, but the effort of moving it from side-to-side was too much and he slumped back in the chair knocking his bifocals out of kilter again.

All this pussy-footing around was too much for Jane and the repeated insinuation that she was wife number two had gone too far. She directed her attack at Robert. 'Get these people out of my house now,' she yelled. She deliberately chose to call it 'my house' to get through to Precious that she was Robert's only wife.

But Precious wouldn't budge. She put up a struggle, refusing to go and that was when Sellie appeared.

She stormed up to Precious and let fly a verbal onslaught, throughout which Precious stood speechless with her mouth wide open. Although Jane and Robert couldn't understand the words, the meaning was clear and had the desired effect on Precious. She immediately stopped ranting and timidly went outside dragging a useless Jimmy to wait for a taxi. Sellie turned to go back to her room, with Robert's grateful thanks following her into the kitchen.

When the taxi arrived, a muted conversation was followed by the slamming of car doors and the vehicle departing.

Sitting in a chair, arms folded across her chest in a defiant gesture, Jane stared directly at her emotionally drained husband.

'They were both drunk… you know I never married her… never… believe me.' He looked despairingly at his furious wife and tried to put on a reassuring smile, as though the whole episode had just been a load of nonsense.

'I'm going to bed,' Jane informed Robert through gritted teeth, 'and you can sleep in the spare room. Do not, I repeat, *do not* come into my room.'

'You're being silly again and…' was as far as Robert got before Jane decided to reveal her other accusation.

'You also lied about having to be married for me to get a visa to live here. It's not true, is it?'

'It's the law,' was Robert's limp reply, knowing what was coming next.

'It may be the law but it's never enforced.'

'Who told you that?'

'Never you mind.'

'We had to get married to get this house. My bosses insisted on it.'

'Ah, I see. It's all clear now. You tricked me into marriage so you could get a better house and have free sex every night. With fucking Precious, you had to pay for it.' With that final declaration, Jane stormed through to the bedroom.

What a mess. Why had his world just fallen apart? Robert tried to work out how he could explain everything to Jane. She was extremely upset over his being economical with the truth over the visa, and now Precious' claim to be his first wife. How could she say that, knowing it wasn't true? After a fitful night in the spare bedroom, Robert left the house the next morning before Jane chose to get up. As soon as she was dressed, she went straight into the kitchen to thank Sellie for her timely intervention the previous evening. Sellie, looking very self-satisfied, told her that the boss had already thanked her.

'Oh, by the way, what did you say to make her go away?'

'I tell her I a witch with special power,' she laughed, 'and if she don't go now I cuss her good. She frightened because I look strange and speak magic tribal words.'

'Will she come back?'

'She not come back to this place, no way, but she get some big-shot lawyer man to make trouble for the boss. She Peelee woman and most law people Peelees. I think Mr Kimber get big money trouble.'

Shortly before noon, Robert phoned Jane to see how she was and suggested they talk about everything after Gilly had gone to bed. She wasn't sure what to do. Should she be highly offended, give him a hard time and threaten to leave, or should she be sympathetic and help him out of the mess? She thought Cindy would be the best person to ask although it was highly likely that the whole sordid story would spread around the compound like wildfire but, was that a bad thing? Probably not. It was bound to get out as the guards would have heard Precious' side of the story, and that would be much worse than Robert's version.

Kath was at Cindy's when Jane arrived so, a little apprehensively, she told them both about Precious. There were a few moments of silence before either of them spoke. Cindy was sympathetic but Kath only sympathised with Jane and thought Robert had behaved badly. They agreed that Sellie's reasoning was correct and Robert would hear more from Precious' lawyer in the not-too-distant future.

'These people will cause as much trouble as they can,' said the holier-than-thou Kath. 'It will cost Robert a lot to settle this problem.'

Cindy came to Robert's rescue and looked coldly at the pious Kath. 'Hey, this kind of thing happens all the time in Buzamba and, as long as you have a decent lawyer, you'll get a reasonable settlement.'

This was the cue to change the subject and they soon went their separate ways after Cindy had told Jane she would be round to see her later. When she arrived, it wasn't long before Cindy attacked Kath's hypocrisy, knowing as did half the compound, that Quentin had been screwing around for years having affairs with several 'desperate housewives'. He was currently seeing the wife of the second secretary at the British High Commission; this was common knowledge amongst the expat community and Cindy couldn't believe that Kath didn't know about it.

'I'm feeling better already,' Jane laughed.

'And this happened before Robert even met you,' Cindy continued, 'unlike Quentin who is still up to his tricks. So don't be too hard on the lovely Robert... promise? I think he's great. And don't worry, Gregg and I will look after you,' she added, with what Jane thought was a knowing wink.

Although Cindy had been tossing it over in her mind for a few days, she didn't tell Jane that Gregg had actually seen Robert in the Kabara Safari Lodge. Robert was so engrossed having dinner with a very glamorous local lady, that he didn't notice Gregg. When they'd finished, they left the dining room together and went upstairs to the bedrooms. Cheekily, Gregg had checked with a young man at reception who'd told him the Mr Kimber was staying in room 202 for five days, and the lady with him in the dining room was his sister.

'Is anything the matter, mummy?' Gilly asked that evening, picking up on the change in Jane's mood. She'd been sound asleep on both the occasions that Precious had been to their house so was unaware of the reason for this tension between her parents.

'No, of course not, darling.' Jane did her best to reassure her troubled daughter.

Gilly's life had changed dramatically since their arrival in Buzamba. She was having a wonderful time with new friends, new school, and especially her new daddy, but deep down, she had an uneasy feeling that things could change – change for the worse. Jane gave her a hug and assured her again that everything was fine. But was it? She knew then and there that she had to make things up with Robert, if only for Gilly's sake.

Facing each other across the coffee table when Gilly was asleep, Jane asked for an explanation of his relationship with Precious and their so-called tribal marriage. Was he a bigamist? Had she really been demoted to wife number two? Were there any children? She was willing to listen calmly as long as he told the truth.

Robert's defence was brief and to the point. He'd met her in a bar a year before, and had finished the relationship six months ago. During the last Easter holidays, she'd begged him to take her to her village so she could give her family a supply of food and other bulky items which were too cumbersome to take on the bus.

Reluctantly, he'd agreed, planning to return to Ouverru the same day. By accident or design, Precious had delayed their departure so that it was almost dark when they arrived, and there was no choice but to stay the night. He had met her father and other members of her family and had some food with them, but he'd slept alone in his car and returned to Ouverru early the next morning. Robert assured Jane that at no time had any agreement or ceremony taken place.

'But she said the food was a gift to the family from you.'

'Rubbish!' Robert paused for a moment. 'I did, of course, give her money from time to time but that was for her – not her family.'

Jane thought for a moment and then softened her tone of questioning. 'Are you certain, absolutely certain that you've told me everything? Because if you have, I'll stand by you. I'll even forgive your deception over the visa.'

Robert looked Jane straight in the eyes. 'I guarantee there is nothing else.' A note of irritation crept into his voice. 'Jane, you've got to trust me on this.'

She did believe him. After all, she, herself, had been economical with the truth about some of her relationships in Ringwood – not that he knew this! He put his arm round her shoulders and she relaxed into his embrace deciding it was time to ease the tension.

'And tell me, why did Precious call you " Bigman"?'

Robert knew where this was leading. 'Only because I'm tall and she's short.'

'Oh, I thought it might be something else, something I hadn't noticed.'

'Ho ho, you cheeky minx.'

She thought he'd better know that the scandal would be all round the compound by now because she'd told the whole story to Cindy and Kath.

Robert shuddered at the thought of his forthcoming embarrassment. 'I won't be able to show my face round here for a long time,' he groaned.

'Of course you will, *bigman,* look them all square in the face.'

'Ha, it's easy for you.'

'It should be easy for you, too. You don't have anything to be ashamed of, do you?'

'I guess not.'

'You'll be pleased to know then, that I've invited Cindy, Kath, and Josie, with their husbands for dinner on Saturday night – and they've all accepted.'

'You're kidding.'

'I'm not kidding, you… bigamist. You'll be able to show them you have nothing to hide. I'll tell you something that will make you feel better,' Jane smiled. 'According to the morally challenged Cindy, Quentin has been having affairs on a regular basis so you'll get no aggro from him. One last question though, what did you ever see in Precious? She looked horrible.'

'Yes, I know what you mean. When I knew her, she looked quite nice, didn't wear makeup, her hair was… you know… normal and she dressed sensibly. But there's one other thing troubling me. Why did Jimmy bring her here? He must have known it would cause trouble.' Robert thought for a moment. 'F-fucking f-fearless f-Faversham.'

'That's the first time I've heard you say the f-word.'

'That's because I don't like it, but in this case… it's the only word to use.'

'I agree,' Jane smiled. 'F-fucking f-fearless f-Faversham he'll be from now on.'

Going straight into the baking hot accounts office the next morning, Jane asked Hani if he'd heard from Mr Wasubu about the missing computers.

'I speak with him yesterday. He say he will have more information next week.'

'Is he just trying to put us off, do you think?'

'No, he a good man. He will have something next week. I'm certain.'

With that slight reassurance, she went through to see Ken and told him the news. 'Why does it take so long?'

'You'll soon learn. One thing all Africans are blessed with is patience.'

Jane laughed. 'Are you sure it's a blessing or a curse?'

This brought a smile to Ken's face. 'Maybe you're right. Anyhow, putting that on one side for the moment, there's one other place you might like to visit and that's the health centre.'

The newly-painted sign on the front of the health clinic 'Ogola Slum Upgrading Project Health Clinic funded by the Federal Republic of Germany' was a very grand title for what, Jane thought, looked little more than a double garage. Outside, a queue of mainly women waited at the counter, which was managed by two smartly-dressed African ladies in starched blue and white nurses' uniforms. Those trying to describe their ailments to them talked loudly, waving their arms and using animated gestures. The atmosphere was more or less congenial and occasionally people added their own opinions, creating laughter amongst some, but irritation in those trying to get treatment.

Guided by Ken through a side door, they entered a small waiting room. Behind a waist-high wall were the two nurses and on the other wall was a door with a sign marked 'Treatment Room'. Ken knocked and a man's muffled voice called for them to enter. The little room was furnished with a small table, two chairs and an examination couch covered with a white plastic sheet.

Ken introduced Jane to Doctor Dieter Blanke.

'*Karibu*, welcome to Ogola and all things beautiful,' Dieter said, with more than a touch of irony. He gave her a cautious glance, 'it's quite an eye-opener isn't it?'

'Yes, it's certainly that.' Jane smiled. 'In fact, I'm really shocked to see how people live. They must be tough to survive.'

'Well, the phrase "survival of the fittest" has a definite meaning here.' Dieter was a tall, thin angular man, not much older than Robert, who spoke with an almost flawless English accent. He had a relaxed manner with an easy smile; casually dressed in khaki shirt and shorts, badly in need of ironing, contrasting sharply with the two smartly dressed nurses. After a polite discussion about Ogola and the many problems faced by all and sundry, Jane learned that Dieter had worked for four years in a Nottingham hospital, hence his good English. He was now a volunteer, sponsored by a German charity which provided doctors and nurses to third world countries on ten monthly assignments. Their services were free but the charity paid all their expenses, and also provided some of the medicines used in the clinic. This was Dieter's second assignment in Ogola and he hoped to do one more before settling down as a GP in Germany. At least, that's what his fiancée believed!

After ascertaining that Dieter had some spare time, Jane told him that Ken had taken her to see a lady desperately ill with AIDS. 'I've read about AIDS but the reality only hits home when you see it for yourself,' Jane said.

'Well, if you spend time here in Ogola, you will see a lot of people dying from AIDS. There are hundreds in Ogola alone, and thousands more... no, hundreds of thousands more in the country.' Dieter replied. 'Would you like to hear some facts and figures?'

Jane hesitated a moment before nodding her head.

Dieter then reeled off some statistics that were clearly embedded in his memory. 'In the whole of Africa, twenty-five million people are infected with HIV, which represents sixty per cent of the world's sufferers. Around sixteen million have already died and there are now twelve million orphans. To put that figure into perspective, more people have died from AIDS in Africa than the combined total of military in both world wars. How's that for starters?'

'Pretty grim and impossible to imagine such numbers,' Jane said.

'In Buzamba, around twenty per cent of the adult population has HIV or AIDS which is not as bad as in many countries.'

As Dieter's figures were slowly ingested, Jane struggled to find a suitable response. 'But everyone must know about AIDS so why can't it be controlled, by using condoms for example? Or can't people afford them?'

'We give out free condoms here in this clinic,' he opened his cupboard and showed Jane a shelf full of boxes of condoms. 'Most men refuse to use them, isn't that right, Ken?'

'Yes,' Ken said bitterly. 'Most men won't use them, it's... well... it's not macho, if you see what I mean. And many top people in Africa, including the politician Thabo Mbeki, do not acknowledge that sexual intercourse and AIDS are connected. So the message isn't clear and it goes against traditional practices.'

'It's still surprising to me that, as Dieter says, sixty per cent of people with HIV/AIDS are Africans.'

'I have a couple of theories about that,' Dieter answered matter-of-factly. Before he could expand on his theories, the door was opened by one of the nurses asking him to see a sick lady at the counter.

'Help yourselves to drinks. Ken knows where I hide them,' and with that he left the room.

Ken pulled a curtain away from the front of the counter to reveal a small fridge. 'There's beer or...' he moved some bottles to look what was hiding behind, '... or more beer.'

'In that case, I'd love a beer, please,' Jane laughed.

'I'll join you and I'll open one for Dieter as well.' Ken neatly prized the tops off three bottles and passed one to Jane.

'There's nothing better in this climate,' she said appreciatively as she lifted the bottle to her lips.

'Prosit,' Dieter said as he returned and took his bottle from Ken. 'Ah, now where was I? Ah yes, my theories. Firstly, people in the West take great care of themselves. They wear seat belts in cars, cyclists wear helmets, all household goods are checked for safety and so on and if, God forbid, a child dies, then the harrowing grief is there for all to see. People aren't like that here; they take risks. On the roads the death toll is horrendous; they play around with electrical wiring often killing themselves, and, if a baby dies... well, it's sad for a day or two but it's soon forgotten.' Dieter waited for their reaction.

'So what you're saying is... well, life is cheap.'

Dieter looked at Ken. 'What do you think?'

He thought for a moment. 'It's part of the problem, but only part. I believe the main reason lies with our traditions.' He then told them about their office girl, Ruth, who'd recently been diagnosed as HIV positive. Like many other women, Ruth had fallen victim to a tradition which dictates that a wife whose husband dies must submit to sex with one of his male relatives – a practice supposed to cleanse her of her husband's spirit. She knew the risk but she couldn't refuse because it's their tradition.'

Jane was appalled, especially as she'd already met Ruth. 'So Dieter, what's your second theory?'

'Pornography.'

'Surely not. Not here in Buzamba.'

'It's not only here but throughout Africa. American-made porn films are freely available and in the films, men never wear condoms.'

Ken smiled sadly. 'The West, especially America, is seen by Africans as setting the standard for just about everything, including sex, so if American men don't wear condoms, then it must be all right.'

'God almighty, that's so sad.' Strangely, Jane didn't feel embarrassed talking to two strange men about sex and pornography because the real issue was AIDS. She looked from Ken to Dieter. 'But isn't there any medication?'

Dieter pulled a face as he replied. 'Yes, there is. Buzamba, along with other countries in Africa, qualifies for antiretroviral drugs from the Global Fund to Fight AIDS, TB and Malaria. If HIV sufferers are caught early enough, these drugs can significantly extend their natural life.'

'Well, that's good. Ruth should be okay then.'

Dieter and Ken gave Jane uneasy looks.

'I'm afraid not,' Dieter said quietly with a sad shake of his head. 'We haven't enough drugs for new patients. The limited amount we have is barely sufficient to cover those already on a medical programme. Our clinic was sent drugs from Germany but here's the rub; we have the documentation for 30,000 euros worth of drugs which were sent to us three months ago, and we have evidence the shipment arrived at Ouverru Airport. After that it disappeared.'

Jane found all this hard to grasp. 'So what happens now?'

'The German government won't send any more drugs until the first shipment is found.'

She shook her head in despair. 'Have you been to the airport yourself to find out what happened to the shipment?'

'No, but the Embassy sent people along with one of my nurses. They found the paperwork but no drugs. The airport workers said they would look into it but it's probably a waste of time. Some big shot has stolen the lot. End of story.'

'We have a good contact at the airport who may be able to help.' She looked at Ken to see if he was going to tell her to forget it, but he kept quiet. Was she getting too involved? Fools rush in, etcetera.

'I can give you the documents if you feel you can do something. I'll send them over to Ken in the morning.'

'Yes, okay then. I expect to be going there next week over another issue so I'll see if anything can be done.'

'And here's another thing,' Dieter said as he took more beers from his fridge and passed them round. 'Manufacturers' prices of antiretroviral drugs have recently fallen, in some cases by ninety per cent. But this has been offset by African governments loading taxes on the drugs before pharmacies sell them on to patients.' He searched in his desk drawer and quickly found what he was looking for. 'Here are some examples,' he read from a paper, 'Kenya imposes taxes of 40%, and Tanzania over 32%.'

During the past few days, Jane thought she had become unshockable but now she knew this wasn't the case. She started to say something but couldn't express her shock. Her brain had switched into neutral.

'As I've already told you, the number of deaths from AIDS is staggering,' Dieter continued, 'but malaria is still the main killer.'

Jane remembered she'd seen a programme on TV about malaria. 'I've heard somewhere that mosquito nets are being sent to Africa.'

'That's correct,' Dieter confirmed. 'Insecticide impregnated nets are donated to African countries free of charge. They go into government warehouses and are then sold to pharmacies.'

'I thought you said they are free.'

'Yes, they're supposed to be, but local officials sell them on and keep the money. The nets are on sale in Ouverru for five hundred shillings.'

Once again, Jane was speechless. How can this happen?

'But they make wonderful fishing nets,' quipped Dieter. 'I even saw some decorating the wedding dress of the Minister of Health's daughter.'

There was a sudden commotion at the counter and one of the nurses asked for Dieter to come quickly, so Jane and Ken also rose to leave. 'Jane, you are welcome to come at any time,' Dieter called as they were leaving, 'and don't forget,' he added with a light laugh, 'if you want some lightly lubricated condoms to make balloons for your next party, I'm your guy.'

CHAPTER SIXTEEN

Although Jane hadn't fully recovered her composure after her many emotional roller coasters, she now had to plan the following night's dinner party. She had given out the invitations on the spur of the moment but she wanted to demonstrate on behalf of her wayward husband, that neither of them had anything to be ashamed of. But how would she manage? She'd never hosted a dinner party in her life and here she was, glibly giving out invitations to people she was somewhat in awe of. She'd already discounted asking Robert to help as he'd probably never done this himself but... ah yes, Sellie had. She'd catered for large dinner parties with her last employer.

Much to her relief, Sellie was more than happy to do all the cooking and they put their heads together to come up with a menu and a shopping list. Jane was almost out of the door when the phone rang. It was Ken asking if she could go to Ogola as two of the three computer quotations had come in. Thinking on her feet, she said she would be there shortly, but couldn't stay more than an half an hour. That way, she could combine her visit to Ogola with a shopping expedition.

At the project office, Jane was shocked to see Kaba sitting on the ground outside the entrance, obviously waiting for her. During the turmoil of the past few days, Jane had completely forgotten that she had asked the Social Department to find out if she was still around. Now she knew she was.

She walked towards Kaba who gingerly got to her feet. Jane was upset when she saw that her face, arms and legs were filthy and her dress tattered and torn. She had an ugly-looking injury on the side of her forehead which had partly healed over with a dirt encrusted scab, but a trickle of blood and some yellowish liquid was seeping from one edge of the wound.

'Ow are you?' Kaba timidly greeted Jane.

Jane held out her hand. She needed help with translation so she motioned for Kaba to stay where she was while she went into the office. The smile disappeared from her face as if she thought she was going to be abandoned again, but Jane smiled encouragingly and held up one finger. 'One minute,' she said, hoping Kaba would understand. She hurried into the office but Ken wasn't there. Lola told her he'd be back shortly. Jane then asked Lola to help and explained the reason for Kaba being there. Lola gave her a very strange look. She asked Lola to tell Kaba that she was sorry her mother had died and to ask her if anyone was looking after her, where was she living and was she still being fed at the feeding station? Kaba was extremely slow in replying and Jane could see Lola getting irritated.

Eventually, she turned to Jane. 'I not sure of all facts but I think all brothers and sisters sent to her village. Kaba stay because she got bad hand and can't work in the fields. The family want children to work. I think it true.'

'So where is she living?'

Lola again asked Kaba more questions. 'She live with street children, she scavenge for food and water.' Lola shook her head in a resigned manner. 'It bad. Many, many children this way. There is orphanage but too full with children. Kaba not eating at feeding station now her ma dead.'

Jane had one last question. 'Ask her which tribe she belongs to.'

Once again, it took Lola some time to get an answer. 'She Gree tribe.'

This didn't help Jane. 'Do you know where the Gree are from, and would she by any chance know the Lindu language?'

This time Lola didn't need to ask Kaba. 'She know some Lindu, Gree tribe close to Lindu lands.'

Jane was wondering what to do next when Ken arrived and, with Lola's help, she told him Kaba's story, ending by saying she wanted to help.

Ken spoke to Kaba who immediately sat on the ground, then he motioned for Jane to go into the office with him. 'Whatever you do, Jane, don't get involved with the girl. It will create enormous problems. You've already given some money for her food, now, leave it at that.'

'But we can't just leave her. Look at the state she's in – she's deteriorating rapidly, she has a nasty injury on her head which looks septic and she can't do much scavenging with only one good hand. Do you want her to die?' As soon as Jane said that she regretted it. She didn't want to upset Ken who had become a good friend over the past few weeks.

Ken was visibly annoyed with Jane's last remark, but he let it pass. 'We can have a word with the Social Department to see if they can help in finding her relatives.'

'I'm sorry I said that about her dying,' Jane said. 'That was uncalled for, so please accept my apologies. It's just that I...' she struggled to find the right words to continue '... as you know, Kaba was the first child I met in Ogola and now her mother's dead and it looks as if she's been abandoned and... she's in such a mess... I want to help her.'

'In what way?'

Jane wanted to take Kaba home with her immediately, but this wasn't the right time to say that. She knew that Ken, and probably all the others, would think she was crazy, Robert would throw a fit, and she hadn't even asked Sellie, so she chose a more sensible approach. 'I'd like to give some more money for someone to look after her for the next few days; clean her up and buy her some decent clothes, arrange for her wound to be treated and give her somewhere to sleep and food to eat.' Jane took a thousand shilling note from her purse. 'Will this be enough until Monday?'

Knowing Jane's concerns were genuine, Ken took the money. 'I'll ask Lola to take her to the Social Department. A thousand shillings will be plenty.' Kaba looked happy going with Lola. She probably thought that someone was going to look after her for the first time since her mother became ill.

In the accounts office, Hani was closely studying sets of documents from two of the computer suppliers.

'I think we should wait for BuzanComp before we make any decision.' Jane knew this delay would give her more time to get

161

everything ready for the dinner party. 'What I suggest is that you give me the two quotes. I'll look at them over the weekend and see you Monday morning.'

Hani thought that was a good idea and passed everything to Jane.

'Any news from Wasubu yet?'

'Yes,' Hani gave a relaxed smile. 'Mr Wasubu will have something in a few days.'

Jane got the feeling that the investigation was reverting to *Africa-Time*. 'We must get a move on because there's something else to chase up as well the computers. Antiretroviral drugs for the Health Clinic also went missing at the airport. If these can be found then people with HIV in Ogola can be treated... including Ruth.'

These last words seemed to energise Hani as his voice suddenly became more animated. 'Ruth is from my tribe and a good woman. She Solu, same- same as Mr Wasubu. I call him now.'

'Thank you, Hani. Try and arrange another meeting with Wasubu for Monday morning, the missing drugs should take priority over the computers.'

'I do that,' was Hani's firm reply.

'Can you come into my office for a moment?' Ken asked. 'We have a problem!' he said, closing the door.

'Oh, what's that?' Jane thought he was going to caution her again about getting involved with Kaba, but it was something completely different.

'All the contractors have left the site.'

Jane struggled to get her mind around that. 'The contractors have gone. Why?'

'In a way it was expected. Our beloved MP for Ogola, Mr K.K. Machuri, has brought charges against us, saying we awarded the contract illegally and his friends at Zanga Construction weren't given a fair chance in the bidding. It's all lies of course but he obtained a court injunction a couple of hours ago.'

'So what happens now?'

'I just spoke to Robert and he wants a meeting with the Ministry of Housing to get this cleared up. In the meantime, he'll contact the German Embassy. Unfortunately, K.K. has already arranged for the radio, TV and newspapers to send reporters here, so we can only guess at the lies he'll tell them.'

'Can't we tell the media our side of the story?'

'Ha, we'll try but K.K. has them all... how should I put it?... in his pocket.'

While Sellie unpacked the shopping, Jane brought up the subject of Kaba, reminding her of her wish to have children, but she didn't respond and silently turned away. Jane waited for a reply but none came. She hadn't discussed it with Robert yet but he wouldn't dare object, because if he tried, she would re- introduce the 'Precious tribal marriage and visa' argument. How could he refuse? She was determined to do whatever she could for Kaba despite Ken's opposition, Robert's certain objections, and the scorn of many of her friends. To most people, it would seem like a self-serving gesture but she was determined to help one child to have a decent life.

A worried-looking Robert didn't arrive home until after eight o'clock. 'The best I could do was to arrange a meeting with the Ministry on Monday afternoon, but at least the German Embassy will be there to help. Ken told me that the residents plan to protest tomorrow and he's concerned there will be rioting.'

'But what will they be rioting against?'

'I honestly don't know,' Robert said shaking his head. 'But K.K. Machuri will think of something. He'll want to show that the wicked white people are trying to exploit them and he's the only one who can stop them – the people's hero.'

Jane let Robert calm down before she dared bring up her bombshell about Kaba. His chin almost dropped to the floor.

'No way, Jane, you can't do that. I know it's sad to see kids living in poverty. If you want, we can give money for someone to look after her, but that's all.'

'I'm not giving up and you owe me one. In fact you owe me more than one.'

'What do you mean?'

'You know very well what I mean. If I say the words 'Amanda' and 'Precious' and 'visa' – do any of those ring a bell?'

'But that's different.'

'Well, I've made up my mind, and if that means bringing Kaba here to stay with Sellie, then I'll do it.'

Robert was too tired to argue and said they would talk about it later. He knew it could never happen.

An infuriated Ken phoned at half past nine the following morning saying that rioters had tried to set fire to the office and had damaged the partly-completed head office. He said it was still dangerous and Robert should stay away for the time being, but he could go in the morning if order was restored. In the meantime, it would be on the radio and TV.

Although Sellie was the epitome of calm composure, Jane and Robert were extremely nervous as they waited for their guests to arrive for their first ever dinner party. Getting dolled-up for such events was not unusual for Jane as she'd had to do the same when she was an escort, and she'd thanked Cindy once again for borrowing another dress from her large wardrobe. They gave each other a quick hug to boost each other's courage.

During their dinner party's pre-dinner drinks, Robert's 'Precious' indiscretion, and his alleged tribal marriage, were quickly dealt with. Most sympathy came from Cindy and Gregg, whilst racist Quentin quietly took Robert to one side to let him know that he should restrict his philandering to members of the white race. Josie and Lester said nothing. From Kath's expression, it was obvious she considered he had transgressed too far; fraternising with local prostitutes was definitely beyond the pale. Robert knew he would have to take it all on his chin – it was certainly big enough. 'Do you have a good lawyer?' Quentin asked.

'Schultec uses Victor Veme for all its legal matters.'

'Wow!' Quentin was impressed. 'He's the best there is. He should be able to sort things out for you as most of the top politicians and even some judges are in his pocket.'

When everybody was at the dining table, Jane changed the subject away from Precious. Robert had suffered enough so she asked what their thoughts were about her new interest of international donors. There was a broad consensus that aid was a two-edged sword, in so far as some aid caused more damage than it solved but, apart from Josie and Lester, none of the others seemed to be concerned. To them the facts were simple: Africa was in a mess and the only way out was to send more and more money, with more and more foreign experts to implement more and more projects.

Lester wasn't convinced and felt the situation was more complicated. 'As most of you know, I was seconded to the World Bank for five years and spent another five years with the EU, so I've a pretty good idea how they operate. If money is poured into poor African countries, their politicians will skim off as much as they can on the way to their bank in Zurich. The poor will be no better off.'

'The problem with ordinary Africans is their willingness to accept the corrupt behaviour of their leaders,' Quentin said. 'There is no tradition of people power. And many of the leaders are evil. Just look at the atrocities taking place on a daily basis here.'

'You mean like Liberia and the Ivory Coast?' questioned Robert.

'Exactly. And don't forget Rwanda. One million people butchered to death in one hundred days. They are bloody evil.'

'It's been suggested that very wicked people have a genetic disorder,' Lester said. 'A chemical reaction in the brain involving inherited genes prevents them from having any compassion for others.'

'Well, they all seem to be in Africa,' boomed Quentin. 'There's just a thin veneer of civilisation. Scratch the surface and you uncover savages.'

'I think, Quentin,' scolded Cindy , 'you should look at the atrocities carried out during the Second World War. You can't get any more savage than that.'

There was a moments silence before Quentin had the good grace to acknowledge she'd made a point.

Although Jane was still on tenterhooks on whether the evening was going well, she couldn't stop herself from glancing in Gregg's direction at every opportunity. What is it about him? She occasionally caught him looking back at her with a knowing smirk on his sexy mouth, making her blush and turn away. She knew she shouldn't encourage his covert attention and forced her attention back to the conversation about Africa's problems by asking Quentin about British companies using slush funds to get large orders in the Middle East and wondered if it was the same here?

'When you've been here a little longer,' he said, 'you won't even need to ask. Every foreign business has its own slush fund to grease the palms of those who matter. If you're not prepared to do it then you might as well pack your bags and go home because you'd be out of business in no time.'

'The press and the dewy-eyed do-gooders in UK are far more vocal in condemning their nation than any other country,' Gregg continued. 'I'm not sure why this should be... maybe it's the famous British "fair play" ethos pushing the politically correct buttons.'

'There's also the Bribery Act which only affects the UK and nobody else,' Lester said. 'Facilitation payments or small bribes are illegal under the Act but America exempts these payments from prosecution. And so do all of Britain's main competitors.'

'I thought it might be like that,' Jane said.

'Every country competing for big business anywhere in the world has to pay to win orders,' Quentin said. 'Whether it's cash, race horses, or loose women. It matters not whether country A's product is better than country B's – it all depends on the sweetener. And for a fraud squad to try and prove that one British company has paid a backhander is the height of stupidity – what planet do they live on for goodness sake? All it achieves is to put British workers on the dole... business that will happily be picked up by the French, Italians, Americans and any other countries which can get their hands on it. The British government's attempts at integrity are nothing but a joke.'

'So all of us… all Western companies add to the corruption,' Jane said.

'Yes, you're right. And that's the reality of international business… or, in fact, any business.' Quentin confirmed. 'It's a wicked, corrupt world we live in, my dear Jane, and I don't see it ever changing.'

Cindy, having been brought up in Jamaica, took very little part in the conversation because corruption was part of the way of life there. She was sure that part of her father's wealth hadn't come just from his salary and pension. 'But what I do find hard to understand,' she said, 'isn't just the odd few millions presidents grab, but many, like Mbuto and Moi for instance, are reported to have billions. How on earth do they get such huge sums?'

'Well, we know they take a percentage from all the aid projects,' Lester replied, 'but that's small fry compared to the really big money. That comes from selling their country's natural resources and foreigners will pay squillions to exploit these.'

'Yes, Lester's right,' Quentin gave a sad smile, 'the potential wealth of Africa is enormous. Not only are all natural resources here, but they have more of them than almost anyone else: oil, copper, iron ore, gold and diamonds etcetera – the list is as long as my arm.'

'Oh, for Pete's sake, I wish I hadn't asked,' Cindy scowled, 'just give me the potted version… please.'

'Okay ma'am,' laughed Lester. 'In a nutshell then, instead of using all this fabulous wealth to develop their countries like, for example, the Middle East, they sell everything at a rock-bottom price to anyone who'll put a billion dollars in their Swiss bank accounts.'

This last statement from Lester puzzled Jane. 'Am I getting this right? Are you saying that if African countries were better managed… well, I mean properly managed, don't I, then they could be as rich as places like Dubai and Saudi?'

'Absolutely,' Lester gave an anxious glance in Cindy's direction fearing another reprimand might be on its way. 'The combined value of all these resources is worth ten times more than all the oil in the Middle East.'

'That's hard to believe,' scoffed Cindy. 'Anyhow, enough is enough. Come on you guys, this is supposed to be a fun evening; loosen up, will you. We've had a fantastic meal and wonderful hospitality from Jane and Robert, and all you do is moan and groan.' Her intervention brought a collective sigh of relief. Talking about the virtually unsolvable problems of Africa had put a dampener on the evening and Jane was pleased that Cindy had lifted the mood.

Being the first time she'd entertained, Jane hardly tasted the dinner but was relieved when there was universal praise for an excellent meal. What would she do without the amazing Sellie?

Josie looked at her watch. 'Let's leave the rest of Africa's problems for another day, shall we? Maybe you would all care to join us for dinner next week when Lester and I can bore you with our thoughts on what should be this wonderful continent.'

Everyone took the cue and left in a group to walk leisurely home through the warm, scented, moonlit evening, thanking their hosts for a great get-together.

Putting his arm around Jane's shoulders, Robert gave her a gentle kiss. 'You did a fantastic job tonight. I won the jackpot when I married you.'

She kissed him back. 'Yes, you did, Kimber, and don't you forget it.'

When they eventually got to bed, Jane wondered if she should be bothered that there was never any earth-shattering gratification when they made love. Sex had gradually become a maintenance thing, like having their ceiling fans serviced, just another part of running a household. Maybe she'd read too many books where love-making had taken the couple into some sort of climactic stratosphere. Ah! she smiled - the fantasy of the novelist. As these disturbing thoughts raced round her head, Jane had no idea that their lives would soon change forever – in a big way – she had just conceived a new generation of Kimbers!

Chapter Seventeen

The leisurely lie-in they'd hoped for after the previous evening's dinner party was abruptly interrupted by the shrill ring of the phone. Robert dragged himself out of bed – it was Ken telling him that everything in Ogola had calmed down, partly due to a fortuitous heavy downpour. It should be safe for him to go there after lunch to inspect the damage. He also had a message for Jane that Kaba was waiting for her.

'I don't like the sound of this, Jane.' He was extremely apprehensive about her interest in this girl.

She decided to say nothing and bide her time.

They heard noises in the kitchen of pots and pans being washed which meant Sellie was back from church.

While Robert hovered in the background, Jane went and gave Sellie a big hug. 'Sellie, you're a treasure.'

This embrace by a *mzungu* was a new experience for Sellie who didn't know how to react, so she just stood still with her wet hands hanging at her sides until Jane eventually released her.

This un-British display of affection made Robert uncomfortable but to show his gratitude he thought he should add his thanks. 'A wonderful effort, Sellie; well done.'

How bloody pompous, Jane thought. The sort of thing an officer might say to his troops who had just beaten the enemy – "wonderful effort – well done chaps".

They discussed the riots in Ogola and the damage that had been done but Sellie had already heard about it.

'The radio man say, German people make our people pay too much rent, and evict many sick people. The radio man say contractor pay corruption money.'

'It's not true, Sellie, believe me,' Robert said. 'The rents are lower than in the rest of Ogola and nobody is evicted if they're sick. In fact, the German government is giving millions of shillings to the project, and the money is a gift, not a loan that has to be repaid, it's free money.'

'I thought it that way,' Sellie acknowledged. 'Many people in Ogola tell lies. Even politician people.'

When Robert went into the living room to check for any more news on the radio, Jane quietly asked Sellie if she would go with them to Ogola to see Kaba.

Sellie was clearly apprehensive. 'Is she good girl, Madam? What happen if she come to this house and be bad girl?'

'I honestly don't know but I think she will be good. I'll talk to the boss and Ken Kasansa and make sure you will be protected. You met Mr Kasansa when he came to the house the night I arrived here. Do you remember him?'

'I remember.'

Jane phoned Cindy to see if Gilly could stay at her house until later that afternoon.

'Yes, of course.' Cindy was more than happy, as having Gilly there kept her two girls from squabbling.

While they were having their morning coffee, Jane told Robert that she wanted to go with him to Ogola that afternoon.

'Yes, I don't see why not. Ken would phone if it wasn't safe.'

'I also want to take Sellie.'

'Why would she want to go?'

Jane took a deep breath. 'It's to do with this girl, Kaba. I've asked Sellie if she would take care of her – in her room.'

This was crazy. Somehow, he had to make her realise that it was impossible, but knowing how strong-willed she could be at times, he thought he'd have to let Sellie meet the girl, but make no promises, and ask Ken to intervene on the side of good sense. He knew Jane had a very high regard for Ken and would accept his guidance.

'How would it affect Gilly if we suddenly took in this Kaba girl?' He wasn't sure if Jane had thought everything through properly.

'Yes, I've thought about that. Kaba would live with Sellie as her little girl so I don't think Gilly would mind at all. In fact she might like having another girl close by they're about the same age.'

'Well, I don't like the idea at all. I don't think Ken does either.'

Arriving at the office, they found Ken waiting for them, and he greeted Sellie in his usual affable manner but gave a puzzled side glance at Robert, as if to say 'what's going on here?' There was no sign of Kaba.

Luckily, the damage inside the office was superficial. Ken showed them where the rioters had forced open one of the shutters and pushed flammable material through the opening. There were scorch marks against two of the metal desks but whatever had been used had burnt itself out on the concrete floor.

'Hardly any damage at all,' Robert said.

'Yes, we were very lucky.' Ken looked grim. 'The sooner we move into the new building, the better.'

He then took them to see the tiled roofs on the new blocks. 'They break so easily when a brick hits them. It's back to the drawing board I think.'

Continuing past the housing blocks to the head office site, they saw that one of the contractor's cement mixers had been pushed through a gap in the partially completed walls. It had been tipped over, a load of hardened concrete covered the openings for the toilet and water pipes. Some of the exposed iron rods supporting the walls had been bent and blocks around some of the windows had been smashed. Other blocks and a lot of the timber had been broken and scattered around the site.

'Will it be a big job to put everything right?' Robert asked Ken.

'We may have to re-site the plumbing but apart from that, it should only take a week to get back to where we were… that's as long as the contractor comes back.'

'Do we really know why they rioted, Ken? Here we are, trying to make their lives better, free of charge, and all they do is run riot and break everything they can. It doesn't make sense.'

To everyone's surprise and before Ken could answer, Sellie gave her opinion. 'It K.K. Machuri.'

Ken gave her a cautious look. 'Why do you say that?'

'Everyone know K. K. He trouble-making man, good at getting stupid people do what he wants. He say "go break this place" and they do it. He say "don't pay rent" and they stop. These people too stupid!'

Although he was of the same opinion, Ken didn't respond, but gave Robert another perplexed sideways glance.

Noticing that dark, threatening-looking rain · clouds were gathering, they hurried back in the direction of the office. Word of their visit had spread and a crowd of about forty people, including a worried-looking Kaba, waited near the office, some of the men carrying heavy sticks. Ken, walking purposefully towards the mob, told Robert and Jane to go quickly to their vehicle, but he didn't realise that Sellie was following closely behind him.

Recognising some of the regular troublemakers, he directed his attention towards them, ordering everyone to disperse. Nobody moved and several shouted back, waving their weapons. There was a collective, angry cry from the crowd that was growing in size by the minute, and it looked as though they were intent on violence.

Without warning, Sellie pushed past Ken and, in a surprisingly deep, throaty voice, shouted and gesticulated at the crowd. The strange sight of a disfigured, seemingly crazy woman momentarily silenced them. Ending her verbal assault, she dramatically thrust her arm in the air, heralding a blinding flash of lightning and an ear-bursting crash of thunder. The effect was extraordinary. With mouths wide open, fearful eyes, and hands placed firmly over their ears, they reminded Jane of Munch's famous painting of *The Scream*. There was an awed silence before the terrified crowd turned and rushed away, leaving one frightened little girl hunched against the office wall.

Jane, Robert and Ken looked stunned, unable to believe what they'd just seen. Still standing on the same spot, Sellie's expression didn't change.

'You Kaba?' she pointed and spoke loudly at the little girl, who somehow managed to nod her head.

'Let's go into my office,' Ken suggested, but Sellie said she would stay in reception to speak to Kaba. Pitiful little Kaba, Jane realised, had just witnessed this scary woman with a scarred face bring down the fury of the thunder spirits, sending a crowd of rabble-rousers rushing away, and now she had to face the woman herself. How would the poor girl manage?

'What was all that about?' Robert almost laughed at what they'd just witnessed although he'd been frightened at what might have happened.

'To be honest,' a bemused Ken shook his head, 'I'm not sure myself. I only understood half of what she said but the crowd was convinced she had special juju powers. There's a well held belief in Buzamba that people get maimed and killed by lightning, and when you see them putting metal pans over their heads to shelter from heavy rain, then it's not surprising. By the way, are you sure Sellie's just a house-girl? She had an extraordinary power over that mob... and even over the thunder gods!'

An equally perplexed Robert told Ken how she came to work for them. Without giving any specific details about his trouble with Precious, he mentioned that when they'd had difficulties with some local people, Sellie had sent them packing. Her explanation was that many primitive people believed the scarring on her face meant she possessed magic powers, like a witch.

Jane quickly made tea, and while the three of them mulled over the events of the last few minutes, they could hear Sellie's raised voice speaking to Kaba.

'She sounds angry,' Jane remarked, 'so I don't think she'll want to take Kaba.'

'Is that what you really want?' Ken asked anxiously. 'Is the idea that your house-girl should take Kaba to live with her... in fact, to live in your house? I don't think that's wise Jane. It could lead to lots of trouble.'

'Maybe it's crazy but that's what I want.' Jane's voice trembled slightly but if Ken hadn't realised her strength of character before, he knew now. 'I know she's only one little girl out of hundreds or even thousands orphaned in Buzamba but if we can help Kaba, then it's one less dying of sickness or starvation. Anyway, it's probably only academic because it doesn't sound as if Sellie is interested.'

173

There was a knock on the door and Sellie put her head round. They waited for her to speak.

'The girl Gree.' Sellie announced.

They waited for her to add to this brief declaration but Sellie remained silent, as though she had said everything that needed to be said.

Jane looked at Robert and Ken but it was fairly obvious neither of them wanted to be involved. She thought carefully before speaking. 'Yes, Kaba is from the Gree tribe and comes from an area close to your village.'

'Not very close.'

'But she understands the Lindu language... doesn't she?'

Sellie's expression hadn't changed since she'd entered the office. 'You want I take this girl?' Her voice had an edge to it.

'Only if you want to.' Expecting the worst, Jane held her breath.

'She need new clothes, money for school fees, her broke hand needs fixing good. If she stay with me she go to school.'

'Yes, of course,' Jane breathed a sigh of relief. 'We'll pay for all of that.'

'Mr Ken to get permit from girl's tribe headman,' Sellie demanded. 'Make it legal. I not want bad police business.'

Jane turned to Ken. 'Would it be possible to make it legal, like an adoption.'

Ken took a big breath and gave an uneasy sigh – this was the last thing he needed. Due to the sensitivity of his tribe's poor relations with the ruling Peelees, he certainly didn't want to be involved. 'I can't do it myself but one of the ladies from the Social Department could probably arrange it.' He turned to face Jane. 'But Jane... please, think carefully about what you're doing. It's a big responsibility for Sellie and who knows what could happen in the future.'

All of a sudden, Jane became angry: angry with Buzamba for allowing this handicapped girl, who had just been orphaned and abandoned, to scavenge amongst the filth and grime of this horrible slum just to stay alive; angry that the very people capable of helping, the rich and powerful Buzambans, only wanted to turn their backs and let Kaba's abject misery continue; angry with Robert and Ken for their lack of compassion, and angry with the world at large. How dare the rich nations live their extravagant lifestyles while only a mere eight hours away by luxury jet, were hundreds of thousands of children trying to exist on scraps and polluted water. But most of all, she was angry with herself for living in the lap of luxury, with the realisation that the amount spent on last night's dinner party would have provided food for hundreds of children like Kaba.

Her voice was resilient and unambiguous and neither Robert nor Ken was about to challenge her again. 'I've thought carefully and if Sellie is in agreement, then I will take Kaba out of this place and give her a decent home... end of story.' The instant Jane finished speaking there was another flash of lightning and a loud thunderclap. It made Ken think that Jane had got the same magic as Sellie – who was he to fight against that? He said that they should give more money to the Social Department, and proposed that Sellie should collect Kaba the following Friday. He hoped that the extra few days would give Robert time to convince Jane that taking Kaba was a bad idea, but he didn't really believe it. Jane had made up her mind and neither he nor Robert were the men to change it.

A sense of déjà vu descended on Jane when, in the middle of breakfast, she had to rush to the bathroom and retch over the basin for five minutes until the nausea passed. As it was the same feeling she'd had when expecting Gilly, it occurred to her that she could be pregnant. Was this a good time, she wondered? Although they had discussed the possibility of having a baby when they were settled, this seemed a bit soon. And there was Gilly to think about. So far, she'd coped marvellously with all the changes in her life but would the arrival of a new baby be too much, especially as their other newcomer, Kaba, would be living in their house with Sellie? There was certainly a lot to mull over, and she decided not to say anything to Robert for the time being but would see the company doctor in the next week or two. Everything could wait until then.

Waving goodbye to Robert as he entered his office, Jane and Basil continued on to Ogola where Ken was just finishing a call with his main contact at the Ministry.

'We may have a problem,' he said wearily. 'The Deputy Minister assigned to our project hasn't arrived at the office and his secretary hinted that he may not be in all day. She did let slip, though, that our friend, K.K. Machuri, has seen the Minister himself and she's in no doubt that he's been stirring up trouble.'

'Does that mean there won't be any work on the project?'

'The contractor won't bring his workers back until he gets the all clear. I can get some casual labour to clean things up and do some minor repairs, but that's all.'

Ken left to round up some workers and Jane, armed with her copies of the two computer quotes, went through to the accounts office. Hani wasn't there as he'd gone to BuzanComp to get the final quotation. The two cashiers, Momo and Amos, were also out and only Lola was at her desk. She told Jane that she hadn't seen Amos that morning but Momo had gone out to remove some doors.

'What do you mean,' a puzzled Jane asked, 'remove some doors?'

'When people not pay rent, we give warning. If still not pay, we take their doors.'

Not sure if she'd heard correctly, Jane asked, 'Do you mean that if people don't pay their rent you remove the doors from their rooms?'

'Of course,' Lola nodded in a matter-of-fact manner. 'If people still not pay we take the roof and door,' thinking it was very funny, she giggled. 'That works good.'

'But I was told,' Jane said, 'that if people were unable to pay the rent, the Social Department would give them some sort of exemption.'

'Ah, that only for sick people. These people not sick but not want to pay – there many, many like that.'

Just then, a woman's angry face appeared at the cashier's grill and started shouting at Jane and Lola, waving her arms above her head and banging her fist against the wall causing clouds of dust to fall from the ceiling. Lola quietly told Jane to leave, so she went into the general office where the ever-smiling Ruth brought her a coffee. After a few minutes, a satisfied-looking Lola poked her head round the door to tell Jane she could go back.

'That one woman had door removed. She pay now.'

'So it works!' Jane wasn't sure if she should be impressed or not.

'Most times it work. That woman, she angry like hell,' Lola didn't seem bothered. 'She also say German *mzungu* woman – that you – should pay the rent. You rob poor people. But I tell her she wrong and you volunteer from England.'

'Did that satisfy her?'

'No,' again Lola laughed. 'She say something bad about you and me and Momo but she had plenty money in her bag. I see it. She rich woman with four rooms and she sublet them for bigger rent. There plenty people like that.'

Jane was rapidly learning more about the reality of life in Ogola. 'By the way, Lola, how much is the room rent?'

'One month rent – 800 shillings.'

Jane quickly calculated that to be about £6.

'Eight hundred shillings is smaller than before project. Some landlords make people pay 1,000 or 1,200 shilling.'

'So really, nobody in Ogola should complain.'

Again, Lola laughed. 'These people do complain… all the time. They say rich German Government spend big money here and German people live in big houses. They should make smaller rent… and many people say rent should be free. That what K.K. Machuri tell them and that how he get many people to riot. He own many rooms in Ogola and make people pay big rent… if people not pay, K.K.'s men beat them.'

'But surely the people must realise that the project is making their lives better with clean water, roads; there's the health clinic and the feeding station. You would think they would support the project and not this K.K. Machuri man who is causing trouble.' Jane had the feeling that every time she said what she thought was common sense, it made Lola and the others laugh. She was obviously missing something.

'Many people impressed by big-shot Buzambans who not listen to white man, who stand up to white man. They think... wow, this man very strong, we do as he say.' Lola was no longer smiling. 'They stupid and not think that if they riot and make damage, the white man go and take his money and they left with bad rooms, no water and pay big rent to K.K.'

The door suddenly burst open and a happy-looking Hani came into the office clutching a large bunch of documents under his arm. 'I get all this from BuzanComp.' He proudly placed everything on the table.

'Have you had chance to check it?' Jane asked.

'Not yet. I bring everything back to you. We check together.'

Jane and Hani spent the next half hour looking through all three quotations and Jane quickly realised she was out of her depth. Luckily, her saviour walked in, albeit looking very dejected. Robert had returned with Ken from the Ministry but all their efforts to meet anyone had failed. In the meantime, the project was on hold.

Jane showed Robert the problems she and Hani were having with the computer quotations and that they really needed expert help. Robert said he knew the manager of Benedicts, the accounting firm located on the floor below his office, and would ask him for advice.

Putting the computer quotes aside for later, Jane asked Hani what time had been arranged for the meeting with Wasubu, about the missing computers and antiretrovirals.

'We can go now but Ken say we see him first.'

Hani's brother, Ben, wearing his police uniform and the customary dark sunglasses, was waiting in Ken's office. 'I've asked Ben to give us some extra help,' Ken said. 'What you're doing, Jane, is commendable but I have to warn you of the potential dangers. We're talking about organised crime, and it's just as violent here in Buzamba as anything you've seen in American gangster movies. And as you've already experienced first-hand, all criminals here have guns and aren't afraid to shoot people if they get in the way.'

For reasons Jane couldn't quite understand herself, instead of Ken's warning making her nervous, it gave her a buzz. God! what is wrong with me? she thought, am I going mad? 'We'll be very careful, Ken. I promise. Any sign of danger and we'll drop everything. Is that why you asked Ben to join us?' She'd already noticed he carried a gun – American style.

'Yes, it is. As you know, Ben and Hani Oburu are brothers. Their uncle is Vice-President and they are all from the Solu tribe, as is Mr Wasubu at the airport.'

'Yes,' Jane acknowledged. 'I know that.'

'But because the Peelees are in the majority,' Ken continued, 'most of the criminal activity is amongst them, as they get the most protection.'

Ben nodded. 'The complication is that most of the police are Solus and prosecuting Peelee criminals is... well, it not easy.'

'Anyhow,' Ken continued, looking serious, 'go and see what you can find out... Ben will be with you. To be perfectly honest, Jane, I'm not really interested in finding those missing computers as we are getting new ones in any case, but finding the antiretroviral drugs would be great.'

With that last thought focusing their minds, all three set off for the airport and were immediately taken to Mr Wasubu's office. There were even more stares and nudges from the crowded office than last time; why was the same little *mzungu* woman still tamely following not one but two big local men? On entering the office, they all shook hands, and a smiling Wasubu had a long chat with the two Oburu brothers. The room was sweltering as there'd been a power cut all day and Wasubu's shirt was see-through with perspiration. Jane could smell the men's sweat from where she was sitting.

Hani turned towards Jane. 'We think we know where the computers are.'

'Wow, that's good, Hani. How did he do it,' she said smiling in Mr Wasubu's direction.

'One of the chief clerks here, a Peelee man called Waltok, has been taking backhanders for several years to send shipments belonging to other people to Peelee companies. Mr Wasubu has known this for a while, but all his efforts to stop him have failed because of... well...'

'Yes, I understand,' Jane interrupted. 'So what's changed?'

'You and the BBC. Once Mr Wasubu knew there was a BBC investigation, he spoke to his boss, a Peelee, and he agreed that Waltok should be charged with theft because if the BBC broadcast this on African radio, he could get into big trouble. To keep himself out of jail, Waltok told them where the computers were.'

Good news about the computers, Jane thought, but was she getting in over her head? Would she get into trouble by pretending to represent the BBC? Did she care? Not for the moment anyway, she was far too excited. 'So where are they?'

'The Basdrink Brewery.'

'Can we go and get them?'

'We can try.'

'What about the drugs?' Jane asked.

'No news. Waltok had already left before he could be questioned.'

'We need to find Waltok then. Get his address will you?'

Mr Wasubu gave them the details. Thanking him for his help, and not wanting to waste a minute, Jane suggested they head straight for the Brewery. Basil had the air-conditioning running so they felt refreshed after the fifteen minute journey.

'That was a good start,' Jane smiled at the two formidable brothers. 'You did well. By the way, Hani, you do know I'm not actually from the BBC but from BBNC.'

Hani and Ben laughed, 'It's close enough, Jane.'

'Good. I have the paperwork here and the Burg brand of German computer is not usually sold in Buzamba.'

The Brewery was a substantial brick-built building and apart from brewing its own brand Equator Beer, they also made countless types of soft drinks. The daunting trio entered reception, where Hani, buoyed by the presence of a BBC *mzungu* and an armed police officer, showed Jane's business card, loudly demanding to see the officer in charge of their computer department.

What happened next was astonishing. They were quickly taken to the head of the IT department who confirmed they had the Burg computers in their office, but they were faulty; the reason being, he claimed, that some of the staff had used them to play pirated computer games on discs infected with a virus. He had no objection to them being taken away.

'No,' Jane snapped passing the IT manager a copy of the invoice. 'Your staff have ruined them so they can keep them but you must pay for the whole shipment.'

Hani and Ben, towering over the diminutive manager, took their lead from Jane and demanded immediate payment. To ease the poor man's discomfort, Jane promised that the four unopened boxes would be sent to him. Crossing her fingers, she then said that unless he agreed, she would report the theft to the BBnC in London. She held her breath.

Jane's mischievous but guilt-ridden blackmail did the trick. After making a couple of nervous internal calls, he authorised the full payment to the Ogola Slum Project. They stalked out of the building grinning widely, and Jane stood on tiptoes to share 'high-fives' with her two enforcers.

On their return to the office, Robert and Ken were pleased but, at the same time, uncomfortable with what had been achieved, and how.

'Let's hope there aren't any repercussions,' Ken said. 'You've all done amazingly well… what do you think, Ben, will we get away with it?'

'Of course,' a confident Ben replied. 'The BBC will make sure of that.'

'Any luck with the antiretrovirals?'

'Not today, but we've got the address of a man who does know what happened to them,' Hani said. 'We try and see him soon.'

Restarting work on the Ogola project seemed as far away as ever, so Jane gratefully stayed at home the following morning, feeling a little groggy after her now routine morning sickness. There had been a fierce thunderstorm overnight, and for the first time since she'd arrived in Buzamba, the temperature had dropped below 20 degrees, leading her to search for a light sweater. Sellie also felt the cold as she was encased in a thick woolly red jumper, striped red and blue skirt and red socks. She also wore a bright red and yellow woolly hat that looked like an old-fashioned tea cosy. All morning, the clouds were thick and thunderous, eventually giving way to a watery sun, forcing its way through the grey.

Jane took a sandwich onto the rear terrace where the air was much fresher, and she could write her latest epistle to Tony. She doubted whether he'd be interested in how they'd found the missing computers, but at least he'd know she was telling him everything down to the smallest detail.

All around, brightly-coloured birds were pecking on the lawn, feasting on the numerous insects forced up by the rain. The weaver birds were busier than ever, especially those whose nests had fallen to the ground during the storm. This was one of the two breeding seasons, so if the male couldn't produce a nest during the next week or two, they would have to wait a further six months to find a mate. Robert had told her that when the males had mated, they would often go to another tree and build a nest for a new mate. Typical male, Jane thought... get one female pregnant and then slope off after another. At least Robert wasn't like that, she said to herself, crossing all her fingers. Since finding out about her pregnancy, Jane had become very emotional and didn't know whether it would be best to give birth in Ouverru or England. She roughly calculated that the due date would be around early July, just before Robert's annual leave, so if it was going to be born in Ringwood, she would have to fly in early May at the latest. And Robert didn't even know yet... when should she tell him?

She thought about Poppy, desperately trying for a baby for years, and here she was, pregnant for the second time without even trying. But, what to do? She smiled to herself, already adopting local sayings like 'what to do?' It was one of those all-inclusive expressions that said everything and, then again, said nothing.

Amazingly, she had only been in Buzamba for three months but it felt much longer – in a nice way. The house was lovely and she relished having Sellie doing all the tedious housework and most of the cooking. The Ogola project was fascinating and challenging and she hoped passionately that Robert, Ken and the German Embassy would soon solve the K.K. Machuri problem. She already had good friends in the compound and, with Sellie's help, would save Kaba from a probable early death. All that in just a few eventful months, from the hard struggle of a life in perpetual poverty in Ringwood, to this cushy existence in a far-off, exciting land – wow, not bad, eh?

As the chattering, nattering birds flew, pecked and perched, weaving their nests in the now sun-filled garden, she knew what she appreciated more than anything else; not the house or the lifestyle, but the man in her and Gilly's life. They were a real family, like those she'd seen in cheesy American films but thought she'd never have. She was glad now that Robert had tricked her into marriage. But, once again, she faced the big question… was she in love with her husband – undisputable, body-tingling love? When she was young, she'd made a checklist of every trait she wanted in her soulmate, and Robert ticked most of the boxes. But one or two would be blank – the main one being a 'love god'. As soon as the phrase *love god* crept into her mind, she immediately coupled it with Gregg. Damn it, you naughty girl, she chided herself. She just wished Robert was a bit more exciting, both in and outside the bedroom; but hey! nothing is perfect.

As Jane was tidying up the following morning, she heard the sound of something being slipped through the letter box; it was a note from Josie Pennicott inviting them for dinner that evening. Gilly was very happy that Sellie would babysit for her, and Sellie had no objections as she'd become very fond of Gilly, and an extra two hundred shillings added to her wages was more than welcome. Unusually, Jane and Robert drove the short distance to the Pennicotts, heavy rain was expected for later that evening. During dinner, Lester asked what Jane was doing to keep herself busy. 'I'm only asking,' he said, 'because I've gathered you've more interest in the problems in Africa than most expat wives.'

'Well, I can't sit around in a goldfish bowl all day like Cindy and Kath and most of the other wives.' Smiling in Robert's direction, she added, 'I told Robert early on that I wanted something to do.'

'Yes, she made that very clear,' Robert confirmed, 'but I had no idea she'd get so involved. I thought seeing the slums in Ogola would put her off, but it seems to have had the opposite effect. She's taken it upon herself to fight corruption and the dangerous job of finding our project's missing computers and antiretroviral drugs.'

Lester considered this before continuing. 'That's great but... as Robert says, it could be dangerous. If you stick your neck out here, you don't get the same protection you'd get back in England.'

'I know I have to be careful,' she conceded. 'But along with the accountant in the Ogola – oh, his uncle happens to be the VP – we've already found the missing computers at the Basdrink Brewery which, by the way, they'd broken, so we demanded they refund the full amount to the project.'

'And did they?'

'Yes, they did.'

'Fantastic. Well done you.'

'And now we're hot on the trail of the missing antiretrovirals.'

'Well, good luck with that, but be very careful,' Lester looked concerned. 'You can be sure that whoever stole them will be very high up in the government.'

'That's what Ken, our local manager and I have told her,' Robert said.

'Well, if there's anything I can do,' Lester said, 'then let me know.'

'There is one thing,' Robert hesitated slightly before continuing, 'We're having problems with a man called K.K. Machuri. He got an injunction to stop work on our slum project on the spurious grounds that we cheated when the contract was awarded; needless to say it's because it didn't go to one of his friends.'

The mention of K.K. Machuri brought a big smile to Lester's lips. 'Ha, old K.K. is still up to his tricks, is he? At the Canadian Trade Commission, we've crossed swords with him several times. If you let me have the details, Robert, I'll see what I can do. Anyway,

I'd be interested to hear more about your slum project because when I worked for the World Bank, we tried the same thing in other African countries but they all failed miserably.'

Robert gave him a brief outline, at the end of which there was a look of astonishment on Lester's face. 'Did you say you've installed showers and flush toilets in a slum?'

'Yes, we've built wetcores on each block.'

Lester's mouth gaped for a few moments. 'It sounds over-designed to me. Was it the German DGA experts who did the design?'

Robert nodded.

'Typical.'

'The local staff told me,' Jane interrupted, 'that the showers aren't being used and some of the toilets are already broken.'

'I'm not surprised. I would have thought DGA would just provide a few standpipes and pit latrines, not showers and toilets. And did you say the units have tiled roofs?'

Robert was beginning to wish he'd never mentioned the slum. 'Yes, it keeps the rooms cooler than corrugated iron and there's less noise when it rains,' and then, almost afraid to say anything else, he added, 'and it looks nicer.'

Lester shook his head. 'A slum is not supposed to look nice, it's supposed to improve the living conditions of the poor so that in ten years' time, water can still be bought at the standpipes, the pit latrines still work, and the roofs are intact.'

Jane saw the uncomfortable look on Robert's face, so immediately changed the subject. She asked Lester what it was like working for the World Bank and the EU.

Lester leant back in his chair and studied the ceiling for a moment before giving an expressive sigh. 'As far as their operations in Africa are concerned, I'd close them down straight away. The main aim of the staff is to stay employed long enough to draw a gold-plated pension. They are brilliant at creating work when none exists. They know every rule backwards yet when a decision is required they refer up, or delegate down, or better still go missing.'

'And what about all the corruption,' asked Robert. 'It doesn't seem to be getting any better.'

'And nor will it. As far as the World Bank is concerned, the USA and UN want things to continue as they are for political reasons. America conducted a lot of its foreign policy through the Bank. In fact, the Cold War was fought in numerous proxy wars all over Africa. Those that rejected the communists received aid, including the most corrupt despots.'

'That's incredible,' Jane said, thinking it would make good copy for her next report to Tony.

Lester's basic premise was that the World Bank was being run solely for the benefit of its employees.

'That's a bit radical, isn't it?' questioned Robert.

'Not really. It's just jobs for the boys. In Washington, there are ten thousand bureaucrats in huge offices on the most expensive real estate. And what work do they do? Just duplicating the work done by the African Development Bank. It's a joke. And then there's the EU's international development section; I've no idea how many it employs but it's certain to be thousands.'

'Is that why you're now with the Canadian Trade Commission?'

'Exactly. It may be a bit top-heavy, but we do get things done. I'm so much happier now.'

'Thanks for that, Lester,' Jane said. 'I've learnt a lot tonight. And thank you, Josie for such a lovely meal. I hope, Josie, we didn't bore you with all the shop talk.'

'Not at all,' Josie smiled. 'I act as Lester's secretary so I'm very interested in the whole aid culture. I'm just so annoyed that most aid doesn't reach the people it's intended for.'

'If you're interested, Jane,' Lester said, 'I could lend you several articles on all aspects of aid to Africa. The lies and propaganda, as well as the truth.'

'Oh, I'd like that,' Jane said. 'Before I came out here, I worked part-time for a news bureau, so every couple of weeks, I send a draft article back to my ex-boss, although I don't think he's had much interest from the media yet. But, anything you have will help me to understand more of what's going on in the world of aid.'

Chapter Eighteen

'Do you want the good news, the bad news, or the very bad news?' Robert asked when he came home for a late lunch.

Jane's heart sank. 'I'll take them in that order, but… dwell more on the good news.'

The good news was that he'd seen his friend at Benedicts who'd arranged that she and Hani should go to their office in the morning to see a computer expert, Lily Sessey. The first bad news was that there wouldn't be a meeting at the Ministry before the following afternoon, and the really bad news was that he'd received a letter from Precious' solicitor with lots of mumbo-jumbo legal jargon saying, more-or-less, that he'd been a naughty boy and would have to go to court, with an underlying warning that he'd have to pay big money.

Jane was happy about the meeting with Lily Sessey, and the bad news was not unexpected. She put her arms around him and gave him a kiss. 'Not to worry, big man, it'll all work out – I'm sure of it.'

As soon as Basil picked up Robert after lunch, Jane quickly changed into her 'modest' bikini and went to the pool for a swim before Gilly came home from school. It was so peaceful here on her own and she thought what crazy people lived in Basu compound. It had turned out to be a beautiful, sunny afternoon and the air was much fresher after the rains – it was perfect, and yet all the wives were somewhere indoors or out shopping. What's wrong with these people? Probably it was too much of the good life and they were used to weather like this for most of the year. Jane thought how much Poppy and Tony would love it and she was so looking forward to their promised visit.

Completing her twentieth length, she had the sensation that someone had dived in nearby and, lifting her head, she saw Cindy's laughing face speeding past. They did another ten lengths together before Jane hauled herself over the edge and flopped onto one of the loungers, waiting for Cindy to join her. She wanted to talk to her about Kaba.

When Cindy finally pulled herself out of the pool, Jane couldn't help but laugh. 'Your bikinis seem to be getting smaller.'

'Gregg doesn't mind when all the men leer at me, and I kind of like it as well. I can tell a lot about a man by the way he looks at me.'

'So who's in the leering brigade?'

'Oh, Robert's a gentleman, a real gentleman, which is a bit disappointing considering all the effort I make. He obviously only has eyes for you, honey! But all the others are *leerers*! Frank and Aaron are leerers and starers, so it's not just the *mzungus* who like to check out my gorgeous, sexy flesh.'

'You need to be careful when titillating these horny men. You never know when they might lose control.'

'Ha, I can take care of myself and anyway, I like the attention. There's nothing like a bit of masculine interest to spice up one's love life.' She sat on the lounger next to Jane, 'Gregg and I have many similar friends.' This was the clearest hint Cindy had given that they were happy to share their affections with other couples. Was she saying that they would be happy for her and Robert to join in their 'socialising'? Jane didn't respond.

Purring past the pool in a large black, chauffeur-driven Mercedes, a smiling Jewel Cooper waved from the window. They waved back.

Jane asked if she or Gregg saw much of Jewel and Frank Cooper or Mona and Aaron Toko, who were the only Buzambans living in the compound. It seemed that they only socialised occasionally but, nearer Christmas, each couple held an open house for drinks and canapés; an event which simply couldn't be missed. 'They compete with each other to produce the best champagne, wines and spirits, and last year Aaron had caviar, fresh oysters and huge prawns supplied by the Plaza Hotel. Frank and Jewel were seething! There's no doubt that this year they will go one better and it'll probably be the best meal you'll have all year.'

'Sounds interesting. Do you know where they work?' Jane asked.

'Aaron's a big fish at the Ministry of Finance – I'm not sure of his official title but he has his own chauffeur-driven limo. He goes to Washington and Brussels quite a lot and attends Pan-African conferences two or three times a year.'

'And what about Frank and Jewel?'

'Well, I worked for Frank for eight weeks a couple of years ago. He was doing one of his *leering* exercises during a barbecue and, out of the blue, he asked if I would help out in his office while his secretary was on holiday. The pay sounded fantastic and, as I was a bit fed up with the kids, I took it.'

'Did he try anything on... you know?'

'Not at first, but it didn't take long. There was the sweaty, groping hand routine and the accidental brushing of my boobs with his arm, but I didn't want to go any further with that relationship: too political! So I told him I had to leave due to a family crisis.'

'So what's his job?'

'Well, Frank is the National Director of ESSA, the charity Education for Sub-Saharan Africa. How he got the job is anybody's guess but the fact that his aunt is the President's wife might have something to do with it! Both he and Jewel have chauffeur-driven Mercs; his office consists of two floors in the ultra-smart Uhuru building in the centre of Ouverru, where he employs about thirty staff, including four female expats,' Cindy gave Jane a big wink. 'The mind boggles! And he spends half his life flying first class around the world.'

Jane was puzzled. 'But surely a charity wouldn't waste money like that.'

'How it works I have no idea but I do know they receive tons of cash from all over the place including the UN, the EU, and even those pop concerts. Providing education for the poor of Africa is very sexy – so everyone gives.'

Jane still felt she wasn't getting the complete picture. 'So what's the money used for?'

'Frank's bank account and palatial offices come first, of course. It's supposed to be used to build and equip government schools but the records are in a complete shambles, most files go missing and they are unable to prepare proper accounts because they don't know where all the cash has gone. One day, the shit will hit the fan.'

'Why's that?'

'The UN, or some other organisation, will send in its own inspectors and find that a lot of the cash has just disappeared. Gone into thin air with no trace. That will be the end of Frank... until his Auntie finds him another lucrative job.'

Jane left it there, but she wasn't sure whether to believe Cindy, thinking that charities should be much better organised than the aid agencies. After discussing some of the other residents in the compound and life in general, Jane turned the conversation to Kaba and her plans for Sellie to take her in. Cindy thought the whole idea was fraught with problems, but when Jane defended her decision, Cindy decided to wear her diplomatic hat and say nothing else.

On their arrival at Benedicts' office, Lily Sessey was waiting for them. She apologised that the meeting would have to be cut short, and asked if Jane would be in charge of the implementation.

'Oh no, that will be Hani,' Jane looked in his direction. 'I'm only a volunteer helping Hani and his staff in any way I can.'

Suddenly, something clicked in Lily's head. 'Ah! are you Robert's new wife?'

'Yes, that's me,' Jane said tentatively.

Although they had shaken hands when they first met, Lily reached over and shook Jane's hand a second time. 'Oh, I'm so glad to meet you. Robert is a nice man and we all wondered what you would be like.' She made this odd statement in a jocular but friendly way. 'We heard he'd married someone on leave. I think he's a lucky man.'

'Well, thank you, Lily. I had no idea Robert was a man of such interest amongst the ladies in this building. I'm still learning new things about him.'

Both Lily and Hani thought this funny and after a few more pleasantries, Lily started to pick up all the papers. 'I'm sorry but I'll have to rush, but leave it all with me – it looks straight forward. I'll let Robert know when I have something for you... probably by next Monday, so I'll see you both then.'

As Schultec's office was on the floor above Benedicts', Jane and

Hani walked up the flight of stairs into the reception area where a beaming Patience Akuku welcomed them. 'Did you see Lily?'

'Yes, she seems very friendly.'

Patience said that Lily would do a good job, *especially* for Robert. This made Patience and Hani laugh again.

'I not tell you this before but I tell you now, because everyone like you.' Patience gave what Jane took to be a knowing smile. 'When Robert went on leave, many people knew he contacted an English agent for a wife.'

'How did they know?'

'I don't know, Jane,' but from her mischievous expression, Jane was convinced she knew but wasn't telling. 'So we ladies in this place – we say Robert will get trapped by some bad woman.'

'So, were you all right?'

This sent Patience and Hani into further fits of laughter.

Robert pushed open his office door and immediately they all stopped and looked guilty, like naughty children caught out at school. 'It sounds like a kindergarten in here.' He turned towards Jane. 'Every time you're in this office, all work stops and it's party time. What is it with you?'

'Sorry, boss,' a chastened Jane said meekly.

Even Robert laughed this time. 'OK, that's enough. By the way, Hani, there's a message from Mr Wasubu. He would like to see you on Friday morning... he has some news for you.'

'That must be about the missing drugs. Can you make it then, Jane?'

'Yes, of course. Get Ben to come as well and put on your best suit and tie... we want to look as impressive as we possibly can.'

'I worry about this crime-busting business, Jane,' Robert said, 'I don't want any incidents.'

'Don't worry, boss,' Jane smiled. 'I'll have my two bodyguards with me, won't I Hani?'

'Well, okay then, but be very careful. Anyhow, my other news is that Ken and I have a meeting at the Ministry at three o'clock, so hopefully we'll be able to get the project back on track.'

Gilly was already asleep when Robert went to kiss her good night. Earlier in the day Sellie had prepared one of her special cottage pies and all Jane had to do was put it in the oven and set the timer. Noticing how stressed Robert looked, she poured him a stiff gin and tonic and helped herself to a glass of lemonade.

'That bloody man Machuri is really trying things on and he's got the ear of the Minister.' Robert described the meeting at the Ministry. 'Machuri insists our project is illegal and we had no right to take the buildings over, even though the Justice Ministry approved everything. He insists that all the buildings should be handed back to the original owners.'

'So what happens now?'

'The question is, do we do a deal with him so we get the project back on track?'

'And....?'

'We don't – not for the moment anyway. I'm hoping Lester and the Canadian Trade Commission might be able to help.'

'Well, good luck with that.'

Full of apprehension, Jane and Sellie went to Ogola to collect Kaba – there was no going back now. Robert had hurried off to his office and Jane suspected that he didn't want to be around when Kaba was handed over – as if it was nothing to do with him. Their friends and the Ogola staff thought she was doing the wrong thing; Kaba wasn't an exception – she was just like thousands of other orphans in Buzamba, so why choose one when there were so many?

Arriving at the office, there was no sign of Kaba. It had been arranged that someone from the Social Department would bring her at ten o'clock. A nervous Jane checked her watch – they were early.

Sellie waited in reception, while Jane went through to see the accounts staff. Momo and Amos were both out with debt collectors removing doors and Hani and Lola were manning the cashiers' windows, attending to more and more irate tenants forced to pay for their doors to be reinstated. Jane thought that if it wasn't so sad, - the scene of the tenants waving their arms shouting insults and, only after venting their rage, reluctantly parting with their money, would be comical.

Ruth came round with cold drinks and asked when Kaba would be coming. She told Jane that they were doing a good thing in taking the little girl, and Jane was so grateful that at least one person thought she was right. Good for Ruth.

A few moments later, she rushed back into the office. 'Kaba… she come right now,' and this time gave her broadest smile.

A very elegant African lady appeared followed closely by a nervous-looking Kaba, wearing what appeared to be a new dress and sandals and carrying a plastic bag. The young lady approached Jane, introducing herself as Constance Wanjiku from the Social Department.

Jane was taken completely by surprise at the woman's confident manner and appearance, so different from all the other women in Ogola. She wore smart, western clothes and shoes and carefully coiffed wavy hair – or was it a wig? They shook hands.

'Oh hello, Constance, we haven't met before,' Jane said. 'I think you were in Italy when I met Nelson and all your colleagues… oh, and thank you for bringing Kaba. Hello Kaba, you look very pretty today.' Jane gave Kaba a reassuring smile and a brief hug. She was pleased to note the injury to her head had almost healed and she looked clean and well looked after.

Sellie said something to her very quietly and, without looking up, Kaba whispered to Jane, 'ow are you'. She looked more subdued than the first time Jane had seen her. She now understood that something important was happening to her and that this *mzungu* lady with a scarred face, and the strange-looking Lindu woman, were going to take her away from the only life she'd ever known. She sat in the chair next to Sellie looking up into her face for some kind of comfort. Sellie quietly said something to her, so she stayed very still, firmly clutching her plastic bag in her good hand.

'You're doing a wonderful thing taking this little girl in and anything I can do to help… well, just ask.' Constance had a flawless accent and spoke with the confidence of a girl from an English public school.

'Thank you, that's very kind. But I'm afraid we're in a very small minority in thinking the way we do.'

'Oh, ignore them.' Constance spoke with an authority which would not counter any opposing view. 'What you and Robert are doing is wonderful – and Sellie, of course,' she added smiling in her direction. 'I just wish other people would follow your example. I was taken into care by an English couple when I was young and I'll be forever grateful to them.' She went on to explain that when she was six, her parents had worked at a Christian missionary station in Ouverru but they both had died in a bus crash. The head of the mission and his wife brought her up, giving her a good education, the last five years of which were at a British-run boarding school in Kenya.

Just then, Basil put his head round the door and said they must leave because Mr Kimber needed the car.

The effusive Constance gave Jane, Sellie and Kaba big hugs and kissed them all on their cheeks as they made their way to the Land Rover. 'May I come and visit Kaba?' she asked.

'You'll be very welcome, Constance, any time.'

'Oh, and one other thing,' Constance suddenly remembered. 'I'd wanted Dieter to give Kaba a health check before handing her over but he's been away all week. I'll arrange for him to see her next week – I'll give you a call.'

So it's Dieter and not Dr Blanke, Jane thought – Constance Wanjiku is full of surprises. She seemed to have taken on the role of a social worker and, for the moment, Jane was pleased someone was showing a positive interest in them. Asking Dieter to check Kaba's health was a good idea, one she should have thought of herself. Getting out of the car at their house, Kaba held Sellie's hand very tightly. She didn't look around and kept her eyes firmly on the ground. Just what was going through her little mind Jane could only imagine.

'Should we show her round the house or wait for Gilly?' Jane asked Sellie.

'No, Madam. I take her now, she stay with me, not in your house, but in my quarters,' and with that Sellie took Kaba round to the back of the house to her own entrance.

Letting herself in through the front door, Jane felt a little deflated. She'd thought of bringing Kaba into the house and seeing her amazement when she saw how they lived. She'd imagined Kaba playing with Gilly in the bedroom and outside in the garden and seeing her laugh and run as she blossomed into a polished young lady. But she now realised that it was just her own conceited dream

– showing the world what a caring person she was. She now felt a bit silly and hoped Robert wouldn't see it that way.

After changing into more comfortable clothes, Jane made tea and looked in the fridge for something to make a sandwich. As the kettle was boiling, Sellie came into the kitchen following her normal routine; there was no sign of Kaba.

The Kimber family stayed around the house and compound all weekend, not even catching a glimpse of Kaba. Sellie carried out her duties as normal and told Jane that the little girl was settling in. They were aware that Sellie had taken her to church on Sunday morning and they occasionally heard Sellie's raised voice as though reprimanding the little girl for something she'd done, or maybe not done.

'Will I be able to see Kaba when I get home?' Gilly asked on Monday morning on her way to join Trish and Susie for her ride to school.

Jane felt sorry for Gilly. She'd been excited at the prospect of meeting the new girl and even went and knocked on Sellie's door after Sunday lunch but she'd been told Kaba was resting.

'She's being a bit strange, isn't she?' Robert commented about the non-appearance of their new resident. Jane couldn't understand it either but said they must be patient and let Sellie handle things her way.

When Robert and Gilly had left, Jane asked Sellie if they could meet Kaba later that day.

'Of course, Madam,' Sellie replied, as if it was obvious they would.

'Gilly will be pleased,' Jane said. 'Oh, changing the subject, can you bake cakes? It's Mr Kimber's birthday on Wednesday and it would be nice to make him a cake. I'd try myself but mine usually come out more like pancakes!'

'Of course, Madam, I make good cakes. I make one cake for Mr Kimber. I get Kaba to help.'

'That would be great. Thank you. Oh, by the way, Sellie, when's your birthday?'

Looking a little uncomfortable, Sellie said she didn't know.

Trying not to show her surprise, Jane asked how she knew how old she was.

'In my culture – in the village – we not have birthdays like you people – we add one year every harvest, so I think I'm...' Sellie hesitated as though she was doing a complex mental calculation, 'about twenty-two.'

'And do you know how old Kaba is?'

'I find out, Madam.'

Just before lunch, Robert phoned. 'Guess what, the contractors are actually back working again! For some reason, which neither Ken nor the German Embassy can understand, K.K. has withdrawn the injunction. It's a mystery,' and then, after a little reflection as though talking to himself he added, 'I wonder how long this will last?'

'That's great news and let's hope it does last. Do you think Lester had anything to do with it?'

'I've no idea. I'll call him later to tell him the news.'

'By the way,' Jane asked, 'have you heard from Lily?' Jane asked,

'Yes. She sent her report to Hani so hopefully you'll be able to make a decision,' he changed his words slightly, 'well, not *you* exactly but Ken and Hani... with your help. Oh, and another thing. I've received a letter from Victor Veme, confirming that he's arranged a settlement with Precious' solicitor, without accepting any liability on my part. I've got to make a bloody goodwill payment to Precious of twenty thousand shillings which will stop a court case and put an end to any claim she has now, or in the future.'

'Ah well,' Jane said philosophically, 'I guess it could have been worse.'

'So that's about f-four-hundred p-pounds f-fucking f-Fearless has cost me. I've now got to think of some way of getting my revenge.'

The two girls met when Gilly came home from school. She did a double take when she saw Kaba alongside Sellie, stopping dead in her tracks. The two girls looked at each other, neither of them saying anything.

'This Kaba.' Sellie quietly announced.

'I'm Gilly,' she shouted, and then turned and ran to her room.

From her bedroom, Jane heard Gilly's excited voice. Going through to the living room she found Sellie and Kaba standing by the kitchen door as if it were a demarcation line that neither should cross. Rushing back, Gilly was clutching one of her favourite dolls, and slowly approached Kaba, holding it out towards her.

'You can have it… it's a present.'

Sellie translated for Kaba, who immediately reached out with her good hand and snatched the doll from Gilly, clasping it as hard as she could to her chest, her eyes never leaving Gilly's face for a moment. The only change in her expression was of a fierce determination to hold on to her new doll – nobody, but nobody was going to take it away from her. The idea of one child giving a doll to another was outside her experience.

Taken aback by the girl's aggressive snatch, Gilly thought she might try to take it back but something in the way Kaba glared at her made her change her mind. She turned and ran into her mother's arms. 'She grabbed it, mummy, she hurt me,' and tears started to well up in her eyes.

'It's okay, Gilly, it's fine,' Jane said embracing her tearful daughter, 'Kaba's very pleased, aren't you Kaba? It was a lovely thing to do and I'm very proud of you.' With these reassuring words from her mummy, Gilly felt better and turned round to face the girl again.

Sellie spoke sharply to Kaba, and although she listened intently to what she was being told, she clung onto her doll and still stared with unblinking eyes at Gilly.

With repeated encouragement from Sellie, Kaba eventually whispered 'tank you 'illy,' and, with that, ran back into Sellie's room.

Sellie started to apologise, but Jane stopped her saying she understood. She then reminded her that Mr Kimber would like to meet Kaba when he came home from work.

'I find out Kaba's age, Madam.'

'Oh that's good, how old is she?'

She explained to Jane that Kaba's mother had kept little cups for each of her children, high on a small shelf just underneath the roof, and each year she put a coffee bean in each cup so she would remember their ages. When Kaba's mother died the eldest child took down all the cups, counted the beans, and told them all their ages. There were seven beans in Kaba's cup.

What a bizarre yet touching tale. Jane thought she would write it in her next report along with all the other extraordinary anecdotes she'd recently heard. 'Can you think of a date… say sometime next year, which we'll call your birthday so we can buy you a present and also a date for Kaba so she can have a birthday too?'

'Yes, Madam, I do that thing for you.'

There was a sense of expectation in the accounts office the next day when Hani gave Jane the report of Lily's submission. Jane read it through three times before she understood it. 'So Hani, what do you think?'

He was unsure. 'It's err… good… isn't it?'

'Yes, Hani, it looks very good to me. So, according to Lily, you should get BuzanComp down here and negotiate a better price for the computer, but the rest of their quote seems to be very good.'

Feeling nauseous, Jane awoke early and crept to the bathroom while Robert slept, snoring slightly. After a few minutes, the sickness passed and she tried to sidle back into bed without waking him. He turned over and, still with his eyes closed, he sleepily felt for her.

'Happy birthday, husband,' she whispered.

A sleepy 'Mmm,' was the only reply.

Even in the dim light she could see he was smiling.

'I've got a present for you.' She took his hand and placed it on her belly.

'Thank you… wife,' he muttered as he felt around for some sort of gift that must have slipped down in the bed.

Jane once more put his hand back onto her stomach. 'Happy birthday… father of my unborn child.'

His head didn't move but his eyes opened wide as he tried to clear the sleep from his fuzzy brain. 'What the…?'

'I'm pregnant. You're going to have a baby.'

'You're pregnant!'

'That's what I said.'

'Oh!'

'Is that all you can say – … "oh"?'

'You mean… you're actually pregnant?'

'Actually yes, I am… actually.'

'Oh!'

'Can't you say anything other than "oh"?'

Despite being wide awake, he still managed to bang his head on the headboard as he sat up. 'How… err… how long have you known?'

'Just over two weeks. I haven't seen a doctor yet but I know the symptoms. Aren't you going to give me a kiss and say something romantic and tell me how clever I am?'

He took her into his arms and kissed the top of her head and held her there swaying slightly from side to side. He then kissed her very gently on her lips and hugged her more tightly. 'Wow,' he smiled, 'a lot of hard work went into that!'

After giving him a well-deserved thump, she nestled into his embrace. She felt loved and secure, unlike the first time she was pregnant when Peter Collins wanted nothing to do with her or the baby.

'What are we going to do?' He sounded worried as if yet another problem had descended on them.

'We're going to get up as usual and have breakfast, and you will go to work and I'll go to Ogola, that's what we'll do. And we won't say anything to anyone until I've seen the doctor. By the way, who is our doctor?'

Still in a state of shock, he mumbled that the company doctor was Dr Patterson. 'He's a very nice chap so I think you'll like him. His father was Scottish and his mother Buzamban, from the same tribe as Ken. Shall I make an appointment?'

'Yes OK, next week'll do.'

He now became worried. 'Are you sure you want to go to Ogola, now that you're… err…? The heat and the bumpy roads might… err…'

'Have you forgotten how to finish sentences now? Maybe too much sex has addled your brain. I'll soon put a stop to that! Anyway, I'll be fine. I'll lead a normal life until much nearer the time, so don't worry.'

At breakfast, Gilly gave Robert a present and birthday card she'd made herself.

'What a beautiful card Gilly, come and give me a kiss.' He

picked her up and kissed her several times which made her giggle. 'And what's in the parcel?'

Enjoying this, Gilly was jumping up and down with excitement. 'It's a surprise, open it!'

He did as he was told and unwrapped a book on Buzamban native animals and birds, full of colour photographs and descriptions of how and where they lived. He picked her up and kissed her several more times, at the same time tickling her under her arms, which sent her into gales of laughter.

After they'd calmed down enough to eat breakfast, there was a knock on the kitchen door.

Putting her head round, Sellie said that Kaba had something for Mr Kimber.

Kaba appeared at Sellie's side holding an envelope. Both of them stood in the doorway as they'd done on previous occasions and Sellie whispered into Kaba's ear. Very slowly, Kaba lifted her hand in Robert's direction.

''appy burfday mista Kumba.'

The 'birthday boy' walked slowly around the table and took the envelope from the little girl. Inside was a homemade card, with a series of coloured scribbles. Robert felt tears coming to his eyes and quickly brushed them away. When he grew up, his parents 'didn't do' emotion and now he felt awkward and wasn't sure what to say. He wanted to pick Kaba up as he had Gilly but knew their relationship wasn't ready for that. His emotions were starting to get the better of him. First Jane clobbered him with the news that he was going to be a father, then Gilly gave him a card and present as daughters do, and finally this from Kaba. How much can a man take?

'Thank you so much, Kaba – it's beautiful.' He reached out and took her hand and then leaned forward and gave her a gentle kiss on her cheek.

A shrill ring brought Jane to the phone the following morning. Constance Wanjiku's well-modulated voice informed Jane that Dieter had seen Kaba. It was a little disconcerting to Jane that Constance seemed pleased that she was in the room when Kaba was examined. What was it with this woman? On the one hand, Jane was glad that Constance was supportive and eager to help but, on the other, she seemed to want to be in control. Later in the morning, Jane decided to find out directly from Dieter how he'd got on with Kaba.

'She's a cute little girl and, like most kids here, she's malnourished but a few weeks living with you and Sellie will soon put that right. I've taken blood and all the other specimens and will have the results within ten days. Things can be a bit slow around here. Anyhow, she seems to be in reasonable health and I'm not expecting any bad news. I'll let you know when I get the results,' he paused for a moment before continuing, 'that's if Constance doesn't get them first.'

Jane laughed. 'Yes, why is it that Constance seems to be trying to take Kaba over?'

'I'm not sure, but one thing I do know is that she is worth keeping on your side. She has some very important Peelee connections and likes name-dropping the President, and the minister for this and that, as though she is on good terms with all of them.'

'What about Kaba's hand? Can it be fixed?'

'I'm not an expert in orthopaedics but strangely, the injury doesn't look very old to me. Both Sellie and Constance asked Kaba to tell them when and how it happened but she wouldn't. She just clammed up as though she wanted to block it from her mind. Anyway, I've given Sellie a note to take to the Victoria Private Hospital where a friend of mine, a Danish orthopaedic surgeon, will x-ray it and see if the damage can be fixed. I'll let you know when Sellie should take her.'

'That sounds promising. Robert and I will obviously pay all the costs as she's our responsibility. Is the Ouverru General Hospital not very good?'

Dieter pulled a face and told Jane about his last visit there. 'How anyone comes out of that hospital alive is a miracle. The corridors are crammed; wards for twenty people have up to sixty being treated; patients lie head-to-toe or under the beds; old needles, dried blood, and other bodily fluids cover the floors and corridors; many taps don't work and sanitary facilities are almost non-existent. I even saw a mangy old dog licking at something stuck to the floor.'

Jane closed her eyes in disbelief. 'That sounds awful.'

'Yet despite all this, most nurses and doctors do amazingly well and my heart goes out to them for their superhuman efforts. The bulk of the funding for the Hospital comes from Britain but the UK Minister, when asked, knew nothing about the dreadful conditions and said something along the lines that *"the British Government takes these matters very seriously and has brought in a task force and introduced tough new accounting systems!"* I'd like to go to London, grab that man by the throat, and drag him into the hospital to see for himself.'

'I'll hold your coat while you do it,' Jane sympathised.

'Like most African nations, the Buzambans used British aid money for absolutely the wrong things – every top official got a new car, but only four ambulances! And to make matters worse, they are desperately short of basic medicines. People are dying from preventable diseases. This makes me so mad.' Dieter slapped his hand hard on his desk – he was very angry. The next sentence he said through clenched teeth. 'Whenever anyone asks you if foreign aid is working in Africa, just remember these simple basic statistics – over the past five decades, donors have given more than a trillion dollars to Africa – try and get your head around one trillion – think of a billion and then multiply it by one thousand, and yet we can't get medicine costing fifty cents to cure a child dying from malaria! Tell that to your minister back in London.'

They sat in silence for a few moments.

'I'm afraid there's one other thing I… err… hesitate to mention. And I haven't said anything to either Sellie or Constance. I can't be sure but Kaba may have been sexually assaulted within the past few months. There's a sign of recent scarring and… she's not a virgin. This kind of injury could have been caused by an accident but I thought you should know.'

Jane slowly sat down again and put her hands to her face, almost prayer-like, and sat very still for a moment. 'Poor little girl. Do you come across this much?'

'Unfortunately, yes, but probably no more than in the rest of the world. Paedophilia and child abuse are some of the horrors we doctors come across far too often.'

She thanked him again and asked if she owed him anything for his time but he smiled and said 'it's on the house.'

CHAPTER NINETEEN

Jane was working with Hani when Constance came to tell her that Dieter had Kaba's medical results. 'He wants you to go to see him before lunch as the surgery is usually quiet then. Would you like me to come with you?'

Knowing she had to be tactful, Jane explained that she would send for Sellie and Kaba to join her and would Constance mind if they saw the doctor alone; Constance accepted this quite cheerfully.

Making a fuss of Kaba, Dieter told them that she was in good health and, much to their relief, she was clear of HIV. The malaria parasite was present in her bloodstream which was common in the slums, but she had obviously built up a resistance to the disease. However, he gave her an injection and said that now that she was living away from Ogola, she shouldn't get the sickness.

As they were about to leave, Dieter asked Jane if she had any news about the missing drugs.

'I'm not sure, but our contact has asked us to go there on Friday morning, so... fingers crossed. Anyhow, I'll keep you informed.'

'Well, good luck with that,' Dieter looked grim. 'We're desperate now and soon we won't be able prescribe to those already on a drug programme. Is there anything I can do to help... or even someone from the Embassy?'

'Leave it with us for the moment,' Jane gave a reassuring smile. 'If we come up against a brick wall, I'll come running but, for the time being, we'll do what we can.'

'Thanks again, Jane. I'd almost given up, so any glimmer of hope is... well, comforting.'

Completely out of the blue, Schultec notified Robert of a change in the agreement between DGA and the Buzamban Government; the water and sewer systems in Ogola would remain in the ownership of the project, and not be handed over to the Ouverru Water Department as had been originally intended. Therefore, he must make a complete set of 'as-built' drawings for this work. And, horror upon horror, DGA wanted the first set in four weeks. There was no way he could meet this… oh, but hang on just a moment, he thought. A mischievous plan was slowly developing in his devious mind. He phoned f-Fearless, who apologised yet again over Precious, but was then thrilled when Robert invited him round for dinner that evening. Jane wasn't keen on the idea but she could see Robert wanted to resume normal relations with his best friend.

After the meal, Robert sprang the surprise on what was, until that moment, a very sober Jimmy. He asked him to prepare a detailed set of documents, including drawings of Ogola's water reticulation system (with all the outlets), and sewer system (both septic, grey water and inspection points). Being the expert, Jimmy could liaise with the contractor, the infamous Zanga Construction, and have it all done within three weeks.

F-Fearless visibly paled. He was on the spot and he knew it. Was this the price of forgiveness? Well, if it was, he knew he had to do it… but what a rotten job. A few stiff drinks later, his shredded nerves on the mend, the three of them gradually relaxed into their old ways and, Robert confirmed, Precious would now be history.

After f-Fearless had gone, Jane gave Robert a punch on his arm. 'You sly, conniving, charlatan. Now I know why you suddenly wanted to f-forgive f-fucking f-Fearless f-Faversham.'

Robert gave her a triumphant grin, and took her into his arms. 'Revenge is mine!'

While preparing for their next visit to Mr Wasubu, Jane thought long and hard about whether she should be getting involved in something that could well turn out to be dangerous. For the first time in her life, she was instrumental in organising other people and, surprisingly, enjoying it; not the danger but managing other people. She felt quite important.

Arriving at the airport cargo section, she followed the smartly-suited Hani and the armed police officer, Ben, as they again made their way through the main workplace towards Mr Wasubu's office, but this time there weren't any nudges and sniggering from the staff.

'Mr Hani… over here.' The young man Jane recognised from earlier visits called over, and they waited for him to join them.

'Mr Wasubu not here,' he said.

'Where is he?' Hani demanded.

'He in hospital. He been beaten.'

Jane's heart sank. Was this her fault? Should she back out now? But how could she… they'd come so far. They went into Wasubu's where the young man introduced himself as John Cole, one of Mr Wasubu's assistants, and told them that his boss had been attacked outside the office on the previous evening.

'Do you know why?' Jane asked.

'Was it to do with the missing drugs?' Ben questioned sharply.

John Cole studied his dust-covered shoes before nodding his head and mumbling, 'I think so.'

'Mr Wasubu had information for us. Where is it?' Ben's voice was getting harder and, probably out of habit on these occasions, he fingered his holstered gun.

A fidgeting John Cole muttered, 'I don't know.'

His reply was so pathetic that Jane could tell he was holding something back. Ben suddenly grabbed him by the lapels of his shirt and brought his face close to his. 'We want this information.' He said it slowly and quietly but with a threatening tone. 'Nobody will hurt you – if there's any trouble just mention my name and you'll be safe. Now, I'll give you one last chance, where is the information on the missing drugs?'

'I think there something in his top drawer,' he nodded in the direction of Wasubu's desk.

Hani tried to open the drawer but it was locked. Ben let go of John Cole's shirt and took a metal lever from his belt… one swift downward push was all that was needed. Ben handed the contents over to Jane.

She and Hani looked at them together. There was a hand-written note as well as photocopies of letters and signed delivery notes to a company called City Pharmacy.

Jane looked at Hani. 'We should take these with us. I think there's some promising information here.' And then turning to look at John Cole said, 'I'm worried about this young man though, will he be beaten as well?'

Hani and Ben had a discussion which Jane couldn't understand,

and every so often, a worried John Cole would nod and say a few words which seemed to be in agreement with what was being said.

Hani stood and said they should go back to Ogola. Jane gave what she hoped was a reassuring smile to John Cole and thanked him for his help.

When they got in the car, Hani told Jane that he and Ben would go to the hospital to see if Wasubu was in any condition to confirm everything. Ben said he'd put a police guard on Wasubu's room and John Cole shouldn't have any trouble as nobody in the office saw him hand anything over. 'He has my name which should help if anyone threatens him.'

'That's good,' Jane said with relief. 'Do you think the drugs were taken by City Pharmacy?'

Hani gave a grim smile. 'Well, if they took them, we'll be in for some fun and games. City Pharmacy is owned by K.K. Machuri!'

While Hani and Ben went to see Mr Wasubu in the hospital, Jane went straight to Ken's office. Luckily, Robert was there as well. She told them everything that had happened.

Robert looked worried. 'You're getting yourself into dangerous territory, Jane, especially as K.K. could be involved. You must stop now. Leave it to Hani and Ben, or Dieter or someone else. What do you think, Ken?'

'Someone is definitely getting nervous, and that's why poor Wasubu was given the treatment. I'll wait to see what Hani and Ben say after they've seen him. And Jane,' he gave her a sympathetic glance, 'you should do as Robert says.'

'And be the obedient wife, you mean,' she almost exploded. 'No way. I'm not letting this one slip away. If we can get our hands on those drugs we'll be able to save Ruth's life and hundreds of others. That's worth taking a chance, isn't it?'

'But why you? Ken's right… let someone else do it.'

Ignoring them both, Jane assured them she wouldn't do anything silly. 'What we need is a plan and I think I've got one.'

'And that is?'

'First, we have to find out if Dieter's drugs are on sale at the City Pharmacy. We'll send someone there to try and buy some HIV medication.'

'Well, you are not going,' Robert said with authority. 'We could send Lola.'

Jane was now pumped up with excitement. 'No, we'll send Ruth. She's the one with HIV so there'll be nothing suspicious. Lola can go with her... she can read whereas Ruth can't.'

'Where's this leading, Jane?' Robert was still looking uncomfortable and annoyed that Jane was not taking any notice of his advice.

'Once we have the evidence,' Jane continued, as though she'd suddenly gone deaf to anything Robert said, 'I'll see Dieter to discuss what should happen next.'

'You've read too many detective novels,' scolded Robert. 'This is Africa, remember, nothing works like that out here.'

'I agree with Robert.' Ken knew he was in a difficult position between the warring couple, 'but she does have a point you know. We might have to refine the plan... Africanise it, if you see what I mean.'

Robert was losing face, and didn't like it. 'If Ken and Hani come up with a scheme, then I'll support that, but you stay out of it, Jane.'

'Yes, boss,' she took his hand and kissed it submissively. 'Whatever you say, boss.' She only did that to make Robert think he'd won a victory, but she knew she'd lied through her teeth. She was determined to be involved at every step of the way.

'Okay, all agreed,' Ken said, relieved that the Kimbers now seemed to be at peace and not at each other's throats. 'It's Friday lunchtime now,' he said looking at his watch, 'let's meet first thing Monday morning to decide what we do next.'

It was turning out to be an extremely busy day for Jane. After the excitement of the morning, she attended her appointment with the doctor later that afternoon. Putting all the Ogola problems to one side, Robert was desperate to find out if he really was going to become a father. He had thought of little else since she'd told him she was pregnant and during that time he'd had periods of excitement followed by apprehension, with bouts of near panic thrown in for good measure. When she arrived home, he tried to put his arms round her while she told him what had happened but she laughingly pushed him away as he hadn't showered. She'd found Dr Patterson (call me Angus) to be a strange little man, with acne and bad teeth, but he'd confirmed her pregnancy. He'd also shown her around the Victoria Private Hospital, including the delivery room, and confirmed that, if she did decide to have the baby in Buzamba, the treatment would be equally as good as she could expect in the UK.

Robert was over the moon wanting to broadcast the news to everyone but Jane insisted that they should leave the announcement for a couple of months. However, she said he could let his parents know; he was sure they would be thrilled, especially if it was a son to carry on the family name. 'When will we know what sex it is?'

'I don't want to know before it's born so you'll just have to wait, Kimber.'

Nothing Jane said could dampen his enthusiasm. 'If it's a boy I'd like to call him after my father – Hubert.'

'You must be out of your tiny little mind. Hubert! No son of mine will be called Hubert. Think again, Kimber.'

After a long phone conversation with his boss in Germany, Robert told Jane that he would have to go to Kabara the following week to sort out some new problems there, but he would only go if she promised not to get involved in her planned 'drugs bust'. With her fingers crossed behind her back, she told him… well, lied to him actually… that she'd let Ken take care of everything.

As they'd had such a hectic week, it was an easy decision for Jane and Robert to spend the weekend at home, calmly reflecting on the testing events that seemed to be stacked up like the planes circling at Heathrow, and then making order out of chaos by eventually landing in an organised fashion. First and foremost was Gilly which, for the moment, was the opposite of a problem. They were both astonished at how well she had adapted to her new life in Buzamba – she acted as though she'd lived there all her life. The old grumpy side of her personality had gone… for the time being at least, replaced by an almost constant sunny disposition. She adored her new daddy but always made sure to include Jane when it was time for cuddles and kisses. She and Susie Bond had already been on a sleepover at Bella's, a Buzamban girl, who was one of their classmates from school. Bella and Gilly were then invited to stay overnight with the Bond girls the following weekend. Jane was pleased that she was making friends with local girls as well as expat children.

Then there was the small matter of Jane's pregnancy, which, much to Robert's chagrin, she insisted should not be broadcast for the next couple of months; not even to Gilly. They agreed that as long as the pregnancy developed normally and Jane maintained her good health, she would have the baby in Ouverru. This would give her about four weeks before they all went on leave.

Although the recent arrival of Kaba had gone against almost everyones' wishes, Sellie seemed to have taken on the job of stepmother as if she was born to it. They were gradually seeing more of Kaba each day, and it wouldn't be long before she had the operation to fix her hand.

Jane's job to help with the computerisation of the Ogola accounts was next on their agenda. Robert realised there was no stopping her even though the hard slog was still to come, but as long as she promised not to overdo things, he was happy for her to continue. He knew how important it was for Ken.

Robert's main concern was Jane's involvement in finding the missing computers and now, seemingly, Dieter's missing drugs. Although she'd told him she'd let Ken handle everything from here, he wasn't sure whether he believed her. She'd done incredibly well so far taking on a task nobody else had even attempted, but now it was getting serious, especially if K.K. Machuri was involved. There could be another shooting rampage in Ogola at any time, and Jane could well be the target.

The rest of Saturday was taken up with report and letter writing for Jane, and catching up with paperwork for Robert. After spending their Sunday afternoon by the pool joining the Bonds, McKeevers, Pennicotts and others for the customary barbecue, Jane made a light tea for them all before an exhausted Gilly fell into her bed. What a great life, Jane smiled after tucking Gilly into bed, and then snuggling up to her lover on the settee. 'I'll miss you next week, Kimber. Don't get into trouble up there, will you?'

'I'll be all right. You be good too. I saw the way you kept ogling the bulge in Gregg's Speedos when he got out of the pool; absolutely disgusting it was.'

'I wasn't,' Jane poked him in his ribs. 'It's not my fault the rest of you men wear baggy shorts in the pool – Gregg is the only trendy bloke there. Anyway,' she poked him again, 'you're not jealous of his bulge... are you?'

'Of course not,' he boasted proudly. 'I'll compete in the battle of the bulge with any of the guys there.'

'And talking about bulges, you dirty old man, your eyes were out like organ-stops every time Cindy leaned forward in your direction. Aren't my bulges of any interest these days?'

'Oh, these things you mean,' he said as he placed his hands over her breasts and caressed them gently. Laughing, she twisted out of his grip and grabbed what she could of his trouser bulge, only for him to pick her up in his arms, cradle fashion, and head for the bedroom. 'I think we should compare our bulges in the comfort of our bedroom. Don't you?'

'Oh, *Bwana*, you are so masterful.'

After kissing Robert and wishing him a safe journey to Kabara, Jane headed straight for Ogola to see Ken. He gave her a respectful smile.

'Has Robert gone?'

'Yes. He's well on his way. So, Ken, I'm bursting to hear the latest.'

He couldn't help smiling at the earnest look on her face. 'Well, we sent one of Dieter's nurses with Ruth to City Pharmacy last Friday afternoon, and, yes... Dieter's missing drugs are being sold over the counter. The cheats put adhesive labels on each box to hide the fact that the drugs are a gift from the Federal Republic of Germany and are not to be resold.'

'The bastards.'

'Dieter was jumping for joy when he heard. I told him your plan... you know, the one you came up with last Friday, and he thinks it's brilliant. He thinks you must be some sort of super sleuth to come up with such a clever plan. A female James Bond!'

'Ha, ha. My boss, Tony, in England would be proud to hear such praise.' She'd previously told Ken about her part-time job with BBNC in Ringwood, so he knew who she was talking about. 'So, what happens now?'

'Well, Dieter contacted the Embassy on Friday afternoon and between them, they agreed it would be a good idea to try and get the Minister of Foreign Affairs, to send a heavily armoured team to the pharmacy's stockroom, and with the help of Ben and his men, surround the place.'

'So when do we go in and seize the drugs?'

'The Embassy thinks it will take until next Monday to get everything ready.'

'But that's too long. They may hear something and move the stuff out. Can't we do it quicker?'

'No, Jane,' Ken said determinedly. 'It will be next Monday. Dieter will give us the time and place to meet by Friday afternoon. Until then, you have to be patient.'

Taken aback by Ken's firm command, Jane reluctantly accepted the delay. Maybe she was letting her excitement get the better of her. 'Okay then, Ken. Please let me know when the arrangements are made.'

'I'll do that. Ben has put a twenty-four hour plainclothes watch on the pharmacy's store room, so nothing can leave without us knowing.'

With that slight reassurance, Jane went through to see Hani to compliment him once again on his and Ben's efforts, and to ask how Mr Wasubu was. She was pleased to hear that his injuries were not life-threatening and he expected to be able to go home by the end of the week. Although neither Hani nor Ben had any evidence of who'd done the beating, all fingers pointed in the direction of K.K. Machuri.

Basil had driven Robert to Kabara, so Jane arranged for Sellie to take Kaba by taxi to the hospital on Tuesday morning for her hand to be X-rayed. The news was encouraging and the next day Kaba went back for the operation and Sellie stayed with her overnight. She came home with her bandaged hand in a sling and a beaming smile on her face, feeling very important, knowing that Sellie and the *mzungus* would look after her – just like a real family. The consultant told Jane that the prognosis was good and he expected her to regain full use of her hand within two or three months.

The ever-eager Constance called to see the patient, bringing her a beautifully wrapped box of chocolates. She seemed genuinely interested in Kaba's progress which Jane did nothing to discourage. She thought that if, heaven forbid, they had to leave Buzamba then Constance with her influential contacts could be of great help to Sellie.

When Jane told Cindy that Robert was in Kabara again and wouldn't be back until Sunday, Cindy decided she should tell Jane what Gregg had seen on his last trip. Cindy had no moral qualms about Robert having a mistress if that was what he wanted and, deep down, she wouldn't have minded if he showed more interest in her once in a while.

'I've something to tell you about Robert which might upset you.'

'What on earth do you mean?' Jane studied Cindy's face for a clue of what was coming.

Choosing her words carefully, Cindy told her that Gregg had seen Robert dining with a woman at the hotel in Kabara and, after dinner, they had gone upstairs together. On being questioned by Gregg, the receptionist said that the lady was Mr Kimber's sister.

Ashen-faced and with her heart in her mouth, Jane asked if the woman was African. Cindy confirmed she was.

'But how could she be his sister?' The dreadful image of Precious immediately came into Jane's head. 'Oh my God, do you think he was with a prostitute?'

'Gregg said she looked attractive and well dressed, unlike a prostitute.'

'Ah well, it definitely can't have been that bloody Precious women. Do you think he's having an affair?'

'I've no idea... but it did look suspicious... don't you think?'

'Why didn't you tell me this before?'

Cindy tried to console Jane by resting her hand on her arm. 'I didn't know what to do. I'd thought of telling you earlier but then again, I didn't want to cause any rift between you two. You are our best friends.'

'I've a good mind to go up there and confront him. Catch him out... if he's screwing another woman.'

'You could fly there tomorrow morning if you want. Sellie and I will look after Gilly.'

Jane wasn't sure what to do. Maybe it was just a simple misunderstanding with a simple explanation. But... it didn't seem to be... going to his bedroom after dinner sounded very much like an affair. And calling her his sister... how stupid is that? 'I think I will go,' she told Cindy. 'I could get a taxi to the airport and...'

'Look,' Cindy interrupted, 'you can't go on your own. I'll tell you what, I'll get Gregg to go with you.'

'You can't do that. He can't go at the drop of a hat.'

'Of course he can. He's the boss, he can do what he likes. And he's always got business to do in the branch office.'

'Are you sure? I'd be a bit worried going on my own, not having been there before.' What Jane didn't want to reveal that she was having early morning sickness.

'Leave it all to me. Be ready with an overnight bag at ten o'clock tomorrow morning, and Gregg will pick you up and accompany you on the flight to Kabara. He'll also make hotel reservations.'

Was she being disloyal? Didn't she trust her husband? Since becoming pregnant, their love life hadn't changed so he had no excuse for needing a temporary sex partner.

'Yes, okay then,' she told Cindy, 'I'll do it.'

During the whole journey through to checking-in at the Safari Lodge Hotel, Gregg had been very attentive and considerate, holding Jane's hand and providing a sympathetic shoulder for her to lean on. She didn't care that Gregg was too tactile... almost intimate... as the support of a friend at this upsetting time was what she needed. He made her feel protected. The receptionist confirmed that Mr Kimber was a guest there and he thought he was presently in his room, number 202, with his sister.

'Do you want me to phone his room to check?' the receptionist asked.

'No thank you,' Jane smiled nervously thinking on her feet, 'we're... err... old friends and we'd like to give him a wonderful surprise.'

Gregg said nothing. In fact, he was very much looking forward to the 'surprise' and was already getting aroused by what may well turn out to be a sexual confrontation. For separate reasons, Jane and Gregg nervously went up the carpeted flight of stairs and stopped outside room 202. There was no sound. Jane knocked on the door.

'Who is it?' Robert's muffled voice called.

Her heart beating ten to the dozen, Jane answered, 'room service.' Her nerves were so bad that her voice croaked and she hoped that Robert wouldn't recognise it as hers.

'Come in. It's not locked.'

Her hand was sweaty and shaking so hard she couldn't turn the handle. Gregg gently pushed her away, grabbed the handle and opened the door wide. They were both there… Robert and the woman, the woman who was his 'so-called sister.' Jane had never seen anyone's jaw drop as far as Robert's. The woman gave a shriek

'We've caught you,' Jane yelled.

For a moment, nobody moved. The nervous tension was palpable as Jane's accusation hung in the air. Wanting to take control, Robert straightened himself to his full height, shoulders back, chest and chin thrust out like a gladiator about to do battle.

'Sit down, Jane,' he ordered in an authoritative voice, pointing to a nearby chair.

'I… err…' was as far as Jane got.

'I said, sit down.' Each word was clearly enunciated to emphasise there was no alternative but to obey his command.

Jane's head was in a whirl. She'd just caught her husband with another woman in his bedroom and here he was, giving orders to her. She had wanted to take the upper hand and lambaste him for his adultery, but his assertive action had taken the wind out of her sails. Half turning to see if Gregg was going to help, she saw him still standing behind her, looking uncomfortable.

'Maybe I should leave… it's none of my….' but Robert stopped him in his tracks.

'You stay where you are, Gregg, and you Jane… sit down.'

Somewhat flummoxed, Jane did as she was told.

'Now Jane,' his voice was quieter but firmly controlled, 'I'd like to introduce Mrs Ambeda from the Multi-Faith Mission Hospital here in Kabara.'

The African lady, Mrs Ambeda, smiled meekly in Jane's direction. 'Hello, Mrs Kimber, I'm very pleased to meet you.' She had a pleasant, educated voice, unlike the guttural accent of that horrible Precious tart, and had the presence of mind to ignore the obvious tension between Robert and his wife.

'And the gentleman,' Robert continued in a brusque voice, 'is Mr Gregg Bond.'

Mrs Ambeda and Gregg exchanged hesitant smiles.

Jane was momentarily halted in her planned assault, as the commanding figure in front of her was so different from the timid husband she was used to. This made her a little unsure of herself but she still felt she held the moral high ground. 'So why did you tell reception that Mrs 'whoever' was your sister?'

'Ha,' Robert gave a self-satisfied smirk, 'so that's what you think.'
'Well?'

'Mrs Ambeda is the Sister at the hospital. The Sister,' he repeated. 'The hospital's medical Sister,' emphasising it again to make sure she understood.

Jane's jaw dropped this time. 'But you told reception...'

'I told reception nothing, but Mrs Ambeda is well known in Kabara and everyone knows she is the hospital Sister.'

Gathering up some of the papers, Mrs Ambeda stood to leave. 'I think I've got all the papers I need, Mr Kimber. And thank you once again for helping with the water connection. If you could call round tomorrow morning, I'll have them all signed for you. Is that all right?'

'Yes, Sister, I'll be there by ten.'

'Goodbye, Mrs Kimber... Mr Bond,' Mrs Ambeda said as she was leaving, 'Nice to meet you both.'

While Gregg opened the door for her, Jane sheepishly stood at a loss for words.

Duly chastised, she sat down again. 'Oh dear, I... seem to have got things wrong.'

'Yes, Jane, you certainly have.'

'But why was she in your bedroom? You must admit it looks strange.'

'When I'm here on business, my bedroom is my office.'

'Yes, I see,' she said timidly.

'Look here,' he pointed to numerous papers laid out on his bed, 'here's my file on the water treatment plant, my file on the transmission line, my file on the distribution system, and my laptop is over there,' he pointed to a small desk in the corner next to the window. 'I do my work and hold meetings here. Even meetings with ladies.'

Not knowing what else to say, Jane sat quietly on the chair. This had been a disaster. When Cindy had told the tale, she should have stopped to give it some thought instead of overreacting like an immature teenager. Now she had egg on her face. And how!

'Have you two had lunch yet?' Robert, quite relaxed now, looked at Gregg.

'No, not yet.' Gregg was relieved the tension had to some extent been relieved with the mention of lunch.

'In that case, I suggest you go now as lunch in the dining room finishes in fifteen minutes. I've already had mine. And it will give me a chance to straighten things out here,' he indicated the files covering the bed. 'Come back when you've finished.'

A compliant Jane and Gregg did as they were told.

After Robert closed the door, his expression immediately changed from hurt to one of triumph. He looked at his reflection in the mirror and gave a double 'thumbs-up'. 'Excellent,' he murmured, 'one nil to me for a change.' His expression suddenly changed as he remembered something he had to do before Jane came back. Smiling guiltily, he walked over to the top of his bed, pulled back the covers and, lifting the pillow, pulled out a pair of ladies' red frilly panties and matching bra. Mmm, poor Sister, going home without her underwear. I'll return them tomorrow.

The hotel dining room was almost empty. Neither Jane nor Gregg felt hungry so they just ordered chicken salad sandwiches and coffee.

It was Gregg who spoke first. 'Oh dear, what a mess. And it's all my fault.'

'I guess you weren't to know,' Jane reflected. 'I should have waited until he got home and then challenged him. I should have trusted him.'

'All I can say is I'm very sorry for all this, Jane. I should have challenged Robert myself instead of telling tales behind his back. I hope he'll forgive me.'

'I hope he'll forgive me as well. He looked very hurt.'

'Yes, he did. He was very composed and… well…confident, wasn't he? I've never seen him like that before.'

'I guess when he's on firm ground, he can hold his own with anyone. By the way, are you still staying here tonight? Because I'll stay with Robert if he'll have me.'

'Yes, I'll stay, but I think it best if I keep out of Robert's way. I'll go to my branch office this afternoon, and as we're both booked on tomorrow's midday flight, I'll see you at the airport.'

'Yes, okay then.'

'And… good luck.'

CHAPTER TWENTY

Promptly, at nine o'clock on the Monday morning, the meeting took place in Deputy Minister Kana's office in the Ministry of Foreign Affairs. Apart from Minister Kana, the group consisted of Hans Schulz from the German Embassy, Dr Dieter Blanke, Hani and Ben Oburu, and Jane. It had only been intense pressure from the German Embassy that had persuaded the Ministry to cooperate.

Earlier, Robert had argued with Jane because he thought this should be a German Embassy problem and absolutely nothing to do with Schultec. It was only after Dieter intervened on Jane's behalf that Robert reluctantly gave in; Dieter's argument being that Jane had been at the heart of the investigation, and could still play a crucial part in the successful recovery of the antiretrovirals.

There was an uncomfortable atmosphere in the room. The unenthusiastic Minister Kana insisted that this was a police matter and that Ben Oburu and his colleagues should carry out the raid. Dr Blanke should go along because he was the legitimate person to identify that the drugs were his. Kana and Hans Schulz would meet K.K. Machuri, and they would arrive at the City Pharmacy stores in one hour's time.

'What?' Jane screamed to herself in apoplectic frustration, 'he's going to meet K.K. Machuri now! Well… that's it then. If K.K. already knows there'll certainly be nothing to find.' Strangely, Kana didn't mention Jane or Hani at all in his directive. It's as though they weren't there.

They set off in their separate cars. 'Will we be too late, Ben?' Jane asked. 'Has Machuri already moved things out?'

Ben shook his head. 'Plain-clothed police watched all the time, Jane, and they see nothing.'

'What do you think, Hani?' Jane's frustration not abating.

'I think it still there.'

Chewing on her bottom lip, she gave a deep audible sigh, knowing she could do nothing but wait. Basil drove them to City Pharmacy, where he stopped on the kerb opposite the store's rear entry.

Ben got out and told Basil to drive to the front entrance and stay in the car until they heard his whistle, and only then should they go into the shop. 'If there's any shooting, it'll be in the store.'

Oh my God. Naively, she hadn't thought about a gun fight which, now that she thought about it, was quite possible. What had she let herself in for? And not just herself – she'd probably led them all into danger.

The three of them sat in the car for what felt like ages, trying to look over the heads of pedestrians as they passed the pharmacy entrance, hoping to see some sign of activity. Suddenly, several gunshots were heard from the rear of the building at the same time as two police cars screamed to a halt on the kerb directly in front of the shop. Frightened pedestrians scattered in all directions as seven or eight policemen rushed into the shop with their pistols raised.

'Let's follow them,' Jane excitedly started to open the car door.

'No,' barked Hani, gripping Jane firmly by the arm, 'we wait for the whistle.'

Jane did as she was told. They could hear shouting and occasional screams from inside the shop before more gunshots which immediately stopped the shouting. Then there were two sharp whistle blasts.

'Okay, we go now,' Hani shouted, and he and Jane ran over the road into the shop's front entrance. Chaos reigned: police everywhere, three white-coated men having their arms tied behind their backs, and the unfortunate customers lying on the floor. Then a triumphant looking Ben appeared from the storeroom, followed by an equally happy Dieter, carrying a large carton in his hands. A collected sigh of relief issued from everyone there, followed by the excitable noise and back-slapping of a successful raid. The bewildered customers got to their feet and quickly left.

Ben, grinning widely, came over to Jane. 'We got them. The drugs are here.' He gave Jane high fives.

'Is anybody dead?' Jane almost shouted her question, frightened of what the answer might be.

Ben smiled again. 'We only fire to frighten them, we shoot no one.'

She was about to question him further when suddenly, there was complete silence. Everyone stopped talking and turned to see Minister Kana, Hans Schulz and an immaculately suited man wearing mirrored sunglasses enter the shop; they were accompanied by three armed soldiers.

'That K.K. Machuri,' Hani whispered in Jane's ear.

Nobody spoke or moved for what seemed to be ages, yet Jane knew it could have only been a few seconds. Removing his sunglasses, K.K. Machuri, followed by the three soldiers, strode up to the counter, his shoulders hunched forward aggressively. Jane nearly jumped out of her skin as his clenched fist thumped on the counter, rattling bottles on the shelves.

'What's all this?' he bellowed. 'What's going on?' His piercing gaze seemed to look into each individual's eyes; Jane wished she had something large to hide behind, and saw her feelings mirrored by Minister Kana who seemed to be trying to make himself invisible behind Hans Schulz. 'You,' he shouted and pointed at Dieter, 'who are you?'

Calmly, unmoved by K.K.'s aggressive manner, Dieter told him his name, where he worked, and that a shipment of important medicines, sent to him from Germany, had gone missing at the airport; the police had now found them in the City Pharmacy storeroom. He showed him the details marked on the carton and, balancing it on one knee, took the paperwork out of his pocket to show he was correct. There followed a staring match between the two men which Dieter eventually won. Machuri snarled something to his soldiers, who slipped their rifles off their shoulders and were about to lower them in Dieter's direction when, at the same time, the policemen, including Ben, raised their pistols. The soldiers stopped halfway, hesitated, and then re-shouldered their arms.

Jane's heart was pounding nineteen to the dozen, her bravado long gone. This dangerous confrontation was too much but she was unable to move.

Machuri, knowing he had lost, tried to save face by turning his aggression on to the taller of the three shop assistants, who still had his arms tied. There followed a discussion between them which Jane couldn't understand, but it was obvious that the poor assistant was being lambasted and probably blamed for everything that had happened.

'This is the man,' Machuri shouted for everyone to hear, and slapped the man hard across his face. 'This is the man who took the drugs. Nothing to do with me. Arrest him now,' he directed his last outburst at Ben. Machuri's shoulders were moving up and down with extreme anger as though they were pneumatically operated. And then, for no apparent reason, he turned and looked at Jane, square in the face. 'Who are you?' he yelled.

'Err, I'm err...' was as far as she got before Hani stepped forward. His massive frame towering over Machuri.

'This Mrs Kimber, she from BBNC,' he said evenly, and took one of Jane's business cards out of his pocket and showed it to Machuri.

He slowly read her card, a puzzled look on his face. 'BBNC,' he slowly mouthed the letters, 'sounds like the BBC. Are you BBC?'

'No,' she had got her voice back, 'BBNC is a British news agency.'

Whether this made any sense to Machuri or not, she couldn't tell, but after glaring once more around the shop, he stormed out followed by a shaken-looking Minister Kana and the three soldiers.

Although shaken-up, Jane was on cloud nine when they walked into the office and she and Hani told Ken everything that had happened.

'You did well, both of you. And now Dieter will be able to treat Ogola's HIV sufferers including Ruth, but....' he let that word linger for a while, 'I hate to think how K.K. will react to this humiliation. He's the last person in Buzamba you want to cross.'

'What can he do?' Jane's euphoria slowly ebbed away as she took on board Ken's warning.

'It's a pity you were there, Jane. He now knows you, and it won't take him long to link you with Robert and this project. Anyway, we'll just have to be extra careful from now on.'

At that moment, Dieter burst into the room, joyfully picking up Jane as though she was a little girl, whirled her round and round a few times before covering her face in kisses. 'You little darling,' he said as he put her down, and then he tried to do the same with Hani, but even lifting him off the ground by an inch was an achievement. This light relief brought smiles to all their faces. 'Thank you so much you two, and everyone else involved. We're back in business.'

Once the ecstatic Dieter had returned to his health centre, Ken told Jane to go and see Robert and tell him everything that had happened. 'It will take him a little time to fully understand the implications of it all,' he said. 'I also suggest you don't come here for a couple of days. Let the dust settle a bit, and Hani and I will use our contacts to try and find out if K.K. is planning revenge.'

That evening, Jane and Robert had an invitation for drinks with Josie and Lester, and as they settled down in their living room, Lester told them he was 'carless' for the time being as his car had been arrested.

'You mean you were arrested,' corrected Robert.

This made both of them laugh. 'No, just my car. Not me.' He told them that he'd been driving in town when he was pulled over by the police. They said that two days earlier, they'd seen him commit a traffic offence, so he was under arrest. Lester had then proved to them that two days earlier, he'd been out of town in Bumunu, so it couldn't have been him. They insisted that they were right and someone else must have been driving it. Again, he told them nobody else ever drove his car so... they arrested the car.

'Will the naughty car be going to court then,' Jane laughed.

'No, but the car has been fined one thousand shillings.'

'I hope it can pay,' Robert said.

'They're clever, aren't they? They know very well I'll have to pay if I want my car back, so let that be a lesson to you. Don't let your car out on its own.'

Jane refused another alcoholic drink on the pretence of a slight headache. She still wasn't ready to tell people she was pregnant. Robert then thanked Lester for his help in getting K.K. Machuri to lift his injunction on the work in Ogola.

'No problem, old chap. In our files at the Trade Commission, we had some of his dirty dealings recorded so a threat that we might release the info to the police was all that was needed.'

'Well, thanks again, and that leads us neatly onto the next Machuri episode.'

'Oh really? What is it now?'

Jane, with some unnecessary help from Robert, told them all about the missing drugs, the City Pharmacy incident, and her role in it all, including Machuri finding out who she was.

'I told her not to go,' Robert said, 'she'd already done enough without going on the actual raid.'

Jane decided not to reply to his criticism but hoped Josie or Lester might come to her rescue.

'What you witnessed,' Lester looked concerned, 'was a classic Peelee versus Solu confrontation. As we all know, the Peelees basically run this shambles of a country but they cannot ignore the one other large tribe; that's why the V.P. is always a Solu. The Peelees control the main source of power which is the army but, as you saw, the Solus, who most people acknowledge are a bit smarter than the Peelees, have managed over the years to infiltrate the police. And this, my friends, is potentially an explosion waiting to happen.'

'You think there could be some sort of civil war?' Robert asked, not totally surprised by Lester's warning.

'Certainly a tribal war. Don't be too alarmed yourselves, though, as all our experience in Africa would suggest that other tribes and foreigners would not be targets. Just don't get involved in the crossfire.'

After Jane had drunk only lemonade for most of the evening, she had the task of guiding her swaying husband back to the home. His amorous advances were quickly given a kick into touch, Jane was not in the mood.

'I've brought you a peace offering,' Cindy said, knocking and walking into Jane's kitchen the following morning. She was carrying a bottle of white wine. 'I hope I'm not persona non grata.'

'No, of course not,' laughed Jane, pleased for something to divert her attention from the Machuri situation. 'Come and sit out on the veranda. It's a real scorcher today.'

Settling herself down, Cindy hesitantly asked if everything was okay between Jane and Robert after the unfortunate incident in Kabara.

Jane assured her that, although he'd been a little cool with her... especially at first, they were now more-or-less back to normal. 'I've learnt my lesson though. I should have trusted him.' She opened the bottle and poured two glasses. 'Thanks for the wine, by the way, it's just what I need.' She just hoped her baby wouldn't be born an alcoholic.

'Well, if I hadn't opened my big mouth,' Cindy took a large gulp of wine, 'none of this would have happened. I had thought of keeping it a secret, but... you know... I wanted to protect you.'

'Yes, I know you did.' They continued their conversation with Jane recounting in general terms how Robert had forgiven her for her outrageous accusation. 'I'm feeling better already,' she said, cleverly masking the fact that she was only taking tiny sips from her glass.

'Yes, and so am I,' laughed Cindy taking another large swig from her refilled glass. 'Oh, before I forget, you know Susie is having this girl Bella for a sleepover this coming weekend, and Gilly is coming too.'

Jane nodded.

'Well, it's changed. Bella's coming on Saturday morning instead of Friday evening.'

'Okay, thanks for telling me. This girl, Bella, seems very nice, doesn't she?'

'Yes, she does. She's also very rich. Her father is some big shot in the government.'

'Oh, that explains it. When Susie and Gilly were at Bella's house, Gilly told us about how fantastic it was with its own pool, spa and tennis courts.'

'Yes, how the other half live, eh? Anyhow, back to Kabara. I'm pleased you've sorted everything out. When Gregg goes away on business, I'm sure he gets up to all sorts of things – including women.'

'Don't you mind?' As Kath had already warned her about the Bond's sexual habits, this came as no surprise.

'Well,' Cindy hesitated for a moment before continuing, the consumption of wine already loosening her tongue, 'me and Gregg… ooh sorry, Gregg and I,' she giggled, 'have an arrangement.'

'Oh? What sort of arrangement?'

Cindy hesitated once again before giving Jane a cheeky grin. 'Tell me, Jane, if you're out and you see a real hunk, you know, a great-looking guy, do you think… wuurrhh, I wouldn't mind trying him out?'

'By trying him out,' Jane laughed, 'you mean making love to him.'

'No, no, no, not love. Love has nothing to do with it. It's lust… it's sex… pure unadulterated sex. I save all my love for my husband.'

'So, you separate sex from love.'

'Of course. That's what I'm getting at. Wanting to have sex with a man needn't have anything to do with love.'

'Well, we… err, that's Robert and I… don't.'

'Don't what?'

'You know. Separate sex from love. We only have sex with each other.'

'Ah, well, you're newlyweds of course. But you know what I mean about great-looking guys and fancying them rotten.'

'Yes, I know what you mean.' All this talk about sex was starting to have an effect on her, and the image of Gregg kept appearing in her mind.

'You must have fancied some of the men you went out with when you were an escort.'

The conversation was starting to get personal and Jane knew she had to be careful… her sordid past had to remain in the past. 'Whether I fancied them or not didn't come into it,' she lied.

'Oh, poor you.'

'Anyhow,' Jane wondered just how open Cindy would be, 'what's this so called arrangement you have with Gregg?'

'Promise not to tell anyone,' Cindy giggled.

'I promise.'

'Well, it's like this. If Gregg meets a woman and has one of those wuurrhh moments, you know, then they have sex together.'

'Wow, the naughty boy,' Jane giggled. 'And don't you mind?'

By now the girlish laughter was getting to them both.

'No,' smirked Cindy, 'because I have the wuurrhh moments myself – with other blokes.'

'Isn't that a bit dangerous?'

'No, not at all. We trust each other. We never have affairs as such, just the occasional one-nighters. It does wonders to spice up our sex lives. And let's face it – there's not too much excitement out here, is there?'

'I'm not really looking for that kind of excitement. I love living here… in this compound, and having friends like you and Gregg.' She was determined not to concede that she fancied Gregg. That can of worms had to stay firmly closed.

Whether it was the drink or the fact that their intimate private lives had now been revealed, Cindy was determined not to leave things there. 'Tell me, oh monogamous one, what did Robert's sister look like?'

'What do you mean?'

'You know, the sister in Robert's bedroom in Kabara… was she a looker?'

'Oh, I see what you mean. I didn't take much notice.'

'Oh, come on now. At first, you thought she was Robert's girlfriend, so you must have checked her out.'

'She was okay, I guess. Young and nicely dressed.'

'Did she have a nice figure or was she fat?'

'I'm not sure. She wasn't fat though.' Jane thought back to the encounter and something suddenly registered with her. Something she must have dragged up from her sub conscious. 'Yes, I do remember something about her. She had to walk past me when she left the room and she didn't have VPL.'

'VPL. What on earth is that?'

Jane laughed. 'Oh it's one of Poppy's expressions. I told you about Poppy, didn't I? She's my best friend back home. VPL stands for "visible panty line". You know if you're wearing a tight dress and the outline of your pants can be seen through it, then that's VPL.'

'I haven't heard that one before,' laughed Cindy, taking another drink. 'Have I got VPL?' she stood for Jane to examine her.

'Yes,' Jane's childish giggling increasing by the minute, 'but with you I think it's VTL – Visible Thong Line.'

They both laughed raucously at their silly conversation, and Jane poured more wine into Cindy's glass.

'I may have VTL,' continued Cindy, obviously relishing their smutty talk, 'but I don't have VBL, do I?' She unsteadily stood up holding onto her chair for support, shaking her bosom at Jane. 'I don't have a 'visible bra line' because I'm not wearing one.

This made them laugh even harder, and Jane could feel her mascara start to run. 'Fanny... err sorry... fancy some more wine?'

'Better not,' Cindy kept laughing and continued to shake her bosom. 'It's too hot to wear bras in this heat. In fact it's too hot to wear anything at all.'

'That would be a sure way of attracting every man in the compound,' Jane laughed. 'But doesn't gravity work with you? Your boobs don't seem to sag very much.'

'Aha, and there's another of my secrets. I've had them fixed.'

'You mean implants?'

'Oh no, my boobs are naturally enormous,' Cindy put on a very self-satisfied smile, 'I've just had them fixed.'

'Fixed?'

'Just tightened up so they don't sag. After two kids and a sex-mad husband who won't leave them alone, I had some minor plastic surgery and – hey presto – I've got teenager's tits.' This last remark made them both laugh even harder, with Jane having to wipe the tears on her face.

Jane wondered what other juicy bits of information were going to be revealed by her drunken friend, but Cindy decided she must try and stagger home before she became completely legless. It wasn't even noon yet.

Before leaving, Cindy put her finger to her lips. 'Ssh, promise to keep it all secret.'

'Of course I will,' Jane lied through her teeth. She'd tell Robert the moment he got home from work... just in case he was a wuurrhh on Cindy's lust list.

CHAPTER TWENTY-ONE

Robert went round to f-Fearless' office at the Water Department to check on how he was progressing with the task Robert had set him on Ogola's water and sewer system. Although he'd been in regular phone contact with him, Robert was shocked to see his friend's harassed and unkempt appearance as he shuffled piles of grubby-thumbed paper and manuals around his desk in a totally disorganised manner. His heart sank. With great difficulty, he put on a confident tone. 'How's it going, Jimmy?'

'Well… yes, I'm… err g-getting close. Still some p-papers to c-come from Zanga, but I think we're almost th-there.' His stuttering was worse. His normal, lazy, laid-back attitude had had a rude awakening. A relatively simple task that most sanitary engineers would have completed within a couple of weeks had stretched him beyond his diminished capabilities.

'I'm up against a deadline here, Jimmy, so we'll have to get a move on. I'll tell you what, bring what you've got to Ogola tomorrow morning and I'll ask Ken and Jane to help with getting everything you still need from Zanga.'

'Yes, that's a good idea.' This was a relief for Jimmy, partly because he knew he needed help and also because Jane might dampen down any tension between them if he failed to complete the job.

Although Robert had warned Jane that f-Fearless seemed to be getting close to a breakdown, she was still shocked at his appearance when he arrived at Ken's office with Robert. The cliché death warmed up and gone cold again was certainly appropriate. His pallor was grey, his hair looked as if it hadn't been washed for weeks, and his shaking hands were almost as bad as old Mr

Tompkins who'd lived two doors away in Ringwood, and who suffered from Parkinson's disease.

'Hello, Jimmy,' she forced a cheery smile and tried not to show how alarmed she felt. 'I'd like you to meet Ken Kasansa – he's the boss here and may be able to help.' Robert had already told Ken the reason for Jimmy's visit.

After studying Jimmy's papers for a couple of hours, and asking a lot of questions to which Jimmy only gave incomplete replies, Ken, pulling a face of frustration in Robert's direction, prepared a list of what he thought was still required from Zanga. He then arranged that he, Jimmy and Jane would visit Zanga's site office to see their chief engineer, Motu. Due to Robert's previous bad experience with Zanga, Ken thought it advisable for him not to go.

It was obvious to Jane that relations between Ken and Motu were not good, and Motu objected to the extra work Jimmy wanted him to do. In the original agreement, all Zanga had to do was preliminary drawings for the Water Department which meant that shoddy work would have been okay. When Ken told Motu that Jane was doing an investigation for the BBC (he purposely left out the letter 'N'), and would be reporting back to London, the tone of the meeting suddenly changed. Politics in Buzamba were such that there were always people ready to stab you in the back if you became foul of the press – especially the international press and especially the BBC, so Motu knew he couldn't palm them off with rubbish. After another heated discussion between Ken and Motu, with an anxious Jimmy only adding his pennyworth when asked directly, and Jane taking notes like a professional reporter, it was agreed that Ken and Jimmy would meet with Motu the following Monday to put finishing touches to DGA's demands.

After enjoying what had become a traditional Kimber Saturday morning breakfast, cooked by Robert but washed up by Sellie, Gilly went to pack her bag for her sleepover at Susie's. In fact, it was more than a sleepover as she'd also be staying for lunch and dinner. Even though she was a regular visitor at the Bonds', she was still excited about going, especially as her school friend, Bella, would be there as well. Susie had been friends with Bella for a couple of years and now that Gilly had arrived, the three of them had a firm friendship.

When the front doorbell rang Jane and Robert were in the bedroom so Sellie answered it.

'Who is it, Sellie?' Jane asked as she came into the living room.

'It K.K. Machuri, Madam,' Sellie using the same guttural tone as when she wanted to frighten people with her juju powers.

'Oh, don't be so... oh... oh, it is...'

Standing in the doorway, wearing mirror lens sunglasses, was her worst nightmare. The very man who triggered off all the unrest in Ogola, the owner of City Pharmacy where they'd found Dieter's stolen drugs, and the very man she'd come face to face with just five days earlier during the raid. Her heart pounded so hard it felt as if it would burst out of her chest; she almost collapsed. So many wild thoughts flashed through her brain. Had he come looking for his retribution for what she'd done? All she wanted to do was scream and run away as quickly as she could. Looking out to the front, she could see a large black limousine parked in front of a pickup truck with armed soldiers sitting in the rear.

'Are you Mrs Bond?' he asked, confused by the look of alarm on her face.

'Err... Mrs Bond. Oh! You mean Mrs Bond.'

'Yes, that's right, are you Mrs Bond?' His look was now more confused than before. Doesn't this *mzungu* woman with the scar know if she's Mrs Bond or not?

Before Jane could reply and before K.K. Machuri could quite remember where he'd seen this scarred white woman before, Gilly came rushing up to the door.

'Hello, Uncle Mack,' she gave an excited laugh as she ran right up to him.

'Hello, Gilly.' He smiled, and immediately bent and picked her up with one arm and gave her a kiss on the cheek. 'Is this your house?'

'Yes. Is Bella with you?' Without waiting for his reply, Gilly said that Susie lived just down the road and she'd show him the way.

'Thank you, Gilly, yes, you can show me the way.' He then turned to Jane, the curiosity getting the better of him. 'We've met before, I think, haven't we?'

Jane nodded. Her 'yes' came out as a quiet squeak.

'I thought so. At my pharmacy?'

Again Jane answered with a nervous 'yes'.

'Mrs…?'

'Kimber.'

'Ah, yes. Mrs Kimber, the… err… BBC reporter.'

She was too stunned to think of sensible reply, so said nothing. Gilly was starting to squirm with impatience.

'Do I have your permission, Mrs Kimber,' his voice was very composed, 'to take Gilly with me and Bella to Mrs Bond's house?'

All through this episode, he was very calm – nothing like his rant last Monday at the pharmacy – and if she'd known nothing about him before, she'd think him an extremely nice gentleman. Gilly certainly thought he was special. Uncle Mack, indeed. 'Yes, of course.' She gave Gilly a kiss and told her to be good.

As he was about to lead Gilly to his limousine, he said, with what Jane thought a slight hint of menace, 'we'll meet again, Mrs Kimber.'

'Yes,' a totally bewildered Jane replied to the retreating villain who was firmly holding her daughter's hand as they walked down the drive.

'Who was that?' Robert asked as he came into the living room. 'God, what's the matter? You look as if you've seen a ghost.'

'Worse than a ghost… it was K. K. Machuri at the door.'

'What! You're kidding. Are you sure?'

'Oh, I'm sure all right. Bloody sure. He's just gone with Gilly to the Bonds' house.' She suddenly had a horrible thought. 'Oh,

Sellie. Please run and see where he's taken Gilly. Hurry please. You as well,' she said to a bemused Robert, 'make sure he's not abducted our daughter.'

Sellie immediately ran out of the house to see where Machuri's limousine had gone, while Robert took hold of Jane as if she'd suddenly flipped her lid. 'What are you talking about. Machuri wouldn't come here and take Gilly.'

Ignoring Robert for a moment, she went down the drive and saw Sellie coming back.

'It all right. I see him take Gilly and his little girl to Mrs Bond's house. They ran inside laughing. They okay.'

'Oh, my God. It was Machuri, wasn't it, Sellie?'

'It him..'

'He's Bella's father,' Jane said. 'Can you believe it? He came to the house looking for Cindy... he didn't recognise me at first... but then he did. Gilly called him Uncle Mack and rushed up to him to be picked up. Can you believe it?'

'I'd better go and see Cindy straight away,' Robert hurried out of the house, his worried expression showing his anxiety.

Without realising it, Jane reached for Sellie's hand. 'You know all the trouble we've had... I've had with Machuri. Will Gilly be all right?'

'I think it okay, Madam. What K.K. do as a father is not the same as his business. He not do anything bad to Gilly. That not our way in Buzamba.'

With that reassurance, Jane didn't know whether to laugh or cry. Laugh because of the unbelievable coincidence that fate continued to throw at her, and cry because now her daughter was somewhat involved with this evil man.

A breathless Robert rushed back saying everything was calm at the Bonds'. Gilly, Susie and Bella were already getting ready to go to the pool with Gregg and Cindy, and Machuri plus his bodyguard had gone. 'He'd told Cindy he would be back tomorrow afternoon.' He flopped down on the nearest chair. 'I need a drink, a strong one.'

The weeks leading up to Christmas in Basu compound were the time of soirées and dinners for the adults and swimming parties, fairy lights, and games for the children. On two consecutive evenings Jane and Robert, together with other expats, were invited to soirées given first by Mona and Aaron Toko and then by Jewel and Frank Cooper. Although Cindy had told them about the amazing spreads put on in previous years, they were still astonished by the extravagance of both couples. Noticeable by their absence were Cindy and Gregg who were in a production of Cinderella, put on by the Amateur Dramatic Society; and Josie and Lester who had found better things to do.

Jane was completely taken aback when the door was opened by the Tokos who, adopting an Egyptian theme, were dressed in pseudo-Tutankhamen gowns with gold lamé headdresses. Their stewards, looking rather uncomfortable, were dressed as Egyptian slaves.

'The bloody slave trade continues,' Quentin whispered mischievously, crumbs on his shirt giving away that he'd already been to the buffet. 'Who the hell do they think they're trying to impress? Pity Gregg and Cindy can't be here to join in the fun – but that's showbiz!'

'Are you and Kath going to see them in the pantomime?' Robert asked.

Quentin gave him an open-mouthed grimace. 'You must be joking, old man. I'd rather be castrated by a syphilitic hyena than watch that rabble of frustrated thespians prance and screech for hours on end.'

The next soirée was at the Coopers', who had decided, not very originally, to adopt the Christmas story for their party. 'There's a novelty,' Quentin's sarcasm was clear. 'From Egypt to the Holy Land in twenty-four hours. Not even Moses did it that quick.'

'Don't be horrid, Quentin,' Jane gently admonished him with a smile, but thinking how over the top it all was.

Deafening Christmas carols blared from the stereo system, effectively stopping any conversation. Frank was dressed as Father Christmas complete with beard and sack of presents, and Jewel, in a very fetching Christmas Fairy outfit, was handing out gifts to the guests: designer leather evening bags for the ladies and Pierre Cardin wallets for the men. They must have thought they had scored one-up on the Tokos!

'Bloody childish nonsense,' Quentin contemptuously remarked to Jane. 'And if you want to know where all the aid money goes, well a lot of it goes towards buying ridiculous presents for the rich bourgeoisie of Buzamba. You can be one hundred per cent certain it didn't come out of Frank's pocket.'

Apart from the different theme, the two soirées were more or less carbon copies of each other, except that Hans Schulz was at the Coopers' which cheered Robert up no end. Hans had been ordered to attend the party by his ambassador (who avoided these events like the plague) but left as soon as diplomatic etiquette allowed. This gave Jane and Robert their opportunity to leave early, giving the impression that Gilly wasn't too well.

'You liars,' Quentin laughed as they left. 'See you both on Saturday at our place, that's if Gilly's better, but you'll get no presents from us!'

A few days before their annual six weeks' leave in South Africa, Quentin and Kath held the third drinks party of the week. There was no 'theme', Egyptian or otherwise, although carols from King's College, Cambridge, as well as a Bing Crosby selection, were played as a gesture to the Christmas season. The guests were all from Basu compound and although the Tokos failed to turn up, Frank and Jewel Cooper put in an appearance.

Loudly proclaiming his views covering every subject from the crisis in Afghanistan to the mess into which South Africa was rapidly declining, Quentin was in one of his more vociferous moods. He burst into song whenever he recognised a carol and Kath had to restrain him when his version belonged more to schoolboy humour than to *The Ancient and Modern Hymn Book*. She was even more concerned when Quentin put his arm round Jewel Cooper's shoulders encouraging her to join him in singing *I'm Dreaming of a White Christmas*. Jewel recoiled from his embrace but Frank, with a beaming smile, joined in the singing, later telling Quentin that it was his favourite carol; no one had the heart to tell him it was only a song.

Making a face in Josie's direction, Jane remarked that Quentin was not being very PC tonight. 'Poor Jewel looked quite embarrassed.'

Josie agreed. 'Quentin gets away with things that most people wouldn't. I don't know how he does it.'

'Yet Frank said *White Christmas* was his favourite – a bit odd isn't it?'

'Probably not as odd as you may think. Many black people believe that when they die they will become white.'

'You're kidding!'

'No, not if they're Christians. I've heard it's because in religious pictures, angels are always white, and when people die they become angels… or something like that.'

Jane was quiet for a moment. 'Do you think many black people would prefer to be white… you know, if they could choose.'

'Yes, I'm pretty certain of it. A bit sad though isn't it?'

Remembering what Ken had said about black people having a chip on their shoulder dating back to colonial times, Jane thought it might be true. Sellie had also commented that black people expected the foreigners to sort out their problems. 'But not Cindy though. I'm sure she's happy being black and that her girls brown,' Jane whispered.

'You know, Jane, Buzamba joins many other African countries in celebrating the Black Awareness Movement, while every street hawker sells skin-lightening cream. So, there's your answer.'

'And just look at Michael Jackson,' Jane laughed. 'He went whiter than white.'

Whether or not it was Quentin's overpowering domination of the conversation, his voice getting louder the more he imbibed, many of the guests, including the Coopers, began leaving at ten o'clock.

Quentin didn't seem to mind. 'Ah, just the hard core left – maybe I offended someone… again.' He gave the remaining company one of his boyish grins. 'The big drinkers. Come on lovely Josie, let me refill your glass. Do you think I upset anyone?'

Getting worried, Kath wished Quentin would stop drinking, anything could happen when he was drunk.

'Maybe the *White Christmas* rendition didn't go down well with everyone.' Josie was also getting irritated with his over-the-top behaviour.

'Ah,' Quentin sighed, 'maybe you're right. But when people talk about racism, they don't really mean bigotry between different races, what they really mean is colour prejudice – especially white against black.'

'Someone talking about me again?' Cindy and Gregg walked into the room having just finished their last pantomime performance.

'Not at all, dear lady, not at all. It's just that Frank and I sang a beautiful duet to *I'm Dreaming of a White Christmas* and some people here,' he paused and looked round, 'thought I was... err... it was... somewhat demeaning to black people.'

'Oh, heaven forbid,' Cindy mocked bitterly. 'Whatever gave them that idea? Anyone would think you were a racist Quentin, and that would never do.'

Kath couldn't stand it any more. While she privately shared her husband's views and both had been supporters of Apartheid, she knew Quentin was at the point where he was saying too much and would cause offence. 'I don't think we should go any further down that route, darling,' she warned him.

Cindy wasn't so easily mollified. 'Oh, I don't know Kath. I'm always keen to hear your views on why we blacks are inferior to the patronising white races.'

'Now Cindy, you know that isn't the case.' Quentin rose to Cindy's bait and ignored his wife's warning. 'Just before you arrived the subject of race didn't arise, and... I don't know what the definition of a racist is. Do you? As I've told you before, I'm not keen on the Germans for the atrocities they committed during the Second World War and the fact that my grandfather died in one of their prison of war camps. So does it make me a racist to say I don't like the Germans?'

'You know very well that's not what we're talking about,' Cindy angrily responded. 'It's nothing to do with the Germans, the fact is you don't like blacks.'

Kath tried once more to stop this discussion which was rapidly turning into a dangerous confrontation, but Quentin shrugged off her attempts to stop him.

'You're wrong, Cindy, my dear, I do like black people. I like a lot of blacks very much. I wouldn't be here in Buzamba if I didn't. More to the point, I like you Cindy, I think you're terrific.'

Coming straight from the pantomime, Cindy was still in theatrical mode and putting her hand over her bosom, she feigned an attack of the vapours. 'Oh, Quentin, at last I've found my true love. Take me away from all this to a romantic love nest and we will be together forever.'

By this time, the remaining guests had gathered around listening to what was becoming a heated exchange.

A smiling Quentin looked in Gregg's direction. 'I think your husband might have something to say about that, my dear.'

'And so might I,' Kath added, looking more relaxed now that humour had replaced confrontation.

But Quentin just couldn't keep his mouth shut. 'My point about the disparity between people of different colour is that the European and Asian races manage to prosper using their own efforts, whereas the black races don't. That's why tens of thousands of European and Asian workers are in Africa supported by money given by the West.'

After listening to this latest slur, Cindy's sense of humour vanished. 'That's all bollocks and well you know it. The whites imposed slavery and colonial rule to exploit the African people and the resources of this continent, to make themselves rich and us poor. Don't forget, Quentin,' and then copying his patronising phrase, '... my dear', I'm a descendant of the slave trade myself.'

'That's enough.' Kath shouted finally to put an end to this verbal altercation. 'I insist everyone,' she glared at her husband, 'and I mean everyone, change the subject. We love you too much to fall out and we want to stay friends with you all. So please...

there's plenty of food and drink and...' she struggled to finish her sentence, '...we're coming up to Christmas, remember... peace and goodwill to all men... and women.'

Now that calm had been restored, the audience broke up into various groups and, as a show of solidarity with Cindy, Jane went and put her arm around her and gave her a kiss on her cheek. 'Good for you. Quentin needed a kick up the bum, and you, my dear, did just that.' Robert also threw caution to the wind and gave her a hug.

'Well, thank you kind people, I appreciate your support. But don't worry, Quentin and I have had these ding dongs many times before. I know he's a racist but there are worse, if you see what I mean.'

Neither Jane nor Robert was sure what she meant, but were pleased that she didn't seem to hold any grudges against the McKeevers.

The Kimbers, Bonds, Pennicotts and many others stayed for another couple of hours enjoying the plentiful food and drink. This was particularly appreciated by Cindy and Gregg who were both famished and thirsty after their final pantomime performance.

'By the way you two, what are you doing for Christmas?' Gregg asked Jane and Robert as he wiped some crumbs from his mouth.

'Nothing special,' Robert replied. 'We thought we'd spend some quality leisure time around the house and the pool.'

'Why don't you join us at InterBank's villas at Lake Arthur. The company owns two villas in the grounds of the Lake Resort Hotel and they're both free. It's beautiful there and the girls love the place, and they'd like it even more if Gilly was with them.'

Robert looked at Jane. 'What do you think?'

Jane explained that she didn't want to leave Kaba so soon after she'd come to live with them, but Gregg assured her that it wasn't a problem because separate accommodation was provided for domestic staff. They themselves were taking their steward and there would be plenty of room for Sellie and Kaba. They planned to drive up on Christmas Eve and stay until the 29th. It was about a five or six hour journey and the town of Lasutu, roughly halfway, had a local restaurant which served a good lunch and, more importantly, the toilets were clean. Jane thought it was a great idea and said she'd speak to Sellie.

'And I promise not to let my silly husband do his usual nonsense on the way there.' Cindy gave Gregg one of her well-practised stern looks.

'And that is…?'

'He stops in every village that has a hardware store and, pathetically trying to mimic Ronnie Barker, he asks for four candles.'

'Oh, I think I can guess what comes next,' Robert laughed.

'You're right, and don't laugh at him, Robert. He stands and watches the poor shopkeeper open a large packet of candles and put four on the counter, and then he says 'no, fork handles… handles for forks. You know the sketch, don't you?'

'Yes, it's funny when the Two Ronnies did it, but I doubt if any of the locals would see the funny side of it,' Jane said. 'Why do you do it, Gregg?'

'It's hilarious… don't you think?'

'In a sad childish way, but all you're doing is taking the piss. I agree with Cindy on this one.'

Gregg looked downcast and looked to Robert for support. Surely he would see the funny side.

After seeing the glares from Cindy and Jane, Robert shrugged his shoulders and said, 'no comment, mate… I've got my shins to worry about.'

Leaving the McKeevers, they wished a now much calmer Quentin and Kath a wonderful holiday in South Africa and looked forward to a reunion in the New Year. They all received kisses from Kath and firm handshakes from Quentin. As Cindy turned her back to leave, Quentin cheekily gave her a quick kiss on her lips. 'I do love you, you know,' he said.

'Yes, I know you do, Quentin,' Cindy smiled, 'and I love you too.'

Racial harmony had triumphed. Thank God for that, Jane smiled to herself. What a strange couple they are.

That weekend, the Kimbers and the Bonds arranged their Christmas holiday at Lake Arthur. Gregg had to be back in his office no later than the 29th but, as Robert had no such constraints, their return was left open. And this Christmas adventure also included the Kimbers' extended family: Sellie, Kaba and Basil, who wouldn't be doing any chores because both villas came with staff. It would be a holiday for everyone.

During their discussion, and after the three girls had gone out to play, Jane announced, with great fanfare, the news that she was pregnant.

Cindy laughed. 'I already knew. I can recognise pregnancy at a thousand paces. Gregg didn't believe me but I knew. By the way, who's the father?'

They all turned to Robert who looked self-conscious. 'Oh, ha, ha!'

'Congratulations both of you... and to the father,' Cindy laughed, and with that she gave them a huge embrace and kisses which, to her great amusement, made Robert feel uncomfortable and, he hated to admit, a bit randy. Had she meant to let her stray hand caress his crotch, or was it an accident? After all, he was only human, and which man wouldn't fancy screwing the luscious Cindy. But no – no way! He wouldn't risk a lustful fling to jeopardise what he had now.

Being more restrained, Gregg planted a polite kiss on Jane's cheek, shook Robert's hand and, at the same time, gave him a wink saying he would give him a kiss later.

Cindy asked the usual questions about when it was due, where it would be born, which doctor, and did they want a boy or girl? She thought it was great that Jane planned to have the baby in Ouverru and promised all her support.

When they were alone, a worried Robert asked if Jane thought the Bonds might try something on with them at Lake Arthur.

'What do you mean?'

'You know what I mean – wife swapping. We'll be together for several days and they may think we're... err...'

'Err what?'

'Well, up for it.'

'Well, hello Dumbo, look at me… pregnant.' And then after a few seconds she added, 'Are you 'up for it' then? With Cindy.'

'No, of course not. Don't be silly,' he retorted probably a little too quickly.

'Well, there you are then,' Jane said not noticing Robert's shamefaced appearance. 'I'm sure they'll reserve their sexual adventures for people with similar interests, and we, my faithful husband, are not that way inclined.' Even when she said it to reassure Robert, deep down, she found the idea of an intimate relationship with Gregg extremely exciting.

On the home front, Kaba was settling in well with Sellie. She was very happy when, three days before they were due to go on holiday, the hospital nurse took the final dressing off her hand and gave her the all clear. Naturally, she was allowed to play in the garden with Gilly and the Bond girls, but it was occasionally difficult for her because she couldn't understand what they were saying. Once, she ran to Sellie in floods of tears, only to receive abrasive words telling her to go back and play. Sellie's unsympathetic response put an end to her tears and Sellie later told Jane that Kaba had to be tough if she was to survive in the foreign community in Buzamba.

While they were packing to go away, Sellie handed Jane a piece of paper. On it she'd written the date she and Kaba had chosen for their birthdays; they had both picked July 1st, when Sellie would be twenty-three and Kaba eight. Jane promised a party for them but didn't reveal that her baby was due around the same time. Well, if she couldn't arrange the party, Robert would have to.

CHAPTER TWENTY-TWO

There was a palpable sense of excitement as the Kimbers, with Sellie and Kaba, left Ouverru for their first African holiday. The infectious mood even got to Basil who, at the wheel, couldn't suppress his wide grin as he followed closely behind the Bond family in Gregg's Toyota Land Cruiser. The first few miles of road were in reasonable condition with an asphalt surface, albeit eaten away at the edges, but there were also sections studded with deep potholes which slowed them down to a snail's pace. Other segments were unpaved and made up of graded laterite. Repair gangs were usually working at regular intervals along the route but all maintenance had stopped for Christmas. Drums of asphalt, heavy rollers, trucks, generators and other equipment were parked haphazardly at each side.

As the road took them further away from the capital, the number of buildings, shops and shacks diminished. Recent rains had created a rich variety of greens and, in parts, the countryside had rolling hills not dissimilar to Dorset and Devon, whilst other areas were heavily wooded and tropical. It wasn't at all like the vast open plains, teaming with herds of wildebeest and other wildlife that Jane had seen in films about Kenya and Tanzania. She couldn't help but feel a bit disappointed.

Although the landscape had not quite lived up to her expectations, one of the first things that struck her was the difference in flora compared to England. Between areas of palm, eucalyptus and papyrus swamps, were cultivated fields of tea, maize, coffee and bananas. It was so wonderfully foreign – so exotically tropical. Every so often, they passed small roadside markets where tomatoes, onions, sweet potato and unusual-looking fruit and vegetables were neatly stacked in pyramids on small trestle tables. Other stalls sold varieties of cooking pots, hardware, recycled engine oil and second-hand clothes. The market women called out to sell their wares, accompanied by loud background African music from what looked like mini ghetto blasters. Women and girls carrying bundles of firewood on their heads shimmied along in time to the music, while men and boys used bicycles to carry huge hands of green *matooke* bananas and jerrycans. In Buzamba, the bicycle had become the modern beast of burden.

Gilly was thrilled when little children with smiling faces waved, and she frantically waved back. Sellie and Kaba ignored them. Robert pointed out occasional mobile phone beacons, all of them solar powered. 'That's why the system works so well here – impressive isn't it?'

It seemed that around almost every bend, something different was happening. The few vehicles they saw were mainly pickups, small trucks and *mutatas*, which were overloaded with sacks of maize and rice, cartons of tinned fish and vegetable oil, as well as green bananas. Buses were crammed full of people, laughing and shouting with boxes, packages and even live chickens filling the roof racks. Looking dangerously overcrowded, they struggled manfully up the slightest incline, resulting in clouds of black, noxious smoke billowing out of the exhausts.

'They go home for Christmas,' Sellie stated the patently obvious. 'They take plenty food. Tomorrow, people eat and drink too, too much,' she laughed.

'It's the same in England,' Jane added. 'Everyone wants to be with family for Christmas. What about the people in Ogola, will they go home?'

'Some maybe, not many. Transport cost too much. In the village, if they take no food and beer, they be too ashamed.'

'When are we going to see the wild animals?' Gilly butted in after she'd been patiently staring out of the window looking for signs of African wildlife.

'Not here, Gilly,' Sellie answered, 'maybe few monkeys or baboons. Big, big animals – they stay in game park where people not kill them.' She laughed again. 'That is… people who obey the law.'

'Does that mean some people still go hunting?' Jane asked.

'There few, Madam. In civil war, soldiers kill everything.'

'But I heard that animal numbers are increasing. Is that right?'

'I think so. Park wardens shoot poachers if they catch them.'
Sellie laughed again. 'The wardens have better guns than poachers.'

'So which animals will we see at Lake Arthur?'

'There two game parks near the lake but people must pay to go inside. Buzamba not have animals like Kenya. I think there be antelope, plenty warthogs, plenty hippos, and maybe elephant.'

'Can we see the elephants, Daddy?' Gilly asked excitedly.

Just then, their little convoy reached Lasutu, the halfway point of their journey, which, for the time being, took Gilly's mind off her hope of seeing elephants. Gregg led them down a dusty side road and after fifty yards they came to the Lasutu Hotel. They stretched their legs and made full use of the (not very clean) washrooms before sitting on the veranda. Jane insisted that all the staff join them at their table; she was still uncomfortable with the servant/master relationship and thought that being away from their home environment was a good opportunity to do away with these barriers.

Isaac, Basil, Sellie and Kaba chose the meat stew, a thick soup full of chunks of meat and dark green vegetables, served in deep bowls. This was obviously their favourite and they noisily soaked up the last of the liquid with chunks of bread. The three girls had pizzas while their parents satisfied themselves with sandwiches. They all felt rested, well fed and watered for the second leg of their journey.

'Hey, Gregg,' Jane said, 'about half an hour before we arrived here, we saw what appeared to be a large factory over on the right-hand side. Did you see it? Robert wasn't sure what it was.'

'I know the one you mean. It was a Scandinavian pulp-paper scheme, which, like so many other wonderful schemes, went belly up a few years ago; the Swedes planted a whole forest, built the factory, imported machinery and recruited staff.

'So what went wrong?'

'One of the President's family wanted half the business and produced papers showing he owned the land. I saw the papers because our bank was involved. The papers were fakes – poor fakes at that, but the court decided they were genuine.'

'Huh, surprise, surprise,' Robert gave a hollow laugh.

'The real owner, who had already been paid, had left the country. After a protracted saga involving the Swedish and Finnish

Embassies, the Scandinavians more or less said 'sod you' and walked away.'

'So what happens now?' Jane asked.

'Nothing. The building will gradually crumble and will be yet another pathetic reminder of the dozens of projects which were started with great wads of foreign aid and goodwill which have collapsed. Africa is littered with part-built factories, housing, clinics, schools and farms which were never finished. Welcome to Africa!'

As they were leaving the restaurant, Cindy noticed a man eating alone at the far end of the veranda. 'Hold on a second Gregg, I think I know him.'

As Cindy drew near, the man stood and they shook hands. After speaking for a few moments, Cindy waved for them all to come and join them.

'This is Tom Smith from ESSA... you know, Education for Sub-Saharan Africa. I met Tom when I worked for Frank Cooper. He's some sort of education expert... isn't that right, Tom?'

He explained that he was a consultant on a technical assistance programme sponsored by the British Department for International Development. 'That's DfID to you and me,' he said. He was on secondment to the Education Ministry assisting with the Rural Education Programme under the auspices of ESSA. His task was to tour the country to inspect government schools outside the eight main urban centres and make recommendations for additional school building and teacher training.

'That sounds an interesting job,' Gregg said. 'How's it going?'

Tom gave a disconsolate shrug. 'It's all a bit... err... disheartening.'

'Oh dear, that sounds bad. Are you out here alone?'

He explained that he led a team of four, the other members being a Ghanaian and two Kenyans, but they had gone to their home countries for the Christmas holidays.

'Are you on your own for Christmas then?' a concerned Cindy asked.

Tom's shoulders slumped. He was staying in Lasutu so that he could write up his report as far as possible before his team returned. He had thought of going to Ouverru but didn't know anyone there and preferred staying in the peace and quiet of the countryside. He also planned to take full advantage of his hobby, photography.

'You can't be alone at Christmas,' Cindy chided, 'come and stay with us at Lake Arthur. We can make room, can't we Gregg? There may be a vacancy in the hotel.'

The idea didn't appeal to Gregg in the slightest but he knew he couldn't object and, although Tom assured them that he didn't mind being on his own, Cindy wouldn't hear of it. So he gratefully accepted and followed them to Lake Arthur in his vehicle.

For the second leg of the journey, the road was unmade and very rough, taking much longer than expected. At half past six, just as the sun was setting, they pulled up at their destination. Gregg collected the keys for their villas and Basil, Sellie, Kaba and Isaac were shown to their accommodation at the rear of the hotel. Tom was able to get a room because the hotel was unusually empty.

In the twilight, Jane saw what appeared to be two large dogs slowly walking in their direction, holding their heads down like grazing cattle. 'What are they?' she said with a note of alarm in her voice.

'They warthogs, Madam,' Sellie gave a soft laugh.

'Are they safe?'

'You leave they alone, they leave you alone,' Sellie added. 'Don't go close, don't feed them, they eat grass.'

As the two animals came closer they could just make out their features. Jane had seen photographs of warthogs but she had imagined them to be bigger – these were only a bit larger than her friend's old Labrador in Ringwood.

'Thanks for that, Sellie, we'll see you in the morning. Not too early, say about half past eleven, and a Merry Christmas to you both.'

'Thank you, Madam… and boss… Merry Christmas.' Sellie gave Jane an envelope containing a card from her and Kaba.

Gilly quickly pulled everything out of her little case, had an amazingly quick wash and, while her parents strolled to the hotel dining room, ran ahead to join the Bonds and Tom Smith.

'Where is everybody?' Gregg looked around at the almost empty dining room, 'I thought it would be heaving by now.'

Apart from one table where nine young, noisy men and women were well into the festivities, all the others were empty.

'This is strange.' Tom was clearly surprised. 'I've stayed here several times and it's always been busy, usually with foreign consultants and NGOs. Maybe they've all gone home for Christmas.'

The waiter who served them explained that fifty-five expats from a big iron ore mine on the eastern border of the country had booked for Christmas and New Year but, because of some violent rebel activity in the region, the women and children had left the country and had, at the last minute, cancelled. The hotel manager was trying to get more guests but it was difficult. Two couples were due to check in the following afternoon but only for five days, and apart from the present company, the hotel would be empty. The crowd at the other table was only having dinner and not staying overnight.

'Well, in a way, it's lucky they're here as it certainly improves the atmosphere,' Jane said looking at the rowdy table. 'They're really knocking back the wine.'

'And look at the prices,' Robert checked the wine list, 'there's nothing under two thousand shillings, and that's just for ordinary French wine. Those people must have a generous expense account.'

'I suggest we stick to local spirits and beer,' Cindy said. 'It's crazy to pay over forty pounds for a bottle of cheap plonk.'

Tom drank beer all evening while the others, except for Jane, plumped for gin. They were tired after their journey and didn't want a large meal so they ordered tilapia, fresh from the lake for themselves, and the three girls had hamburgers and fries.

While they were waiting for their meals, they watched with growing interest the shenanigans at the increasingly noisy table, where alcohol had obviously worked its insidious effect on the group. There were only three young women in the party and it looked as if the six men were competing to see who would end the night with more than a stocking on his bedpost. Trish, Susie and Gilly looked wide-eyed at some of the aggressive flirting and their parents hoped they were too young to understand the competition for sexual favours taking place in front of them.

Just as their meals arrived, the boisterous group got up and hurried outside, the three happy-looking women each having more than one suitor eagerly escorting them through the doorway. A few seconds later they heard the sound of vehicles being revved up and the screech of tires as they headed for their base, wherever that was.

'I wonder who they were?' Jane asked.

'I know them.' Tom had a look of satisfaction on his face. 'They're volunteers from a US Christian charity called WATCH, which works with local people to teach them how to be self-sufficient. And the joke is that Africans have survived through their own self-sufficiency for thousands of years and could teach those young Americans more than they'll ever know.'

'Have you met them before, then?' Cindy asked.

'No, but I've heard of them. And did you see how much wine they drank? I counted eleven empty wine bottles, so with the meals added, I'll bet they must have spent around £1,000 tonight... just for dinner.'

'So much for charity. The collection plates in American churches will need to go round twice to keep those tearaways in food and drink.'

'Actually, as charities go, WATCH seems to be one of the better ones,' Tom said.

'How do you mean?'

'They steer well clear of politics, unlike some of the others. Over the years, I've found several charities have a strong left-wing agenda, but anyone who has studied the recent history of Africa knows that socialism doesn't work here.'

'So, you've come across quite a few charity workers over the years?' Jane asked.

'Yes. There are aid workers with charities and NGOs, who shouldn't be confused with workers on aid projects, who are expats like Robert and me.'

'So how do they differ?'

'I call the charity aid people 'adventurers'. They are usually young single people who are here for the experience, not for the money, unlike we expats who like to be well rewarded.'

'How do you mean – adventurers?'

'Many of them are amazing people. They often live in terrible conditions in dangerous regions and do fantastic things for the poor suffering masses. I take my hat off to them. I've noticed over the years that they seem to get a kick out of danger and discomfort. Strange, isn't it? They seek out the most inhospitable places because, to them, it's an adventure.'

'A bloody dangerous adventure, if you ask me,' Gregg said.

'And that's why they get front page headlines when things go wrong. But in many ways, they're asking for trouble.'

'What sort of trouble?'

'For example, look at those young women in Iraq and Afghanistan. These are countries where men can abuse and even murder their own women with impunity, so why the hell do they choose to go there? Their chances of being raped and murdered are much higher than in non-Muslim countries.'

'So you think it's partly their own fault when things go wrong?'

'Don't you?'

It was Gregg who reintroduced the definition of expatriates. 'So we go back to Quentin's question: are we missionaries or mercenaries? After what Tom's said, I guess we're all in the latter group.'

After dinner, they wandered through the warm scented night to their villas. There was a slight breeze coming off the lake and an amazing clear, starry sky. After the children had gone inside, Cindy and Gregg took the opportunity to give their holiday guests all-embracing Christmas kisses, which included Gregg pressing himself suggestively against Jane and cradling her breast in his sweaty hand, while Cindy's hands were busy caressing Robert. The Bonds' invitation to continue the seasonal festivities once the children were asleep was politely, but firmly rejected.

'Phew! That was a bit much, wasn't it?' Robert took Jane's hand to walk the few yards to their villa.

'Yes, they didn't leave us in any doubt about what they had in mind.' Jane didn't mention Gregg's intimate embrace because... damn it, she'd liked it.

When they went inside, they found Gilly in a tearful mood. It seemed that Trish had told her she wouldn't get any presents because Father Christmas wouldn't know where she was. It took their combined efforts to assure her that they'd already told Father Christmas where she would be.

'But Trish said letters won't get to Lapland from Africa.'

'I think she's teasing you, sweetheart.' Robert was quite touched, seeing her tearful little face.

Gilly sat on Jane's knee and snuggled down into her embrace, wiping the tears from her eyes. There was so much going on in their lives, and Gilly had gained so much confidence since arriving in Buzamba, that Jane had forgotten that her daughter still needed reassurance that she was still the centre of their attention. Last Christmas in England, it had just been the two of them in their cold little house in Ringwood; their only excursion was to the carol service in the Parish Church and to Poppy and Tony's for tea. And now she was in the middle of Africa with a new daddy, new friends and a completely new life.

A tired little smile replaced her tears. They settled her down in bed and left the door open so that she could call them. Within minutes, she was sound asleep which gave them time to put up a small artificial Christmas tree and place her colourfully wrapped presents underneath.

Robert was awake first on Christmas Day morning. He checked his watch and saw it was already eight-fifteen. He lay on his back and gazed at the stained paintwork on the ceiling, which looked as if the roof had leaked during the last wet season – or several wet seasons for that matter. But now the weather was dry and the next rains weren't due until March. He idly wondered if anybody would ever get round to repainting it.

Carefully putting his arm around Jane's shoulders, he turned to watch her gentle breathing as she slept with a contented smile on her face. He thought of his pathetic last Christmas with f-Fearless and some of the other lonely reprobates in Ouverru, whose only thought was to get totally pissed and tell each other silly jokes they'd all heard before. And now his life had changed… dramatically so.

Quietly slipping out of bed, he crept into Gilly's room. She must have sensed him there as she immediately opened her eyes and, after a moment taking in her surroundings, remembered what day it was and jumped out of bed with a look of guarded excitement on her face.

'Has Father Christmas been?' she asked in a little voice, desperately searching Robert's face for a clue.

'I'm not sure,' Robert replied. But even at that young age, Gilly could tell that her daddy already knew and... he had been. 'Let's go and see mummy first.'

Racing into her parents' bedroom, Gilly took a flying leap onto the bed and, if Jane had been asleep, she was certainly awake now.

'Merry Christmas, darling,' Jane said, giving Gilly a big hug and kissing her face all over.

In the living room, Gilly's eyes fixed on the Christmas tree, immediately seeing the presents underneath. She stopped and stood very still, tightly clutching her mummy's and daddy's hands, staring at the mound of presents. She started to cry.

Jane picked her up. 'What's the matter, darling, why are you crying?'

'I thought... err... Trish said Father Christmas didn't know... he... he has been, hasn't he Mummy?'

'Yes, darling, he came when we were all asleep.'

Gilly wiped her eyes, smiled and tentatively started to open her gifts. 'Oh look, she cried out with amazement, there's one here from Auntie Poppy and Uncle Tony. They must have told Father Christmas as well.'

Robert made tea, and they sat on the rickety bamboo sofa watching Gilly's excitement. 'Merry Christmas, husband,' Jane gave him an affectionate kiss to show her thanks for everything he'd brought into her life. Up until six months ago, she didn't believe such men existed.

They took their time getting dressed, enjoying the moment, before strolling over to the hotel for breakfast, skirting past a bunch of warthogs contentedly grazing near their villa. Much to their surprise, the dining room was empty, the waiter informing them the Bonds had already eaten and gone back to their villa. Choosing a table on the veranda with views of the lake, it felt surprisingly fresh and Jane couldn't imagine a more perfect setting for Christmas Day breakfast.

It was great fun when they later joined the Bonds, exchanging season's greetings and noisily opening presents and thanking one another. Nobody wanted to venture far – it was too perfect here – so they stayed in the hotel grounds and walked near the lake to work up an appetite for a special Christmas dinner. Jane again insisted that Basil, Sellie and Kaba should be with them at their table, even though she knew Cindy and Gregg disagreed.

'They'd prefer to be on their own, you know,' Cindy said crossly.

'That may be so, but I want Kaba to start to feel at ease with us, and this is a good opportunity, don't you think?'

Cindy didn't think so, but said nothing.

A hesitant knock on their villa door shortly after eleven o'clock, revealed Sellie and Kaba, looking very smart in matching dresses, sandals and hair bands, smiling uneasily as Robert shepherded them into the room, like two nervous sheep. Jane immediately hugged and kissed them both, while Robert stood awkwardly by, wondering if he should do the same, but deciding not to. Gilly knew which presents were for Sellie and Kaba and this time Kaba accepted the parcel without a desperate grab as she had on the first day they'd met. It was then Kaba's turn to give each of them a present, the labels reading 'Bestest Christmas from Sellie and Kaba'.

Before Gilly could ask what they were, Jane butted in. 'Look Gilly, Sellie and Kaba have made each of us a bookmark. Aren't they nice! They're made from palm leaves. Isn't that right, Sellie?'

Just what a bookmark was, Gilly wasn't sure but she knew she had to look pleased and politely said thank you. Jane told Sellie that dinner would be at five thirty and, after gulping down their glasses of orange juice, they made a quick exit.

Supervised by Isaac, the two Bond girls and Gilly played with their presents while their parents wandered down to the placid lake. December was the best time of year for flowering trees and shrubs, with masses of bougainvillea, hibiscus, and frangipani. There was also the unmistakable jacaranda and bottlebrush trees, yellow-blossomed cassia and the startling red-flowered African Flame Tree. The air was a heady mixture of exotic scents. Several of the taller trees had weaver bird nests precariously attached by only thin strands to the tips of the branches.

'It's so beautiful here,' Jane observed looking around at the kaleidoscope of colours, 'and so peaceful... except for the busy weaver birds,' she laughed. 'Oh look,' she pointed, 'there's even a tree the same as Ogola's famous African Tulip Tree.'

'I wonder if this one flowers all year round and cries?' Robert laughed, enjoying teasing her about her belief that the Ogola Tulip Tree cries for the poor. She ignored his puerile comments.

The morning was overcast but warm, and it wasn't long before the tropical sun forced its way through the clouds, the heat enveloping the four of them sitting on a bench watching local fishing boats paying out their nets in the distance. A flock of ibis, screeching frantically, flew past heading for the far bank of the lake.

'Wow, it's getting hot,' Jane wiped perspiration from her brow, 'I wonder what the weather's like in Ringwood now? I wish Poppy and Tony were here.'

They then noticed Tom Smith, who had set out early with a guide to take photographs of the lake and its surroundings. Now on his way back, he'd paused to take a couple of pictures of them sitting in the sunshine. He checked the screen on his digital camera and seemed satisfied with the results.

'I'll send you copies when I get back to my office. Memories of Christmas at Lake Arthur.'

'Come and sit down, Tom, and tell us about your schools project. Will the British taxpayers be sending more of their hard-earned cash to educate Buzamban children?'

He didn't answer Jane's question directly. 'My problem, which is shared by most consultants, is that I've already been told what my report must say.'

'How do you mean?'

'Before I left UK, two chaps from DfID told me on the quiet that my conclusion must be that more money should be sent to support education in Buzamba, regardless of whether it's needed or not.'

'I still don't understand.' Robert said. 'It doesn't make sense.'

'DfID has to spend its money somehow and, unbelievably, it's only the foreign aid budget that will continue to increase.'

'But, what is the actual situation here? Do they need more money?'

'That's difficult to answer because in most cases, state schooling is lousy and, of course, additional funding could help. But it doesn't work like that. I know that ninety per cent of the money donated will be wasted and end up subsidising the corrupt rich of this country. The money will not improve the kids' education.'

'But your report will still recommend extra funding.'

'Yes. This will satisfy the politicians who can show how much they care.'

'That's no surprise to me,' Cindy said. 'Remember, I used to work for Frank.'

Tom shifted nervously. 'I keep promising myself to tell the truth and send copies of my report to all the newspaper and TV editors so that DfID won't be able to secretly delete the facts. The trouble is, I've got a wife and kids, plus two ex-wives back home who depend on the alimony, so I'll shamefully write what they want. The truth will have to wait until I retire.'

They all sat quietly for a few moments thinking about what Tom had said. The beautiful surroundings had momentarily masked the reality that was Africa. Light clouds were now floating towards the sun and the first stirrings of a slight breeze ruffled the surface of the lake, giving some relief from the noonday heat. It all seemed a million miles from the suffering and hardships that most Africans endured. Jane remembered what Dieter had told her about women from this very area selling themselves to fishermen, just to feed their families, and ending up getting AIDS.

Cindy put an end to their thoughts and turned to Tom. 'When I worked for Frank, all the reports sent to ESSA and the various aid agencies were very positive. Were they all lies?'

'All lies and half-truths, but in the currency of today's vernacular – it's *spin*. There are as many spin doctors in Africa as there are witch doctors. Spin is one thing the West has taught them very well. Most of the money meant for schools and teachers somehow seems to… well…disappear.'

'Where does it go?'

'Ha, good question. Some of it sticks to ministers' palms; then there's that wonderful phrase 'administrative expenses'; some goes to phantom teachers who don't even exist, some to teachers who never turn up in class because they have other jobs. Oh, the list is endless.'

'I heard some children have to bribe teachers just to stay at school,' Cindy said.

'Absolutely right. And that's another thing the donor doesn't want to hear – corruption starts in the classroom. You may find this a little hard to believe, even pathetically sad, but the most cherished gift for any African child isn't a toy but an exercise book, with a set of pens and pencils, and a text book which doesn't have to be shared with the rest of the class.'

'I must remember that. I'll get some for the kids in Ogola,' Jane glared at Robert just in case he dared to challenge her. He didn't.

'Imagine, eighty plus children crowded into a dingy classroom, four to a desk meant for one, no electricity and so dark that those at the back cannot see the blackboard. Many children so hungry they cannot concentrate properly. The teacher reads from an English textbook he barely understands; the aid money to cover the costs of providing every child with books in their own languages, as well as English, never arrives. That's the reality.'

Apart from a few exasperated sighs, the others were silent. Nobody was surprised by what Tom was telling them as they'd heard similar stories before, but every chapter on corruption and bad governance still managed to jolt them out of their equanimity… that's until they heard the next one.

'What about private and missionary schools?' Robert asked.

'Ah! They are different but outside my brief. There are some excellent Catholic and other charity schools, and some of the private boarding schools are as good or even better than in UK. I've even heard of some expatriate Africans who live in UK, sending their kids back to Africa for a better education, because their local English comprehensive is so bloody bad! How's that for irony?'

'That's unbelievable – well – no it isn't really.' Gregg looked bemused. 'So, are the African elite educated in private schools?' he asked.

'I would say most of them are and the university intake is mainly from that sector. And therein lies another problem. Seventy thousand graduates leave Africa every year. So those lucky enough to benefit from a good education are quite likely to up sticks for Europe and America as soon as they can.'

'And Europe and America send their graduates as aid and charity workers to Africa.' Robert continued with Tom's theme.

'And as far as DfID is concerned, one third of its budget is handed to the EU!'

'Ha. The bloody EU again! We must hand over vast amounts of our cash for those buggers to waste on our behalf,' Gregg said. 'What a joke!'

Tom smiled. 'One definition of madness is a readiness to keep repeating the same mistakes, while each time expecting a different result. On that basis, lunatics have taken control of the West's development asylum.'

As usual, Cindy was already bored with the subject and led the way back to their villas to dress for dinner. 'That's enough gloom for one day, I only want to hear happy news from now on. It's Christmas Day for Christ's sake!'

The special Christmas dinner in the hotel was a big let-down. Jane had hoped that Sellie, Kaba, Basil and Isaac would have enjoyed dining with them but clearly, they didn't, being ill at ease, trying to act properly and being careful to use the cutlery instead of fingers which poor Kaba found very difficult. They refused any alcohol and ate very little of the turkey dinner and Christmas pudding. Jane knew they would have been much happier eating meat stew in the local café. As soon as they could, they hurried from the empty dining room after arranging to accompany the families on a trip to one of the game parks early the next morning.

'I don't blame them for rushing away,' Gregg pulled a face as he pushed away his dessert plate. 'The bloody turkey was like rubber, the soddin' roast potatoes were as hard as bullets, and the veg was inedible. And this bloody pudding... well...'

'OK, OK Gregg,' Cindy was already in a bad mood, 'we get the picture – it wasn't the best meal we've ever had but we're only here because of your recommendation, and... stop swearing, there are young children at the table AND it's Christmas Day.' Cindy knew it would have been better if Jane hadn't insisted on their staff joining them. She just hoped she'd learnt a lesson for next time.

The atmosphere in the dining room was distinctly flat and the only other guests, two middle aged couples sitting at the far end, were far from lively. The Christmas spirit was well and truly missing. Feeling a bit disgruntled, they went back to the Bonds' villa where they tucked into a couple of boxes of chocolates and started their last bottle of brandy. A little later, Isaac knocked on their door to see if they would like to go back to the hotel while he sat with the children. Without the slightest hesitation, they headed for the hotel bar collecting Tom on the way; maybe the evening wouldn't be a total waste after all.

The two couples they'd seen earlier had already moved to the bar. They explained that they were with the Global Wide Bible Organisation, or GLOWBO for short, and were based in Nairobi. They were involved in translating the New Testament into every language known to mankind and, although there were two other larger concerns doing exactly the same, GLOWBO managed to pick up some of the more obscure and remote dialects the big guys had missed.

Cindy, looking at Jane, pulled a face. This introduction hadn't cheered her up one little bit; they would obviously have to make their own fun that evening.

Tom bought a round of drinks. 'Are you working in this area? I believe there are about twenty different languages in Buzamba.'

'No,' one of them replied, 'we're just here on R&R for a week. We'd heard from friends that this was a jolly place to spend Christmas and New Year but...,' he shrugged his shoulders and surveyed the empty dining room, 'it's dead.'

It transpired that the two men were 'administrators' for GLOWBO and their wives were 'counsellors'. Every summer, they spent four months fund-raising in Europe and the USA, and were in Africa from mid-September to mid-May. The administration work involved identifying new languages to be translated, organising the translators, and then printing and distributing the finished bibles. Tom had a strong suspicion that the counselling was a ploy to keep the wives on the payroll. Around midnight they left their 'Bible' friends who were ordering yet more drinks from the bored-looking barman.

Boxing Day morning dawned with a magnificent orange and yellow sunrise surpassing anything Jane had ever seen, she was totally awestruck. Ripples on the lake were sparkling and shimmering like strings of multicoloured diamonds, set in rows of ever-changing tints; morning rays burnishing leaves in colourful trees, every branch and twig seemingly covered in tiny sparkling fairy lights. What a breathtaking spectacle.

The dazzling splendour injected a sense of wellbeing into all of them. Compared to the flatness of the day before, breakfast was a cheerful affair; everyone, including the adults, was in high spirits, which grew into excitement during the drive to the Nelson Mandela Game Park. Gilly and Kaba were so animated, that their squeals of delight had to be tempered so that they wouldn't frighten the animals. Jane, equally thrilled, managed to mute her reaction as a family of magnificent elephants slowly crossed the road in front of their vehicles, the massive matriarch trumpeted a challenge directly at them. Although it was breathtaking, it was unnerving and left them almost speechless, while the two drivers prepared to reverse quickly… just in case. It was all amazing; they saw herds of zebra, impala, kudu, other antelopes, and a family of savage-looking hyenas, as though they had been choreographed to appear as they drove around each corner.

Lunch was at a traditional safari lodge in the middle of the game park. Under a roof of palm leaves, they sipped chilled white wine or lemonade, and it wasn't long before grilled steak and salad, followed by fresh mango dessert was served. Life couldn't get any better than this; the adults felt totally relaxed. Kaba's face was a picture as she happily sat with the other girls, listening but not understanding their conversation. Jane felt so happy: this scene was one she was determined to place in her memory bank and their video camera was working overtime to record these moments for posterity.

Rousing themselves in time to join a few other visitors for a boat ride, they drifted lazily on the channel linking Lake Arthur and Lake Ellwood. Dozens of hippos swam and repeatedly surfaced around them, harrumphing and snorting with their mouths wide open, yawning at the intruders. The guide explained that the flat-bottomed steel boat was specially built so that hippos couldn't tip it over.

'Hippo too, too fierce, Madam,' Sellie informed them, 'they kill many people.'

'Yes,' Tom said, 'I've heard that. They kill more people than any other wild animal, even lions.'

With that disturbing thought in mind, Jane was rather relieved when they disembarked leaving the hippos happily enjoying their channel undisturbed. 'Are there any hippos in Lake Arthur?' she asked.

'Oh, yes, Madam. Many,' Sellie replied.

'Do they tip over the fishing boats?'

'I not sure, but I find out.'

It was very early the next morning, just as another splendid sun was rising, that Basil took Sellie and Kaba in the Range Rover to Kaba's family village, promising to return before sunset. The Kimbers and Bonds were happy spending the day at the hotel, enjoying the gardens and swimming pool. By the time the Range Rover returned, the sun was about to disappear below the horizon. Noticing Kaba's eyes were swollen as if she'd been crying, Jane was worried, especially when she saw Sellie's dour expression, similar to the time when she'd cleared the crowd of troublemakers in Ogola.

Putting her arms around Kaba, Jane asked Sellie what had happened.

'I tell you, Madam... the man been fixed good.'

'What man?'

'It Kaba's uncle what did bad thing to the girl.'

'I still don't know what you mean, Sellie. What bad thing?'

It took a little time but eventually Jane heard the full story. When Basil had found Kaba's village, Sellie sought out the headman who gave final confirmation that Kaba could live with her in Ouverru. She also met other family members, most of whom Kaba never knew existed, but the little girl was happy that so many people spoke well of her late mother. Just as they were sitting down to eat a meal, Kaba's uncle Toma Obayo arrived. The effect on Kaba was shocking as she immediately ran screaming into Sellie's arms. Toma stopped in his tracks, turned abruptly, and ran off. As he frantically tried to hide, some of the elders wrestled him to the ground, dragging him in front of the headman.

'Ah, I remember,' Jane interrupted. 'Toma was the man who told the people in Ogola not to give Kaba any food as she had evil spirits and must die.'

'I didn't know that.' Sellie's eyes narrowed in deep thought. 'I understand it better now.'

While the men were holding Toma, Sellie hugged Kaba until she had calmed down. Still shaking, she managed to tell the crowd that this uncle had done bad sex things to her in Ogola and during her struggle to escape, he'd broken her hand – the hand that had just been mended. The villagers all gathered round for a big palaver, everybody having a say, including Toma who denied everything. The village witch doctor performed some juju to see if Toma was telling the truth. He first took some special powder out of a small pouch and rubbed it on Toma's leg, then he put the blade of a knife into a fire and then directly onto the leg; he cried out in pain as the hot blade burnt him, which was proof that he was lying; no burn would have shown his innocence. After the guilty verdict was declared by the witch doctor, Toma was forced to swallow a juju potion. A curse was put on him, which Sellie said would be the end of his sex life and he would never be allowed back into the village. Kaba, sitting on Sellie's knee, cried throughout the ritual.

Although Basil wasn't from the Lindu tribe, he had witnessed the whole thing and confirmed everything to Jane.

'What will Toma do now?' Jane asked. 'Will he return to Ogola?'

'I go speak to people,' said Sellie. 'They tell me if he come so I myself can fix him. We not afraid, Madam – he been cussed good.'

During dinner that evening, Jane repeated the tale to the others.

'Wow, what an amazing story,' Cindy said. 'Poor Kaba has been through a lot. It makes you realise how lucky our girls are.'

It seemed no time at all before the Bonds had to return to Ouverru and Tom went back to Lasutu. The Kimbers used their last day in Lake Arthur to visit Sellie's home village of N'Burunda. They drove on very poor, unpaved roads, throwing up clouds of dust as they passed through forests of eucalyptus and great swathes of bamboo, broken by open, arid, scrub areas, more barren than anything they'd yet seen. In the distance were large herds of Buzamban Cob, a small timid antelope common in that area. At a road junction, Sellie told Basil to stop. She was looking for the many baboons with their babies which appeared whenever a vehicle stopped for a meal break. Today, there were already two *matatus* there with some of the passengers throwing bananas and bread fruit to the waiting animals. When the bravest got too close, the drivers forced them away by running and waving their arms.

On approaching Sellie's village, the first sign of habitation was the concrete Anglican church of Saint Francis. Outside, several well-dressed parishioners were chatting, saying goodbye to the Danish priest, Father Thomas, who was well known to Sellie. Robert, Jane and Gilly followed Sellie inside and found the Father and a helper clearing up after the service. He gave a big smile when he saw Sellie.

'*Karibu* Sellie, *karibu*,' and Sellie awkwardly genuflected before shaking the priest's hand.

She introduced him to the Kimbers and then to Kaba, explaining to him that she was going to bring her up as her own. Father Thomas was delighted to meet new visitors as very few foreigners ventured this far from Ouverru. Sellie laughed when Father Thomas teased her about her occasional absences from school but he added, for the Kimbers' benefit, that families often took their children off during harvest times, or to look after sick relations. Not only did he hold services in N'Burunda, but he was also responsible for churches in three neighbouring villages, assisted by five local lay-preachers. He also trained two children's choirs and taught English and religious studies at all four village schools.

'You obviously keep very busy, Father. How big is your congregation?'

'Yes, I do keep busy. Unfortunately, I've not been too well recently, so I rely more and more on my assistants. As far as I can tell, the population in all four villages is between seven and eight thousand and well over half are children. It's the AIDS, you see.'

'Are many orphans?' Gregg asked.

Father Thomas nodded. 'Yes. It used to be just malaria that kept the population down, but now...'

Jane thought about asking him if he encouraged men to use condoms, but felt it would be impolite.

During a lull in the conversation, she did ask whether he'd heard of GLOWBO and, if so, which language his bibles were written in.

'We did have that organisation here four or five years ago, but we already had bibles in Kiswahili and English and, in truth, that's all we needed. But they still asked the head teacher to help with translations into Lindu.'

'So, did you get anything from GLOWBO?'

Father Thomas gave an uncomfortable smile. 'Come with me, I'll show you.'

Trooping after him, he led them into a storeroom at the rear of the church where there were some chairs in need of repair, a couple of trestle tables and some untidy tea chests. Ignoring these, he pointed to some cartons in one corner.

'These arrived from GLOWBO about two years ago.' He pulled a couple of books out of the top carton and passed them to Jane and Robert. The quality of binding was poor and, although they appeared to be new, some pages were already coming loose.

'We assume they are bibles but we're not sure because they are written in a language we don't understand. It's certainly not Lindu or any other Buzamban language. We wrote to GLOWBO but apart from an acknowledgement, nothing has happened. And as you can see, they are already deteriorating in the humidity.'

'That's too bad,' Robert said. 'All that effort and expense wasted. And there's probably an area somewhere else in Africa with bibles they can't understand because they're printed in Lindu.'

'Welcome to Africa!' said Father Thomas which made Jane and Robert laugh – how many more times would they hear that maxim?

She didn't tell him that people from GLOWBO were staying at the Lake Resort Hotel as it might ruin their holiday!

Sellie then took them to the school, which was an improvement on Tom Smith's description of the typical school. The walls were brightly painted, with examples of the children's schoolwork fixed to parts of the wall, looking very much like Gilly's classroom in Ringwood. Sellie said the school wasn't crowded when she was a pupil but she reminded them that it wasn't a government school but was provided by an Anglican charity and funded from overseas, which would have been outside the scope of Tom's project.

Before walking into the village, Father Thomas suggested that Jane and Robert might like to join him later for tea, so that Sellie would have longer with all her family members. Sellie spoke to the many people who greeted her as she walked into her home village. They were mainly Lindu, but inter-tribal marriages meant that there were a few from other tribes. Sellie estimated her extended family was over sixty.

Although proudly introducing the Kimbers, she made it obvious that Kaba was very special to her. This took a long time and some villagers scowled at Kaba as though she had no right to be there, which Sellie explained was because Kaba was Gree, and they thought she should have chosen a child from her own village. Apart from that, everyone was friendly and welcomed the *mzungus* from England.

The village was so much nicer than Ogola – very little litter and everywhere swept clean. The mud and thatch houses, although small, were in a good state of repair and not crowded together. As in Ogola, most activities took place outside, and large bowls of water were on the ground for washing and cooking.

At Sellie's suggestion, Basil brought the vehicle into the village so he could unload several five-litre cans of cooking oil, a sack of rice, and two large bunches of *matooke* bananas. These gifts were well received, and any antagonism towards Kaba soon disappeared.

Although they had spent little more than an hour in the village, it did give them an insight into Buzamban rural life. Compared to the squalor and poverty of Ogola, it helped to balance Jane and Robert's view of Africa and Africans. Village people, with little or no material wealth as measured by the Western model, seemed to live contented lives, subsistence farming providing their everyday needs.

Leaving Sellie with her family, they accepted Father Thomas' invitation for tea. His house-girl had prepared a table with a crisp white cloth, a bone china tea service and a matching cake stand. He apologised for not having any cake but his cook of over fifteen years had never managed anything beyond rock cakes. There was a glint of humour in his eyes as he emphasised the work 'rock'. Instead of cake there were biscuits and crackers stacked on the stand. 'Not very inspiring, I'm afraid,' he observed apologetically. 'The local shops don't stock anything fancy.'

'Oh, it's lovely,' exclaimed Jane. 'It looks beautiful.' Sitting in his sparsely furnished living room, she suddenly felt very sad for this kind-hearted man who had given his life to his ministry. She wondered what life was really like carrying out God's work in remote African villages?

'We were very impressed with your school,' Robert said. 'Someone we recently met is doing a survey of government-owned schools, and he was very depressed by what he saw.'

'I'm not surprised,' Father Thomas replied. 'Our advantage is that our four schools are funded by the church. That's no guarantee though.'

Slightly puzzled by that, Robert asked what he meant.

He shook his head slightly before replying. 'We had this amazing Australian girl here a few years ago – she was only young, about twenty-three I think, but a good Christian girl. Anyhow, she had been backpacking around Buzamba with a friend and stayed a few days in the adjoining village of Saniquell, which has a good Catholic health centre, but no school. When she returned to Australia, she raised enough money to build a school there and stayed on for six months to organise the teachers and all the teaching aids.' He paused to refill their cups and take a drink himself.

'What a wonderful thing to do,' Jane was very impressed,

'We were all thrilled... for a while.'

'Oh dear, do I sense there was some sort of problem?' Robert asked.

'Have you ever seen the film, *The Wizard of Oz*?'

Robert and Jane looked at each other, wondering if the good Father's mind had suddenly flipped.

'No, I'm not crazy,' he laughed, when he saw their expressions. 'But you'll remember that Dorothy's house was blown away by a twister.'

They both nodded.

'Well, the same thing happened with the school in Saniquell. It vanished.'

'Vanished? How do you mean, vanished. Was there a storm?' Jane asked.

'Yes, there was, but nothing out of the ordinary,' he sighed, taking another sip from his cup. 'I've heard a hundred versions of what happened, and which one was true I couldn't say, but when I went to see for myself, all that was left was the concrete floor.' He repeated 'just the concrete floor' in case they hadn't heard him properly.

'Dare we ask what you think happened?' Robert ventured.

'I do think the school had been damaged; the builders had taken advantage and made a botch of the building – you can't blame the girl for that – part of the zinc roof had blown off and one of the walls was down. However, twelve hours later, everything had gone. Everything.'

'And…'

'The village headman told me in a very aggressive way, daring me to challenge him at my peril, that the school had blown away. He said it was sorcery.'

'Like witchcraft, you mean.'

Father Thomas nodded. 'But one of my parishioners quietly pointed out that the headman's house had a brand new roof, and his brother's house had been completely renovated.'

'Oh, my God,' Jane's exclamation sounded like a prayer. 'After all that Australian girl had done.'

'Yes. And what was also strange was that the head teacher had disappeared as well – with all the books!'

'So is there a school there now?'

Father Thomas gave them a poignant smile. 'The Anglican Church built a new school using the same concrete floor, and everything is fine now.'

'But won't the same thing happen again?' Robert queried.

'Not a chance,' Father Thomas replied. 'It will be there forever,' and gave a hearty laugh. 'I would never admit this to anyone, especially my bishop but…' he put his index finger to his lips as though he was telling them a huge secret, 'I paid the local spirit man, or sorcerer, or whatever he's called, to put a curse on anyone who tampered with the school. He did so in front of everyone in the village, including the headman.' He laughed again, and recited, 'The Lord works in mysterious ways, his wonders to perform,' and then added, 'using any means, fair or foul. Amen'

'That's a wonderful story,' Jane laughed. 'But very sad at the same time. Robert and I always think of the powerful politicians in Ouverru who, through their own greed, place every obstacle in the way of improving conditions for the poor, but even here in the rural areas, there are people who would deprive children of an education, just to repair their houses.'

'Yes, I'm afraid that is the case.' He went on to tell them other stories about his parishioners, their spiritual and health problems, and his prayers that peace and harmony should prevail. One other concern he highlighted was that in Buzamba and throughout Africa, young men and women were being lured away from their villages by the bright lights and excitement of the cities, and false expectations of monetary wealth. 'They often end up hooked on drugs or alcohol,' he continued, 'and the girls in prostitution. That's why Ogola and all the other slums are becoming more and more overcrowded, with the consequential increase in crime.'

They were interrupted by a knock on the Father's door and Sellie, with Kaba, said they should set off soon as it was important to reach the hotel before it got dark. Father Thomas agreed, saying the roads were very dangerous in the dark, so they said their goodbyes and thanks and headed for the car.

On the way back to Lake Arthur, Jane and Robert reflected on their day, especially on the discussion with Father Thomas.

'What did you make of him?' Jane asked.

'I think he's amazing. He and dedicated people like him are doing their utmost to provide schools and health facilities in the rural areas.'

'Yes, I agree. I particularly liked the bit he said about aid. Not a penny he has received through the Anglican Church and other charities went missing. If only it was like that with DGA's money in Ogola.'

'That'll be the day. It's a salutary lesson to all donors to ensure the greedy paws of despotic leaders should be kept away from all aid. But, how to do it?'

Their fascinating experiences were beyond anything Jane could have imagined just six months ago, and they were all sad to leave Lake Arthur the following morning. The Christmas holiday had been a great success as well as an adventure; Sellie and Kaba had visited their home villages and the mystery of Kaba's damaged hand was resolved, and the culprit punished. Leaving aside the flirting, the friendship between the Kimbers and the Bonds had stood the test of being together for several days and Gilly, as well as her mummy, had seen amazing wild animals in their natural surroundings for the first time.

On New Year's Eve morning, Robert called at the office to find out from Akuku what had happened during his brief absence, and then made a quick visit to Ogola to hear the latest news from Ken.

'Everything's fine,' Robert told Jane when he got home. 'Hani hopes you will be able to go down on Monday as they have one or two problems, which he thinks only you can put right.'

For their first New Year's Eve together, Jane and Robert were alone. The Bonds had gone to the golf club party, the Pennicotts had an invitation to the British High Commission, and most of their other friends were either away or at parties. Having a romantic evening together was much more important.

'So, Mrs Kimber, did you do the right thing six months ago in marrying me?'

'Mmm, let me think now. Did I or didn't I? That is the question.'

At the time they'd agreed to get married, she'd been honest with him, saying that although she was very fond of him, she didn't love him, and he'd accepted it on the basis that love would come later. Well, that 'later' was now. She turned to look at him and gave him a kiss. 'Of course I did the right thing.'

His smile said it all. 'You know I fell in love with you the first time I saw you and my love has grown week by week.'

She gave him another kiss, but deep down she wasn't certain she was being completely truthful; she did love him for what he was – a kind, considerate and caring man, and a brilliant father to Gilly. What she was confused about was the difference between love and lust. While she did love Robert, she didn't lust for him, any lust she felt was for Gregg.

CHAPTER TWENTY-THREE

The temperature had increased noticeably since the end of the last rainy season and the next few months were particularly hot and humid. Jane found that the mornings, up to about eleven o'clock, were just about bearable but from then until late afternoon she struggled, especially in the office, baking under its corrugated-iron roof. She wondered if her pregnancy was partly responsible. As it became hotter, without rainfall to dampen things down, clouds of dust were blown by even the slightest breeze, eddying in the air and leaving a brown haze on every surface.

Even worse than the heat and dust was the smell. It was the distinctive odour of an African slum; unwashed humanity urinating at will, defecating onto scraps of plastic, tossing the results in the air or onto fetid heaps of rubbish, naked infants playing in ditches running with sewage. It was virtually impossible to avoid inhaling the essence of Ogola and Jane tried not to dwell on the matter.

Although the locals and those expats who'd lived in Buzamba for many years did suffer from the heat, many had grown accustomed to the high temperatures and humidity, managing to work normal hours, even through the hottest time of the day. Fortuitously, most offices, where the bulk of the foreigners worked, were air-conditioned but that was not a luxury available in Ogola.

In order for the computer deadline to be met, Hani asked Jane to work as much as she could, plying her with bottled water from a cooler box which he filled with ice first thing every morning. The new office would have a tiled roof, fans and a fridge, but until it was ready they had to soldier on in conditions which were like being in an oven on a high setting.

The heat gradually took its toll on Jane and she decided that in future, she would only work in the mornings. She told the staff about her pregnancy so they would understand when she needed to take a break to walk outside in the air which, although anything but fresh, was less oppressive than inside. During one break, Ken took her to see the new blocks that had been finished before Christmas and were now fully occupied.

'Looks great, Ken,' Jane smiled, 'I can actually see progress since my first visit… and the road is starting to look good.'

'Yes, we'll be putting in the first set of street lights next week.'

'That should cause a bit of a stir. And what about the head office, will that be finished on time?'

'Yes, God willing. We're still planning on moving in six weeks.'

Because Amos hadn't been to work since mid-December, he'd been given the required number of warning letters so that Ken was able to fire him. He recruited a young man called Joshua, who had worked in the office of a wholesale flower company until it moved to a new site five miles out of town. It was obvious from the start that he was a much better worker than Amos and was prepared to work late with the others to get the paperwork back on track.

'Does anyone know what's wrong with Amos?' Jane asked.

Momo said that he'd seen him at Christmas but he looked poorly. His clothes were torn and dirty, one of his eyes was badly swollen, and Momo thought he was either drunk or on drugs. He'd told Amos to go and see the doctor but he'd refused.

'I try and find him later,' said Hani, 'but I think he not listen to me. He mix with bad people.'

Ken continued by telling Jane that six months earlier, Amos had arrived for work one Monday morning with his right arm in an improvised sling, without which it just hung useless at his side. Ken sent him to the doctor and two hours later he came back with a sick note – he was excused work for two days because his ailment was 'Saturday Night Palsy'.

'What on earth's that?'

He gave her a cautious smile. 'Actually, it's not all that uncommon. On a Saturday after payday, some men get very drunk; they crash out on the floor and when they sleep, they rest their head on their outstretched arm, using it like a pillow. They can lie in that position for hours, cutting off the blood supply to their arm. Hence the paralysis and hence Saturday Night Palsy. The arm is back to normal in about two days.'

'I must remember that one,' laughed Jane, making a mental note to put it in her diary. 'So Amos is a heavy drinker.'

'Very much so and, like Hani said, I think he's joined a bad crowd.'

Ruth arrived late for work that morning and her usual happy manner was noticeably missing. She told Hani that her eight year old son had been injured in the quarry and she'd taken him to the clinic. Dieter is away for a few days but one of the nurses attended to him.

'But what about Ruth's son. Was he playing in the quarry?'

Ken shook his head. 'No, he was almost certainly working there.'

'But what work can an eight year old do in a quarry?'

'To make extra money... to buy food, they break the rocks into very small pieces, like the gravel used in concrete.'

'And children do that?'

He nodded. 'The boulders are too hard to break with a hammer so the rocks are heated with burning tyres so they fracture easily. They then take a chunk of rock and beat it into powder. It usually takes four or five days to fill one sack and for that they get one hundred shillings, or two pounds in British money. I sometimes pass the quarry after work,' he added, 'and there are dozens of men, women, boys and girls, hacking away at rocks with choking black clouds of smoke all around them. It's terrible and reminds me of a picture I once saw *Dante's Inferno*, it's like that.'

'It's probably a silly question but why doesn't the boy go to school?'

'He help his ma and grandma get food,' Lola answered, 'so he get up at dawn and work till school start. He leave school at noon and go back to the quarry to work till it dark. Many children do the same-same thing.'

A disheartened Jane asked Ken if she could give Ruth some money each week so that the boy could stop working in the quarry but, even before Ken shook his head, she knew the answer.

'If you do it for one, you will end up doing it for everyone and you'll get no thanks, only demands for more money. And they'll only despise you for being rich. And once you start, you can't stop. You'd be hounded out of Ogola. You've already taken one girl to look after and we weren't happy about that.'

It was difficult for Jane to get the image of Ruth's injured son out of her mind, an eight year old boy, breaking rocks just to get scraps of food for his family. Feeling totally helpless she clenched her fists, screwed up her eyes and prayed; 'please God, tell me it's not true... please'. Not only did she know it was true but there were thousands, maybe millions like him. There was another question Jane wanted to ask but she was almost too afraid. She knew Ruth was HIV positive, so she anxiously asked if the boy was the same.

'No,' Lola replied, 'but her daughter is.'

'Oh my God!' Jane felt as though the stuffing had been knocked out of her. At least Dieter had his antiretrovirals and Ruth and her daughter were now being treated.

Jane couldn't wait for Robert to arrive home so she could tell him about Ruth's son working in the quarry. He wasn't surprised. 'It happens. The UN reckons that around fifty million children under fourteen work, either full or part-time, in sub-Saharan Africa.'

'Fifty million! I can't believe that. Not all in quarries, I hope!'

'No, most work in agriculture of one type or another, including spraying toxic pesticides, but others work in construction, mines, as servants, or worse still, as prostitutes. But don't forget, we in the UK sent young children down the pits and into mills less than two hundred years ago, just the same as in Africa today.'

'Oh, I wish you hadn't mentioned that,' Jane said, knowing it was true.

Every time she heard of a new horror, in this case, child labour, she found herself doing a reality check on her very existence. How can this happen? How can the rich live next to half-starving humanity, who suffer from diseases which they could easily afford to treat. How much would it cost to provide everyone in Ogola with enough food and send all children to school? Certainly a lot less than the aid sent to Buzamba, which disappeared into the pockets of corrupt officials.

Strolling to the pool the next afternoon, Jane met Josie and Cindy and told them about Ruth and her children.

'Don't get involved,' was Cindy's stern advice. 'You can't solve the problems of Africa. Just accept there's nothing you can do about it and make the most of your life out here. Enjoy yourself.'

Jane didn't like being preached to by Cindy but, not wanting to fall out, said nothing. Although they had become best friends, Jane was continually surprised at Cindy's apparent lack of sympathy towards the suffering of the locals and wondered if most expats were the same.

Having heard enough about child labour, poverty, and all the other depressing subjects, Cindy went for a swim. She'd decided within a few weeks of arriving in Buzamba that she didn't want to know about the problems the locals endured as she and Gregg couldn't do anything about it anyway. All she wanted was to live the good life while it lasted.

'Westerners,' Josie said to Jane, 'look on child labour as a bad thing. But is it?'

'What do you mean? Surely it's a terrible thing.'

'I know it's bad but what's the alternative?'

'The alternative is that all children should be in school.'

'But here in the real world we all know this doesn't happen. For many reasons, lots of kids don't go to school. They have to work to help the family survive and if they don't – they starve.'

'Yes, I guess I was being naive.'

'And the sad thing is that do-gooders from the West want to stop companies using child labour… but then who does that help? It helps the conscience of the West – that's all.'

'How do you mean?'

'I can give you a good example. A documentary on Canadian TV portrayed children in developing countries being used to sow lace ribbons on ladies' dresses for a major department store. There was outrage in Canada and there were even questions raised in parliament. The department store said it knew nothing about it but immediately cancelled all orders from that particular third-world company.'

'I'm sure they did.'

'But who suffered?'

'Well, I guess the shoppers who had to pay more for their dresses.'

'Absolutely not,' Josie broke off with a sigh. 'It's the child labourers and their families who suffered. Nobody condones children being forced to work, but if the alternatives are starvation or prostitution, then…' Josie left her sentence unfinished. 'Lester wants the so-called sweatshops to open in Africa.'

'But isn't that taking advantage of the poor?'

'That's how it appears. The liberals despise sweatshops as exploiters of the poor, whereas the poor see them as opportunities. Lester says that anyone who cares about fighting poverty should campaign in favour, demanding companies set up factories in Africa. If Africa could establish a clothing export industry, it would fight poverty more efficiently than aid.'

'I hadn't thought of it that way.'

'No, most people haven't and it almost certainly won't happen. So they'll take their sweatshops to Asia – it's much easier.'

'What a world we live in,' Jane sighed. 'Coming out here and meeting so many new people has really opened my eyes to so much.' She smiled when she saw Josie's sympathetic expression. 'Anyhow, we can discuss it tonight over dinner. Is half past seven okay with you and Lester?'

'Yes, we're looking forward to it. Are Cindy and Gregg also coming?'

Making sure Cindy was out of earshot, Jane whispered that it was only them as Cindy would be bored stiff with any serious discussion. Josie laughed.

'Thanks so much for these reports, Lester,' Jane handed him back his file, 'I'm learning more and more each day.'

The four of them had finished another of Sellie's celebrated dinners and were relaxing with some of Robert's precious stock of imported brandy. Not having either the Bonds or the McKeevers with them made for a congenial, less confrontational atmosphere. Robert certainly found it less stressful and Jane, as well as wanting to develop their friendship with the Pennicotts, was keen to learn more from Lester's significant experience on all matters African.

'I'm impressed you've read them,' Lester smiled. 'I don't think many wives are interested.'

'And it's not only the wives,' Josie added. 'Many expat men are only here for the money and don't know, or even care about the political side to the work they're supposed to be doing.'

'Well, I'm certainly getting clued-up,' Jane said, 'but it's the background to aid that's a bit of a puzzle. There seem to have been huge changes from colonial times.'

'Oh, that's for sure,' Lester acknowledged. 'It depends on how far back you want to go. A lot of Africa's problems date back to the

Berlin conference of 1885 when the Europeans drew arbitrary lines dividing up the continent between them. Then there was colonial rule up till the early nineteen-sixties.'

'We can't be very proud about that era, can we?' Jane reflected, 'but I was thinking about post Second World War and the creation of the aid agencies like the World Bank.'

'Yes, you're right, I think that's more relevant to where we are today.' He gave them a potted history of the origins of the World Bank and how he believed they got it wrong from the very start at Bretton Woods, nearing the end of the Second World War. The British recommendation was to create a balance of trade between nations to avoid some becoming creditors and other debtors; there would be a compulsion to maintain a balance of trade. Unfortunately, the British advice was ignored.

'So you believe the failure to agree to the British proposal has resulted in the poverty and corruption in Africa today?' Jane asked.

Lester followed Robert's example and rubbed his chin thoughtfully. 'Well, let's say it contributed. And now, no African country is solvent after borrowing from the World Bank and the IMF. They are all debtors.'

'Will things get any better, do you think?'

'Not unless there's a root and branch change in the philosophy of the donors.'

'It's all a bit depressing,' Robert added, refilling everyone's glasses. 'Are we all wasting our time here?'

'Hmm, maybe. We are just using sticking plasters whereas major surgery is needed.'

'You mean like our slum project,' questioned Robert. 'I wonder if there'll be any permanent improvement in Ogola – especially after we've gone.'

'I do hope so,' said Josie wistfully. 'It's really helping so many poor people.'

'Going back to what Jane was asking, I think the decline in Africa set in when decolonisation took place. Initially, the plan was to devolve power to the traditional rulers but this changed when a new class of European-educated big shots came along. They had developed a taste for material comforts but still retained the African mentality.'

'They took over at independence with one priority.' Josie added, 'to make themselves rich, and they did it very well.'

'Indeed they did,' Lester sighed. 'And the World Bank, EU and others did nothing to stop them. I blame the whole UN ethos.'

'Oh, how's that?'

'The UN is like a club where bribery and corruption are the meat and veg. Corrupt governments are given the same voting rights as democratic countries, and there are more of them so... what chance has it got? None.'

'I read in one of your reports about the Millennium Development Goals which plans to end poverty by 2025. Is it realistic?'

'Not a snowball's chance in hell,' Lester replied. 'The main problem with poverty is population growth, but it's very un-PC to say so. The population in Africa doubles every twenty years so... if we take Kenya as an example, the present-day population of forty-five million will be ninety million in twenty years.'

'Wow, that is staggering,' Robert said. 'So the demand for food and material goods will double as well.'

'Or probably more,' Jane reflected. 'There isn't enough food now and if in twenty years' time, you want everyone to be well fed, educated and live in decent houses with all the trappings of modern life, then demand for food and everything else will probably treble.'

'More than that,' Josie said. 'That's why in our opinion,' she looked at Lester as she said this, 'birth control should be by far, the main priority of every African government and every aid agency or donor or charity. Unless there's a dramatic reduction in the birth rate, then... well, I don't know, there'll be chaos and mass starvation on a scale we just can't imagine.'

'And yet birth control is rarely mentioned,' Jane placed her hands on her chin and gave a big sigh.

'You're absolutely right,' Lester said. 'And if this problem isn't tackled soon, then all the waffle about reducing greenhouse gases will have been a waste of time.'

There was silence for a few moments. Robert went round to refill their glasses but everyone opted for water.

'And then there's the African Union – a union with no unity,' Lester continued. 'Just like the UN, it's full of self-important, corrupt leaders like Mugabe, full of self-congratulations and big budgets, but nothing to show for all their blather. And no African country has donated funds to help drought victims even though the continent's richest economies sent aid to Haiti and even Japan!'

'You know what,' sighed Jane. 'I think we need Cindy here to do her exotic dancing. It's easy to get bogged down with gloom and despair, and I don't think Robert's dance of the seven veils would help very much.'

'Oh, I don't know,' laughed Josie. 'He looks a sassy mover to me. What do you think, Lester?'

'Without wishing to be cruel, old chap. I think I'd need a lot more to drink to see you as titillating as Cindy. She does like bouncing her bosom around a bit, doesn't she?'

'Well, with that thought,' Josie said, 'I'd better take my filthy-minded husband home before he confesses to any more of his pubescent fantasies.'

'Ah, just before I'm dragged away,' Lester gave a jolly smile to his wife, 'I thought I'd leave you with this poser. A chap I know – he's a sort of American Redneck if you know what I mean – has a Doberman, and feeds it on fresh meat every day. Well, he's going on four weeks leave and has left £150 to feed his dog and £20 to feed his houseboy! Are we all mad?'

'Mad or bad,' Robert said.

'And the other thing is he sent the dog to a special training school to teach it to kill.'

'Wow, that sounds a bit scary.'

'Yes, there's a secret word and if he says the word and points to a person, the dog will go in for the kill.'

'What's the word?'

'Ha, of course he won't say. We just hope we don't say it by mistake.'

Puzzled and also worried about what Lester and Josie had said about population growth, Jane popped in to see Dieter the next day. He was pleased to see her and opened a couple bottles of beer from his fridge.

'You're going back to Germany soon, I think,' Jane said.

'Yes, in ten days. I'm really looking forward to it.'

'You certainly deserve it. And will you be back?'

'Yes, I've agreed to do one more tour, and then that's it.'

'It must be a strange comparison between working in Ogola

on the one hand and in the highly developed environment of Germany on the other.'

Dieter didn't answer straight away. He sat in contemplative mood gazing at the ceiling before looking back at Jane. 'Yes, it is. Out here I can save hundreds of lives but… for what?'

'I'm not sure what you mean,' a puzzled Jane said.

'It's difficult to get my head round this… conundrum,' he took another drink from his bottle of beer. 'What am I saving them for? For more suffering… more poverty… more misery, so they can produce dozens of kids who'll be in an even worse state than they are.'

'Phew, that's quite a philosophical dilemma you've got there, Dieter' Jane sympathised. 'A friend of ours, Lester, was saying population growth is the biggest problem facing Africa, more important than all the aid for poverty reduction or development or anything else.'

'Lester's right,' Dieter heaved a sigh and took another gulp of beer. 'We promote the use of condoms… in fact we give them away, but not many men use them. And not only that, they won't let their women take the pill or be sterilised.'

'So why do poor families want lots of children?'

'That's a hard one, Jane. When I first came to Africa, I posed this question to a chap who had eleven children and who complained that having so many made him the poorest man in the village.'

'What did he say?'

'He said so some of them will look after him in his old age. His wife said nothing… it was his choice, not hers.'

'So what can be done about it?'

He smiled as Jane stood to leave. He was wanted by one of his nurses. 'I don't know, Jane, but I'll think about it when I'm in Germany.' He laughed and said he'd send her an e-mail when he knew the answer.

Before breakfast, Sellie came in with a beaming Kaba, who was dressed in her new school uniform; a dark blue blouse, khaki skirt and sandals, carrying a schoolbag with pens and pencils clipped to the side. Sellie was going to walk with her to school every day for the first week and then she would be able to go on her own. Two other children from the compound went to the same school, and they would look after her. Jane had never seen Kaba look so happy, and the normally unemotional Sellie looked very proud.

'Which languages does the school use?'

'Everything English, Madam, children learn everything in English.'

'Is that good?' Robert ventured.

'Oh yes, very good.'

When the phone rang, Jane's first thought when she heard Hani's voice was to expect the worst. She held her breath.

'It the tree,' Hani almost shouted down the phone, 'it crying.'

'You mean the Tulip Tree?'

'Yes, yes, it crying.'

What should she do? She'd love to see it but was aware of Ken's warning. She decided to throw caution to the wind. 'Can I come and see it?'

'Come now, now. I take you. Come quick,' Hani ordered.

She didn't tell Robert who was at his office. She asked the security guard to get her a taxi and within forty minutes she was in Ogola where Hani was waiting for her, his arms full of pieces of material.

'Put this on,' Hani commanded. 'We hide your skin!'

One piece of cloth wrapped round her waist acted as an ankle length skirt and another covered her head and shoulders similar to a Muslim headdress. She was able to hold onto her cover from the inside so that her white hands were hidden.

Hani's huge frame led the way while Jane, holding tightly onto her improvised cape, did her best to keep up, giggling to herself because she could only take short strides like a Japanese Geisha. They were part of a huge throng of noisy, excitable people all heading in the same direction and nobody noticed there was a *mzungu* amongst them – they were too busy ducking between and under structures to get to the tree as quickly as they could.

By the time they reached the high ground overlooking the tree, Jane was sweating as never before. Hani found a good vantage point and put his arm round Jane's shoulders to protect her from those pushing past. Fortunately, they were all too preoccupied to notice them.

The sights and sounds they met were incredible. The whole area under the tree was a mass of jostling humanity and the noise was amazing: excited shrills, shouts and singing seemed to blend into a continuous cacophony of sound, the likes of which Jane had never heard before. It wasn't deafening but what made it different was that it was a 'happy' noise. All their faces were either laughing or wreathed in smiles and those whose arms weren't squashed to their sides, were pointing up at the tree. She looked up and saw that now, unlike the last time, every branch was covered in bright yellow and red variegated flowers. It looked absolutely wonderful set against the deep blue sky. But... where were the tears?

Then she saw one. A single drip fell from one of the flowers and the nearest hands of those underneath stretched upwards to catch it; the lucky recipient immediately putting her fingers in her mouth to taste the 'tear'. There was another and then another, each tear receiving the same euphoric response from those nearest to where it fell. Jane tried to count the tears, and there seemed to be six or seven a minute. Not exactly crying, she thought to herself, but it was the excitement of the crowd and the intensity of the noise as every drip fell that made it so exciting.

After about ten minutes, Hani thought they should go before someone spotted her. Pushing through the energized crowd, and keeping her face well hidden, a hot sweaty Jane arrived safely back at the office. Thanking Hani enthusiastically, she only just managed to stop herself from putting her arms around him and kissing him. That would never do.

'So you went,' Ken said seriously as he came in the door.

'I hope you don't mind but it was fantastic. Something I'll remember for the rest of my life.' Jane looked in Hani's direction and gave him a big wink.

'As long as you're safe, that's the main thing. Does Robert know?'

'Not yet but I'll tell him this evening. But how many days do the tears fall?'

'I think it only one day,' Hani answered. 'The day each year when we feel God cries for our suffering. That's why everyone is happy. We not forgotten by God.'

Chapter Twenty-Four

In the early morning light, the Victoria Private Hospital looked quite impressive. Jane was having her first scan and the nurse carrying out the procedure showed them the image of the new Kimber in her stomach. They collectively made sure that all the limbs seemed to be in the right place and the heartbeat sound.

'Everything looks good,' was the nurse's assessment after checking Jane's blood pressure. She took some blood for tests and said Doctor Patterson would get in touch if he felt it necessary. Otherwise, she should arrange another visit in two months' time.

From Robert's ear-to-ear grin, it was only too clear that he was over the moon about his impending fatherhood. 'Oh! I forgot to ask if she could tell the sex.'

'I've already told you, I don't want to know. All I want to know is that it is healthy – that's all. Is that clear, Kimber?'

'Yes, oh mother of my child, I'll... err, we'll wait to see if it's a Hubert... ouch.'

Relations with Jimmy f-Fearless had returned to normal during the past couple of months, the lovely Precious incident was, for the moment, consigned to history. Even so, Robert restricted Jimmy's invitations to once a week, these were accepted with good grace; he knew he'd committed a stupid mistake and was grateful that both of them were still speaking to him.

Still perturbed by what the Pennicotts and Dieter had said about population growth, Jane decided to ask Jimmy what he thought.

'I agree, you have a very good point there,' f-Fearless said. 'I also believe that population growth is the greatest challenge facing Africa. If you get a chance when you go on leave, fly over Africa at night and you'll see fires making way for more people.

And if you think about it, it's population growth that's the main contributor to global warming, but the politicians would never say it – they're afraid they'd be accused of racism or some other non-PC comment.'

'But isn't chopping down the Amazon rainforest worse?'

'Yes, probably. But the population growth in Africa is a much bigger problem than in South America. Africa can't feed itself – I think your friends are right.'

Robert's next trip to Kabara was due and Basil collected him at five o'clock in the morning so that they could reach their destination by noon. After his bags were stowed in the car, Jane gave him an affectionate kiss and asked him to give her very best regards to Sister Ambeda.

'You will be seeing her, I expect,' she asked, carefully looking to see if Robert's expression changed which might indicate that there was more to the relationship than he'd admitted. She was almost certain that everything was above board but the lack of VPL still puzzled her. Surely a respectable hospital Sister wouldn't go around without any underwear.

'I'll only see her briefly,' he answered. He'd expected Jane to say something about Mrs Ambeda, so was prepared with what he hoped was a guilt-free response. 'And it will be in her hospital office, not in my bedroom, so you needn't try and catch me out again.' He tried to smile but he knew it didn't look natural.

'I trust you, you silly boy.' But did she? She wasn't sure whether his awkward reply was to cover up his guilt or just the memory of how she and Gregg tricked their way into his bedroom.

'Bye, darling,' he said. 'I hope to be back early Friday afternoon.'

It suddenly registered with Jane that to put her mind at rest, she knew exactly how to find out if Robert's relationship with Sister Ambeda was just business. She would ask Sellie to find out from Basil… he would know if she went to his hotel room again… and for how long. Even if Basil tried to hide anything, he wouldn't stand a chance against Sellie.

On the drive to Kabara, Robert had plenty of time to decide what to do about Lucy Ambeda. He'd known her for three years and their affair had started on his second visit to Kabara... long before he'd met Jane. At first, he'd thought himself in love, but she was married to the town's deputy mayor, and had told Robert that she definitely wouldn't leave him; she was happy to see Robert once a month but that was all. He knew he should have stopped seeing her as soon as he met and married Jane, but the promise of wonderful sex... she had the most amazing body... with no strings attached and, he'd mistakenly thought, no chance of being caught, was too much of a temptation. But now everything had changed. He would tell Lucy that it was over. Being married to Jane was the most wonderful thing that had ever happened to him, and he didn't want anything... even his African Queen of Passion... to spoil it. He could manage without Lucy Ambeda but he couldn't manage without Jane.

Two days after Robert went to Kabara, the excited residents of Ogola gathered to watch eight concrete lampposts, complete with street lights, being erected on the first part of the newly-constructed road. At seven o'clock when it was dark, Basil took Jane and Gilly to have a look. They were met by crowds of animated people milling around admiring the new look to their slum. It was almost a carnival atmosphere and everyone thought it was wonderful. They were already imagining how it would be when the road was finished, with street lights lining both sides and small businesses, market stalls, and cafes improving the amenities.

The following morning, the eight concrete lampposts were still in place, but not one of the street lights. They had been stolen.

An angry Ken called an urgent meeting with the security staff and the contractor who had installed the lights. He was the only angry person, the others just shrugged their shoulders as it wasn't a surprise. In fact, they felt it was Ken's fault for not putting razor wire around the lampposts. The security people had seen nothing, and the contractor knew nothing, swearing that none of his staff was involved. The consensus amongst the others was that the *mzungus* would buy replacements – no problem. Meanwhile, a wealthy residential area of Ouverru, where the high and mighty lived, would be like Blackpool illuminations.

After Robert had returned from Kabara, Sellie asked Basil whether Sister Ambeda had visited Mr Kimber in his bedroom. Basil told her that Mrs Ambeda regularly stayed for several hours in the hotel with Mr Kimber. She already knew that *mzungu* men and women occasionally had affairs, but Sellie thought there was a danger that this might end in divorce for Mr and Mrs Kimber. The last thing Sellie wanted was for their marriage to fail because they were very good employers and she liked working for them. The following day she told Jane that Basil had confirmed that Mrs Ambeda had only been twice to the hotel, and on each occasion had stayed for less than five minutes. Sellie was delighted to see the look of relief on Jane's face, and she hoped this lie would be the end of the matter.

Having completed his school survey, Tom Smith was leaving Buzamba and the Bonds organised farewell drinks for him. Jane and Robert were invited as well as Kath – Quentin was out of town on business. It had been the hottest day since Jane had arrived in Ouverru and she was grateful she hadn't been needed in the office that morning. After enjoying a couple of hours sitting in the shade on their rear terrace, she spent the afternoon at the pool, with most of the other residents; the only ones absent being those with air-conditioning. She hoped her baby would enjoy the cooling effect of the water, although she didn't know whether the temperature in her womb ever changed.

It was uncomfortably hot even ambling along the road to the Bonds' that evening, and indoors with the ceiling fans on full blast Jane, in her coolest cotton kaftan, still found the heat oppressive. Robert, Gregg and Tom were sensibly dressed in T-shirts and shorts, Kath also wore a loose-fitting kaftan, while Cindy, as was her fashion, wore a revealing short dress.

Glasses were quickly filled by Gregg with lethally strong gin and tonics, topped up with ice cubes to help cope with the heat and humidity. Even Jane was tempted by Gregg to have one glass.

'So what's in your report, Tom?' Robert asked. 'Will you tell the truth, the whole truth, or aren't you ready to retire yet?'

Tom gave a rueful smile and confessed his punches would be well and truly pulled. The recommendations would be what DfID and the Buzamban authorities required. Namely, to justify more money for education.

'The travesty continues,' Cindy gave a frustrated smile. 'I know,' her voice perked-up as she changed the subject, 'after the cake, we'll play charades. Tom should be brilliant at bullshit!'

'Ho, ho,' Tom pulled a face and tried to keep his eyes away from Cindy's cleavage.

'Cake, what cake?' Kath pricked up her ears at the sound of something interesting.

'Dear Tom here has baked us a cake – with his own fair hands,' replied Cindy. 'It should have cooled now. I'll go and get it.'

Cindy staggered into the living room holding Tom's work of cake artistry to murmurs of surprise.

'Wow, it's huge,' Kath was clearly impressed. It's as big as... err... Cape Town.' Kath was in fine form this evening, speaking in an unusually confident manner. Whether it was the drink or the absence of her husband was difficult to tell.

'It's my own secret recipe,' Tom announced. 'At home I call it Smith's Chocolate Surprise.'

'Well, you can surprise me by giving me some,' Kath had thrown her normal inhibitions out of the window.

Cindy cut generous portions and handed them around. Jane thought it very dry and the chocolate taste was flavoured with something indefinable. It reminded her of a cake she'd had years ago but she couldn't quite remember what it was. They all congratulated Tom on his masterpiece and quickly washed it down with more strong alcoholic drinks. Definitely too dry, Jane decided.

Having helped himself to another slice, Robert asked Tom if anything interesting had happened since they'd met at Christmas.

'Not really.' Tom said that DfID had funded a three-day workshop for rural teachers at the Forest Side Hotel in M'Basara, a town two hours' drive from Ouverru. By a remarkable coincidence, the hotel was owned by the President's family and the rates charged for rooms, meals, drinks and hire of the conference room were inflated to match the Plaza's tariff. Frank Cooper had assured Tom that the rates were fair so, no doubt, he got his percentage.

Thirty-five teachers had attended at a cost to British taxpayers of five hundred pounds per head, plus extra for Tom's team, and expenses for three of Frank's staff, plus two men from UNDP. A total of around twenty-seven thousand pounds.

'Bloody hell. Was it money well spent?' Robert asked.

Tom gave him a mocking look. 'What the fuck do you think?' His hurried intake of alcohol was making him slur his words. 'It was great for all those who attended, probably the best three days of wining, dining and fornication they've ever had but from the project's point of view, it was a total waste of money.'

'Fornication!' A surprised Kath asked with a girlish giggle. 'You mean you provided women as well?'

'As far as I know, we didn't directly pay for prostitutes but the 'ladies' appeared as if by magic and most of the delegates' spent their expenses on satisfying their carnal lusts, so indirectly... maybe we did!'

After more cake and another gin refill all round, he gave them more details. The workshop consisted of a series of educational films from UK, a questionable propaganda UNDP film, a couple of question and answer sessions which Tom let his team run, and a visit to the nearby Catholic boarding school; the latter being an example of the standards they should all strive to achieve.

'Did they actively take part with questions and comments?' Jane asked.

'Oh, bloody hell, yes. They loved it. Most African teachers are articulate and good public speakers, and don't suffer the shyness of their counterparts in England. The trouble is, once they start, it's hard to get them to stop. Not only are they good speakers but they're also argumentative. No place for a *mzungu*! That's why I excused myself and found refuge with the mini-bar in my room.'

'Didn't you learn anything new from the teachers?'

Tom slowly shook his head from side to side. 'Not a fucking thing. I've been round many of the schools and it's clear what's required. Most school buildings are too small and in a poor state of repair.'

'Sounds a bit like England,' Jane said with a touch of irony.

Tom ignored her interruption. 'They are overcrowded; eighty or so in one dark room, and it's quite common for the kids to have no text or writing books. Teachers are several months in arrears with their pittance of a salary, so they often go AWOL for days at a time. And that's despite bloody millions of pounds, dollars, euros or cowrie shells being sent to the government to provide these basic necessities.'

'So, what's the solution?' It was Gregg's turn to ask the obvious.

Tom emptied his glass and passed it to Gregg for another refill, in the process sneaking a peep at Cindy's neckline. 'No bloody idea,' he slurred. 'The money just evaporates – you all know that – and doesn't reach the kids who need it. The only good schools are those run by charities and religious groups. They manage to keep the government's hands off the money.'

'So the solution is to cut out the government altogether.'

'Yes. But try telling that to Frank and all his chums in ESSA. The government insists that DfID funds pass through them – end of story.'

'And if they try and bypass the government?'

'Then take your money along with your rules and go stuff yourselves. That's what Mugabe does.'

Cindy was getting bored with the men talking doom and gloom once again. 'For goodness sake, you people – lighten up.' Her *sex on legs* image quickly refocused their attention. 'Can't you think of anything better to talk about?'

To everyone's surprise, Kath, who had been keeping pace with Tom and Gregg in downing her drinks, happily agreed with Cindy. 'Yes, let's funny... err... fun... have fun,' came her mangled reply. Kath usually gave the impression of being sober and straight-laced, but whether she intended it or not, she was letting her hair down tonight.

'Sorry for the monologue everybody,' Tom said staring appreciatively at his hostess, his alcohol intake making him bolder than usual. He reminded her of the offer of playing games. Just what kind of games he had in mind was open to conjecture.

'Nothing energetic for me,' Jane said. 'And as I'm the only sober member of the party I'd prefer to pass. In fact, I wouldn't mind going home soon. It's so hot tonight... but I wouldn't want to break up the party.'

'Let's all go and get a little fwesh air,' Cindy's slurred speech sounded as though her tongue was stuck to her back teeth. 'We could walk you home. It's bound to be cooler outside.'

Cindy linked arms with Gregg and Tom, extra support being needed to keep all three upright as they stumbled along the track. Kath grabbed hold of Jane and Robert for support but Jane noticed Robert was also staggering a little, so it was left to her to keep them all vertical. What a drunken lot.

There were only four street lights in Basu compound and these automatically switched off at ten o'clock, so there were only the stars to show them the way. When the lights were on, they seemed to attract every flying insect and moth from a ten-mile radius, most of them incinerating themselves on the hot bulbs.

All but Jane were sublimely intoxicated and laughed and sniggered like teenagers out on their first pub crawl. The compound was very quiet with most sensible residents already sound asleep. A slight breeze had sprung up making all of them feel more comfortable and Tom was *feeling* more than he should.

'Stop it, you naughty man,' Cindy giggled as she pushed Tom's straying hand away. Gregg didn't seem bothered. Jane hated being sober when everyone else was well away, but she didn't think she'd ever let herself get legless like the others.

As they passed the pool, Cindy suddenly had the mixed-up brainwave that they should go swimming, or more precisely skinny-dipping.

'I've got the key,' chortled Gregg. 'Let's go.'

Jane's swaying group followed the three inebriated musketeers through the gate and started to undress. They must be mad, Jane thought. Anyone could come by, especially the guard who was supposed to patrol the compound throughout the night. A confused Jane stood rooted to the spot and could vaguely make out Tom and Gregg stripped to their underpants while Cindy went to a nearby chair and unzipped the back of her dress. A very unsteady Kath went and sat next to her and proceeded to take her kaftan off. All of them, except Jane, were giggling like a bunch of adolescent schoolchildren.

The next thing Jane knew, Robert had also stripped to his pants and jumped in the pool. She wanted to yell at him to get dressed and come home but, for some reason which she couldn't fathom out at the time, she did neither. She was confused and light-headed. Everything was fuzzy. She rapidly blinked her eyes a few times to try and clear her head.

Robert didn't even look to see where she was. How could he? This was the man who'd promised she was the only woman in his life and now, just a few weeks later, he was ogling, with lascivious intent, one of her best friends. She was convinced that the sexual allure Cindy had paraded all evening had mesmerized him, and the possibility of seeing her naked had robbed him of his senses.

Jane thought about going home but, although she'd only had one alcoholic drink, she felt a tinge of excitement about swimming in her underclothes amongst near naked men. And then there was Gregg, her Mr Excitement. She saw Cindy slip into the pool telling them to join her, *au naturel*, but it was too dark to see if she was wearing anything. It was obvious she hadn't worn a bra that evening so her top half was certainly bare.

A very unsteady Kath wearing only a bra and pants, slowly lowered herself into the pool. 'This is lovely,' she said. 'Come on in, Jane, it's fucking marvellous.'

What on earth had got into Kath? Jane had never seen her like this before... and her language... is this crazy and seedy and to be stopped now? Were Cindy and Gregg planning an impromptu wife swap? Or was it just harmless fun and a good way to cool down? Jane couldn't decide – she was confused and her brain gradually went into neutral. She heard her own voice saying she would join them but whether she'd said it aloud, or to the voices in her head, she couldn't be sure. At least she was wearing a full set of underwear.

Just as Kath had said, the water felt marvellous; it was wonderfully refreshing and Jane just floated, letting the water cool her body. She leant back to let her head cool down and she could see a sky full of twinkling stars which she wanted to believe were sending her a message to enjoy herself. She felt dizzy.

Her tranquillity lasted only a few seconds before she heard Gregg telling everyone to take off their pants.

As Jane looked round, she saw all the others, still giggling like adolescents, happily removing whatever they'd kept on and placing the soggy articles on the poolside.

'May I molest your husband, Jane?' came a drunken cry from Kath at the other end of the pool, followed by the muted sound of laughter from the others.

What kind of question was that? Jane knew something was wrong with the way she felt but it was a pleasurable, heady sort of wrong. She didn't know whether she replied or not.

She felt someone swim up to her – it was Gregg. 'He'll be all right,' Gregg whispered as he came alongside. 'He can handle old Kath.'

'How do you mean 'handle'?' Jane suddenly thought that was the funniest thing she'd ever said and laughed uncontrollably as Gregg gently put his hand on her bare shoulder, sending tingles of excitement through her body.

'May I be the perfect gentleman and help you out of your underwear?' Gregg's hand slowly went to her bra strap. 'You're the only one dressed.'

Jane later thought that the answer couldn't possibly have been hers; it must have been someone else who had taken possession of her mind and body. Gregg gently removed her bra and pants and placed them on the nearest edge of the pool; a very relaxed Jane, or whoever it was who'd taken over of her body, let herself float, unencumbered by any clothing. She felt wonderful.

'You're very beautiful,' murmured Gregg as he very lightly put his hand on one of her breasts. Why didn't she resist? She thought she should but... nothing. He then gently took both breasts in his hands and kissed her on her lips.

Knowing what was happening but powerless to stop it, Jane wondered if she wanted him to stop? She was floating languidly in her own remote private kingdom. She felt Gregg manipulate her so that her legs were round his waist and her arms on his shoulders. Part of her mind was missing; she was in a sphere where everything was taken apart and put back together slowly. Gregg was about to make love to her and that was the only thing to concentrate on. He entered her and she leant back to enjoy the full sensation. It was fantastic. After a brief pause, Gregg continued his love-making, the water sloshing around them making little wavelets. Suddenly, the mistiness in her head cleared, hitting her like a slap in the face, knowing this was wrong. Very wrong. She was willingly being fucked by another man. No, it had to stop. She didn't love him; she loved Robert. Robert.

'I want you to stop... please.' She was back inside her own body again.

Much to her relief, Gregg immediately pulled away and she was able to stand on the pool floor; her head and shoulders clear of the water.

'Robert,' she called, 'I want to go home. I'm... err... not well.'

He appeared at her side within seconds and helped her out of the pool. She knew they were 'on-show' but all she wanted was to dress and go home. She was aware that Gregg had now gone over to the abandoned Kath, and Cindy and Tom were huddled together doing goodness knows what at the other end of the pool.

Just how they got home and in the front door, Jane couldn't remember but she had the presence of mind to push a befuddled Robert towards their bedroom before going into the kitchen to thank Sellie for looking after Gilly. Sellie was surprised to see a wet and bedraggled Jane but wouldn't ever dream of questioning her employer, even in this unusual state.

Robert lay semi-comatose on the edge of the bed; only opening his eyes when Jane poked him, and giving the most inane grin she'd ever seen. She was gradually regaining her senses and... began to realise what had happened to them – Tom's cake had been laced with cannabis, that familiar flavour was the same as she'd tasted when dating Peter Collins, when almost all her friends in Ringwood were also using it. So it was the combination of too much alcohol and 'cannabis cake' that had made everyone behave in that way. Certainly Robert, and poor old Kath, had acted totally out of character, but maybe this is what Cindy and Gregg did regularly, when they met with their wife-swapping crowd.

But what had she herself done? Unfortunately, she remembered exactly what she had done – she'd let Gregg make love to her... only briefly but... now she was full of guilt. Guilt because she'd allowed him do it, guilt because she'd enjoyed it but, most of all, guilt because she'd cheated on her husband. He might even call her a whore and who could blame him? He might even send her back to England and get a divorce. Jane prayed that this was one secret he would never know; her only hope was that the whole evening would be a blur, or even a complete blank to Robert, especially as he'd drunk far more than usual, and had eaten several slices of Tom's cannabis cake. But what if he does remember? Will he know what he and Kath were doing? Maybe he and Kath... err... no...she didn't think so but the thought did at least bring a slight smile to her face. The very idea... Robert and Kath... prim and proper Kath.

Robert had started to snore so Jane made him comfortable before showering and getting into bed. She had a bad night and had to shake Robert awake the following morning. He looked terrible. He didn't mention anything about the previous evening's high jinks, only complained about a hangover. It was as if the frolicking in the pool had never happened. She wondered when his memory would return.

The Bond's car arrived as usual with Solomon at the wheel and Trish and Susie waving, so at least somebody must be up in the Bond household.

Jane told Sellie she was tired and went back to bed for a couple of hours. Should she try and ignore everything? But how could she? She thought that if nothing happened that day and she heard nothing from either the Bonds or Kath, then she would wait until Robert came home and deftly try and delve into what he could remember.

It was after six-fifteen and starting to get dark before a subdued Robert came slowly into the house. Gilly, making her usual effusive fuss, momentarily improved his mood to the point where he even managed to laugh. After she'd gone to watch TV, his smile disappeared and he avoided looking directly at Jane.

Sellie cleared the dinner plates away, Gilly went to bed and they each sat in their usual places on the sofa, but this time there was a gap between them.

It was Jane who broke the silence. 'How do you feel?'

'A b-bit groggy, I'm afraid,' he stammered.

'Yes, I've not been at my best either.'

Neither of them looked at each other during this brief exchange and, for their own reasons, neither knew whether to add anything.

It was Robert who broke the ice. 'You're not mad, then?'

'Should I be?'

Robert was beginning to stutter like f-Fearless. 'Well, it's about w-what happened l-last n-night – in the pool – with Kath.'

For a moment, Jane thought it sounded a bit like Cluedo – 'I think it was Kath, in the pool, with a candle stick' – or more likely with a bra strap. Jane realised that Robert wasn't aware of what she'd done with Gregg. She'd play it cool.

'Well, what did you do?'

'I'm n-not too sure… but…'

'But what?'

'We were both nak… undressed. Have you heard from her?'

'No.'

This time Robert turned and faced Jane. 'Honestly, darling, I d-don't know what… h-how it happened. B-but I didn't do anything… w-well except…'

'Except what?' Jane knew her tone was accusing which wasn't how she'd meant it to come out.

'W-well we… err… it was her mainly; s-she w-wouldn't stop touching me.'

'Where?'

Robert was going through another trauma of remorse. 'Well, all over r-really.'

Jane knew she should stop her poor husband's excruciating confession; she was the one who should make the main declaration of guilt, one she hoped she would never have to make. She reached over and took his hands. 'I've a suspicion that Tom's cake contained cannabis and that's why we all behaved the way we did – cannabis mixed with alcohol can make people do crazy things.'

'Cannabis?' questioned Robert. 'Oh, bloody hell!'

'I'm going to phone Cindy in the morning and, if it's true, I'm going to give her hell.'

'And what about the baby? Will it affect you?'

'Fortunately, I only had one piece.'

'Did you feel a bit funny then?' a concerned Robert asked, 'what happened to you? What did you do in the pool? Who were you with?'

'Like you, I don't remember much,' Jane lied. 'I think it may have been Gregg.' As soon as she said 'Gregg' she knew it was a mistake.

Robert's mind was slowly coming round to the fact that perhaps he wasn't the only one full of guilt. 'And were you both naked?' he asked.

'I... err... don't remember,' Jane said defensively.

The pendulum had swung and it was now Robert on the attack. 'You were naked; I remember when I helped you out of the pool.' His stutter had now gone. 'What did you do with Gregg?'

'Nothing.' She wasn't sure how convincing she sounded. Where was her 'spin doctor' when she needed one? 'I was dizzy and felt sick, that's why I called to you that I wanted to get out,' was the best she could do.

Robert was way out of his depth. Jane's answer was unconvincing but what he should do or say next was difficult. Had she had sex with Gregg? He didn't think so because Jane had only been in the pool a short time before she wanted to get out.

'I'm going to bed,' he suddenly announced, and strode off to the bedroom. Although he'd lied to Jane about his affair with Lucy Ambeda and any sexual misbehaviour was more his than hers, he felt good about making Jane feel guilty. His memory of the previous night had returned, and he recalled enjoying his encounter with the naked Kath. They were almost at the point of no return when Jane interrupted their *not quite* coupling by calling out to him. Phew, that was a close call, he smiled to himself. Unfairly, she had given him a hard time over Precious and Amanda, so it was good to get his own back. He was sure they would both be more careful in the future.

An angry Jane phoned Cindy the next morning to tell her she'd kill Tom if he ever set foot in Buzamba again. Whilst the threat of death was probably an exaggeration, she told the unusually silent Cindy that she would certainly report him to the police and the British High Commission. For her part, Cindy said that she'd had no idea that Tom had put cannabis in the cake and was mortified that it had happened in her house, with her guests. She'd been round to see Kath to apologise and make sure she was all right. Apart from a hangover and a complete loss of memory, Kath claimed to be OK.

Even two days after what had become 'the pool incident' in her mind, Jane was still very muddled about her feelings and emotions. Does a leopard ever change its spots? Was she still a whore? She had so many questions but not many answers. When she'd married Robert, she knew that he wasn't the most electrifying man she'd ever met but he was kind and a good father for Gilly. For the first time in her life, someone put her first and foremost and provided the financial security she'd always craved.

So now it was clear; crystal clear. She would not have an affair with Gregg. She would work on her marriage and somehow, put a bit of fire in Robert's belly and spice up their love life. She wasn't sure how but there was plenty of time for that. In any case, it wouldn't be long before anything sexual would have to take a back seat in preparation for the arrival of 'it'.

There was an anxiety between Jane and Robert for a couple of days. Although being conscious of his own transgression, Robert still had a suspicious feeling about Jane and Gregg.

Gilly, feeling the tension between them for a second time, was aware that adult relationships could go wrong. Some of her friends' parents in Ringwood and also here in Ouverru had split up. There was a small, niggling doubt in the back of her mind that it might affect her mummy and daddy – a daddy she'd only had for six months. 'Are you all right, Mummy?' she asked, running to Jane after school.

Jane wasn't sure what she meant. 'Yes, of course, darling, why shouldn't I be?'

'Do you still love Daddy?'

Jane's heart missed a beat. It was obvious she had picked up on their stress. 'Oh, Gilly, yes, of course I do. We love each other very much. It's just… well…' she tried to think of the best way to explain away the last two days of friction, 'I've been a bit tired, you know, with the new baby, but I'm feeling better now.'

Gilly looked relieved as Jane picked her up, giving her a cuddle.

'Mummy and Daddy love each other very much,' she repeated, 'and we both love you too,' making Gilly giggle as she squeezed her tightly.

It was abundantly clear that they must patch things up, so when Robert arrived home, she behaved as if nothing had happened and he seemed pleased to be back in the old routine. It was only after Gilly was in bed that Jane told him what had happened.

'Oh dear, we weren't very smart were we? I do love you. I do not, and I emphasise the "not", fancy Kath… or Cindy or anyone else.'

'And I love you… and only you. I also promise.'

Her response gave Robert a lift. This was the first time she'd told him to his face that she loved him. Equanimity returned to the Kimber household and Gilly soon forgot her worries. Mummy and Daddy were back to normal.

CHAPTER TWENTY-FIVE

The news came through confirming the dates of a mission from the German aid agency, DGA. They would arrive in Buzamba in a week's time. During their visit they would check on the Ogola Slum Project and also Kabara.

'Are you happy about that?' Jane asked.

'No, not at all. Herr Priem and Bauer are awkward buggers who find fault with almost everything. Last time they were here, they went out of their way to give Ken and me a very hard time. And this time, they'll want to check the accounts and the computers.' Robert scratched his head while updating the diary on his computer. 'I hope it's not going to tire you too much.' His chin got its customary rub, almost a caress, as he gave Jane what he hoped was a reassuring smile.

'How long will they be here?'

'I'm not sure but I hope it's no more than a week. We'll be in Kabara for one or two days, at least one day in Ogola, and one day at an agricultural project in Sanga – thankfully, nothing to do with me. Finally they'll have meetings at two or three ministries, as well as the German Embassy.'

'Why doesn't the German Embassy take care of them? DGA is part of the German Government, isn't it?'

'It is, yes, but Priem always pulls a face when I remind him that the Embassy is expecting them.'

'That's strange, isn't it? At least, they shouldn't complain too much as you'll have some progress to show them.'

'Don't you believe it. They love to find fault, especially Priem, and there's a lot to criticize in Kabara. I think Ogola should be okay but… who am I kidding? They'll find something to rant and rave about. Oh, and another thing, you shouldn't go to Ogola while they're here.'

'Why not?'

'I never cleared it with Schultec for you to work there. Even as a volunteer. It's better if they think the work has been done by Hani, plus of course, BuzanComp and Benedicts. They may not like the idea of my wife sticking her nose into things that don't concern her.'

While not surprised, Jane still felt a bit miffed. If it hadn't been for her, the computerisation of the accounts would be in a complete mess. 'I hope you haven't forgotten that Hani and I are meeting Lily and Tamba from BuzanComp on Monday and we'll be with them most of the week.'

'Oh bugger! I had forgotten, and I'll have the car.'

'Don't panic,' Jane joked. 'And, for goodness sake, when you're with the Germans, *don't mention the war!*'

Robert's humour button was temporarily out of action. 'I'll have to try and think of something.'

'Don't worry, darling, I can easily take taxis.' She could tell he was already getting stressed, and the last thing she wanted was to add to his worries. 'Anyhow, what else is on your list?'

'The move into the new head office – maybe we should postpone it.'

'But why? Let them see you move into the new building. Ken will have it well organised. You never know, they might be impressed,' she paused for a couple of seconds, 'and one other thing.'

'What's that?'

'Stop stroking your chin – you'll wear it out!'

Robert grinned and tried to relax. 'At least when Poppy and Tony arrive, the Germans should be well away.'

Robert duly met Herren Priem and Bauer off the plane and spent two hours with them at the Plaza, organising the programme for their stay in Buzamba. 'I'm taking them to Kabara first thing tomorrow morning,' he told Jane when he got home, 'but only for one night. Is that OK?'

'I can't very well say "no" can I?' she laughed.

He pulled a face. 'I'd have a problem if you did.'

'Only teasing, Kimber. I'll be fine.'

The following morning, the compound guard organised a taxi to take Jane to the meeting with Lily and Tamba. Hani was already there. They sat around the boardroom table whilst a nervous Tamba confirmed that all the procedures had been finished. Jane sensed there was something lacking in his presentation and that all wasn't well. But what was it? Was it to do with Tamba's shifty-eyed delivery or the fact that Lily didn't have any notes to refer to?

Jane opened the folder Tamba handed her. Her eyes almost glazed over as she tried to read the first few paragraphs – it could have been written in a foreign language as far as she could figure out. She was utterly baffled by it all and somewhere, deep down, her own personal panic button had been given a mighty thrust. It was complicated with jargon, graphs, and charts. What did it all mean? She tried to remember what 'control accounts' and 'accruals' were? She'd come across these terms during her studies but couldn't for the life of her remember what they were. She'd stupidly set herself up for what was almost certainly going to be an almighty crash. What should she do?

The others looked to her for a reaction. She tried to stay calm and hide her unease. 'I… err…think I need a couple of hours to quietly read through it all.' This feeble excuse would give her some time but she knew the timetable was tight and the Germans would be examining everything later in the week. 'Can we meet again at two o'clock this afternoon?'

Whether the others realised she was out of her depth, she couldn't tell but they agreed to her suggestion. She left the office in a daze and walked to a nearby taxi rank but - where could she go? She thought of going home and then sending a message that she'd suddenly been taken ill - being a coward may just about save her face. But everything had to be ready for the Germans and she couldn't let Robert down. While waiting for a taxi to appear she looked around and saw she was outside the InterBank building. Gregg's workplace. Lovely, sexy Gregg! On a whim, she went inside and his secretary ushered her into his office; a big, posh air-conditioned room, with more leather on show than on a herd of cows.

Gregg's eyes lit up. 'What a welcome sight,' he said, as he closed the door. He took her in his arms and gave her a gentle kiss on her cheek. Under different circumstances Jane would have pulled away but right now she needed the reassurance of a friendly embrace.

'Can I get you a drink? Coffee maybe?'

'Oh, yes please Gregg. If I wasn't pregnant I'd have a stiff scotch.'

'Oh dear, what's the problem?'

Jane started to sob, 'I've made a complete idiot of myself.' Little by little, she told him how she'd foolishly involved herself in setting up the computer system and now she was out of her depth. She'd let everyone believe she was an expert, she'd even kidded herself she was, but Tamba's report was double-dutch to her.

Gregg took her in his arms again and gently kissed away her tears. Jane snuggled into his embrace not caring if anyone might catch them. She was beyond that. She wanted him to kiss her and say he'd make everything better. They stayed like that for a minute before a knock on the door heralded the arrival of coffee.

'Show me what you've got there,' Gregg picked up the folder and briefly flicked through it. 'Is there a list of contents anywhere? A schedule of the procedures they've designed? I've no idea from this what they are trying to do.'

'I don't know,' she said uneasily.

'Hang on, I'll call my systems specialist. I'm sure it's just a straightforward computerised accounting system.'

InterBank's systems expert was Emmanuel Obowanji and for the next forty minutes the three of them went through Tamba's report.

'It looks like a load of bull shit wrapped in pages of rubbish.' Emmanuel was very disparaging. 'Typical consultant's garbage. It's looks to me as if it's all been taken straight from a text book,' he added, putting a pencil line through most of the pages. 'All irrelevant!'

Gregg had to go to a meeting but Emmanuel spent the next hour going through it with Jane so that she got a better idea of what she had to do. He was brilliant, explaining what all the terminology meant and, when he translated the jargon into the terms she'd been taught, it started to make sense. Not only did she understand most of it, but she was able to see for herself what was missing. Together, they made a list of everything that still had to be done.

Feeling totally relieved, almost euphoric, Jane returned to Benedicts armed with Emmanuel's schedules. It only took fifteen minutes to deliver her scathing comments on Tamba's report.

Lily looked uncomfortable. It was her job to check Tamba's work, and it was obvious she hadn't. They spent the next hour and a half going through the report with Emmanuel's list of missing information.

Taking a big breath, Jane looked in Lily's direction. 'Lily, I think you'll agree that there is still a lot of work to do.'

Lily took her time before answering. 'I'll go through it with Tamba. Let me have a list of what you think is missing.'

'I'll get the full list to you before five o'clock this afternoon, but here's the important thing, Lily. DGA arrived yesterday and later this week, probably on Thursday, they'll want to see everything to do with the computerisation. And I mean everything.'

A nervous nod of her head showed Jane she understood.

'You know DGA has paid BuzanComp to supply the computers and modify its accounting software for Ogola,' Jane continued, 'and is paying you – well Benedicts actually, for your expertise in making sure everything works. They believe all documentation and staff training is already underway so you have a massive amount of catching up to do.' Jane didn't feel at all sorry for Lily as, after all, she'd let her down badly.

After leaving Benedicts, Jane and Hani went back to her house to organise the list which Hani could hand-deliver on his way back to Ogola. Using Robert's computer they prepared a four page letter listing everything that Lily and Tamba had to finish.

The following evening, Robert arrived home late from Kabara after dropping his DGA 'friends' off at the Plaza. His expression was grim. 'Get me a drink, please darling, and make it a treble.'

'Oh dear. Was it that bad?'

'Both Priem and Bauer tore strips off our staff in Kabara and I haven't come out of it very well. They were mad. They want a new project manager there immediately.'

'Poor you.' Jane put her arms round her gloomy husband. 'So, what will you do?'

After downing his drink he sank slowly into the nearest chair. 'Schultec knows the problems – I've told them about this for the past few months so they shouldn't be surprised when they get a rocket up their fat arses from Priem.'

'But it's not your fault,' Jane tried to reassure him.

'No, it isn't. I just hope Schultec see it that way. At least I won't see either of the Germans tomorrow. Basil is taking them up to Sanga but they'll be in Ogola first thing Thursday morning.'

'I hope they'll be in a better mood by then.'

'Well, we have some progress to show them and the new head office will be more-or-less ready, even if we haven't actually moved in. Priem will certainly say it's all wrong,' he added pessimistically.

'Isn't Bauer the financial analyst? Will he look at the accounts?'

'Ah yes, that reminds me. He wants to see the computers and the new systems in operation on Friday morning. Will Hani be able to show him everything?'

Jane's jaw dropped. 'I thought you knew,' her voice went into distressed mode. 'Nothing's ready!'

Robert looked dumbstruck. 'I thought ..'

'You thought what?' Jane felt sorry for her poor, tired husband. 'The computers are still in BuzanComp and won't be delivered until next week.'

'Can't they come earlier?'

'But we have nowhere to put them. The office isn't ready... remember?' Holding her breath and taking hold of his hand, she then dropped her bombshell about her saga at Benedicts.

'But I thought you understood it all.'

'So did I but... I was being stupid, very stupid. I thought it would be the same as the work I did in Ringwood, but it's not.'

'Oh bloody hell. So what happens now?'

'Not to worry big man, I've got it sorted. If it hadn't been for Gregg though, I'd have been in a bloody mess.' She told him how Gregg had come to the rescue and how Emmanuel had helped to explain everything so she could crack the whip with Lily and Tamba.

Robert wasn't convinced. 'But what about Hani? Will he be able to explain everything to Bauer?'

'Tell Bauer that Tamba and Lily can do that in BuzanComp's office. Hani and I are going to Benedicts in the morning and we'll spend all day there.'

Robert was still worried. 'I'll tell you what, I'll phone Alan Swanson at Benedicts – he's the senior partner there. He'll have to rattle Lily's cage a bit.'

An anxious-looking Tamba and po-faced Lily were already there, still leafing through Jane's schedule, when she and Hani arrived. A none-too-happy Mr Swanson had laid down the law to Lily and he wouldn't accept any excuses. The report had been completely rewritten in draft form but it didn't take Jane long to work out that it was nowhere near complete.

'Lily, you know what we want.' Trying to remember what Emmanuel had told her, Jane emphasised that there had to be a schedule starting at the beginning of process – the beginning would be the tenant's ledger, and then a logical step-by-step procedure through the total process to the month-end report. This is what had been agreed. When Lily responded, again using accounting jargon, Jane knew she was losing it. More panic. What could she do?

'I'll tell you what, Lily. I'm feeling a bit headachy, so I'll go and get some fresh air, and I'll take this report with me. Can we meet again at one o'clock?'

Lily and Tamba had no alternative but to agree. Jane told Hani to go back to Ogola and she'd see him back here for the afternoon meeting.

Jane went straight to InterBank and hoped and prayed that Emmanuel would be there – she deliberately avoided Gregg's office. Yes, she was in luck – Emmanuel was in and was more than happy to help. After spending two hours carefully going through the report, Emmanuel called in his secretary and got her to type up his notes. He then took Jane for a quick lunch so that she'd be at Benedicts in time for the second meeting.

Taking the deepest of breaths, Jane stood and started her instruction of what had to be done. 'It needs more work... yes, that's right... look at page six, make it clear... no, no, I've already told you... no, that's wrong... this must balance with that... yes, computerised receipts… of course… yes, good… but that's not right… for credit control… only at the month end…'

By six o'clock, all the points on a totally exhausted Jane's list had been ticked but Emmanuel had told her that it was imperative to do a dummy run of a month's accounts.

Tamba's tired face dropped and he rested his head on his arms. 'If we do a dummy run, it'll take at least four hours.'

With her boss's words still ringing in her ears, Lily had no alternative but to support Jane's demands, and if it meant burning the midnight oil, then so be it.

Only after Jane was in the taxi did she realise how tired she was. The last few days had been exhausting; she had been giving out orders on subjects beyond her capability. On paper, both Lily and Tamba were better qualified than her but fortunately, neither of them knew it. You can fool some people some of the time, but… can you fool all the people all the time? If Herr Bauer found mistakes or just didn't like what they were doing, everyone, especially Lily and Tamba, would point the finger at her. She mentally conjured-up every swear word she knew… she may need them. What had she done? What had she let herself in for? What would Robert say if the shit hits the fan? He might even get fired!

Sitting on the terrace with her cup of tea after breakfast, Jane chewed over how she'd been so incredibly naive as to think she could mastermind the new computer system. It was another hot day and she sat watching the heat waves making swirly patterns on the ground in front of her. She raised her cup and silently toasted Emmanuel which prompted her into phoning Gregg to thank him once again for letting Emmanuel help.

'You owe me one,' he said in such a way that made her feel very awkward because she wasn't sure if he was serious or just joking.

Searching for a suitable reply she managed. 'I do owe both you and Emmanuel for what you did.' She felt deep down that she wanted to thank him in a more personal way and had a fleeting vision of the two of them lying naked in each other's arms. Was it sexual frustration, being pregnant, or just her jumbled-up hormones making her fantasise in this way? She pushed the unwanted images out of her mind.

The swimming pool was very inviting and, after a light lunch, she joined Cindy in some gentle exercise, after which she unburdened herself telling her how she'd become too involved with the project, and that Gregg and Emmanuel had been her saviour. Evidently, he hadn't mentioned any of this to Cindy but she gave a sly wink which did nothing to ease Jane's guilt complex or her feelings for Gregg.

A shattered-looking Robert dragged himself wearily up the steps to the front door. It was almost nine o'clock when he dropped onto the sofa, patting the seat for Jane to join him. Relishing his first cold, reviving taste of a stiff gin and tonic, ice clinking in the glass, he gave Jane a brief summary of the day's events. The two Krauts had been only moderately pleased with the new head office, finding fault with the room layout. They insisted that some internal walls should be changed, so that the accounts staff could be moved to the rear.

'But they need to be next to the cashiers' booths,' Jane exclaimed, 'that's crazy!'

Robert shrugged his shoulders as if to say there was nothing he could do about it. 'They won't change the specification of the wetcores because they're sure that, within a short time, all the residents will be queuing to use the showers.'

'They won't listen to reason then?'

'No, not at all. Both Ken and Nelson tried to tell them but they wouldn't listen. They complained that litter was blocking the drainage channels; the demolition of the old buildings was taking too long, etcetera, etcetera. But the worst thing happened on their walkabout. They came face-to-face with a delegation complaining that the rents were too high and that we'd evicted poor people. Someone from the rear threw a plastic bag filled with god-knows-what, which only just missed hitting Priem on his head.'

'Quite a day then.'

Sellie put dinner on the table and Robert refilled his glass. He felt he was more in need of alcoholic sustenance than food but nevertheless polished off a huge mound of beef stew and mashed potatoes. His appetite never deserted him for long.

'And what about the accounts?' Jane asked, with fingers crossed.

'All that happens tomorrow. Hani is taking Bauer to BuzanComp at nine and then Tamba will join them at Benedicts for a meeting with Lily.'

This news sent Jane's stomach churning out enough acid to burn a hole in the dining table. The poor baby, she thought. I won't be able to sleep tonight, worrying about it.

Jane was sharing a sandwich lunch with Sellie when Robert phoned to tell her that Priem and Bauer wanted to see her.

Her heart sank. 'Oh shit! Am I in trouble?'

'It's not looking good. When the Krauts got back from Benedicts, Hani looked scared stiff. They asked Ken what work Mrs Kimber had been doing.'

'Oh, bloody hell,' Jane's panic button kicked in for the umpteenth time in the past few days. 'What did Ken say?'

'Something about you volunteering to help out and how supportive you'd been, or words to that effect. He even gave them a copy of your CV.'

'Oh no, that's the one you sexed-up with all my phony qualifications?'

Robert didn't answer, only saying that Basil was already on his way to collect her. Driving slowly down Cutty Road towards Ogola, Jane forced her mind away from negative thoughts of doom and disaster. Sod them, she thought. She'd done her best and if she hadn't helped out they would have been in a huge mess by now. So they can stuff themselves and if it means Robert loses his job then…tough shit. How dare those German bastards complain about me? She was angry; as angry as the night at Quentin's when Rex Potts had groped her. She took no shit from randy Rex and she'd take no shit from those two lousy Krauts.

Her bravado sustained her until she entered one of the bare rooms in the new head office, where a temporary table and a few odd chairs had been set up. Robert and Ken were standing, as were the two other men in the room – the nauseating Krauts. All eyes were on her and she felt herself wilt – her comfort zone was somewhere way over the horizon. Robert and Ken both gave her a supportive 'hello' as the two strangers came to meet her.

'My name is Priem,' said the taller of the two. He managed something approaching a smile, shook her hand and, at the same time, gave a slight bow moving his head downward in a jerky gesture, while keeping the rest of his body upright.

Typical Nazi, Jane thought. She was half expecting him to click his heels and give a Hitler salute.

Herr Priem gestured to the other storm-trooper, 'and may I present Herr Bauer, our financial analyst.'

'Good day, Mrs Kimber.' Mr Bauer was considerably older and his bow was more pronounced than Priem's.

'Please have a seat, Mrs Kimber,' Priem said, 'and get her some tea or coffee,' he ordered sharply, looking in Ken's direction.

When they were seated, Herr Priem gave a slight cough to clear his throat, paused for a moment, then spoke directly to Jane. 'We have toured Ogola and the execution of our project is progressing, although there are many issues which need attention.' He spoke very good English with only the slightest trace of an accent. 'The main problem we have – not only with this project but with all DGA projects in Africa – is accounting.'

Oh *hell's bells*, thought Jane, here we go. She vaguely looked round for signs of thumb screws or other Gestapo torture equipment.

Herr Priem continued. 'The local engineering people are usually of a satisfactory standard but there are no good accountants.' As he spoke, he looked neither at Robert nor Ken, but directly at Jane, who thought they might be consoled by being described as at least 'satisfactory'. 'We have been told that good accountants either emigrate to Europe or seek top jobs in government, where they have the opportunity to… err… how do you say – I think the English expression is "to feather their nests".'

What was all this dilly dallying leading up to? Why couldn't they just spit it out and tell her what a bloody mess she'd made? Her dander was well and truly up. Her nervousness was rapidly being replaced by rage. She was now ready to defend herself.

Herr Priem turned to his colleague, 'please continue Herr Bauer.'

'I haf checked thoroughly ze preparation for ze execution of ze new computer system mit Mrs Lily, Mr Tamba und Mr Hani.' His German accent was very pronounced although Jane had no problem understanding him. She thought how strange it was that Germans used the word 'execution' instead of 'implementation'.

'I would like to say what an excellent job you haf done here. It is the best I've seen in Africa. The system is well documented and has logic. Herr Priem und myself would like to thank you for all your work. Mr Kasansa tells me you haf worked very hard and long hours, und you are a volunteer without pay.'

For a few seconds Jane was speechless. Had she heard it right? Both Robert and Ken were trying to hold back smiles while her two new German gentleman friends gazed at her as if she were Saint Jane of Buzamba.

'But you are a professional, of course,' Bauer added.

'Well… err… thank you,' her voice unusually quiet. 'It's not just me, it's the accounting staff here, as well as Benedicts and BuzanComp.'

Both Germans smiled and their body language indicated that it was typical English modesty on Jane's part.

'You are so highly qualified, Diploma Accountant, that is fantastic. We find it almost impossible to get such highly qualified accountants to work in Africa, even with exorbitant salaries,' dearest, darling, Mr Priem said.

'Ya, if you ever feel you vant, ve vill employ you as consultant in many of our projects throughout Africa,' dear, sweet Mr Bauer laughed.

Do they know what they're talking about? I'm not well qualified. They must be mad. Wonderful, but mad. It must be her sexed-up CV that Robert doctored. Alastair Campbell couldn't have done any better!

What could she say? 'Well that's very kind of you but I'd prefer to stay here.'

'We only joke Mrs Kimber, and we are very grateful for you to do this.' Mr Priem continued, his respectful gaze at Jane, totally ignoring Robert and Ken. 'I assume this is your first experience of an African slum?'

'Yes,' was all the bemused Jane could say.

He shook his head in a resigned manner. He went on to explain that the huge population growth in Africa was a major problem. 'It's urbanization without growth.'

'Why do people put up with it?' Jane had just about calmed down enough to join in the conversation.

'Our experience in other African countries shows that when the slums get too big, the governments decide to clear great swathes, usually quoting that they are a breeding ground for crime. Mugabe, however, cleared them because slum dwellers voted for the opposition.'

'Yes, I saw some of that on television,' Jane murmured.

'If they did the same here we would protest strongly; we would threaten to stop more funding, but the Buzamban Government has heard it all before and they would do whatever they want to do.' He then smiled, 'in any case, our threat would be... how you say... hollow.'

With that, they signalled that their meeting was over.

Mr Bauer said to Jane. 'Please send copies of ze first month's results to me in Germany. It vill be very interesting.'

'I think the first month's results would be too soon,' responded Jane, her confidence fully restored. 'I think it would be best left until, say, the third month as there are bound to be teething problems at first.'

'Ya, of course. That is a much better idea.'

Jane was feeling great and brimming over with self-confidence. She took another chance. 'I hear you want the accounts section to move to the rear of this new building.'

Robert and Ken looked nervously at each other. The two darling Germans said nothing but clearly listened to what she said.

'It would be more efficient for them to be located adjacent to the cashiers.'

Messrs Priem and Bauer looked at each other and scowled in Robert and Ken's direction. 'You are correct Mrs Kimber,' the talented and handsome Mr Priem said, 'see to it Mr Kasansa,' he spoke sharply, 'please listen to Mrs Kimber, she is the expert.'

After exchanging a few more pleasantries, the two charming German gentlemen excused themselves, as they were due at the Ministry of Housing, accompanied by staff from the German Embassy, and were scheduled to leave for Tanzania that evening. They both fawned before the brilliant Jane Kimber but were distinctly offhand in their farewells to the 'merely' satisfactory Robert and Ken.

As Jane's two German idolaters were leaving the room, Ken handed Herr Priem a brown envelope.

'These are the photos,' Ken said.

'Ah so, yes,' and he put the unopened envelope in his brief case.

After they'd gone, the three of them sat down in a shell-shocked silence. Jane was the first to speak. 'What highly intelligent and charming gentlemen they are.' And then slyly to Robert and Ken, 'don't you think?'

'No, we don't.' Ken said ruefully. 'They gave us a hard time, but you... you genius accountant, you had them eating out of your hand. How did you do it? Did you get Sellie to put a spell on them?'

Jane gave him a Machiavellian smile. 'I didn't need to, I make my own potions. How do you think I trapped young Robert into marriage?'

Ken laughed. 'Well, whatever you did, it certainly worked.'

'By the way, what is the qualification they think I have?'

'It suddenly dawned on me,' Robert laughed. 'In Germany a diploma engineer is the same as a university degree in UK, except it's better. It takes five years to qualify in Germany. Herr Priem is a Diploma Engineer. So, when we put on your CV that you held a diploma in accounting – I changed bookkeeping to accounting – your German friends believed you had completed a five year university degree course. End of mystery!'

Ken also got the joke. 'You're probably better qualified than Bauer!'

Jane felt fantastic. After dreading the encounter, she was now a star – a megastar. She made a mental note to phone Lily and Tamba to thank them for their efforts – they really must have pulled out all the stops.

'So from now on you two,' Jane said, addressing Robert and Ken, 'do everything I say or I'll write to my dear friends in Germany and then you'll be in big trouble. Remember, I'm a professional and expert and you two – well, you're only just 'satisfactory'.'

'Yes, oh mighty one,' a subservient Ken replied, giving her a humble bow, 'whatever you say.'

Robert's reply was not so submissive. He threatened to expose her phony credentials unless she did as she was told. They eyeballed each other for a second before Jane gave in.

'Whatever you say, *Bwana*.'

'But here's something they didn't tell you,' Ken said, regaining his natural authority, 'they insist that room rentals must be increased by fifteen per cent.'

Jane thought about that for a moment; it came as a complete surprise. 'And how will that go down?'

'Very badly,' was Ken's sombre reply.

'Sounds like more trouble to me,' she said. 'Oh, by the way, Ken, what were the photos you gave Herr Priem?'

Ken smiled. 'Every time the Germans come here, they arrange to have their pictures taken in the slum, amongst the poor but eternally grateful peasants, who are posed gazing up at their benefactors with a look of religious fervour.'

Oh, that's terrible, was Jane's first thought, but Ken's droll sarcasm made her smile. 'Have you got copies?'

Ken pulled a large envelope from the bottom drawer of his desk. 'Have a look at these. They like to get them printed in their internal magazines in Germany.'

There were about thirty A5 size photos of white people posing with a group of slum dwellers, against a backdrop of the worst blocks. Jane recognised three pictures with Priem and Bauer taken a couple of years earlier.

'But who are the others?' Jane looked questioningly at Ken.

'Each German delegation wants a photo-shoot, and our tame cameraman is on hand so they can then show the folks back home what a wonderful job they are doing in Africa. It's what's called 'a good photo opportunity'. My cynical view is that they want to show how superior they are in comparison to a bunch of useless black people.'

'Oh, Ken, surely not.' Jane was shocked although, on looking at the photos, it did seem a bit like that.

'You'll notice it's more-or-less the same residents in every shot. The photographer has tutored them over the years to look suitably humble.'

Jane leafed through the other photos. 'There's a couple here with several bare-breasted women in them. What happened there?'

Ken's expression was hard to decipher. 'A certain Herr Reichslinger from the health charity asked the photographer if he could get some women to remove their tops for him. After a good deal of negotiating, some women agreed but demanded one thousand shillings each, which Reichslinger paid without a quibble. Next time he came, the word got round and about thirty women turned up all willing to do the same.'

Jane shook her head from side-to-side. 'And you say he's from a charity! Oh my God, how degrading is that? A good photo opportunity! Bloody hell. When you see things like this, it tends to put these so-called well-meaning donors in a different light. They're the scum of the charity workers.'

Over the weekend and throughout the following week, the new head office gradually took shape and, by mid-February, the staff had desks and chairs (new); filing cabinets and cupboards (mainly new), and BuzanComp had installed the computers. A standby generator was also fitted for use when the power supply failed. But the big difference was the inside temperature. With a tiled roof, high ceilings and wide-bladed fans, Jane felt conditions in the office were almost as good as in their home. The main drawback was that on windy days, the windows couldn't be opened wide enough because of the dust blowing in.

Ken shared an office with Robert and they had already stocked the new fridge with beer and soft drinks. The staff kitchen also had a fridge, an electric hotplate, a microwave oven, and a kettle.

Every member of staff, from Ken to Ruth, walked around with huge smiles on their faces. Before they left for their homes late on Saturday afternoon, Ken and Robert opened the bar and toasted themselves and staff in their gleaming new offices.

The next time Jane went shopping, she ignored the horrendous costs and bought two bottles of single malt Scotch Whisky. Basil dropped her outside InterBank and she was again shown into Gregg's office by his secretary.

'I've brought you and Emmanuel a small token as a thank-you for all the help you gave me.'

Gregg rose from his chair and went over to close the door. 'Wow, a present like that deserves a kiss. Come here and lean against the door so that I can show you my appreciation. It'll also keep out unwanted guests,' he laughed.

What was she to do? She innocently held up her face for a kiss on the cheek but Gregg had other ideas. He took her face gently in his hands and kissed her full on the lips, his tongue playing tricks in her mouth. Jane felt herself succumbing and gasped as his hands started to stroke her breasts. Her heart was pounding and her body quivered as though every caress was electrically charged. His hands moved down and lifted up her dress and then he started to take down her pants. That trollop, the one who'd temporarily taken over her mind and body in the swimming pool a few days earlier, was powerless to do anything about it. She desperately wanted him then and there.

His phone rang. 'Shit!' Gregg paused for a moment. It rang again.

'Mr Bond, it's Chet Pilger from New York,' Gregg's secretary announced from the other side of the office wall. 'I'm putting him through.'

Gregg left a shaken Jane, leaning against the door, her dress still above her waist and her pants half way down her legs. She tried to catch her breath and pull herself together.

'Hi Chet, how are you, you old rascal.' Jane could faintly hear a muffled response on the other end of the line.

'No, nothing much,' Gregg grinned as he responded, 'just massaging a few figures.' The faint guffaw from New York was matched by loud laughter from Gregg. 'Remember Chet, my name's Bond, Gregg Bond, *On Her Majesty's Sexual Service*.' He gave another dirty, degrading laugh.

His smutty and childish behaviour jolted Jane back to her senses. Feeling cheap, she slowly rearranged her clothing, smoothed down her hair and wiped her mouth on a tissue; she was back in the real world again. He didn't even look up as she left. Feeling ashamed and red faced, she told the smirking secretary she was going to Emmanuel's office. She knocked on the half-open door.

'I've just come to thank you so very much for helping me out. You were wonderful.'

'Hey, that's my pleasure Jane. How did you get on?'

'It was fine. Once you deciphered the jargon and explained the route we had to take, it all seemed to fall into place. Thank you again.' Jane handed him the whisky and hoped he would accept it as a token of her gratitude. He said he would look forward to sharing it with his girlfriend and with that, they shook hands and Jane left the Bank without checking to see if Gregg was free.

Sitting in the back of the car as Basil drove her home, her mind was racing. What was it about Gregg that made her behave like that? Was it because he was good-looking? – yes. Did he have massive sex appeal? – yes. Was he more skilled sexually than Robert? – yes. Did she want him instead of Robert? – hell no. Gregg was a sexual predator who'd fuck anything in a skirt that still had a pulse. He didn't love her. He only wanted another notch on his bedpost.

What is it about sex – damned, sodding sex – that makes normally sane people act like randy animals on heat? Every action seems to have a sexual accelerator and is always skulking around in the shadows of our minds. We pretend that we have superior, more rational things to think about, but no… it's sex. Jane thought of all the broken marriages and devastated children that modern society seemed to produce.

She'd read somewhere that when men and women meet for the first time, their brains make thousands of calculations about whether to have sex together, as if it was hard-wired into their DNA to breed at every opportunity to produce stronger children than the last generation; better able to survive. Natural selection as Darwin had put it. Was this why she and Gregg had had a brief fling? She thought back to the time when Gregg had made love to her in what she thought of as their *swimming pool incident*.

She knew nothing like that would ever happen again. Never. She'd come to terms with the fact that while Robert was a good husband and father he was not, and never would be, the most exciting personality either in or out of the bedroom. She did love him, but her love was more like the way she loved her favourite cardigan rather than the love, or lust, of a macho super-stud. But now they were a family… an expanding one, financially secure and, as she sat in the back seat of the car, she made a solemn pledge to God, not dissimilar to the female lead in Graham Green's *The End of the Affair*, that she would remain faithful. She still thought it acceptable to have secrets, even within a loving relationship. Telling Robert she'd had sex with Gregg could ruin everything. So why tell him?

CHAPTER TWENTY-SIX

'Wow, what a beautiful place you've got.' Poppy and Tony were taking an early morning stroll in the garden, admiring the brilliant colours of the flowers and shrubs. The purple and red bougainvillea seemed to be on fire, the powerful morning rays burnishing the colourful leaves and blooms. The sense of serenity was enhanced by the variety of birds, busily flying in and out of the bushes, and building nests in the tallest palm trees. 'You didn't tell me it was so fantastic,' Poppy remonstrated with Jane. 'I've never seen such colours. Maybe it's because Ringwood is so dull at this time of year.'

Poppy and Tony had arrived the previous evening. Jane had been looking forward to this day for a long time and she could hardly believe that her oldest friend was actually here. Poppy had brought a suitcase full of clothes for Jane, as well as a smart dress and jacket for Sellie, and new dresses for Gilly and Kaba.

'Anything in there for me?' Robert asked mischievously.

'Not a chance, mate,' replied Tony. 'In fact, there was hardly room for my stuff but Poppy said I could borrow from you! Are there any good charity shops here?'

'We've got better than that – we've got a used clothes factory.'

Tony looked puzzled. 'Are you serious, how can you make used clothes?'

Robert laughed. 'In Africa, old chap, we can do anything. Evidently, charities in Europe sell in bulk to traders, who then send them on to Africa where people pay good money for them. They should have called it a used clothes warehouse but… hey, this is Africa.'

Jane had planned a relaxing morning so that the visitors could acclimatise and swap all the latest news.

'So, Tony, how many of my stories have you sold?' Jane asked. 'And oh, I've arranged for you to meet the editor of our only impartial paper later in the week.'

'That's good, I'll look forward to that,' he said. 'But so far, I haven't had much interest from any of the editors. Can't you get Robert to run off with the President's wife, or something similar? It would make a great story.'

'What Robert! I somehow don't think so,' she laughed. 'Anyway, I won't put any ideas like that in his head… just in case.'

'Ah well, just a thought,' he mused.

Not wanting to develop that fantasy storyline any further, (the image of Precious briefly came into her head), Jane suggested that after lunch, they should all go and relax round the pool.

Shortly after they'd had their first swim, Cindy joined them and Jane was pleased that her two best friends hit it off straight away. Their personalities were very similar, both being gregarious, which probably had something to do with them loving the theatre.

Sellie outdid herself by preparing a special meal of roast lamb with red currant jelly and she and Kaba joined them for dinner. The gradual adjustment of Sellie and Kaba mixing with them on special occasions was working well and any awkwardness of the earlier attempts was steadily disappearing.

After the two men had gone to bed, Jane and Poppy talked late into the night catching up on all that had happened during the past six months; their risqué sense of humour completely unchanged.

'Just look at you, Mrs Kimber,' Poppy said. 'Here you are, living a life of luxury with Mr Wonderful. Didn't I do well?'

'You did good.'

'And are you eternally grateful to me, Mrs Kimber? The pregnant Mrs Kimber.'

'I guess so.'

'What do you mean, you guess so. Did I, or did I not find you the perfect husband? I think a spot of grovelling is called for here.'

'You did fantastically well, Mrs Partington. I'll recommend you to all my desperate friends.'

'I should think so too. Oh, and one other thing. I'd like to borrow Robert for a few days.'

'Borrow him… for what?'

'To make me pregnant of course.'

'I do take it you're joking' Jane gave a surprised laugh, although she wouldn't put anything past her outlandish friend.

Poppy kept a straight face. 'It's no joke. I want a man with good sperm… and lots of it. And obviously, Robert's got sperm that works. How else am I to get up-the-duff? Tell me, is he Tarzan in the bedroom?'

'Never you mind.'

Poppy looked coquettishly at Jane. 'I bet he's Tarzan – swinging from the chandelier – beating his chest and shouting "me Tarzan, you Jane".'

'I warned you not to read any more of those Mills and Boon books. If poor Robert heard you, he'd have a heart attack… poor love. But I've missed you so much,' Jane said. 'There's nobody here quite as disgusting as you. Now, what's all this about Robert's sperm?'

Poppy told her that because she still hadn't conceived after years of dedicated screwing, she and Tony had been for tests at the fertility clinic. While she was in perfect nick, poor Tony's sperm-count was low. The doctors said that a normal ejaculation had enough sperm to repopulate the whole of Western Europe, but the number Tony produced could just about repopulate Ringwood Town Football supporters club.

'He didn't say that.'

'Well, not in so many words but my chances of becoming a mum are pretty bleak.'

Jane was very sad as she knew Poppy and Tony desperately wanted children.

'Let's not talk about my problems,' Poppy changed the subject, 'I want to hear more about you and Mr Wonderful.'

Jane's expression must have given her away as Poppy quickly picked up that all was not well.

'He is all right, isn't he?' Poppy said. 'You both seem to be very happy.'

After a little coaxing, Jane told Poppy about Robert's lack of sparkle in the bedroom and how she found other men more stimulating.

'I think you fancy somebody else.'

Jane denied it but Poppy wouldn't be put off. 'Who is it?'

After a little more persuasion, Jane told her about Gregg and how he'd tried it on with her in his office and their night time skinny dip. She denied that any sex had taken place but acknowledged

315

she fancied him. She also warned Poppy about the Bonds being 'swingers', so she and Tony had better be careful.

'Wow, this place sounds better and better.' Poppy saw the funny side of Jane's confession but also realised the danger. 'You'll have to watch yourself young lady. No messing around – understood?'

'Yes Ma'am,' was Jane's compliant response.

It was back to normal the next day for Gilly and Robert. Basil came back with the vehicle at eleven o'clock to take Jane, Poppy and Tony to see the sights of Ogola. But first, Jane took them into the new offices and introduced them to the staff. Afterwards, Jane showed them the old office where she had worked for six months.

'Wow, Jane, it's terrible. It must have been awful. How did you do it?'

'Pure dedication!'

Jane then introduced them to Ken and asked if a tour of Ogola was possible. He thought it would be better not to go far because word had spread about the increased rents and trouble was already brewing. He asked Nelson and Momo to take them. 'But at the first sign of trouble, come back straight away.' Ken warned.

In fact, they didn't go far as Poppy was horrified by the squalor and filth. Whilst trying to hide her feelings from the locals, it wasn't long before she asked to go back to the office, on the pretence of having a headache. She also avoided holding hands with the children who came running up; they were too dirty, especially those with runny noses. Jane couldn't help but be disappointed by Poppy's reaction. Tony, on the other hand, would have liked to have stayed longer feeling sure that there must be a story somewhere, but Nelson diplomatically suggested they all go back together. He didn't want any incidents.

It was nearing noon so Jane asked Ken, Nelson and Momo if they would like to join them for lunch. Ken cried off, explaining he had a meeting with the contractor but Nelson and Momo were happy to take up the invitation. Just then, Constance Wanjiku appeared, cheekily announcing that she was available for lunch as well.

Leaving behind the grime and smells of Ogola, Poppy felt much better and she and Tony enjoyed talking to the staff about life in Buzamba. After lunch, Jane invited Constance to join them for dinner one evening the following week which she gladly accepted.

At the weekend, Basil drove the five of them to the Lake Resort Hotel at Lake Arthur for a two day holiday. Sellie and Kaba stayed at home this time. Unlike their Christmas trip, the hotel was full; the dining room a great deal busier and, fortunately, the food much better. The following morning at the crack of dawn, they all appeared for an early breakfast, prior to visiting a game park. The Kimbers still enjoyed seeing many different animals, and when a mixed herd of kudus and zebras slowly crossed the road just in front of them, Tony could hardly believe it and excitedly took what seemed like hundreds of close-up photos.

Jane's arranged meeting for Tony with Elphic Chuchu, the editor of the *Buzamban Times*, took place the next day. Tony was impressed that Elphic managed to do so much himself, especially when he noticed that the Monday to Friday paper was not only well produced, but also a good read.

'Are any of the stories Jane sent you of any interest?' Elphic asked.

'To be honest, the UK media is swamped with dire stories from Africa and I've had no luck so far. To get them interested, the story has to be big. A bloody coup especially if any Europeans are caught up in it… I could sell that. Or European tourist attacked or mugged or, heaven forbid, killed… that would also sell.'

'Really?' Elphic feigned surprised. 'So your press is only interested in the suffering of white people and not the suffering of blacks.'

'Oh dear, I hope you don't think I'm being racist…' he looked anxiously at Elphic to see if he had taken offence, 'but I can't dictate to editors what they print… I'm just the middle-man.'

Elphic laughed and gave Tony a comforting embrace. 'No, of course not, Tony. Don't worry, I understand completely. And, strangely enough, it's more or less the same here. My readers don't want to read about corruption or stolen drugs, they also like reading about foreigners.'

Relieved that he hadn't upset Elphic, he confided that he didn't want to disillusion Jane by telling her what he'd told Elphic, as she was still learning her craft and she was on the spot if anything big did break. 'I guess you can't organise a coup for me, can you?' he teased.

Elphic took his jest with a relaxed smile. 'Actually, Tony, the reality is that we are not far from major unrest in this country. I'm getting a feeling that tension is building up between the Peelee led army and the Solu run police force.'

'Oh dear. That could be nasty,' Tony looked solemn. 'You know I'm not wishing it to happen but… if it does, then keep me posted.'

Before Tony left, he and Elphic went through the *Times* headlines for the last two weeks to see if there was anything that might appeal to an editor in UK.

'Here's a beauty,' Tony said holding up a paper. 'Can I see your file on this?'

'Yes, of course, but this isn't what you said you wanted.'

'I know, but anything to do with magic or…'

'Black magic,' Elphic interrupted, guessing where he was heading. He sent one of his clerks to locate the file and he was quite happy for Tony to take it with him and return it later.

Humming happily to himself, Tony walked into the fan-cooled interior of the Kimbers' house where, not wanting to waste any time, Poppy was already savouring her first gin and tonic of the day whilst an envious Jane gulped her fifth glass of water.

'This Elphic chap, Jane, seems a great guy.' Helping himself to a beer, he asked them to listen while he read an extract from Elphic's newspaper.

Resurrection from the Dead? Fourteen year old Kerri M'bassa died four weeks ago but, two days later, she came back to life. During the days when her parents mourned, her body failed to decompose. Kerri claims to have gotten powers to cure people. Now crowds of sick people come to her from every corner of the country. They come to her on stretchers and on crutches. The blind, the lame, the crippled, the infertile, the disease-ridden.

Last week she told our reporter of her experiences with God's angels. She was taken to heaven and met John the Baptist who baptised her in the River Jordan before taking her to meet Jesus, who blessed her and gave her a strand of his hair. She held up a golden thread but wouldn't let anybody touch it – if they did they would die and go to hell.

Tony continued reading about the number of people she had cured, including many Europeans and two government ministers, but the reaction from the churches was hostile describing her as an evil sorceress.

'I think I may be able to get one or two editors interested in this, and I could ask Elphic to give you any follow-ups, Jane. What do you think?'

'Yes of course. I remember reading that article myself, but I didn't think you'd be interested.'

'It's all a load of old tosh.' Poppy was totally unimpressed. 'Nobody in England would be interested in that rubbish, it's utter nonsense. What do you think, Jane?'

'I'm not sure - but Tony's the expert.'

'Thank you, Jane,' a satisfied Tony replied, 'I'll give it a go when we get home. You never know, the tabloids may lap it up.'

Still doubtful, Poppy said that if he was serious, he should go and see the girl himself. When Jane asked Sellie what she thought, she barely glanced at the paper before saying she'd heard about the girl and thought it was true. 'Many people get spirit powers in Africa but I never hear Jesus speak to Buzamban girl.'

Explaining that Tony was a journalist, Jane wondered if he could talk to Kerri as he wanted to write a story for the British newspapers. Sellie said she would arrange it for early on Saturday morning.

Originally, when Jane had planned a dinner party so that Poppy and Tony could meet their new friends, Robert had argued that he didn't want Quentin because he would try to dominate the evening and, at the same time, insult their other guests, especially Constance Wanjiku. Josie and Lester Pennicott, who were much more affable, couldn't come as they were busy. So the welcome dinner would be much smaller than intended. In fact, Jane was happy that as well as the four of them, there would only be Cindy and Gregg, Constance and f-Fearless. Robert had warned the latter in no uncertain terms that he had to arrive sober, drink moderately, and leave sober-ish.

Since becoming pregnant, Jane had made-do by altering and letting out her clothes to accommodate her ever-increasing bump, so this evening was the perfect occasion for Jane to show off one of her new outfits. But when Poppy gracefully made her entrance into the living room, Jane gawped at her dress which had an exceptionally low neckline.

'Does my bum look big in this?' Poppy asked as she pirouetted in front of Jane.

'Yes, it looks bloody enormous, but it's the front that needs fixing. I can just about see your knickers!'

'Do you think I should alter it… a bit? Oh! And thanks a lot for the compliments - not.'

'My pleasure,' was the sarcastic reply.

'But isn't this the kind of dress Cindy wears? You've told me so many times about her daring creations.'

'First of all, you are not Cindy. For goodness sake, hitch up that neckline a bit and make yourself more respectable. And hurry, our guests will be here soon.'

As dinner parties go, Jane thought that this was one of her best efforts. Poppy and Tony got on very well with Gregg and Cindy. Whenever there was the slightest lull in the conversation one of them would come up with an amusing anecdote, usually relating to their experiences on the stage, and all four of them had the gift of making even ordinary events sound funny. A more confident Robert was also on fine form, and he and f-Fearless managed to add a little of their unique humour which Constance completely failed to understand, but accepted must be funny because all the others laughed.

After dinner, Tony, the ever-enquiring journalist, asked Constance about her job and what she did in Ogola. What she told them was a big surprise, especially to Robert who'd known her for over three years. She told them how she'd recently visited Italy, one among the many overseas trips she had made at donors', usually UNDP's, expense. During the past seven years she'd spent three months in the Philippines, five weeks in Burma followed by a month in New Delhi, one month in China, six months in Johannesburg, and several weeks in Nairobi, Kampala, Lilongwe and Lusaka.

'Wow, what a job! I'd love one like that,' Tony said. 'How did you manage it?'

Constance gave them a knowing smile. 'I'm well connected,' and then she laughed out loud.

Tony persevered. 'And what do you do in those places?'

'Oh, many, many things. I attended seminars and workshops; I worked with study groups in various universities, and presented papers on my specialist subject.'

'Is that to do with slums?' Cindy asked.

'More to do with immunization programmes related to squatters, such as cholera, malaria and other tropical diseases.'

'And has it helped your work with Robert's slum project?' Poppy asked.

'No, not a lot, but it's helped me,' Constance laughed again and this time they all joined in. 'I've been all over the world with all expenses paid; stayed at the best hotels and received a good per diem on top of my stipend.'

'Well, you did say you were well-connected,' f-Fearless was impressed.

There was a mischievous twinkle in Constance's eyes as she smiled at f-Fearless. 'It's often hard to start Western health programmes amongst the uneducated; it goes against their traditional healers,' Constance continued, her smile undiminished. 'You people call it witchcraft, but traditional healers believe disease has supernatural causes which require supernatural remedies.'

'But surely immunization programmes work,' Gregg asked.

Constance kept smiling in what they now took to be her 'knowing look'. 'All African governments encourage them, and yes – they do some good, but the main reason they are given the go-ahead is not because they save lives but because they bring overseas training programmes for the well-connected.'

Yet again, Cindy had heard quite enough of *African Problems* and shady wheeling and dealing. Every time they were with Jane and Robert the conversation always seemed to turn to something depressing. Already quite intoxicated, she wanted to enjoy herself and maybe flirt with Tony… if she could.

As the consumption of alcohol increased and the four thespians started their yarns again, Constance was ready to leave, so Robert ordered a taxi for her. Much to Jane's surprise, f-Fearless also decided to go and suggested sharing the ride with her.

'What's going on there, then?' Jane said, when they'd gone. 'Do I sense romance in the air?'

'I bloody hope not. She'd have him for breakfast,' Robert added.

'Maybe I could take them both on as… crients of my expanding international infroduction agency,' Poppy was starting to slur her words. 'I could even open a branch office in Ouverru. Yes, I could use your office, couldn't I, Robert?' Poppy reached across the table and took Robert's hand. 'You wouldn't mind, darling, would you?'

A totally sober Jane suddenly felt tired. It had been a long day and hosting the dinner party had taken it out of her so, shortly after Constance and f-Fearless had departed, she excused herself and went to bed. As soon as her head hit the pillow she was fast asleep, not even waking when Robert fell heavily in beside her.

The staccato of pounding tropical rain on the roof woke them during the early hours of the morning and it was still pouring when Jane wearily followed Robert out of bed to get Gilly ready for school. She heard Robert, who was running late, pounding down the steps to the car. There was no sign of Poppy and Tony, but three empty gin bottles on the dining table stood testament to the fact that some heavy drinking had taken place long into the night. By the time a shattered-looking Poppy dragged herself into the living room demanding strong black coffee before she died, it was almost ten o'clock.

'And what happened to you last night?'

'Ooh, I don't know… and don't shout… please. Even my hair hurts.'

'I take it you stayed up late. What time did the Bonds leave?'

Poppy drank some coffee before answering. 'Err, it was about midnight, I think, when we went swimming.'

'Swimming… you naughty girl! You went skinny dipping with Cindy and Gregg – didn't you?'

Even with the effects of a massive hangover, Poppy's face lit up at the memory of what had happened. 'Yes, it was great – we were in there for ages. The water was so warm; it felt like velvet,' she paused dreamily.

'Naked, I assume.'

'No.'

'I bet you were. Cindy would have made sure of that.'

'Well…'

'And the boys?'

'Oh yes, I think so… no, I know so. I'll tell you all about it later.'

Jane hated herself – but she was jealous. Jealous that naked Poppy had had naked Gregg's undivided attention. And did that include sex? Dare she ask? Her curiosity got the better of her. 'Did you get off with Gregg then?'

'Get off! What does 'get off' mean?'

'You did, didn't you? I warned you about the Bonds. And did Cindy and Tony get it off as well?'

'You've got a very dirty mind, Mrs Kimber – I'm shocked. Nothing… err… happened… I'm certain.' Poppy gave Jane a reproachful gaze before saying, 'well… I think I'm certain – it's all beautifully hazy.'

'It's a good thing you're leaving next week or you and Cindy would soon be holding swingers' parties. You're two of a kind – in fact, I think you're four of a kind.'

'You're just jealous… and probably frigid now you're pregnant. Poor Robert.'

'Well I hope you didn't do anything you'll regret.'

Poppy brushed off the veiled accusations with disdain. 'And before you go on any more, I'll take a coffee through to my beloved.'

'But Gregg's not here. Why not take it to your husband instead?'

'Wow, we are sharp this morning aren't we?' and with that, the slightly improved Poppy found her way back to the bedroom.

Just as Poppy left the room, Jane felt the first kick from Robert junior. Gently placing both hands on her stomach, she waited for another. There were two small kicks before 'it' must have decided to go back to sleep. She felt so happy. There had been no thrill all those years ago when she'd first felt Gilly kick. This time was different, married to a loyal and loving husband who didn't go skinny dipping with loose women. If only her dear friend Poppy could get pregnant. She smiled to herself as she gradually enlarged on a plot – a very devious plot – which had already taken seed in her head.

The pool area was a hive of activity. The barbecue was lit and Robert and Lester were preparing the meat and vegetable skewers, their stock of provisions increased in readiness for Quentin and Kath, who planned to join them later. Jane was rather pleased that Cindy and Gregg wouldn't be coming, they were both playing in a golf tournament.

When Tony returned from visiting the girl 'resurrected from the dead', who was now, by some accounts, healing the sick and infirm, the wine was already flowing and ice-cold beers were ready in the coolers. A glass of beer was thrust into his hand while he told them about the visit he and Sellie had made that morning. He'd taken his camera with him, not only to look the part of an international journalist, but also to take some shots of Kerri M'bassa in her village.

'It was an amazing sight that met us when we entered the village. The atmosphere was incredible – almost electric. There was this queue of cripples, blind and lame and variously bandaged people all impatiently waiting their turn, but good old Sellie took me right to the front, telling all those who complained that I was from the BBNC. Even though I couldn't understand what they were saying, I kept hearing *BBC, BBC* being murmured around. This really impressed them.'

'So, what was she like?' Poppy asked.

'Quite strange really. Her skin seemed to have an oily sheen, almost greyish in colour. But it was her eyes that immediately struck me.'

'What do you mean?' Jane asked.

'They seemed to be almost too big, as though she was forcing them wide open, but the irises were quite small. I think she was high on drugs.'

'Drugs! What sort of drugs?'

'Oh, I don't know, but something bloody strong. I reckon those days when she was supposed to be dead – they said due to a 'heart-breakdown' whatever that's supposed to be – she was probably in a coma from an overdose.'

'What about the strand of hair Jesus gave her?'

Tony laughed. 'It looked more like a silk thread to me. But I didn't try and touch it… you know… just in case.'

'Did you tell Sellie the hair looked like a thread?'

'No. Of course not, I could see Sellie took it all very seriously, so I kept quiet.'

'That's hard to believe,' Poppy laughed. 'You've never been quiet in your life!'

Ignoring his wife's disdainful comment, Tony continued with his story. 'I was able to ask Kerri about when she met Jesus and her new powers, but her story was exactly the same as Elphic's. She seemed to understand my questions in English but all her answers were in gobbledegook. Sellie did the translation.

'But what about all those people she's cured?' asked Josie.

Tony shrugged. 'It beats me. It could be some sort of auto-suggestion I guess. You know – the placebo effect.'

Quentin and Kath arrived during Tony's tale and were intrigued with his bizarre story.

'So, have you enough for a newspaper?' Poppy asked.

'Oh, yes. As long as the photos are OK. But I haven't got to the weird bit yet,' he ruefully put his free hand onto his crotch and held it there for a few seconds.

'Tony, what on earth are you doing that for?' scolded Poppy.

He exchanged a glance with his wife. 'Well, just before we left, after Sellie had been rabbiting on in whatever language it was, Kerri suddenly reached between my legs, grabbed my wedding tackle and gave them a very firm pull and a squeeze.'

There was loud laughter and a variety of crude remarks from the men.

'Why did she do that?' a startled Poppy said.

'I don't know. She did it so quickly I didn't have a chance to stop her.'

'Well, lucky you,' was all Quentin could say. 'Do I take it you're a journalist?'

Jane introduced them.

'Well go on then,' said Poppy. 'What did you grab in exchange?'

'Don't be so crude woman. I'm an upstanding gentleman.'

'You probably were 'upstanding' when she squeezed your tackle,' Robert laughed.

Ignoring the general hilarity interspersed with various course remarks, Tony told them Kerri had given him a drink of what looked and smelt like cat's piss with small green leaves floating on the top. It had been made by a dirty old bloke with a face like a festering haemorrhoid. Although he'd felt like vomiting, Sellie had insisted he must drink it. He'd tried to refuse but Sellie said he had to, otherwise he would offend Kerri as well as the whole village.

'It was very bitter but I did as I was told and drank most of it. I didn't want any witch doctor's spell put on me.'

Everyone thought it hilarious but also very intriguing and looked forward to seeing his story in print – especially the part where Kerri squeezed his gonads.

By then the barbecue was ready. The men had shared the labour over the hot grill, the vagaries of the wind wafting the tempting aroma of grilled steak and chicken around the pool, whetting the appetites of those lazing under a raft of umbrellas. Delicious salads had been prepared by several house-girls and the only contribution from the wives was to manage to stand up all on their own and hold out plates for the men to fill. What a life!

Smiling to herself, Jane tucked into her meal; Sellie had obviously done as she'd asked while they were clearing away after dinner the night before. Jane had mentioned that Poppy had been trying to have a baby but the problem was Tony's low sperm count. Sellie seemed to understand, so Jane suggested that when she took Tony to see the miracle girl, she could ask if Kerri could improve his fertility; hence the bitter drink and the attack on his genitals. She knew it was ridiculous, but... one never knew.

After the barbecue and more drinks, there was only one thing to do - be semi-comatose in the shade of the huge umbrellas, enjoying the peace and quiet, broken only by the bird song, and letting one's thoughts drift like the fluffy white clouds above.

'I could get so used to this,' Poppy was in her seventh heaven soaking up the heat of the day.

As the hot afternoon gradually gave way to early evening, the ladies slowly roused themselves and slipped into the swimming pool while the men put the world to rights dominated, of course, by Quentin.

He turned to Tony. 'Here's a story worth printing, although I'm not sure whether it should be in the political section or the comic supplement.' He'd recently had lunch with the first secretary at the British High Commission who had told him, in confidence, about the time he had accompanied the High Commissioner to a meeting with President Amos Mutua. The Commissioner had received a directive from the British Prime Minister stating that he was expected to talk tough regarding the abuse of human rights in Buzamba. The President laughed at the Commissioner's opening statement by saying that he didn't need a lecture about human rights or emergency powers, reminding him that it was during

British colonial times that Africans suffered human rights abuses. The Commissioner tried to ignore this and started to say that he had evidence of torture by the police but, before he could finish the sentence, the President told him to 'shut up and listen'. Mutua then said 'let's talk about moral values. I assume the equipment you sold us was for our defence and had nothing to do with saving jobs in marginals, and with respect, Mr High Commissioner – go tell your PM to go stuff himself'.

'Wow, your President sounds to be a tough cookie,' Tony said.

Quentin agreed. 'He's a cunning old fox, is our Amos. Our spineless Commissioner didn't stand a chance. Completely outsmarted.'

'So what did the High Commissioner do?'

'Exactly what his training as a diplomat taught him to do. He reported that the President had responded favourably to his request for an enquiry into civil rights abuses and emphasised the importance of the long-standing ties between our two countries.'

'You're joking!' said Robert.

'No you're not, are you?' said Tony, shaking his head in disbelief. 'Unfortunately, it's not the sort of story I can sell. I usually deal with minor accidents, child abuse, factory fires and any story that's not big enough for the nationals to send their own reporters. Pity though – it's a bloody good yarn.'

'Amos and the other top brass are smart people,' Quentin continued. 'The abuse of human rights has a degree of rationality about it.'

'How do you mean?' Tony asked.

'Well, it's pretty obvious really. If overseas funding is used to help the poor, there's less money for themselves. And that would never do.'

With his glass refilled, Tony sat looking at the ladies coming out of the pool and suddenly realised he felt very randy. He touched his crotch again, which had now recovered from the mad girl's grab. Josie, looking fantastic in her one-piece costume, took a towel and started to vigorously dry herself, not realising that her wet, clinging costume left little to the imagination. Jane looked very pregnant but still sexy, and even matronly Kath made his pulse race. But best of all was his beautiful Poppy and, in his intoxicated imagination, she looked naked as she stood with her arms outstretched, embracing the sun. After some quiet but persistent persuasion, he convinced Poppy they should go back to the house for a rest. All else having failed, he pretended to have a headache.

When Jane, Robert and Gilly eventually got home, there was no sign of Poppy or Tony but, as they walked through the living room, they heard a muffled sound of moaning coming from the bedroom. Gilly was worried that one of them might have a tummy ache and was about to knock on their door before Jane stopped her just in time.

'Leave them alone - they'll be all right.' She had seen the look in Tony's eyes before they left the barbecue and knew exactly what was on his mind when he persuaded Poppy to come back to the house for a rest. She was, of course, in possession of certain information known only to Sellie and herself.

The three of them had a light meal and when they'd finished there was still no sign of their guests. Long after Gilly had gone to bed, and Jane and Robert were almost asleep on the sofa, a dishevelled-looking Poppy came out wearing her robe. Her normally neat hair was in total disarray as though she'd been fighting a hurricane for the past few hours, and her makeup was all smudged. There was no sign of Tony.

'Can I get coffee and sandwiches?' she asked sheepishly. 'We're feeling a bit peckish.'

Jane accompanied her into the kitchen, put the kettle on, and got bread and ham out of the fridge.

'Everything all right?' Jane gave her best friend a sly smile.

'Fuckin' great, thank you.'

'Is Tony coming out?'

'That's not Tony in the bedroom. It's a sex mad turbo-charged love machine in there, who's insatiable.'

'Wow,' was all an envious Jane could think of to say until an afterthought struck her. 'I think I'll send Robert to see this Kerri girl… you know… just in case!'

Poppy gave her usual dirty laugh. 'A good bollock squeeze and a cup of piss is probably all he needs.'

A laughing Jane helped carry the refreshments to Poppy's room and held the tray while she opened the door.

'Well, see you in the morning then. Sleep well!'

Poppy gave her a parting wink. 'Not a chance.'

Long after the Kimbers had finished breakfast, Poppy and Tony appeared walking hand-in-hand, looking rather pleased with themselves.

'Are you feeling better?' a concerned Gilly asked.

'Yes thank you, darling,' Poppy replied without any embarrassment.

'Just a little weak,' Tony added smugly, to which he received a sharp poke in the ribs from his wife.

'Are you well enough to have a little breakfast?' a smirking Robert asked.

'Oh, yes please,' Tony responded ignoring the looks he was getting. 'A full English would go down a treat.'

The morning was grey and overcast and shortly before noon, light rain started to fall. They thought it would be best to spend a leisurely day at home and plan the last few days of the holiday. In the morning, Tony wanted to go with Jane to see Elphic and for the evening, he suggested that he and Poppy should take the family out for dinner to the Plaza as a 'thank-you' for their holiday. The next day, Jane had arranged for Josie and Lester to come for dinner, and on their final day they wanted to say goodbye to the people they'd met in the compound, especially Cindy and Gregg.

When Jane and Poppy were alone, Jane asked what had got into Tony the day before. 'Do you think it could have had anything to do with the girl in the village?

'I don't know, but whatever it was, I'd like to bottle it and take it home with me. I was as surprised as you were… well… you know.'

'No.'

'He's never been like that before – not even on our honeymoon. It's as though he was on weapons grade, industrial strength Viagra.'

'Well, apart from your sexual Olympics, have you enjoyed your holiday so far?'

Poppy said they'd had a wonderful time and she was jealous of their lifestyle in Buzamba. She loved the house and she was pleased that Robert had turned out to be such a good husband and father. She liked the people they'd met, especially Cindy and Gregg; the trip to Lake Arthur and the game park had been fantastic and… they wanted to return again next year – if they'd have them, she added.

'Of course we will, even though your behaviour has been disgusting. Anyhow, you'll have to behave yourself this evening as the Pennicotts are coming for dinner, and I'd like Tony to have a discussion with Lester and Josie. Apart from being an exceptionally nice couple, Lester's had more experience of Africa's aid problems than most.'

'So it's boring newspaper business, is it? Or does Lester...?'

'No he doesn't,' Jane sharply interrupted, 'they're both respectable... like Robert and me.'

Lester was a gifted raconteur and, at first, even Poppy enjoyed listening to his tales of World Bank and EU debacles he'd had the misfortune of being involved with over the years. Not to be totally outdone, Tony was also able to add a few of his own anecdotes from his life as a journalist.

'So what do you think of my protégé?' Tony cheekily nodded in Jane's direction as they settled down with their after dinner brandies.

Lester laughed. 'Jane is pretty rare amongst the expat wives I've met as she's genuinely interested in trying to help the poor, instead of living in the goldfish bowl of lotus-eating indolence which most women eagerly grasp. Did you find the articles she sends you interesting?'

'Let's say she's getting better,' Tony laughed. 'But basically local papers don't print international news and so far, I've found it very hard to get the nationals interested. I think I'm missing some of the background, like how the stories Jane sends fit into the bigger picture, if you see what I mean.'

'Yes,' Lester looked thoughtful. 'It took me a long time to get my head around it all. Firstly, there are far too many organisations dealing with aid, from the big ones like the World Bank all the way down to the minnows, there are literary thousands of aid agencies, donors, NGOs and charities, all more-or-less trying to do the same thing in a totally uncoordinated, chaotic manner. They constantly get in each other's way, duplicate and triplicate aid to the same project, which conveniently lends itself to government officials pocketing most of the money.'

'I hear more-or-less the same from a chap I know at the Ministry of Finance here in Buzamba,' Robert said.

'Well, here's an example of my point,' Lester read from a small note he took out of his wallet. 'I keep this with me wherever I go,' he smiled. 'The Ministry of Finance in Tanzania receives over one thousand delegations... that's donors, charities etcetera every year, and is obliged to issue over two and a half thousand progress reports to these agencies. It valiantly tries to keep tabs on each project but... well, let's face it... it can't, it's just chaos. Now then, if all aid... and I do mean *all*, was channelled through one organisation; let's say for argument's sake the UN, then there would be one office in Tanzania to coordinate all funding, whether budgetary support or whatever. And as a result, the only source of aid for Tanzania would be one properly run un-corruptible agency – ergo, we solve corruption overnight.'

'Fantastic!' Tony was already taking down notes. 'And will it work?'

Shaking his head and with a cheerless smile, Lester told him it would never work. 'And it's not just Tanzania, it's the same in every sub-Saharan country. There are too many vested interests. Every donor organisation wants its own power-base, highly paid directors, first class travel to every corner of the globe, sitting at the top table being wined and dined in five star hotels, by countries where half the population is starving to death. With my proposal, they'd all be out of a job. Not only that but every African dictator would scream like hell as their source of illicit wealth would be lost. No, it'll never work.'

'Oh, I was just starting to get excited.' Tony put down his pad and pen.

'Well, just look in your country at DfID,' Lester said.

'Go on then.'

'Did you know that the British government through DfID spends a bigger share of its national wealth on aid than any other G20 economy.'

'Why would they do that?' Jane asked.

'Ha, I was hoping you could tell me,' Lester shrugged. 'And the UK's debt will soon reach 1 trillion pounds, but it continues to borrow from China and then giving aid to... guess?'

'China?' hazarded Robert.

The look of satisfaction on Lester's face said it all. 'They give aid to China so that Chinese children can be fed propaganda about man-made global warming.'

They all looked blank, even Poppy.

'What a bloody mess,' was Tony's only comment. 'But didn't I read that DfID's budget is the only one the new coalition government has agreed to increase?'

'Yes you did… unbelievable, isn't it?'

'Does that mean that the West will continue to give billions away but nothing will improve?'

'Quite probably. But if I'm not boring everyone here, I'll give you my thoughts on what could be done.'

Although Poppy was now getting bored with the way the conversation had developed, she played the dutiful wife – said nothing – and helped herself to more brandy. 'So what would you do?'

'Stop aid altogether.'

'What!'

'Africa has massive natural wealth – far more than the Saudis and all those Arab countries. Far more. And do the Arabs need aid?'

'No, they're rich.'

'Exactly. A programme should be started straight away to wean Africa from its aid dependency. Say over a five year period – ten at the max.'

Robert looked puzzled. 'But how would that work?'

'They'd obviously need a lot of help at first but that's what the World Bank should be concentrating on. Weaning them off aid. You could use the Middle East as a model – in fact, Africa could eventually do better than the Middle East.'

Robert still couldn't follow Lester's logic. 'What about the skilled staff? They simply don't exist.'

'Oh yes they do, mate. Over ten million Africans live in Europe and America and many are skilled and highly intelligent. They would come flooding back if they believed they would have power to control the destiny of their own country. Do you think the Arabs were skilled and talented back in the 1950s and 60s? No way.'

Robert turned to Jane. 'What do you think?'

Putting down her pen she looked enquiringly at Lester. 'I read about the lack of land rights in Africa - but I didn't really follow it.'

'In most African countries all land is owned by the state; not the farmers who cultivate it. Now, seventy-five per cent of the world's poor depend on agriculture to survive. If farmers were allowed to own the land, they could use the capital value to generate all the money they needed to completely modernise the farming industry.'

'I understand most of what you said, and I think it's a fantastic idea. You're absolutely right that foreign aid doesn't work but... maybe it's Robert who's got the wrong end of the stick.'

'Have I indeed young lady. And why is that...if I may be so bold?'

'The stumbling block isn't the African dictators, it's the World Bank and all the other aid agencies.'

'So what do you think about that Robert?' Tony asked mischievously.

'If it worked, I'd be over the moon . . . of course I would.'

Tony's next question was about the regular scenes of starving Africans on TV and he wondered if Lester had ever been involved in food aid.

'Food aid is the most farcical of...' Lester struggled to finish his sentence.

'Why's that?'

'Because,' there was a sad tone to Lester's voice, 'Africa can grow all the food it needs. Easily.'

This was confusing to them knowing that throughout Africa, millions went hungry. 'Are you sure?' Jane ventured.

'I'll tell you. All over the continent, foreigners are growing enough food to feed every African man, woman and child.'

'Well, where is it then?' Robert asked. 'Certainly not in Buzamba.'

'You are so very wrong, my friend,' Lester replied. 'I'll give you an example. In Ethiopia, where TV cameras always show people starving, and the West sending plane loads of food aid to help them, foreign companies grow every vegetable you can imagine and ship out one hundred tons of the stuff every day – that's from Ethiopia.' He paused to see if they had understood. 'One hundred tons of food every single day.'

Robert shook his head in disbelief. 'I've never heard of that. Where does it go?'

'Saudi and other Middle Eastern companies have deals with the Ethiopian government to lease its most fertile land at one dollar per hectare. They build huge steel framed hothouses covered in plastic, where they grow masses of food.'

'So what you're saying then, is that foreign companies grow hundreds of tons of food which is exported, while the local population starves. Is that right?'

'Exactly. Exactly' he repeated. 'And it's not only Ethiopia, but it is also Kenya, Tanzania, Congo and even Sudan which have the same arrangements with China, India, South Africa and many European countries, including the UK.'

'Where did you hear this?'

'I got it from our office. There's an organisation called the International Institute for Environment and Development funded by Western governments.'

'Well if it's true, I've never heard anything so crazy in all my life. Why isn't it in the papers and on TV?'

Lester smiled. 'Because, dear friends, too many people have special interests. If it got out, it would make all the pop stars look silly – heresy, heresy! Most aid is senseless and a total waste but it keeps a million people in work.'

'That was very interesting, Lester, thank you very much.' Tony turned towards Jane. 'Now you've got all the ammo, you can write your next article and send it straight to Number 10, Downing Street.'

'Yes,' laughed Robert. 'That'll put the cat amongst the pigeons.'

Not unexpectedly, the cold and gloom of the English winter came as a nasty shock to the Partingtons, but life in the Kimber household returned to what, during the past months, had become as near normal as possible when living in a developing country. Jane spent a few mornings in Ogola checking on the new computer system with BuzanComp's John Tamba who, after the showdown with him and Lily, was now spending everyday with Hani; seemingly having struck up a good working relationship.

The civil works in Ogola were on schedule and the road had been extended by a further fifty yards. But there was a deepening cloud hanging over the project and it had nothing to do with the weather.

'I think we're in for trouble,' Ken told Robert when he called at the office, 'there was more gunfire last night.'

'Damn. Just when things seemed to be calming down. What was the shooting about? Does anyone know?'

'I only hear a little from Hani, but it looks as though K.K. is taking over more of the structures. He and his Peelee clan are fighting it out with the Solus.'

'But I thought the Solus were the majority in Ogola.'

'Yes, but the Peelees have more guns.'

'Does that mean we're in for a tribal war?'

'No, I don't think so. K.K. is too smart for that, and he knows only too well that the police in Ouverru are mainly Solus.'

'I'd better tell Jane to stay away for a while. What do you think?'

Ken was put in another awkward dilemma. He'd been around long enough to know that even with Tamba, the computerised accounts would probably collapse unless Jane could keep her eye on things. And as Priem and Bauer had told him just a few days ago, if the accounts failed, then the whole project would also fail. 'We'll miss her if she does stay away, Robert. What I'll do is pay for two policemen to be here during the day. That'll make her feel safer.'

Robert wasn't sure what to do. 'Yes, okay then. But Ken, if you think there is any danger, please get her away as quickly as you can.'

'Yes, of course I will, Robert. Of course I will.'

'Well, what other tidings of great joy have you got for me?'

'I wish I had some. The other main problem is the rent increases. The grumbles are growing by the day, and Nelson's Social Department think we'll soon have riots on that front as well. The TV cameras were here yesterday interviewing the usual troublemakers, and two newspaper reporters asked me why we were forcibly ejecting the poor people.'

'The same old lies.' Robert was worried. 'Should we notify Priem now, or wait? Protests are one thing, but do we know how to handle them?'

'I think you should get Priem to approve more cash for security, so we should double the number of guards.'

'I agree. I'll send e-mails off to DGA and Schultec today. I'll also let Jane know the situation, but I'm certain she'll still want to come.' He smiled when he added, 'the success of the computerisation is her new goal in life.'

A happy-looking Gilly gave her mummy a card and a large bunch of yellow roses early on the morning of Mothering Sunday.

'They're gorgeous, Gilly, thank you very much, darling. How did you know it was today?'

'They told us at school,' Gilly replied, 'and Daddy bought the flowers out of my pocket money.'

'You did well, Kimber,' Jane smiled at her grinning husband.

They had enjoyed breakfast, which was specially prepared by Robert, the self-proclaimed world's greatest waffle maker, when there was a knock on the kitchen door. Sellie appeared holding Kaba's hand, both dressed in their Sunday best ready for church. Sellie was holding a bunch of roses the same size as the one Gilly had given Jane but this time the roses were pink.

'Kaba here, she give me these for Muvver's Day.' The smile on her poor blemished face lit up the room.

'What a good girl you are,' Jane was almost as excited as Sellie. 'Enjoy the rest of the day.'

After they left the room, Jane turned to her self-satisfied-looking husband. 'You're starting to frighten me, Kimber. Come here, I want to pinch you just to make sure you're real.'

'No pinching, I'm far too perfect for that.'

An excited Gilly had her seventh birthday party with ten friends, including Trish, Susie, Bella and Kaba. The rain kept away, so they played in the garden and Robert, with some much needed help from Gregg, provided a special barbecue. Jane was pleased to see Kaba enjoying herself. This was made easier as two other girls besides Bella were Buzambans. After everyone had gone and a very tired Gilly was in bed, Jane and Robert settled down with their well-earned drinks.

'Thank you, lover,' Jane gave her man a long lingering kiss; he had become a wonderful father. 'You're marvellous.'

'Yes, I know... bloody marvellous.'

'But your kid is kicking again.' She placed his hand on her belly, 'tell it to go to sleep will you?'

Robert leaned over and placed his mouth over the prodding movement. 'Go to sleep Hubert, it's not time to come out just yet... ow, that hurt!' he yelled, as Jane's hand slapped his backside.

'Don't call it Hubert. Under no circumstances will it be called Hubert. Understood?'

'Or Hubertina... ow, you've hurt me again!'

'It was meant to. Now, finish your drink and let's go to bed.'

CHAPTER TWENTY-SEVEN

The first real test of the new computer system was the results for the month of March, which were eventually printed in mid-April. Everyone poured over the print-outs trying to make sense of them; Hani thought the great swathes of paper looked fantastic, until a dejected Jane and Tamba pointed out the numerous errors. None of the control accounts balanced, in fact nothing balanced. What could she do? She thought about going to see Gregg and Emmanuel but Gregg would certainly want 'payment-in-kind'. She had a momentary flashback to Gregg's office when she nearly succumbed to his charms. No, she told herself, that's not the answer, she would do what she could but Lily and Tamba would have to sort it out; they were well paid for doing it.

The atmosphere changed from euphoria to despair. Jane asked Ken to call an urgent meeting with Lily and Tamba, who were ordered to stay until a new set of reports was prepared. Jane wanted Lily to know that if they were still wrong, then Robert would suggest that her boss would replace her with someone more competent. Jane told Ken she would keep her eye on their progress, but privately questioned her own capabilities.

Unknown to them however, forces were already at work to disrupt the project – forces like K.K. Machuri. Two days after the doors of some late-payers had been removed, there was a mass protest, gleefully reported by the media. The reports were wildly exaggerated but the damage was done. The following day, the Minister of Housing phoned Ken, ordering him and Robert to a meeting and said that he was halting the project until his staff had investigated the matter, because of the illegal increase in rents.

'What happens now?' Jane asked Robert.

'We'll carry on as best we can, doing maintenance and accounts. The only difference is that the contractors have gone.'

'And the poor will continue to suffer,' Jane added. 'Only the Germans care about the poor, certainly not the big-shots in government.'

It took almost three weeks, but the crackdown on Lily and Tamba eventually worked. After Jane had checked the first week's total lack of progress, she angrily asked Ken to lay down the law with Benedicts and BuzanComp. This resulted in a software professional being flown in from Uganda, and after a further ten days, the new set of month-end reports were acceptable. The added benefit was that Hani had worked with them in this exercise and now had a much better understanding of the whole system. This was a huge relief as Jane didn't want her dear German friends to think that the highly qualified whiz-kid had fallen at the first hurdle. She was now confident that when the reports were sent to Herr Bauer, he would be a very happy man. In fact, the whole of the Bundestag would be thrilled; maybe she'd even get a Nobel Prize. I can dream if I want to, she said to herself.

As Jane's pregnancy progressed, she spent less time in Ogola. Hani and the other staff were now proficient with the new computers, and it felt rather futile working when there was no guarantee the project would ever start up again. The *big wet*, which brought more rain than on the previous three years, had finished so everyone was happy, especially the farmers. The selection of local produce in the supermarkets was the best Jane had seen since she'd been in Buzamba, especially the strawberries which tasted even better than any she'd had in Ringwood.

'I think I'll finish my A-levels after 'it' is born,' she told Robert as they sat relaxing after dinner. 'What do you think?'

'Yes, a good idea. It'll help to fill your day instead of suffering down in Ogola.'

'And after that I think I'd like to start a degree course in something. My interest now is not history and geography but overseas development, especially Africa.'

'As long as you don't get smarter than me,' Robert laughed.

She poked him in the ribs. 'And what makes you think I'm not already the brains of the family? The dear Germans think I am.'

Robert knew there was no answer to that and as he was no longer allowed to tickle his wife with child; he would ignore her last comment – it was safer that way.

When Basil brought the post, Jane recognised Poppy's writing. Poppy was pregnant! After hesitating for a few weeks before seeing her doctor, she discovered she was seven weeks pregnant. 'And guess when and where conception took place?' Poppy wrote. Could it have anything to do with Kerri M'bassa, the miracle girl? Jane did a quick calculation; the timing was right but common sense told her, surely not. Europeans don't believe in African witchcraft… or do they? It would be just one of those coincidences. But according to the health experts, the chances of Tony fathering a child were very low, and unless Poppy had been with another man… ah…that thought stopped Jane in her tracks, knowing that the only other man it could possibly have been was Gregg. Oh wow! Double wow! No, treble wow!

Poppy obviously wanted to believe it was the actions of the miracle girl and the marathon shag-a-thon that had followed. Jane quickly made up her mind that she would never question Poppy about the nights she'd been skinny dipping with Gregg. Never.

Sellie's expression didn't change when Jane told her; she just nodded her head as though it was bound to happen, once Kerri M'bassa did her medicine.

After reading Poppy's letter, Robert laughed out loud. 'Well, well, that's really good news.' He looked at Jane's questioning face. 'Oh, for goodness sake, Jane, you don't believe it was that miracle girl – do you?'

'Well, it may…'

'Don't be crazy. I think all this witch doctor business is turning your head. It must be your hormones.' He carried on by saying he hoped she would recover her common sense after the baby was born. Jane was not amused but decided to ignore it.

Mystery surrounded the next riot to erupt in Ogola. Late on Friday evening, Ken phoned saying there had been a massive gunfight and that several buildings in Ogola were on fire, shops and houses were being looted and a mob was stoning the office. He would go and see if he could stop further damage but Robert should stay away until he was given the all clear.

Nothing was heard from Ken on Saturday but Robert listened closely to the radio news. There were graphic reports about the poor, exploited inhabitants demonstrating against the sharp increase in rents imposed by the German landlords. The police had been sent to quell the demonstrators, but the fire engine couldn't reach the burning buildings. Hundreds of people had to leave the area.

Poor Hani was completely out of breath when he arrived at their house. His news was bad. From what he could tell, the trouble had started between two rival drug gangs and had nothing to do with rents or German landlords. It was Amos who had started throwing stones saying that it was the Germans' fault.

'Amos? You mean the Amos who used to work in the office?' Robert asked.

'He with bad crowd.' Hani confirmed. 'He angry Ken Kasansa fire him.'

'Have you seen Ken?'

'No, I not see him.'

'He went down there on Friday evening.'

Hani said he would go and look for him. Two hours later he returned with disturbing news. Ken had been arrested and was in gaol; he had been charged with murder.

'Murder!' gasped Robert. 'Who did he murder?'

'Amos!' replied Hani.

'You mean Amos, the same Amos?'

'Yes. He found shot dead just outside the office this morning. Some bad people say Ken kill him dead.' Jane gave Hani a cold drink and then he told them everything he knew from the beginning. Evidently, the trouble first started in one of the bars on Friday afternoon when rival gangs of Peelee and Solu drug dealers fought for control of Ogola. Shots were fired and property set alight. The gangs continued fighting throughout Saturday and into Sunday, and many people were thought to be dead. However, the only dead body found by the police was Amos; all the other bodies had been dumped in the quarry or the Sambula River. Hani was told that three men carried Amos's body to the office so they could shift the blame onto the Germans. And that was why Ken was accused.'

'Why do you say that?'

'My neighbour say many witness people saw drug people shoot Amos. So he not do this thing.'

'But why accuse Ken?'

Hani was slightly embarrassed before replying. 'It easy, he from wrong tribe.'

There was no answer to that, but they had to do something to get him out. Robert phoned Victor Veme but was told that he was out of the country for four weeks, so he arranged to see one of Victor's solicitor colleagues the following morning.

'Will this be expensive?' Jane asked.

'Yes, but Schultec should pay for everything. If they refuse, I'll pay myself.'

'It's not only the legal costs but will there be the police and many others to bribe, especially when they know a *mzungu* is involved?'

'Yes I know, but I'll worry about that when he's free.'

The following morning while Robert went to Victor Veme's law firm, Jane kept her appointment with Dr Angus Patterson. He looked up and smiled as he checked Jane's notes. She inwardly grimaced at the sight of his stained teeth thinking a doctor should look after them better – or keep his mouth shut.

'We thought 3rd July was the due date, didn't we?'

Jane nodded.

'Well, everything seems fine and you are looking great.'

'Thanks very much,' Jane smiled at such a curious compliment.

'From the position of the baby I'd say it might arrive a few days early so… err… be prepared.'

'The sooner the better as far as I'm concerned.'

Seemingly unaware of his less than perfect molars, he smiled again. 'I trust you will breastfeed the baby.'

'I'll do my best. I struggled a bit with Gilly, so I used bottles some of the time.'

'The reason I'm asking is that we have our own little club of new mothers who meet every afternoon to feed their babies.'

Jane was puzzled. 'A club! I planned to feed at home, where… I'll… err… be comfortable.'

Angus laughed. 'Yes, I know it sounds strange but there is a very good reason. It is essential the local women, especially those who are less well-educated, breastfeed their babies and don't resort to bottles. The death toll for bottle-fed babies is very high. It's the hygiene you see,' he added, as if an explanation was necessary.

'I'm still not sure I understand.'

'You probably don't remember but several years ago, one of the world's largest food companies opened several dried milk plants in Africa and promoted its product by showing Western women bottle-feeding their babies. There was an international scandal – an outcry – in fact it's still ongoing. It's estimated that thousands of local women wanting to copy the *mzungus*, used any kind of milk in unsterilised bottles. I heard many stories; some women thought that anything white would be good and some used milk of magnesia or even powdered chalk. You can imagine the result. And we are still fighting to stop all promotions of bottle-feeding.'

'Isn't there any way of stopping them?'

'Sadly no. These companies are the unacceptable face of globalization and are the most boycotted companies in the world.'

'How can they get away with it?'

Angus shook his head. 'They're too big and powerful. UNICEF says bottle-fed babies are twenty-five times more likely to die from diarrhoea than breastfed. So our little club sits in a shelter near the street showing the local passers-by that *mzungus* and educated black women all breastfeed their babies. The club is called 'Suzama Mamas' because *suzama* means mother's milk in the Solu language. I also publish leaflets asking all the supermarkets and stores to boycott everything made by these companies.'

'Do they listen?'

'Most do because many Suzama Mamas tell them they have to, and they don't want to lose their custom. We even have a marquee at the Great Ouverru Show in July.'

Jane couldn't stop herself from laughing. 'A breastfeeding marquee! Wow, that's something you wouldn't see in England.' She knew one newspaper man who would love to carry that story – with photos!

There was no sign of Robert when Jane arrived home. She tried his mobile but it was switched off and there was no point calling the office as the rioters had damaged the land lines. There was nothing she could do so she sank gratefully into her favourite chair on the terrace. The dry season was already having a browning effect on the lawn but most of the shrubs were ablaze with vibrant colours, especially the bougainvillea. She thought how lucky she was to live in such a lovely home and temporarily managed to block out thoughts of the people who lived in dreadful squalor just a short distance away. Her reverie only lasted a few moments before her thoughts switched back to Ken. She'd heard terrible stories of torture and brutality in African gaols and she prayed to any gods listening, to protect Ken from harm. He was such a dear man whose main interest was to help the poor of Ogola. And now he was in gaol on a trumped up murder charge because he was from the wrong tribe.

When Robert arrived home he looked very worried. 'I've tried everything to get Ken released but the lawyer wasn't much help. His only suggestion was to pay to get Ken out but how much to pay and to whom he wasn't sure. There will be several layers of police to buy off and at least one judge. It's a pity Victor Veme is away.'

'What are you going to do, then?'

'I don't know but I think we should go and see Rose as soon as possible. I've spoken to her on the phone and she's very upset. Are you up to it?'

'Yes, I'm OK. Let's go now.'

The Kasansas lived in a good suburb of Ouverru called Saint Ives. A row of magnificent blue-flowering jacaranda trees lined the street, which had obviously seen better days, the road now having several potholes, and litter blowing in the wake of every vehicle that manoeuvred its way around the various obstacles. Rose met them at the front door of her bungalow, which was spotlessly kept and looked out of place next to tatty neighbouring dwellings. Her smile was unsteady as she shook Robert's hand, and gave Jane a gentle hug, being careful not to squash 'the bump'.

'Please come in. Have you any news?'

Robert brought her up-to-date with his efforts and didn't gloss over the problems.

'I think they treat him bad in that place,' Rose said gravely.

'But why would they? As far as we know he's not been charged; he's only being held,' Robert tried to be positive.

'We Busti people,' Rose said, 'we always keep a low profile and... how you say... keep our heads below the parapet.'

'But surely Robert or the German Embassy could help,' Jane said.

'You white people are also from the wrong tribe and the Embassy will only look after *mzungus* – not Africans.'

'Yes, I'm afraid you're right,' Robert said. 'The Germans won't get involved, I've already tried.'

'So what are we going to do?' Jane was exasperated as there didn't seem to be anyone who could help.

'I've tried to contact a lawyer friend to see if he can do anything but he hasn't returned my calls,' Rose said. 'I'll keep trying and let you know if I hear from him.'

The next morning, Jane went with Robert to Ogola. Nelson Lamu looked as if he hadn't slept for days. 'I know where Ken's held but whether he's getting food and water, I can't say. The people there are too bad.' Nelson's voice croaked with emotion.

Hani joined them in the office and Ruth brought tea, coffee and biscuits.

As Ruth handed round a plate of digestives, Jane suddenly had a brainwave. 'I know,' she said, 'surely Constance could get Ken free. She knows everyone.'

They sat nibbling their biscuits letting Jane's words sink in.

'Yes of course, why didn't I think of that,' Nelson suddenly said. 'You're right Jane, Constance knows everyone worth knowing. I'll go and ask her to join us.'

The very elegant Constance did not immediately respond to the cry for help. 'I don't know,' was all she said, her hands nervously folding and unfolding on her knee.

'But we have to get Ken out as soon as possible. Surely, there's something you can do?' Jane felt justified in pressing her.

Unusually, Constance's demeanour was subdued and it was clear she didn't want to get involved. Jane wasn't sure if her expression was showing worry or fear but something was wrong. But why? All she had to do was to get some big-shot to make a few phone calls and Ken could walk free. Constance had been only too willing to name drop before, but now she showed no confidence at all. Something was obviously worrying her.

'I make enquiries,' Constance eventually said, 'and I let you know tomorrow. That's the best I can do.'

As Constance left the room Robert started following but Jane put her hand on his arm and gestured him to remain.

'Don't put pressure on her. She knows Ken is locked away and probably being mistreated, but she obviously thinks it'll be difficult to get him released.'

'Let's wait until tomorrow.' Nelson said, his initial optimism appeared to be waning. 'I'm beginning to wonder if we're asking too much from her.'

Just what he meant by that Jane wasn't sure, but she decided to say nothing.

Waiting for Constance Wanjiku, they were just about to give up when she lethargically walked into the office. They were shocked at her appearance; instead of the upright posture, immaculate hair, elegant clothes and smart shoes which were her trademark, she appeared drab and shabby and, as she sat down, her shoulders sagged like those of an old woman.

'Are you all right?' Jane asked, worried that she might be ill.

Constance gave them a baleful look. 'I go and try to get Ken released,' was all she said, looking down at her cheap flip-flops.

'Do you know where he is? Nelson thinks he's at Kenchea Police Station.'

Again Constance nodded. That was the only acknowledgment she gave.

Neither Jane nor Robert could understand the sudden change in her appearance. Maybe there was more to it.

'Can I give you a lift?' Robert asked.

'No, I walk.' Constance spoke using a strong local accent instead of her usual good English. 'It better that way.'

'But it's about three miles to Kenchea and it's very hot today.'

'I walk. I go now,' again spoken like an uneducated person. And with that, Constance rose and went out of the office. They saw her amble away with her head slightly bowed and shoulders bent as though she was carrying a heavy burden, her flip-flops kicking up small amounts of dust as she dragged her feet along.

Robert rubbed his chin, baffled at what he had just witnessed. He sent Lola to find Nelson. Maybe he could explain.

'I think she expects a bad time,' Nelson spoke solemnly after they'd told him.

'What sort of bad time?' Jane wasn't sure what he meant.

Nelson hesitated before answering. He had a very high opinion of the Kimbers and was grateful that they were doing everything they could to get Ken released, but explaining to *mzungus* how certain people behaved in Buzamba was complicated. 'She has to find out who has the authority to free Ken. It's not easy. And everyone who tells her anything of use… well… there is a price to pay … favours and things.'

'What kind of favours?' It still wasn't clear to Jane what Nelson meant.

He looked uncomfortable and paused before answering. 'In Africa things are different from where you come from. To ask this thing… this big favour, Constance might be badly treated.'

'They will beat her?' Jane pressed.

He nodded. 'She will probably be beaten and…' he hesitated before adding, 'she will be raped.'

Jane's jaw dropped and she put her hand in front of her mouth and gasped. 'Oh my God! I had no idea. Should we go and stop her?'

'No. She will survive, whereas Ken might die if he's not released soon.'

They didn't talk about Constance and Ken for long; Jane felt sick and wanted to go home and pray for their safety; she only prayed when things were exceptionally bad, when she didn't know what else to do. She would ask Sellie if they could pray together.

Ken's release, when it came, was sudden. Robert received a phone call from Rose saying that Ken had been dumped two hours earlier, without any warning. A police car had slowed down in front of their house, the rear door opened and Ken was pushed out, falling heavily onto the road. The bruises from the fall were mere scratches compared to the other injuries he had on most parts of his body, including his genitals. He was in a bad way but their doctor, a neighbour, had checked him over and said there was nothing life-threatening. All he needed was rest. He hadn't been charged with any offence and, it appeared, he was a free man.

Robert asked if he could go and see him but Rose said Ken wanted to rest for a few days, and she would let him know as soon as he felt like having visitors. Rose also asked Robert to thank Constance for helping out; it seems it was her intervention that allowed him to be released.

'Do you know where Constance lives?' Jane asked Robert after he'd given her the news, 'I think we should both go and thank her.'

'I'll get the details from Nelson in the morning.'

Constance Wanjiku lived in a small ground-floor apartment in the UNDP-gated compound located in an up-market suburb of Ouverru. Above was the impressive dwelling of the UNDP resident officer, but her apartment looked as if it had been built as an afterthought as it was hemmed in on two sides by a garage and store room, with only the front and one side having windows.

A house-girl answered Robert's knock. Yes, Constance was in but no, she didn't want to see anyone. She was resting.

Jane took the initiative. 'I promise I will only stay two minutes and my husband will wait outside. Please let me in.'

The house-girl hesitated. She knew she was under orders not to let anyone in but by *anyone* she didn't know if that included a white woman. She felt intimidated by this *mzungu* with a scar on her face and couldn't bring herself to refuse her entry.

The curtains were closed and the room the house-girl led Jane into was dark and gloomy. Jane found Constance curled in a foetal position on the sofa, her knees were tucked under her, almost to her chin and her two hands were clasped over her head as if cushioning it from a forthcoming attack. She didn't move or say anything but Jane knew she sensed her presence.

'I've... err... come to see how you are, Constance. Ken is home now and Rose wants to thank you for your help.' Jane hesitated as she got no response. 'Can I do anything to help... or get you something?'

Again there was no response. Jane walked a few paces closer and reached out with her hand to rest it on Constance's shoulder.

Constance's reaction was instantaneous, as she angrily straightened up to face Jane.

'Don't touch me,' she yelled. 'Go away and leave me alone.'

As soon as Jane saw Constance's face she almost cried out in shock. It was badly swollen with dark discolouration around her eyes and cheeks and the bright red of her bloodshot eyes looked as if red paint had been forced into the sockets. She had a wild, terrified expression on her beaten face. Jane instinctively fingered her own scarred cheek as the memory of her own frightening rape suddenly flooded back.

'Oh Constance, what have they done to you? Can I call a doctor?'

'Go away and... ' Constance wavered for a moment, '... and leave me alone.'

Knowing it wasn't the time to ask any questions, Jane wanted to help in some way. She knew it was partly her fault that Constance had gone on her rescue mission. Jane suggested that Constance could stay with them for a few days and be looked after, but she was adamant that she wanted to be left alone and was angry that Jane was interfering. Her curt order to leave left Jane with no alternative other than to go, but she asked Constance to call her just as soon as she felt better.

'I think y-you should g-go now, Jane.' A man's voice came from behind her – a voice she recognised.

She turned and saw Jimmy entering the room carrying a tray with some dishes and a glass of water. Jimmy? f-Fearless Jimmy? What...?

'She's very t-tired and needs s-some sleep. I'm t-taking care of her.' He put the tray down beside the sofa and gently stroked the top of Constance's head. She slowly reached up taking his hand and placed it gently against her cheek.

Jane was utterly flabbergasted. 'Jimmy, what are you doing here?' She instantly regretted asking such a silly question. It was obvious why Jimmy was there.

'I've taken a w-week off work t-to look after her. It will take t-time but she'll recover. We'd like y-you t-to go now... please.'

We'd like you to go... was this the royal we Jane wondered? Jimmy was clearly speaking on behalf of them both and from the way Constance got pleasure from his caress, Jane knew she was not wanted. As Jimmy showed a perplexed Jane to the door, she repeated to let her know if there was anything she could do but Jimmy assured her that he was in charge.

When Jane got into their car, she held Robert tightly and cried silently into his shoulder. Between her sobs she managed to tell him that f-Fearless was in the house taking care of Constance and she would tell him the rest later – she didn't want to go into details.

Robert wasn't sure if he'd heard right. 'Did you say f-Fearless… our Jimmy is in there looking after Constance?'

'Yes he is. And she doesn't want anyone else. Just Jimmy.'

It took Robert a couple of minutes for it to sink in. 'Bloody hell!'

Exactly two weeks after Ken and Constance had been released from their respective ordeals they returned to work on the same morning. Robert thought they had probably arranged this beforehand. They still had slight swellings around their cheek bones but the main difference was that they both seemed crushed, their previous self-esteem having been beaten out of them. They had obviously each been through unimaginable traumas. In Constance's case, she had the wonderful f-Fearless f-Faversham to coax her back to her old self, and Ken had his loving wife, Rose.

The staff were fully aware of what had happened, so there was no need to ask any questions. Although stopping the project was a bitter blow to the upgrading scheme, the delay gave them the chance to heal their wounds, both physical and mental.

During Ken's convalescence, Robert had visited him a couple of times to update him the latest news. Rose had met the head of the local Busti community to see if it would be safe for them to continue living in Ouverru. The general feeling was that Amos's death was already filed away as another unsolved murder and that the police would now leave Ken alone. Robert hoped that he would continue to take charge of the project as nobody else was anywhere near as capable.

The situation was different with Constance. She was a Peelee, from the right tribe, and so she still had some 'Peelee friends' in high places. Unluckily for her though, they weren't in the police force which was mainly run by Solus. During one of Jane's visits, Constance had eventually given her the name of the man who had abused and beaten her. He was a Solu - Lieutenant M'Sala, the head of the Buzamban Police Force.

'Wow,' said Jane when Constance told her his name, 'he's very important. I've seen him on TV and read about him in the newspapers many times.'

'He's important all right – the bastard – he treated me like an animal,' Constance sobbed. Just the mention of his name brought all the horror back to her. 'I'd love to kill him – very slowly with a great deal of pain. I'd happily do what the rebels did to President Doe in Liberia – cut off his penis and stick it in his mouth.'

Jane took a sharp inward breath at the very thought. She cautiously broached the subject of f-Fearless and asked if he was still living with her. Constance, looking very pleased with herself, said they were a couple, and they had been since they'd first met at Jane and Robert's dinner party. 'He's a very kind man and we like each other a lot.'

Jane said how pleased she was to hear it and that hopefully, when she felt well enough, they would come round for dinner – as a couple.

When Jane told Sellie about Lieutenant M'Sala, she was very angry.

'Him no good, that M'Sala. I hear many bad things about him. I try punish him.'

'But you can't go after such an important man, Sellie. You would put yourself at risk.'

'My power is small, madam, but,' here Sellie gave a cackle like a witch, 'I think I know someone who can. M'Sala has many enemies, he thinks his juju strong – but there are ways.'

'I won't ask any questions but don't do anything to put yourself in danger. Please Sellie... promise.'

Although Jane was fairly certain this story would not be of interest to the British press, she sent a full account to Tony, partly because he'd met Constance and Ken. She would also keep him updated on any developments.

CHAPTER TWENTY-EIGHT

Gilly's and Susie's friendship with Bella became even closer when both girls were invited to the Machuri's for Bella's birthday slumber party. In a ridiculously gaudy, gold-embossed invitation, Mr and Mrs K.K. Machuri asked the girls to join in a swimming and diving gala in their private thirty-foot pool. For obvious reasons, neither Jane nor Robert wanted her to go back to her 'Uncle Mack's', but Gilly was so excited there was no way they could stop her, especially as the Bonds had no such misgivings. What made it even more difficult was that K.K. knew Jane was instrumental in Dieter's stolen drugs being recovered from his pharmacy, his last comment to Jane being that they would meet again. Although said in a polite way, she felt it was more likely a threat; a threat which could not be taken lightly. And, not only that, K.K. had once again stopped the Ogola project, and because he had the Minister of Housing in his pocket, it didn't look as if it would restart for a long time.

'Why Machuri?' Robert almost screamed as he looked heavenward. 'Why couldn't it be someone else? That bastard of an evil man has us by the short-and-curlies, and he bloody well knows it.'

'I told Gilly to be careful and try not to answer any questions Uncle Mack might ask about us,' Jane said, 'but she's too young to understand.'

On the Sunday afternoon, Gregg was due to go and collect the girls when the phone rang. It was a nurse from the Victoria Private Hospital saying Gilly and her friend had just been brought in and they should go round urgently.

'Oh my God,' Jane shrieked, her heart missing a dozen beats. 'He's killed her. He's killed Gilly.'

'No,' corrected Robert, trying to control his rising panic, 'the nurse didn't say she was dead... she's...'

'She's what?' she yelled. 'What did she say?' As she yelled her question at Robert, she felt a huge number of kicks in her belly. Oh for God's sake, don't come now... please she pleaded silently to any god that might be listening. Not now.

Unaware of his unborn child's rumpus, Robert was too upset to think clearly. 'I don't know, but for heaven's sake, let's just go, and we'll pick up Cindy and Gregg.'

Their combined panic attacks made Robert's furious drive to the hospital as dangerous as any journey any of them had ever taken, but Sunday afternoon traffic was light, and somehow they made it. Ignoring any parking regulations, they stopped outside the front entrance and the four of them raced inside. Jane trailed behind, both hands supporting her outsized bump, to stop an unwanted early delivery. It was the blind leading the blind as Robert, Gregg and Cindy raced down different corridors trying to find the children, so it was Jane who found them first.

'Mummy,' cried Gilly as she rushed up, clinging to her sobbing her eyes out; an equally distressed Susie followed and held onto Jane and Gilly as hard as she could.

'Are you all right, darling,' Jane eventually managed to say as she held her at arm's length to get a good look at her.

'Yes, Mummy. I'm fine.' Relief flooded every part of her body. Thank God.

She then turned to Susie. 'And you, Susie, are you okay?'

'Yes, it's Bella. I think she's dead.'

'No, silly.' Even at that age, Gilly remonstrated with her friend. Turning to her mother she said, 'Bella was in a... commer.'

Just then, the three others saw them and came racing down the corridor.

'They're both fine,' Jane managed to shout before Cindy hoisted Susie into a smothering embrace with Gregg hugging them both, while Robert picked Gilly up covering her face with wet kisses.

'It's Bella who's been hurt,' Jane managed to get her voice

heard above the mayhem. 'I think she may be bad. We should go and find out.'

The relief amongst the Kimbers and Bonds was palpable and, after composing themselves, they went in search of Bella and, presumably, her parents. A passing nurse showed them the way. Sitting on a chair outside a private ward was K.K. Machuri. He stood when they approached.

'How's Bella,' Jane asked gently.

'She's in a coma. The doctor is with her now.'

Just then, Dr Patterson came out of the ward, a look of surprise on his face as he saw the Kimbers with another family waiting with Mr Machuri. He only paused for a second before going to K.K. and the others distanced themselves to give them privacy. Whilst the others conversed quietly, Jane's eyes were drawn to Machuri and Patterson, the former clearly agitated by what was said. After a couple of minutes, Machuri stormed into the ward leaving Dr Patterson outside.

He walked towards them. 'Hello Jane, are you friends of Mr Machuri?'

'Hello Angus. No, not exactly, it's our daughters who are friendly with Bella.' Jane introduced him to the Bond family.

'Oh, I see.'

'How is she?'

His shoulders sagged as he gave a despondent sigh. 'She has a bad head wound. We've x-rayed her and there doesn't appear to be any serious damage but she's lost a lot of blood.'

'Can you give her a transfusion?'

This brought another sigh and he shook his head. 'There should be a stock here but we only have one lot of her blood group – B, which she is getting now, but she needs at least one more. The general hospital hasn't any. Can you believe it? I despair at times like this. They should have big stocks of all blood groups.'

'But surely you could get some more from other donors.'

'We're trying. I've got two nurses phoning our list of B donors but either they're out or the phones don't work. It's Sunday afternoon after all.'

'I'm B,' chimed in Robert. 'Can I help?'

'Are you sure?' Angus asked.

'Oh, yes. I've given blood over the years so I know for certain my blood group.'

'Come with me then,' Angus suddenly had a new sense of urgency, 'and we'll get you fired up.'

'That's fantastic,' Gregg said. 'It's a pity we can't help because both Cindy and I are A group.'

'And I'm AB,' added Jane.

'But I couldn't take any from you, Jane,' Angus said, 'you're too close to giving birth.' As he led Robert into the next room, Jane asked Cindy and Gregg to take Gilly back with them as she wanted to wait. With final hugs and kisses, they all left Jane alone outside the ward. Five minutes later, she was joined by K.K. Machuri.

'Your husband is giving blood,' he said and Jane noticed a slight quake in his voice and his whole body seemed to have shrunken.

'Yes, it's lucky he's the same blood group as Bella.'

He rested his head in his hands, and Jane noticed a few tears seeping between his fingers. What then possessed Jane she had absolutely no idea, but as he straightened up, she put both her arms around his shoulders and held him as close to her as she could. Ever so slightly, he returned her embrace. She knew the man was as evil as they come, but at this moment he was suffering like any other human being. Was she mad to care in the slightest? Bella was a lovely little girl but Machuri was her father – would she grow up differently? Was evil inherited or just learnt? Answers to those and a dozen other questions were beyond Jane at that moment.

'She'll be all right, I'm sure. Doctor Patterson is very good,' she said quietly but with sincerity.

'Thank you,' he just about managed as they released each other.

They sat with their own thoughts for a few moments.

'Gilly and Susie saved Bella,' he said matter-of-factly.

Puzzled, Jane asked him what he meant.

Machuri briefly explained that while Bella was playing on a

diving board, she had slipped and banged her head on the edge of the pool and fallen in. Gilly and Susie saw what happened and shouted before diving in after her. We were sitting on the terrace talking and didn't take any notice as there had been shouts and squeals all afternoon… as children do. Only our maid realised what happened, but she was slow in coming to tell us. By the time the two girls had brought Bella to the surface, we got to her and rushed her here.

Jane decided not to say anything for the moment, and it was only then that she realised Machuri was holding her hand.

'Thank you so much,' he said. 'Gilly helped save her life. And now your husband is doing the same.'

It was almost nine o'clock before they eventually left the hospital going straight to the Bonds to pick up Gilly. Jane told them what she knew, feeling extremely proud of her daughter and Susie. Helping a friend in distress was one thing, but actually saving a life was something else.

'Well done, Gilly and Susie. Bella came out of her coma and Doctor Patterson feels confident she will soon be as right as rain.'

'So, your new best friend is the legendary K.K. Machuri,' Gregg laughed.

'I don't know about that, but let's say we're on amicable terms.' She didn't even want to tell Robert yet about her warm embrace with their sworn enemy. That could wait until she'd got it straight in her own mind.

CHAPTER TWENTY-NINE

Baby Kimber burst forth into the world on July 1st, with minimal effort from his mother; Jane's labour had lasted less than ninety minutes. One slap on his bum, and he was complaining loudly that he'd been kept waiting far too long. The whole of the maternity unit was in no doubt that this was one little boy who was determined to be noticed in life, probably as a future army sergeant major. At seven pounds twelve ounces, all his wriggling limbs were there and functioning like those of a prize fighter.

'Wow,' laughed Angus, while a pale-looking father looked on with immense pride, 'you've got a real handful here, Robert.'

'He looks… amazing,' was all he managed to say.

What seemed like a lorry-load of flowers was delivered to her room the next day with a simple child-written note saying 'with my very bestest love, Bella'.

'How the hell did K.K. know you were here?' Robert asked.

'I think you can be sure he knows everything there is to know in this town,' she replied, telling the nurses to distribute the whole lot around the other wards. She had her own simple bunch of flowers next to her bed from Gilly, and that was all she wanted.

Mother and child stayed in the Victoria Private Hospital for three days before a frustrated Jane decided enough was enough, and she wouldn't pander any longer to Angus's eagerness to keep her in, just because she was having difficulty breastfeeding. He was concerned that the ever-demanding baby Kimber was not getting enough milk. Jane had suggested supplementing her own milk with a couple of bottles a day but Angus wouldn't hear of it.

'No Jane, you must persevere. Give the baby the best possible start in life and don't risk any sort of infection. No matter how careful you are, remember – this is Africa – and it is so easy to pick up germs even in the most spotless of houses.'

Jane hadn't wanted any visitors other than Robert and a highly excited Gilly, so her homecoming was a big event. Very few white babies had started life in Basu compound.

First to greet the new arrival were the beaming Sellie and Kaba. Under the watchful gaze of Jane, first Sellie and then Kaba cradled the baby in their arms, swaying slightly from side to side, softly singing a lullaby they both knew from their tribal homelands. Jane soon relaxed when she saw how expertly they held him, as though they'd both done the same thing a hundred times before. It was reassuring to know that she would have so much help in bringing up Master Kimber; when Gilly was born there was only Poppy.

'Me and Kaba – we pleased the baby born on our birthdays,' Sellie said happily.

'Of course,' a startled Jane replied, looking sharply in the direction of her husband. 'Yes of course. Did you get your cards and presents from Mr Kimber?'

'Thank you, Madam. Kaba and I got our birthday presents, from Gilly and Mr Kimber. Thank you,' she added again.

Jane smiled at a grinning Robert. 'Well done Kimber, I confess I'd forgotten,' and then turning to Sellie, she added, 'we'll have a party for all three of you next week. Mr Kimber will arrange it all, won't you, darling?'

Shortly after Robert and Gilly had left for the day, there was a knock on the door and Cindy walked in carrying a huge bunch of flowers. 'Well done, you two. Let's have a look at what you've got there. Wow, isn't he gorgeous,' she cooed. 'So what's his name?'

'At the moment he hasn't got one.'

'No name! That's crazy, you must give him a name. You can't just call him 'it' or 'hey you' all the time. What's the problem?'

'The problem is… Robert wants to name him after his father.'

'So what's wrong with that?'

'His father is called… now, don't laugh or I'll scream.'

'I promise,' Cindy solemnly replied, getting ready to laugh her head off.

Jane hesitated before saying, 'Hubert'.

Cindy's straight face lasted for only a couple of seconds before she tilted her head back, opened her mouth wide, and gave the loudest, shrillest laugh she could muster. 'Hubert! Nobody's called Hubert, please say you're joking.'

'You horror, you promised not to laugh. Anyway, I can't let the poor lad be called Hubert. He'd be a laughing stock… especially if he's got Robert's chin as well as the silly name. He'd have no chance in life.'

After Cindy had got her breath back and wiped the tears from her eyes, she suddenly came up with the perfect solution. 'Instead of Hubert, why not call him Hugh?'

'Hugh... Hugh Kimber!' Jane tested it aloud and it sounded quite good. 'I think I like it, Hugh Kimber, or the Right Honourable Hugh Kimber QC, or Sir Hugh Kimber MP. Yes, it's quite distinguished isn't it?'

'Do you think Robert will agree?'

'He'll have to. It's as close as he'll get to Hubert.'

After Cindy's visit there were so many callers, including Kath and Josie, that Jane soon became tired but that didn't stop her loving all the attention; the congratulations, flowers, chocolates and cards, and everyone saying how handsome baby Hugh was. Jane felt proud of her new baby: life couldn't get much better than this... as long as she behaved herself.

When they had all gone, Hugh started to exercise his sergeant-major's lungs demanding food. She tried her best to satisfy his hunger but she knew it was difficult for him to take enough. Feeding had become stressful and Jane wondered if Hugh sensed her anxiety. It would appear that her bosoms were not particularly well designed for breastfeeding but she would persevere, even if it took all night.

Unfortunately, Hugh (Robert had happily agreed to the name compromise) howled most of the night keeping all three of them awake, he was only quiet when Jane fed him and was frustrated and unhappy when the continuous supply of milk didn't come quickly enough. He had no problem in fulfilling his part of the 'joint venture'; Jane painfully acknowledged the strength of his suck but she was obviously failing to supply enough milk.

A very tired Robert and Gilly left as early as they could; even work and school would be a relief. Whenever Hugh slept for an hour or two during the day, Jane did the same while Sellie provided her with as much support as she could.

The next night was a repeat performance. Fortunately, Gilly was so exhausted that she slept through all the noise. Jane and Robert were relieved as it was her special concert at school that evening. She had been chosen to sing a solo in front of all the parents and

Robert and Jane had promised to be there. This was one event that even Hugh couldn't prevent them from attending. Forewarned that the birth was due a week before the school concert, Jane had planned to take the baby with them. She had imagined a quiet, sleepy, perfect baby but, as Hugh cried most of the time he was awake, she thought it best to leave him with Sellie. They would be away for less than two hours so she gave him the best feed she could before they left and hoped he would sleep in Sellie's care.

What they hadn't planned for was the fiercest July storm Ouverru had witnessed in living memory. Gilly and the other children had done their pieces (Gilly did moderately well although she was out of key and flat most of the time) and the concert was approaching the finale when the first crack of thunder, followed by several flashes of lightning, caused everyone on the stage and in the audience to jump with shock. After that, the thunder was even louder followed by sudden torrential rain pounding on the school's zinc roof.

Jane looked at Robert. 'I think we'd better go as soon as we can.'

'You wait there and I'll get Gilly.'

'Please be quick,' Jane's voice tailed off as Robert hurried backstage.

But Gilly was too keyed-up to hurry. She dawdled as she changed out of her costume, chatting excitedly with her friends and only after several pleas from Robert did she eventually take his hand and they rushed to find Jane. Outside, the rain was hurtling down and they didn't have raincoats or umbrellas. Luckily, Basil spotted them by the main exit and, after a lot of manoeuvring, he eventually got them into the car.

'Well done, Basil,' Jane said thankfully, looking at her watch and noting they'd already been away two hours, 'let's get home as quickly as possible.'

The torrential storm had caught everyone out. Very rarely was there any rain in July, and this was exceptionally heavy, resulting in far more vehicles on the road than usual. For about half a mile they managed to crawl along at walking pace, but then, all the cars in front of them stopped. Several impatient drivers leant on their horns in the African way, even though it was a total waste of time. Basil followed suit but Robert soon stopped him.

After being stationary for about five minutes, Jane was getting desperate. Hugh was already overdue a feed. If only she'd ignored Angus Patterson and prepared some bottles. She borrowed Robert's mobile phone to call Sellie but the reception was very poor, which wasn't helped by the fact that the batteries needed recharging.

'Can you hear me?' she shouted down the phone.

All she could hear was crackle, crackle followed by a faint sounding Sellie asking something about food. But even with all the static and above the weak signal, Jane could clearly hear Hugh yelling his head off. She started to panic. 'We have to get home quickly,' she shouted unreasonably at Basil. 'Take another road, or force your way through.'

'There's nothing Basil can do, Jane,' Robert said. 'We're boxed in on all sides.' He didn't mention the even worse news that the road was gradually flooding. 'We'll just have to wait here. It's over three miles to our house and there's no way we can walk in this weather.'

Jane was almost at bursting point. She tried, once again, to phone but the batteries had run out. Over the past twelve months she had developed a huge amount of trust in Sellie but now the situation was beyond her. Sellie mustn't give him cow's milk as it would need boiling – but she had no bottle feeders, in any case. Even if she had, they had to be sterilized before giving him water or milk; Sellie wouldn't know about that. And she couldn't give him solid food either. How long could a six day old baby hold on without being fed? She looked at her watch for the umpteenth time; it was nearly three hours since they'd left the house.

Because of the chaos, the massive traffic jam and the flooding of several roads, it was half-past one in the morning when Basil finally got them home. By this time Jane and Robert were beside themselves with worry and Gilly had cried for the last fifty minutes. She didn't understand why her mum was so frantic but she knew her baby brother must be hungry.

The sight that greeted them as they burst through the front door stopped them dead in their tracks. Sellie was standing by the armchair with a tentative smile on her face - the sort of smile a child might adopt when it isn't sure if it's in trouble or not. Sitting in the armchair was a total stranger: A woman, a black woman, her dress unbuttoned down to her waist, breastfeeding Hugh. The strange lady looked up as they entered and gave a 'Basil type' smile.

'What...' was about as far as Jane got, her face a contrast between panic and horror.

'Who...' was also as far as Robert got before stepping forward to take Hugh and then hesitating because the woman was bare breasted. He turned to Jane. He was out of his depth here and instinctively knew he would have to leave everything to her.

'This Regina,' Sellie said.

Jane recovered her self-control and quickly stepped forward to take Hugh from the woman – Regina. Just as she was about to snatch him away, Hugh let go of Regina's nipple and Jane saw a look of contentment on his shiny little face. He was full. As she picked him up and put him over her shoulder, he gave the most enormous burp which made Sellie and Regina laugh out loud. Even Gilly thought it was funny and joined in; she knew that her baby brother was well fed and there was nothing to worry about.

But this woman was a stranger and Jane and Robert's immediate thought was who the blazes is Regina? Is she free of infection and, more importantly, free of HIV? Could the storm and being late home lead to Hugh contracting AIDS?

Jane didn't know what to do. She looked as sternly as she could at Sellie as if to say 'how dare you do this, you had no right,' but instead, she rushed Hugh out of the living room and into their bathroom. She vigorously washed him all over and tried to rinse out his mouth, but for what? Would scouring his mouth and scrubbing him pink get rid of AIDS? In fact, can a baby pick up an infection by feeding from an infected woman? All of these questions flashed through her mind without any answers.

Robert joined her in the bedroom.

'Go and get Gilly ready for bed.' Robert did as he was told. Their anxiety must not upset Gilly.

After washing and changing Hugh, Jane went back into the living room. Sellie was alone.

'Where's Regina?'

'She gone, Madam. She go home.'

Jane had moderately calmed down by now and knew she must choose her words carefully. 'Who is Regina?'

'She a friend. She live outside compound gate. She have baby boy age two, so I know she have plenty milk. That's why I bring her

362

for baby Hugh.' Sellie looked at Hugh who had closed his eyes and was fast asleep in Jane's arms. 'He happy now.'

'Yes, I know that but…' Jane tried to think of a way of asking what she desperately needed to know 'but… err… how well do you know her? She may be… infected.'

'Oh no, Madam. Regina a good, clean woman. She not sick – she got good health.'

What else could Jane do? She couldn't bring herself round to thank Sellie for what she did, because in her eyes it was wrong. Dreadfully wrong. All she did was ask her to bring Regina back in the morning so that she could take her to Dr Patterson's clinic to get her checked out.

For the first time since he was born, Hugh slept through and Jane and Robert had their first good night's sleep. Hugh was cross when Jane got him up to give him a morning feed and wailed loudly when he couldn't get enough milk. Jane was almost at the point of tears. Why wouldn't her own baby feed from her but do so from a stranger?

When Basil returned with the car, he took Sellie to talk to Regina and returned with a beaming Regina who was only too willing to cooperate and see Dr Patterson.

Angus Patterson had no such feelings of diplomacy as he spoke to all three of them. 'Even if Miss Regina is HIV positive, which I very much doubt, there is very little chance that Hugh will contract the disease.'

Jane cringed in her chair. That was not what she wanted him to say in front of Regina, she must be furious. Jane took a breath and slowly turned to look in Regina's direction. But neither Regina nor Sellie seemed to have taken any offence. In fact they were looking in her direction, waiting for her to say something – it was not their position to speak before her.

Apprehensively, Jane turned to Regina. 'Would you mind if Dr Patterson has you checked?' Jane chose not to add 'for AIDS'.

'I happy,' replied Regina, giving another of her big smiles.

'I'll give her Nevirapine as it might help. It blocks the transmission of the virus from mother to baby. I know Regina isn't the mother, but…it won't do any harm.'

While Regina and Sellie went with the nurse, Angus wanted to know if Jane was successfully breastfeeding.

'Not very well, I'm afraid. I had the same problem with my first child and eventually put her onto a bottle. She was much happier then.'

Sensitively, he gave Jane an examination and could see no reason why she had a problem. 'Are you stressed or tense?' he asked. 'Is anything troubling you?'

'Not that I know of,' was all Jane could say, thinking I'm only stressed because you won't let me bottle-feed.

Angus again encouraged a fretful Jane to persevere and suggested that if baby was not getting enough milk from her, then she could ask Regina to step in again. She should not use a bottle.

Before they left, Angus reminded Jane about the Suzama Mamas and hoped to see her the following afternoon. Jane said she'd think about it.

This was one decision she couldn't make on her own, so she waited for Robert to get home. 'Angus thinks it would be safe to let Regina feed Hugh. What do you think?'

'Oh, I don't really know,' Robert put his arms around her and held her close. 'If Regina is infected, then it's probably too late anyway. And if anybody knows about the dangers of HIV/AIDS, then Angus is the man.'

'Yes, you're right, but this must be our joint decision, darling.' She snuggled into his embrace and gave him a tender kiss. 'If I can't give Hugh enough milk, then I'll ask Regina. Do you agree?'

Still holding her tightly, he only took a few seconds before saying he agreed.

Neither Jane nor Robert were surprised when Ken told them that the project was back on track; assurances had been received from the actual top man, the Minister of Housing himself, that there would be no more interruptions. Ken couldn't understand this change of heart, especially as the original building owners who'd maintained that the project was illegal had now dropped the charge. Jane and Robert thought it best not to tell them the real reason – it would be too complicated. Instead, they said Sellie had used one of her magic potions on K.K. Machuri, which, of course, he didn't believe for a minute.

With encouragement from Robert and everyone at Ogola, a tired Jane, after another sleepless night with Hugh, took him to show him off to the staff and give him his first whiff of Ogola. There had been no rain since 'the storm' and the air was particularly pongy. Jane hurried him into the office which was somewhat protected from the outdoor odours. Baby Hugh was a big hit with everyone and showed his appreciation of all the attention by howling his head off.

'Here, I take him,' Lola said and, without asking, took him from Jane, deftly tightening the light blanket around his body and energetically swinging him to and fro like a swing-boat ride at a fairground. At the same time she made slight swishing noises close to his ear. Immediately, Hugh stopped crying.

They all laughed at Jane's perplexed expression.

'How did you do that?' Jane grinned.

'It what we do in our village when baby cry. You see – it work for *mzungu* babies just like African.'

'I must remember that,' Jane said appreciatively. 'He cries a lot of the time – except when his tummy's full.'

After the excitement of baby Kimber's arrival, when everyone, including Ken, had a turn to hold him, Jane took advantage of the lull to say goodbye, knowing that she wouldn't visit again before going on leave in ten days' time.

She was just about to leave when an angry-looking Constance Wanjiku came storming into the office and, ignoring everyone else, went straight up to Ken.

'Why you do this thing?' she yelled.

Ken's expression was of total surprise. 'What thing? What are you talking about?'

'You fix Lieutenant M'Sala. You crazy! That was a dumb thing to do.'

Ken stared angrily back at Constance. 'Constance, what are you talking about? What fix – Lieutenant M'Sala?'

'You mean you haven't heard?' she said, turning round to look at all the others. 'Has no one heard?'

Everyone's expression was the same, nobody had any idea what Constance was talking about. They only knew that it was Lieutenant M'Sala who had abused Constance and he was also the officer who had Ken locked up and beaten, but nothing else.

'He in hospital – he almost die.' Constance told them.

'What happened?'

'You know the big storm the other night?'

They all nodded as it had been the worst dry season storm they could remember. 'M'Sala was struck by lightning, on his head, his eyes burned in the sockets, he blind now, forever. You honestly didn't know?' she demanded.

'My word of honour, I didn't know anything.' The expression on Ken's face showed he was telling the truth.

'Because everyone say it witchcraft by one of his victims and we were his latest victims, so everyone say it was me… or you. And, I swear, it wasn't me.'

'It wasn't me either. I promise,' Ken said vehemently.

'M'Sala's family want you and me to go and see the Solu Comus.'

'I'll go. I don't want to but, I'm innocent. I'm not a Solu though so they may trick me, and blame me.'

'No, I'll make sure it's honest. I'll have friends with me, I promise,' Constance tried to reassure Ken because she now believed him.

Ken reluctantly agreed, and all the staff, with the possible exception of Nelson, thought it was necessary to get this witchcraft charge sorted out as soon as possible. If he refused to go he would be in even more trouble. By this time, Jane and Hugh had been forgotten, so Jane said her farewells and left.

When she arrived home she told Sellie all that had happened to Constance and Ken, and the fact that the hated Lieutenant M'Sala had been struck by lightning, losing his eyesight. 'Could it be witchcraft?'

Sellie was silent and looked uncomfortable, nervously fiddling with her hands and shifting her feet in an anxious manner. This was most unlike her as she usually liked to talk about witchcraft, spirit people, and traditional customs – but not today.

'Do you know what the Solu Comus is?'

'Yes, Madam,' Sellie nodded. 'Comus is a sort of big, big magic man; something like the top judge in your country. He tell if Constance or Ken did this thing.'

'You mean like a trial?'

'Remember, I tell you about Kaba's uncle who was accused of doing bad things to her?'

'Yes, in Kaba's village at Christmas.'

'Yes, Madam, local medicine man proved he guilty.'

Jane said she remembered.

'Well, Comus like that man but with strong, strong power, nobody has strong power like Solu Comus. He hold trial, maybe with fire or poison, and if guilty, then…'

'What?'

'It's OK, Madam. Constance and Ken not do this thing, so they be OK.'

Jane wasn't sure whether to ask her next question. 'How do you know they are innocent?'

Again, Sellie twisted her hands nervously. 'I know it.'

Was it because she was tense and stressed, or was there some other unknown cause for her dread of feeding Hugh? He still couldn't get enough milk and she and Robert had another terrible night. She wished she'd ignored Angus Patterson's pressure to continue breastfeeding because it just wasn't working. And to make matters worse, she was coming down with some kind of fever. She had a bad headache, her limbs started to ache, and she felt really ill.

As the morning light crept around the bedroom curtains, she started to cry.

'Hey, what's the matter,' Robert woke up and gently put his arm around her shoulders.

Between sobs, Jane, who rarely succumbed to crying, told him she was a failure, unable to feed their baby. She just couldn't give him enough, and she was his mother. 'He won't sleep until he's had enough milk and he won't feed from me. I'm so tired.'

Robert did his best to reassure her although, being short of sleep himself, he wasn't feeling at his best. Incredibly, Gilly slept through all of the ear-numbing howling.

During a brief lapse in Hugh's protestations, Robert went through to the kitchen and gently knocked on Sellie's door. He asked her to please go and see if Regina would come and feed Hugh, and would she be available for the next few days? He was too tired to question if there was a slight chance of infection being transferred from Regina to the baby. If by some tragic stroke of bad luck, Regina was infected, then it was probably already too late.

When he went back to bed he told Jane what he had arranged. She accepted his decision and immediately went back to sleep as if a huge weight had been lifted from her shoulders.

Jane stayed in bed all day. Her temperature was over 100 degrees and Angus recommended that she should drink plenty of liquids with Paracetamol and go to see him if she was no better in a couple of days. He did have some good news though – Regina's test result had come through and she was clear of any disease, including HIV.

Now that Hugh had his new *milk machine* on tap, he changed from being a complete monster to the happiest baby in Buzamba. Jane was able to relax and her fever went after three days. She fed him once a day to keep her milk, but waited another two days before attempting to feed him all by herself. Although it was not a total success, it gave her confidence that, until they went on leave, she would be able to cope.

On the day that Jane was back in the land of the living, Gilly finished school for the summer holidays. Her report and test results were better than her teacher had predicted, which was exactly what they wanted to hear. Her education had not suffered since moving to Buzamba. In fact, Gilly seemed to thrive in a smaller class and, it seemed to Jane, she was ahead of where she would have been in England. She was already looking forward to the start of the next school year, even more than her holiday. In her mind, her life was in Buzamba with her mummy, her daddy and baby brother and she didn't associate this all-inclusive life with the past in Ringwood.

Kaba also finished school and, in the last six months, Jane had noticed a huge change in her. She had grown in self-confidence and the improvement in her grasp of English was amazing. She now had little difficulty in holding conversations with Gilly and her friends. Her school report was encouraging but Jane felt the teachers had not fully appreciated her background and the baggage she had come with. Sellie and Jane discussed her report at great length, Sellie being as proud as any mother would be. Her 'child' was being educated which, in the future, would give her so many opportunities. Sellie hoped that when Kaba completed her education, she would be like Constance Wanjiku, who was her role model.

CHAPTER THIRTY

Four days before they were due to leave, Sellie asked to speak to Jane privately. She had a troubled expression on her face and Jane noticed again her nervous habit of folding and unfolding her hands.

'I need fifteen thousand shillings,' was her brief but staggering request.

Jane wasn't sure that she'd heard properly or understood. 'Did you say fifteen thousand shillings?'

Sellie hesitated. 'Yes, Madam, I pay you back something each month.'

'But why?'

'I cannot say, Madam…'

Jane sat on the stool and remained quiet for a few moments while her mind raced with anxiety. Why on earth would Sellie ask for such a huge sum of money just before they went on holiday? Was it greed, knowing that it was too late for them to make alternative arrangements? Surely not. Not Sellie – wonderful Sellie who had helped to make their life so enjoyable over the past year. She was still struggling to make sense of this strange request when a sudden thought struck her. She looked Sellie straight in the eye. 'Is this anything to do with Lieutenant M'Sala?'

Sellie didn't reply straight away but Jane knew she'd hit the nail on the head. Eventually Sellie said lamely, 'I want to help.'

'Did you arrange for some witchcraft… some magic for the lightning to strike M'Sala and make him blind?'

'I want to help,' she repeated.

'But you knew that Mr Kasansa and Constance Wanjiku would be suspected of doing this.'

Sellie nodded. 'I know this thing. I know Comus say they innocent.'

'How do you know?'

'I know Comus, Madam. I met him.'

Jane had thought that nothing about Sellie would surprise her, but this time she'd outdone herself. It was Sellie who'd arranged for M'Sala to be struck by lightning and now she had to pay-up. Secretly, Jane was pleased M'Sala had been punished as he was clearly a cruel man who took pleasure in abusing and torturing people, and now he'd been seriously punished. And maybe, just maybe, anyone else in authority with the same sadistic leanings as M'Sala would think twice, knowing what had happened. Also, the authorities would hesitate to abuse Ken and Constance ever again, knowing that someone on their side had stronger juju than the head of police.

'OK, Sellie,' Jane said, but in a reproachful manner, 'I'll ask the boss to get the money today.' She would never ask Sellie to pay any of it back. Fifteen thousand shillings or three hundred pounds was money well spent, and when she explained it to Robert, he totally agreed with her.

Making the effort to take part in Angus's breastfeeding charade with his so-called 'Suzama Mamas', was worrying Jane. She imagined her stress levels going through the roof, struggling with a whinging baby in public. How embarrassing would that be? Hugh would complain like crazy and that would not impress any onlookers, and what sort of onlookers? Voyeurs?

Could Regina? Would Regina? After a great deal of soul searching, Jane tentatively broached the subject.

'I happy, Madam, very happy,' the ever-beaming Regina replied.

Good old Regina. What a relief.

Luckily, they were a little late arriving after Basil had been held up by a minor traffic accident, but the scene that met Jane was… she struggled to find an appropriate word… bizarre was the best she could come up with. Next to the clinic was a thatched-roofed shelter which was enclosed on three sides by the clinic building and a garage, the fourth side being completely open to the pavement and road. There were some small round tables with two or three wicker chairs at each one, all facing the road so there was no chance of turning one's back to the public. Around fifteen women of various hues and races were monopolising most of the seats, feeding their offspring under the watchful eye of two of Angus's nurses. Angus himself, was nowhere to be seen.

'Come, Mrs Kimber.' Comfort, one of the nurses beckoned her, 'you sit here.'

Jane took a spare chair so that she could sit next to Regina. She explained to the nurse that because she had been ill with a fever and couldn't feed her baby, Regina would feed him for her.

'She your wet-nurse?' Comfort wasn't sure if this was what the doctor expected but it was clear that Jane wanted it that way.

'Shall I start, Madam?' Regina asked.

'Yes please.'

And with that, Regina followed the example of all the other ladies and clasped an eager *mzungu* baby to her milk-engorged bosom. All the other babies were more-or-less the same colour as their mothers but Jane thought that white baby Hugh looked fantastic feeding on a black breast. If only she had a camera!

And were the public interested? You bet they were. There was a large crowd of locals watching, some stood rooted to the spot and others slowed down as they went on their journeys. Jane estimated that three-quarters of the onlookers were men and boys which somewhat defeated the object.

Jane spoke to the lady next to her, quickly giving her excuse as to why she wasn't breastfeeding. Her neighbour, an Australian of Korean origin called Mae, told Jane she had been coming to the Suzama Mamas for over four weeks and was already on friendly terms with several of the other regulars; and not only were some of the mothers regulars but so were some of the onlookers.

'You see that man there?' Mae pointed in the direction of an elderly man, looking shifty and wearing scruffy shirt and trousers, 'he comes here every day,' she laughed. 'We call him Mr Peeping Tom.'

'It's probably the highlight of his day,' Jane laughed with her. 'Someone should go round with a collection plate.'

All the time the mothers were feeding, the two nurses were talking to the watching women, explaining the dangers of bottle feeding.

Feeling awkward, being the only mother fully covered, Jane noticed Comfort taking drinks to the ladies so she volunteered to help. She spoke to several of the mothers, introducing herself and repeating what was rapidly becoming her lame excuse for not joining in.

'Hey, you're cheating,' a blond woman with a strong Australian accent called out to her. 'Trust a ruddy Pom to keep her kit on.'

Jane explained again about her recent illness and that her friend Regina was filling in for her.

The Australian was not satisfied. 'Well in that case you can still strip off like us – you could be a topless waitress.'

'Maybe next time,' Jane replied, showing she was not fazed by the woman's whinge, knowing very well that was one thing she definitely would not do.

There were continuous comings and goings of mothers and babies but by five o'clock there was only Regina and one other lady left. Hugh, who was totally and utterly full, fell asleep while Regina was trying to persuade him to take more.

'Thank you, Regina,' Jane smiled. 'I think it's time to go.'

Regina passed the sleeping bundle to Jane and fastened her top. The crowd had almost gone; all except for Mr Tom.

'See you tomorrow, Mrs Kimber,' Comfort called as they were leaving.

'Is that okay with you, Regina?' Jane asked.

Regina was only too pleased to cooperate. She was really enjoying herself and the promise of a substantial payment for her services was very welcome.

The last few days before their holiday went quickly. Although Jane felt better after her fever, she still asked Regina to feed Hugh as often as she could, and it followed that all the Kimber family slept soundly every night. With regular feeds and a lot of attention, Hugh was a happy and contented baby. For Jane, the first item on her UK shopping list would be bottles and baby milk formula.

Gilly had a farewell party for some of her school friends, including a now fighting-fit Bella, as well as Susie, Trish and Kaba. In fact, the nationalities of her friends were becoming a minor United Nations. Jane and Robert were pleased that some of the ever-growing circle were not British, and English was not even their first language. What a change from Ringwood and what a fantastic experience for Gilly.

Josie and Lester Pennicott gave an evening drinks party for them and their Basu friends. Two weeks after the Kimbers, Cindy and Gregg would be on leave for six weeks, so it would be a couple of months before they would see each other again.

When the party broke up about midnight, Jane and Robert were ready to leave to flop on their own settee, swirling their nightcaps of Buzamban brandy around and around in the balloon glasses.

'So, Mrs Kimber, are you looking forward to your holiday?'

'Yes, of course. Catching up with the pregnant Poppy will be fun, but I wish we could see more of them.'

'Yes, that would be nice. It's been quite a year hasn't it?'

'It's been absolutely amazing. You know it was Poppy who saw you as my perfect partner, long before I did.' Jane raised her glass to her contented-looking husband. 'Little did I know then what the year would bring.'

'Yes, we owe a lot to Poppy's Introduction Agency. That bribe I gave her to make you marry me really worked… I love corruption!' he smiled.

'You what?'

'Only kidding. Anyway, you haven't achieved anything while you've been here… well, apart from retrieving all the money spent on the first computers and that little matter of finding the stolen antiretrovirals and so saving a few hundred lives.'

Laughing at his droll, condescension, Jane gave him a kiss. 'And don't forget I gave birth to your child.'

'Did you really,' he pretended to look puzzled. 'I must have missed that... ouch!'

'Why do I put up with you, I wonder?' she gave him another kiss. 'And what else did I do?'

'Mmm, let's see,' he pretended to think deeply. 'That incredible, not worth mentioning, matter of the new computerised accounting system which many government departments want to copy... and DGA thinking you're God's gift to the whole continent...is hardly worth a mention... and taking a dying girl from the slum and turning her into a brilliant young lady.'

'I'd like to help more kids on our next tour,' Jane said, a serious tone in her voice. 'Maybe get some charity money to set up a home for all those poor scavenging street children... I could get Sellie to help.'

'Phew... if it's you and the amazing Sellie, nobody would stand a chance.'

'Hey, you missed out one thing, Kimber.'

Robert thoughtfully sipped his brandy. 'And that is...?'

'That our daughter has finally put a stop to K.K. Machuri causing any more problems in Ogola. Purely because of her, the project will now speed along, improving the lives of many thousands of poor people.'

'Oh that little insignificant thing. Besides, it was my pure, beautiful British blood that did that.'

'Only because yours is common and mine is rare and precious.' Laughing, Jane launched herself on Robert resulting in one of their tickling and poking romps as they rolled on the rug. 'And don't think you'll be getting any sex for a long time... it's far too early. Anyway, I think we should do our bit to stop the population growth. When we resume our night time adventures, I think I'll go on the pill. What do you think?'

'Yes, my darling, I agree. Anyway, if I don't get enough sex from you, I'm sure Cindy will... ouch, that hurt. I'll get you for that...'

Before he could resume his attack, a cry came from Hugh's bedroom.

'Now look what you've done,' Jane gave Robert one last poke in his tummy, 'you've woken Hugh, you moron. You can go and get him back to sleep, and you can breastfeed him this time.'

Two nights before leaving, Jane invited F-Fearless and Constance Wanjiku for dinner.

'Are they coming as a couple?' asked Robert.

'Of course they are, dummy. F-Fearless certainly stayed at Constance's house after her ordeal and I wouldn't be surprised if he's still there.'

'He hasn't said anything to me.'

'Well, maybe he's shy! – know the feeling, Kimber?'

They were both shocked when f-Fearless and Constance arrived… shocked in a special way. Jane had never seen F-Fearless look so healthy, Constance had fully regained her poise and confidence, and when she glanced in f-Fearless' direction, there was no doubt that Cupid's arrow had struck home.

'We have some news,' Constance beamed and held up her left hand revealing a glittering ring on her engagement finger. 'We're engaged!'

Two open-mouthed, stuffed dummies stood rooted to the spot, staring at f-Fearless and Constance as though they were two Martians who'd lost their way. It was Jane who eventually reacted first.

'You… you're engaged… to each other?' she gasped.

'To be married?' Robert croaked.

The emboldened, shiny-new f-Fearless f-Faversham put his arm around Constance's shoulders, gave her a quick kiss on the lips and, without the slightest stutter, said, 'Yes, we're engaged… to be married.'

'That's fantastic,' squealed Jane and she rushed up to them, hugging and kissing them for all she was worth.

Robert's reaction was less frenetic, but he gave his silly ear-to-ear grin, shaking f-Fearless warmly by the hand, and timidly kissed Constance on her cheek.

Jane wanted all the details and demanded to know how it all happened. She and Constance went to sit on the settee and their excited chatter excluded Robert and f-Fearless who sat near them looking lost for words.

'Open the wine, Kimber,' demanded Jane. 'And the good stuff, let's celebrate.'

Gradually, calm was restored and a glowing Jane repeated for the umpteenth time how pleased she was. 'It's the best news I've had since...' she paused to try and remember her last piece of exciting news... 'since some guy, or other... I can't quite remember who... proposed to me a few months ago.'

'Oh, ha, ha Miss whatever your name is, how very droll.' Robert laughed.

'She only wants to marry me to get a British passport,' f-Fearless quipped.

'Liar,' Constance joked back. 'He wants me because I'm so beautiful and he's madly in love with me and... well, nobody else would have him.'

'I see you're learning our rather peculiar sense of humour,' Jane laughed.

'Yes, I'm gradually getting there but... oh boy... I find it very strange. It seems that the closer friends men are, the greater the insults they hurl at each other. Is that really the British sense of humour?'

'It's not all like that,' Robert answered, 'but it's part of it. For example, when I was at university, I had a really good friend who was Scottish – we played rugby together – and he called me a gormless English wanker and I called him a bloody, ignorant Scottish plonker.'

'And yet you say you were best friends?' Constance struggled to make sense of this.

'Absolutely. But I would never say anything like that to anyone I didn't know very well, or didn't like.'

'And we could be mistakenly labelled racist if we were to make a similar comment to a close African friend. It's meant to be a term of affection.'

Constance still looked puzzled. 'Don't you ever call me a plonker, f-f-f-Faversham,' she said, looking directly at her fiancé, 'or I'll get Sellie to use her powers to turn you into... err... let me think... into a mouse.'

After a moment's reflection, Robert added. 'Maybe she already has.'

Constance understood that, and erupted into gales of laughter before poking her fiancé in the chest. 'I think I might enjoy your British sense of humour after all.'

After their guests had gone, Jane and Robert marvelled at the change in f-Fearless. Not too long ago, he'd been a washed-up, sickly man who spent most of his life depressed, becoming a drunk-depressive, not an alcoholic in the medical sense but life was a meaningless waste of time and the only way to get through each day was to drink.

'And there goes another of our achievements; we brought those two together. All f-Fearless needed was the love of a good woman,' Jane said looking round at her husband.

'Yes, I think you're right, I must look for one myself... ouch!'

Jane rose very early the following morning – departure day. Although she was looking forward to the holiday, she was also desperate to return to Buzamba. Any earlier doubts she'd had were gone and everything in her life was falling into shape. She had made a lot of new friends and had gained tremendous satisfaction from her work in Ogola. But could all this last? She'd first met Robert as a penniless single mother with no prospects and now, here she was a secure and self-assured wife and mother.

The dusky, red orb of the sun was just rising above the horizon, burning through the misty pink and pale blue morning haze – it wouldn't be long before the whole sky was a vivid blue once again. She strolled onto the terrace and standing by her favourite chair, watched the African sunrise, remembering her many experiences; some happy but some profoundly sad. Sellie suddenly appeared at her side and Jane held out her hand to her. Together, they stood in silence for a while, as Jane had done so many times. She watched the busy comings and goings of the weaver birds flitting from tree to tree, the male birds putting the finishing touches to their nests hoping to entice a prospective bride to its highly desirable residence. 'You'll find me where the weaver birds fly,' she said wistfully to herself, not realising she'd said it aloud.

'Pardon, Madam.'

'Oh, Sellie,' Jane's voice croaked slightly as she turned to face her. 'This is my favourite place on earth. I think... when I die, this is where I want to be and, when it's someone else's time to pass away, I'll tell my family and loved ones they'll find me where the weaver birds fly.' She felt a bit silly as she put her arm around Sellie's shoulder. 'Can you arrange that for me, Sellie?'

With a smile as wide as Africa, and a tear rolling down her disfigured cheek, Sellie did something she'd never done before and put both her arms around Jane and kissed her on both cheeks. 'I fix it for you, Madam. I get the best juju spirit man to make it happen.'

They held each other tightly for several seconds, their tears intermingling like blood brothers as a token of true friendship.

'Thank you for everything,' Jane finally managed. 'You've done so much for my family, and I hope that you and Kaba will be with us for many years to come.'

'I hope so, Madam.'

As Basil drove out of Basu compound, taking the Kimber family to Ouverru International Airport, Sellie and Kaba, with huge grins on their faces, waved frantically at the departing vehicle. After the car had finally disappeared, they walked, hand-in-hand in the garden, when suddenly, a weaver bird's nest fell to the ground just in front of them. As Kaba picked it up saying she would keep it for Gilly, Sellie knew that Africa's mystical soul, older than history itself, had sent her a sign... a sign from Jane that her spirit was with them in that garden where the weaver birds fly, and she'd soon be guided back to where her heart belongs.

EPILOGUE

Dear Tony

This is my final report... my valedictory before the Fabulous Kimbers leave for their first holiday back in Ringwood. I thought I'd write my verdict on what I've seen and learnt in my year here, and in the words of the Beatles, I've written it 'with a little help from my friends'. Quite a lot of help, actually. Lester provided a lot of the data but I also got bits from Gregg and Quentin. More importantly, I received excellent help from Ken and Hani in Ogola. And my dear Robert helped me put it into a presentable format.

What I've written is from the personal experiences of those who actually work in the nitty-gritty of Africa, and not gleaned from academic works written by so-called experts who spend a couple of weeks hob-nobbing with government, NGO and charity officials who push their own agenda to support their vested interests.

Now, here's the big thing... not only have I written what's wrong with aid, I've also come up with a fantastic solution – okay, it's not just my idea, but I haven't seen or heard of anyone spelling it out quite as well as little modest me.

So, as your humble apprentice, I hope you think I've done okay... maybe even gold star material. I've called it....

AID TO AFRICA
MAINTAINING THE STATUS QUO
By Jane Kimber

Since the end of the colonial era in the early 1960s, one thousand-billion dollars of aid has been sent to Africa, which is equal to US $1,000 for every man, woman and child on the planet today. Regrettably, there is little evidence that this generosity has helped to 'make poverty history' in sub-Saharan Africa, the main beneficiaries being corrupt dictators, expatriate consultants, and bureaucrats. We can only shake our heads in incredulity and ask – how could this happen?

The general public has a deep-seated but mistaken belief that foreign aid is always virtuous, mainly brought about by politicians craving Tinkerbell's stardust that attaches to various celebrities and pop stars. In private, even the World Bank admits it has failed to deliver its aim which was to generate economic growth and alleviate poverty in Africa. Our own government through the Department for International Development (DfID) boasts that aid from UK has helped take thousands of people out of poverty. The truth is that the number of Africans in absolute poverty increases year-on-year. Our cash-strapped coalition government has increased funding for DfID. Why? Presumably Cameron and Clegg thought it showed their caring side. And it gets worse, until recently DfID evaluated its own performance so there was no independent check on whether or not its £7.6 billion (and rising) annual funding was being wasted... but there is a mountain of anecdotal evidence to show that it was. The more money given to countries with corrupt dictators, the less incentive they have to change their ways.

Whilst many individuals within the world's donors are genuine in their attempts to help the poor, the structure they work within thwarts them at every step. The donor agencies are: international (e.g. World Bank), national (e.g. DfID), or nongovernmental organisations (NGOs) and charities. The latter two groups can often bypass African governments and, consequently, have had marginal success, although many of the benefits have proved to be only short-lived.

In the main, donor agency staff have *jobs for life* – well-paid, privileged jobs which they hold onto at all costs. Not for them the need to be judged on performance; when things don't improve, they point to the corruption in the African countries they serve, their argument being that aid has failed because of the crooked dictators – nothing to do with us Guv! Their backs are well and truly covered.

My argument is that corruption and bad governance have not only been condoned by the West but, through pure inertia, actually encouraged. As most of the corruption money comes from the developed world, it could have been stamped out, but it was easier to turn a blind eye and pretend it wasn't happening.

We all know there is irrefutable evidence of corruption by African leaders. Swiss banks are stuffed to the gunnels with billions of dollars in numbered accounts. The World Bank, IMF, DfID and all aid workers know this to be true – but that doesn't stop them from using more of the West's taxpayers' money to swell the despots' coffers.

So – what's the solution? The solution is this – stop aid to Africa. I can already hear the screams of outrage – how could any caring person even contemplate such a drastic step? After all, we are bombarded with pictures on our television screens of starving African children, scavenging for scraps in the rubbish tips around most African towns. Surely, you would think, these poor people need more aid, not less. But alas, the money you send doesn't reach the poor, but it does reach the corrupt dictators. I am making this proposal because I care about the welfare of all Africans and I'm not the first person to suggest such a radical plan. A growing number of African academics want a cessation of aid coupled with the abolition of the EU's Common Agricultural Policy which keeps African agricultural exports out of the EU markets.

To start, all current aid for Africa should be channelled through one single organisation instead of thousands. The World Bank/IMF has had its chance and can't be reformed. The answer is to create a new agency made up of the 30 or so benevolent countries which would actually give aid and not expect a return on their handouts. For argument's sake, call it D30 (Donor 30). The D30 would include countries like Denmark, Finland and Norway which give aid but so far have had little or no influence amongst the big-boys like the G20. The D30 would directly manage the programme to stop aid gradually over the next ten years, and be the only source of future investment. China would be excluded from the D30 as it doesn't recognise the continent's need of help or assistance, only selfishly exploits its natural resources.

So, how would the shortfall be covered? By (a) reducing non-essential expenditure (cars, private jets, palaces etc) and (b) increasing income.

Africa has enormous natural wealth which the rest of the world desperately needs. 90% of the world's diamonds and phosphate, 50% gold, 40% platinum, uranium, oil, gas, agriculture, fisheries, timber – the list goes on. This wealth, instead of being exploited for the benefit of foreigners, should stay in Africa. African countries have the potential to be economically self-sufficient, and D30's role should change from being a provider of aid to that of a vehicle to undertake this change.

D30 could open offices in every country to implement the reduced aid programme and help the locals with the development of their resources. Any dictator refusing to cooperate would be warned that assistance to his country would stop immediately – he would then have nowhere else to go. The first dictator to be overthrown by his people would be the catalyst to warn other hesitant rulers.

Africa could enter the world's capital markets, using its natural resources to acquire credit ratings. Some countries are already issuing bonds; emerging markets are always of interest to investors. African equity markets are some of the best performing in the world; asset rich countries can deliver the high returns which markets look for. There would be no shortage of investors because they would know that the D30 would be supporting and, in some cases, guaranteeing the investments. The cost to the West of providing such guarantees would be a fraction of the current aid budget.

Then there's Foreign Development Investment which creates jobs, stimulates capital markets and helps local companies to trade around the world. Internationally, this business is huge but because of corruption, bureaucracy, red tape and 'vested interests', Africa only receives a small percentage. With the backing of D30, this would increase and enormous economic benefits could flow to Africa.

These are only two of a host of initiatives that could be undertaken with the help of the D30. In giving aid, the donors' pockets are never empty but, if a ruler used private money in the same way, lenders would foreclose – it's a self-correcting programme. Without aid, rulers like Mugabe, would never have existed.

The question then is… would it work? I headed this article 'Maintaining the Status Quo' and therein lies the probable answer. Would it work? Almost certainly not – there are too many vested interests. In the developed world, hundreds of thousands of people earn their living from the 'aid industry'. They will fight to keep their jobs, pensions and other benefits – that is their priority. And in Africa, the rulers are happy with the way things are - they have no compassion for their starving citizens.

Could it work? Yes it could. Will it work? Africa awaits the answer.